I0554111

IOU A HORSE

Lisa Annette Powell

ISBN: 978-0-9906428-5-5

Cover art design and background photo by author; graphics by Brian Busse; Acara (horse) photo courtesy of Victoria Grindle

Lisa Annette Powell

Other titles available on Amazon or by contacting author

CatSkill Trilogy:
CATSKILL First of CatSkill Trilogy
Winner of Certificate of Excellence

CATSKILL'S LIONESS Second of CatSkill Trilogy

CATSKILLS TANGO Third of CatSkill Trilogy

ROAD TO FEARLESS
Winner of WORLD'S BEST CAT LITTER-ARY AWARD

IOU A HORSE

Dedicated to T.C. AHLAM

My Dream and Soul Mate for
32 WONDERFUL years

Ahlam and Lisa
Photo courtesy of Nan Rawlins Equimage.com

**Irish Amber Version- my Bubbly Girl, my Guardian, and me
Photo courtesy of Helen Meiser, my great aunt!**

IOU A HORSE

Nugen Leah Jamaal- ACARA, my new friend
Photo courtesy of Nugen Arabians Jeff and Matt Brown

Perhaps I was four or five when my impatient mother tried to teach me how to read. Regardless, it was the book she chose which ignited the passion.

For as soon as I knew there was such a wonder as a horse-well, the magic took hold...

IOU A HORSE

There is something about the outside of a horse that is good for the inside of a man.
Winston Churchill

Species need species f****** specific communication!
Sierra Sorenson

You are part of everything and everything whispers for you to accept this.
Teacher

LET GO!!!
Cloud

1

I hate being sucked down the drain to my first years. Helplessly spinning, until I'm numb. Beyond my control- for provocation unexpectedly and relentlessly spits at me.

The unlimited sadness of loneliness, or is it lonely sadness. Is there a difference? In those early years, I didn't even know what it was that lingered in my sidelines, quietly heckling.

Why is it, that for me, the latest sad incident magnetizes all past ones to it? Why isn't it enough to endure what's happening now and let the past episodes remain passed?

But for me, it's never worked that way.

The trigger could be as simple as the latest innocent creature dead on the road, or inadvertently hearing the wrong news flash before I can quickly change the radio station- consequently, I never watch or listen to the news. There should be a genetic anomaly in all beings that keeps them away from hurtling objects and harmful individuals and deadly situations.

I try not to see/hear it, but a sorrow in me surfaces and suddenly my mind spirals back. I've learned to control myself, at least until I'm alone.

And then the door swings wide. A floodtide of every past disheartening moment viciously sucks me back- ignoring all intermittent good. A whirlwind backlash. A tragic falling domino game of memory. Toppling, tears toppling...

The monstrous rattling of the old car. Its belching, hissing and crotchety loose parts are all frighteningly hideous to my ears. Perched alone on the back seat, I shiver at the wind and sleet alternately sluicing and whistling through the window that refuses to close.

IOU A HORSE

"I'm c...c...cold," I cry. "C...cold," a little louder, vying to be heard over the rush of winter battling the insufficient glass.

"Shut up! Shut up, you hear me?" My father screams over the radio which always seems to produce an obnoxious noise all its own.

An aside to my mother, "Why didn't you bring her a cover?"

"She peed on it. What good is a wet blanket?"

Curses.

"Serves you right, you stupid kid, now shut up!" The sting of a slap on my bare leg as I whine one last time.

My mother cranks the radio further to smother any more noise issuing from the back seat. But there isn't a peep.

Instead, a numbness having nothing to do with the cold steals the breath from my body. I will become well acquainted with this mechanism.

I've learned my first valuable lesson. I am cold, I whine and life gets worse. Perhaps there were other lessons, previously administered, but I don't remember them. At least, my brain doesn't recall.

I am three years old.

"I'm hungry." I stumble from the room I share with a stack washer and dryer and utility sink.

My mother is on the phone, father absent. Normal. She is busy prattling on about some TV show or new eyeliner or my father's latest escapade.

"I'm hungry," I try to get her attention by approaching, not too close, and raising my voice.

With an over-dramatic sigh, she momentarily halts her conversation.

"Then find something to eat," she points toward the kitchen. I feel the frown on my forehead before wrinkles manifest.

"Go on!" she orders, as I turn away toward the room usually reserved for food storage. At least, that is how it appears on TV shows. "And do the damn dishes!"

Another lesson. When you need or want something, shut up, find it yourself, and clean afterwards.

My mother considers me a diversion worthy of a few winter afternoons. She's brought home the means to her end- a small book with a gray horse on the cover. The pony is ridden by a boy in a red jacket, weird black hat, and a huge smile. I'd like to be him.

The horse has a silver-white mane and lighter gray circles on a darker gray body. Horse and boy are sailing over a jump- right off the cover, it seems. Don't come here, I think.

It makes her laugh to see me struggle with sounding out words, trying to read the story of the boy and his pony. It makes her curse when I don't seem to remember one sound from another.

I shrink at her foul words and even more from her reddened face and raised hand.

But something miraculous clicks inside my head and before the winter's cold finishes bandying about and sneaking into our un-insulated home, I am reading.

Everything I can find words on. Labels, telephone books, cereal boxes, cast-off books... New books are never gifted to me. If I'm lucky, I may retrieve books from the garbage once in a while. I still smell the discarded volumes. Rarely were the stories worth ignoring the scents.

I am four and have learned vital lessons.

A succession of new, old homes or apartments, but nothing replaces the arguments between my father and mother. Nothing like the families on the TV shows is like what I grow up with.

IOU A HORSE

What is real? At what age does a child realize that something is out of the ordinary? Missing? An ingredient the heart longs for, but my tongue can not voice. Until it is chucked into a corner of the mind and forgotten.

Then, I discover the magic.

2

I didn't grow up with a Godly rapport. My parents never spoke of God, except to damn Him. But I saw a picture, abandoned probably along with faith, in the last home I shared with them.

Not knowing it was supposed to be of God, I called Him the Kind Man. An enigmatic smile and gentle eyes drew me- that and the lamb held safely in His arms. The colorful print wasn't very big. My small hands extricated it from its simple gold frame and broken glass– broken hopes of the former tenants?

Losing myself in those gentle, brown eyes, until I was summoned by my mother to obtain something she could not leave her chair to get, I knew what I'd do.

Carefully, I folded the unharmed print making sure not to crease the sympathetic face. And I kept it with me. A friend? At that age I'd yet to conceive of what a friend might be.

Only one other instance of kind rapport comes to mind during that early time: a new neighbor, an elderly man, offered me a donut one morning when I was playing on the doorstop. I got quite a thrashing for accepting, and screamed at, "Don't talk to people you don't know!" Lesson learned– keep quiet and to yourself. The quiet part also involved my not waking my sleeping father who slept most of the day. I guess to make up for being gone all night.

The magic came shortly afterwards. Perhaps the Kind Man in the old picture with His lamb in His arms gifted the magic to me.

Magic is precocious. It doesn't always present itself when you might like it to. Don't bother calling- rather like a Pavlovian experiment. But it may sneak into your life when you need it. If you're lucky.

In the same apartment where I found the print there was a bed, couch and a cushiony wingback chair. "No recliner," my dad cursed and griped. When he was like that I knew to make myself

IOU A HORSE

scarce- invisible was most advisable. Until I was hollered for- then, hop to it.

We never seemed to have furniture of our own to bring with us. Lost in the latest eviction and hurried abandonment. As there was only one bedroom, the cushiony wingback was relegated to me for a bed. My bladder wasn't to be trusted with the couch– the chair could be hidden away. Shoved in a closet.

That first night when I climbed out, actually to go to the bathroom, the thick seat cushion shifted. Upon adjusting it, I discovered a surprise hidden underneath- a sizeable tablet of mostly blank pages and several pencils with a rubber band around them.

Opening the cover, I found the first pages had multiple, small drawings. Stick people carrying sticks graduated to attempts at kittens and puppies. Expressive examples of an arched cat, a nut-grasping squirrel and a begging dog on the second page were drawn on the left hand side of the paper as if a teacher presented a student with artwork to copy.

Totally absorbed, I turned page after page, intently studying. Five pages in all were filled with small drawings. Along with the attempts to imitate the artistic renderings, there were many other small drawings. Flowers, bees- I knew them from their stripes, more kitties and puppies, a skillet?- a pig with letters for ears and feet and a curlicue for a tail, and more.

So few pages... Perhaps the artist wished to conserve the paper. Why had it been left behind, hidden under a cushion in the chair I was supposed to sleep in?

I unfolded the picture of the Kind Man with the lamb in His arms. In the dim glow of a night light, I pushed a pencil from the tightly bound group and touched the sharpened tip to a corner of a blank page.

My crude endeavors to duplicate the lamb in His arms made me frown. Erasers were quite handy, as the previous artist had also learned- hence the nibbled pencil tops. Ruefully, I tried again. Sleep was forgotten until my last attempt met with weary approval. Unfamiliar facial muscles produced a smile. I could do this.

Replacing the pencil, I closed the book, hid the magical items under my short stack of bagged apparel, and crawled into my chair bed.

Uncharacteristically, I received a present the next day. A box came in the mail addressed to the previous tenants. Didn't stop my mother from tearing into the box, grimacing at the contents and tossing it my way.

Imagine my astonishment when twirling through the air came a lamb, its reclining position the exact duplicate of my drawing attempts! All white, tiny fuzzy tail resting alongside its hind legs, little ears down, a hint of a happy smile.

"You might as well have that," she muttered and promptly went back to her cigarette and the phone.

In grateful wonder, I hid my smile in the lamb's curly fleece. Magic!

"Get me a Coke," my mother interrupted my reverie.

It had worked once, maybe it would work again. I tried my luck with a puppy, doing my best to imitate the teacher/artist's example. Nothing. I tried a kitten. Nothing. I tried a smiling stick family. Nothing.

One afternoon, upon waking from a nap, my stomach growled fiercely. I knew from my morning's search for breakfast materials that the cupboard was bare. My parents had stayed out late the night before and were sound asleep. Would be until nightfall. I was hungry, but I knew better than to wake them.

I pulled out the tablet. I didn't know how to draw chicken noodle soup, but hunger compelled me to give it my all. For a moment it seemed as if the pencil took on a life of its own, scratching upon the white paper, shading in appropriate areas. The final results were certainly recognizable. Closing the tablet, I hid it and the pencils in my bag and slowly advanced to the kitchen.

It wasn't that I believed in magic. I'm not sure that I believed in anything, but there was such a thing as wholehearted hopeful necessity, residing like a lump in my chest.

IOU A HORSE

I began my search with the cabinets I could reach- under the counter. A scattering of roaches as the light brooked their love of covert operations. Too used to their antics, I never thought maybe there might be a kitchen somewhere without those creepy crawly bugs.

I pushed aside the few pots. Nothing. The same for the other cabinets and drawers. An old can of Comet cleanser, two faded dish towels, empty Saran-wrap box, odds and ends of silverware...

My stomach protested more vigorously. Quietly, I pulled a chair over the linoleum floor. Mustn't wake my parents. Cabinets of glasses and plates. I searched behind all of them. Nothing. Another grousing pang in my mid-section. Without breakfast, my head felt pretty light and my hands had developed a shakiness.

On to the next. The double cabinet over the sink. I had to climb in the sink and then perch atop the stainless steel divider, holding onto the cabinet doors. Bowls and more bugs.

To thoroughly check what was beginning to seem a lost cause, I tiptoed on that divider and tilted my chin up. There. All the way in the back corner. I almost cried.

Taking a fork from the sink I nudged the can to my hand. Chicken noodle soup. Of course. Magic, or coincidence? What was the difference? I was five years old.

3

Not that every day and night afterward assuaged my hunger– the physical hunger– the only kind I recognized early on. But the gnawing, hunger pang episodes were definitely fewer.

On those rare occasions when grocery bags entered the kitchen and it was my job to put things away, I'd sometimes find an extra can of soup or peanut butter. Once, I'd drawn brownies from an old magazine I found on a closet shelf and the magic must have felt especially inclined, for at the bottom of a bag there rested a box of brownie mix. This was a tricky one.

Granted I could read, but other than heating soup or making a peanut butter sandwich or frying a hamburger or eggs– rare items- I'd not cooked using an oven.

One night when my parents were absent (most nights), I borrowed an egg from the neighbors– a sure-fire punishable offence. I recalled how melted butter looked like oil, stirred the batter, set the oven number indicated on the box and produced a batch of brownies. Nothing had ever tasted so good! I cleaned the pan and hid the leftovers.

It wasn't long before a different hunger took hold. I'd begun to draw the little gray pony from my first reading book. Over time, the lines came easier from the pencil in my fingers. Soft lead created curves- ears, neck, a hump, back, hips and tail, and by turning the pencil different ways I learned the intricacies of detailing.

Experiments had me turning the black spot of an eye into a living, alert eye with the simple, strategic allowance of a speck of white. With the pencil in my hand, I not only reveled in the horses I went on to draw, but I began to sense a feel of silky skin, thickness of mane, softness of muzzle, whisper of breath, looking into and through the soulful depth of equine eyes.

IOU A HORSE

My imagining fingers curled into mane, and I laughed- when alone, as a figment tail, chasing a fly, flicked my arm. The satiation of this particular hunger beguiled me for hours. Page after page. Four horses or more to a page. Must conserve the drawing papers.

I sketched the different movements of the pony that the artist had painted inside the child's book. All of this without knowing the proper terms. I lived in all of this wonder without ever seeing a real horse.

More sure than I knew magic came calling once in a while, I knew I'd befriend a horse one day.

Sometimes, the magic had ideas of its own. By now you're thinking coincidence. Just coincidence? Who's to say?

The first time it happened I'd picked up a pencil and touched paper and suddenly, my hand was not mine. My fingers were no longer under my command. The pencil took on a life and ideas of its own to manifest...

By this time, I was about half-way through the sketch pad and quite fearful of using all the pages. Surely the magic wouldn't stop on the last page? I unequivocally knew I'd reserve the very last blank space for drawing another sketch book. But right then...

A woman's face appeared, took form under my moving hand. When complete, she gazed back at me. Where had this individual come from? No one I'd met or seen anywhere before.

Short hair hugged her skull; lines creased her forehead and the space between her nose and top lip, the corners of her eyes- bright, miss-nothing eyes. Thin nose, thin lips, freckles...

Who was she? My pencil wasn't finished. With a few strokes, a black muzzle pushed against her cheek. A very large horse head marched out of the pencil tip. There was a peculiar twist of hair upon his forehead between forward-perked ears. The same twists graced the arch of his immense neck. An eye larger than the woman's mouth focused completely on her.

My fingers were but willing adjuncts to the pencil. As the drawing finished, I retraced every line of the woman's head and then, the rendering of the horse. Over and over again I let the pencil, resting lightly in my hand, retrace the entire drawing.

Quickly, I turned the page. I'd completed a rendition of the boy in my book riding his pony in a prancing gait. Alongside this, on the next page, my magic-inclined pencil raced across blank space. My fingers seemed to buzz with energy...

To reveal the woman astride the huge horse. His legs were symmetrically lifted. Hind legs reached far under his body, lowering his back end. His neck arched proudly with the tiny, curious twists of mane evenly placed there.

The woman's arms were extended by means of thin lines to the horse's mouth. Her legs lay gently at his sides. Her chin and eyes were up, her back straight. I almost felt and heard the footfalls as a cadence of music.

A smile rested on her lips. Yes, if I were her, I'd smile, too. To be part of such magnificence!

My fingers shaded his lower legs and tail and her tall boots and jacket and an elegant hat with curved edges upon her head.

Carefully, I set the pencil down and admired both images-the first one the pencil called into being on its own and the second, of the woman riding, that I'd had a more than equal part in producing. This was two days before irrevocable change charged into my five years.

IOU A HORSE

4

Children have no concept of death. It's not a natural, innate understanding. I suppose if a child had something to miss- hugs, kind words, support, special times spent together with parents, then death might mean something...awful.

My parents were generally absent to me in mind if not physically. Once my mother lost the brief diversion she obtained teaching me the rudiments of reading, I became a non-entity or an object to curse at or order to do the dishes, heat soup for supper, do the laundry, bring her a Coke...

I'd never experienced any warmth from my parents unless it was the remains of a slap. No happy family baby makes three moments. So when flashing lights and a pounding on the door woke me one night, I calmly watched men in dark blue clothes with guns on their sides check the rooms, and I wondered why they were there and at such an odd time.

One knelt in front of me, asked my name. I'd already learned via drastic means not to talk to strangers or neighbors. So, I simply cocked my head and kept my distance.

"Listen, little one, we're police officers. Do you know what police are?"

I nodded, hadn't my father made it abundantly clear, "Pigs." Oops! I shouldn't have said anything.

The man kneeling smiled patiently; his companion rolled his eyes.

"My name is Ken, won't you tell me yours?"

At his gentle urging I gave in, "Dove."

"Pleased to meet you, Dove," he continued to smile- a sad smile.

"She's in here," I heard the other man call.

A tall, thin, sleepy-eyed woman stepped around my courtier and offered her hand accompanied by another sad smile.

"She's very shy," Ken affirmed.

The woman called me by name and asked if I'd go with her. Too tired to think of a reason not to, I nevertheless backed away and studied her.

Sensing her harried benevolence, I still had to say, "I'm supposed to stay here and be quiet. My parents will holler."

Nodding at my forthrightness, she addressed my concern with patient gravity, "I promise you it will be OK."

I forced my eyes to stay open by use of my fingers as she gathered my things, watched the men fade into the background.

"Am I missing anything?" She presented me with a box of my few clothes. In answer, I promptly lifted the old cushion of my chair bed, retrieved my pencils, sketch book and the book with the pony and little boy- all tucked inside a bag with a few other books I'd picked up along the way of life.

With my lamb tucked under my arm and my thumb firmly ensconced in my mouth, I refused her hand, shied away from close proximity with her, but followed her out to the car, nearly napped on the short drive.

My memory stretched back to the car incident when I was three and learned my first important lesson- about cold and quiet and something else- I'd slept in a bathtub until I stopped wetting myself, then a floor, and at last my favorite- the wingback chair that housed the magic.

The woman ushered me to a bed in a warm house- a small bed with layers of colorful covers and pillows and stuffed animals. Why hadn't I drawn a bed into my world? Perhaps I'd not considered it more important than horses or food? I slept soundly, comfortably, able to stretch out completely. And it smelled so good- like flowers.

In the morning, I woke to the sun popping through lacy curtains and the smell of... What was that? My stomach growled- hurry up and find out!

After a breakfast of scrambled eggs, a tasty thing called bacon, and toast and an orange drink she called orange juice, the woman began to explain things to me.

"Your parents have gone to be with God," she opened with.

IOU A HORSE

"Who's God?" I felt my face scrunch up, puzzled. I'd heard Him mentioned along with bad words, but never figured my parents wanted to visit Him.

"Uh," she clasped her hands together and her smile further saddened. Opening a black book she showed me a picture- the same one that I'd carried with me since freeing it from a broken frame!

"The Kind Man," I murmured, hesitantly touching the page.

"Yes, dear, the Kind Man. Your parents won't be...coming back, but your great aunt will be here on Monday. You'll go and live with her. She has a farm and horses."

The woman tried to paint a picture for me. But she didn't have to, I already knew. My parents were on an extended absence and the magic was at work.

"This is Dove Gray. Dove, this is your aunt, Victoria Zimmer."

I gazed up at the no-nonsense, older lady dressed in jeans, flannel shirt and tweed jacket, old, but clean, brown boots. I'd missed a few spots on her face, but it was her. Without any sign of emotion I nodded hello, and heard the nice lady, who knew the Kind Man, sigh with relief.

"You're a wee mite of a thing, aren't you?" The magic-contrived woman asked in her deep, gravelly voice.

"Dove is very independent and quiet..." the nice lady began, but my aunt broke in.

"Good! Shall we go? I've got lots to do," and she turned, expecting me to follow.

The nice lady who'd cooked for me and provided me with my first bed had given me an old suitcase which she'd filled with more clothes, books, colored pencils and a toothbrush and comb. She'd looked at me rather strangely when she discovered I didn't know what to do with either one.

By way of parting, her hand rose as if to brush the top of my head. My innate reaction was to duck.

"Good-by," I said. "Thank you for being nice." I took my suitcase and followed my aunt, but something urged me to turn at the last minute.

"Don't be sad," I calmly offered. Her fist went to her mouth and although her head bobbed, I thought she was about to cry.

As I was to learn, my aunt's car was very old, as was everything she owned, but all of her things were in perfect working order and in immaculate spic and span condition. She held the door open for me.

"Don't forget the seatbelt," the kind woman shouted from her doorway.

"Hmmph," my aunt snorted. But she complied in strapping me in. "Well," she started the car. "You can call me Miss Vickie or Aunt Vickie, if you prefer. I don't do family. I had to answer a lot of questions before they'd allow you to come with me. Right now I'm going to ask you one. Do you wet the bed?"

"No," I answered agreeably, relieved at my recent status, and watched the city give way to subdivisions, and finally, countryside and farms.

IOU A HORSE

5

After a long, silent drive and stirring up dust on a gravel path, we stopped beside a small house. "C'mon." She watched me exert my independence as I grabbed my new suitcase and followed her inside. "This is your room."

I eyed the single brass bed with its colored-circles quilt, bedside table with a large clock face perched on three brass feet, a chest of drawers, chair, closet, one window, and shelf upon shelf of books.

"I'll pack up the books. Eventually," Aunt Vickie stated, matter-of-fact.

"I...I like books," I shyly admitted. Would she care?

"You can read? How old are you?" She earnestly studied me with pursed lips.

"Five."

"Hmmm... What else can you do?"

If I were useful she'd let me stay. I had to stay. The magic had brought me this far.

"I can read, cook, do laundry, sweep, do the dishes..."

"All that, huh? The bottom two drawers are empty. You can put your things there. Closet is half empty, too. I have to, uh. . .care to see the horses?"

She eyed my sneakers with misgiving before we walked down an immaculate barn aisle-way. Ten horses of various sizes and colors poked their heads out, greeting us with snorts, whinnies and whiffles. But my eyes sought the magic.

"Listen up, Dove. You will never run or speak loudly around horses. You will always approach with a calm voice and never directly from the rear of the horse. Best to approach from the side, the way horses see. . .oh, never mind for now, but you do understand?"

Quiet to the core, I simply nodded, but as she seemed to require a vocal affirmative, "Yes."

There! Head swinging, the giant loudly, adamantly demanded Aunt Vickie's attention!

"Coming, Marshall, coming," a note of affection basked in her manly voice.

The huge head accepted his due of her gentle hand and lowered over the stall door, down to my height. My body could nearly fit inside his equine skull. Languorously, he sniffed at my shirt and whiffled, stirring my hair, allowed me my first inhalation of that wondrous horsey scent. I stood stock still, fascinated, unable to contain a rare burgeoning smile.

My smiles had been reserved for the magic moments supplied by pencil and paper and the magical end products. Inside, I writhed to touch this magnificent horse- the best magic so far!

"You're not afraid," my aunt murmured.

I shook my head, too enthralled to speak. She showed me how to scratch between his jawbones, fondle his ears, gently stroke above his eyes- all of the giant's favorite spots.

"He's named for a famous knight, William Marshall. You really can read? I've a book about him."

I had no doubts about that. Her small, two-bedroom home was shelf after shelf full, tables topped, and books stacked underneath- loads of books. Perhaps she'd let me read them.

"You're a strange child," she mused. "Come and meet Pippin." Aunt Vickie moved to the next stall which did not set well with the famous, show-stealing Marshall. He flung his head and snorted loudly- spewing me with flecks of horse snot. I startled myself when I giggled.

The odd-to-my-ears sound was cut off when the magic intensified. I caught my breath, for the finely structured, small, gray head that peered over the door was the spitting image of the pony in the book I'd learned to read from. For a second, I felt a strange choking sensation. My eyes watered.

"Pippin, meet Dove."

Aunt Vickie never allowed reins in the hands of her students until she was completely satisfied with the "state of their seat"- her words.

IOU A HORSE

Within minutes of meeting Pippin, she had him saddled and me astride. Issuing a few precise directions about sitting up, heels down, breathing and legs relaxed on the pony's sides... breathing?- she had me moving congenially, joyously, with Pippin, as he walked on a long lead around her.

"Tell me what you feel." Normally a quiet person- virtually spanked into me, I found myself voluble all of a sudden.

"I feel my legs swing from side to side with his...belly. I feel his head stretch. My butt..."

"Your seat," she corrected, without harshness.

"My seat feels when his hind legs move off the ground and come forward."

"Hmmm, hmmm."

Apparently, I was doing fine, and why not? At some point in time, I'd stopped drawing the boy astride the gray pony and produced a rough sketch of what I thought I looked like in his stead.

She stopped Pippin with a "Halt," and walked toward us. I hoped we weren't through already. I never wanted to stop.

"You're not the least bit afraid, are you?" I shook my head, absolutely not. "Then we'll proceed to trot. This gait will feel much different. I want you to grab the front of the saddle with both hands. Breathe," she added.

Interesting command- breathe. I was breathing. This time the circle was smaller. A few soft springy footfalls in the sandy dirt and...

"Trrrot!" Pippin moved off.

I knew this feel, too. I'd drawn the pony with diagonal pairs of legs raised off the ground. We were circling to the left and my seat felt compelled to lift out of the saddle when Pippin's left hind leg came up under him. It felt silly to hold onto the saddle- I was entirely...at home in the magic. So I did as my body was directed by Pippin's actions, gracefully shifting my seat out of the saddle and softly retouching leather to sit.

"I'll be damned," I heard my aunt as if from a great distance. "All my life I've wanted a child prodigy and I seem to have inherited one."

On Pippin I was in a special place- a magical, special place.

"I think we should celebrate," Aunt Vickie said, without a celebratory tone, once she'd finished instructing me in how to care for Pippin after a ride: how to brush him in order to massage the muscles he'd used, sponging off sweat if he had sweated, how to pick his feet- the proverbial gentlemanly school pony let me hold a hoof without bearing down on me-, the proper storage of the saddle and bridle after wiping off any dirt, rinsing the bit, how to hang the saddle pad to dry, and how to give treats- which the expectant Pippin gingerly accepted from my hand.

"Do you like ice cream?"

"I don't know. What's ice cream?" So we began.

A most unusual child. What business had I with a child? But, there was no one else. I could afford her; however, I was a solitary person- not one given to family matters.

I stepped into her room. Not once today did her thumb travel to her mouth as the social worker indicated. Not a single complaint or whine or cry. And she's a natural with horses!

In a fetal position on her right side she lay covered, with a stuffed lamb under her arm. Her suitcase set open on a chair. With the dim glow of the nightlight, I sorted through the few changes of clothing.

Shopping was definitely on the list. We'd need paddock boots, breeches... What's this?

Setting aside an unsuitable romance novel, several children's books- one I recognized with a gray pony on the cover, his rider a small boy in jumping position- I drew out a sketch book.

IOU A HORSE

I thumbed through valiant efforts at drawing various animals and plants. A can of soup- odd. The drawings improved page by page. A picture of Jesus holding a white lamb- a white lamb resembling the one she held. Sketches of a boy riding a pony. Walk. Trot. Canter. The rider eventually replaced by a girl.

The last two drawings caused my heart rate to leap. A woman's face- mine, and...and Marshall's dear, big head nuzzling me. The details! How in the world? A sketch of me mounted on Marshall. His glorious, proud piaffe. I stared in wonderment at the drawings and at the girl. Child prodigy or...?

6

My initial lessons in complete self-sufficiency, via my parents, stood me in good stead as Aunt Vickie's first concerns were the animals. She fed and doctored strays and drop-offs- a continuous supply, and tended all horses- boarders' and hers, like well-loved children.

She never cursed, but had a way of delivering instruction that always got her point across, and the only time she ever raised her voice was if a horse, or any animal, was misused and then, all hell descended on the transgressor.

"Cool your horse out," she'd shout if she believed a mount wasn't properly walked- at least 15 minutes. "Then check him."

"You're on the wrong lead! Fix it this instant!" She would command across the covered riding ring.

"Your horse is unbalanced with your hanging on him like that! The inside rein is not meant for a death grip! Open the door and allow your horse to go forward. Straighten yourself to straighten your horse."

When Aunt Vickie rode a student's horse you could not see the corrections she instigated (talk about knowing horse language), but the results were awe-inspiring to all onlookers. Everyone around always hastened to watch when my aunt stepped up to a stirrup.

Within minutes of lightly sitting in the saddle, she knew if the horse needed further exercises to supple his body, or chiropractic attention first. Years of passion practiced- my aunt's life with horses.

And when my gruff aunt rode Marshall, sighs of pure pleasure applauded the perfect ballet of the pair. Marshall, with prideful grandeur, made jaws drop in envy as he effortlessly gave his all to Aunt Vickie's imperceptible asking. Poetry in motion.

IOU A HORSE

They were favorites of the show judges. She took Marshall all the way up the ladder into Grand Prix dressage- an extremely complicated pattern of movements that must be performed in complete harmony of horse and rider.

I heard many an onlooker state that if she were younger the pair would have been shoo-ins for the Olympics. When I arrived, she was probably in her 60's- no one knew for sure, and she never told. But students flocked to her. She had patience and an eye. If she believed you had a passion and empathy for horses, she'd teach you. If you were spoiled or whiny, she had no time to spare and quickly let you know. Her students ran the gamut from the greenest of beginners of any age up to the highest level riders.

"Balance. Everything is about balance, and listening. Listen and your horse will tell you if you are correct."

Aunt Vickie, called Miss Vickie by everyone but me, was the height of organization. Always on time. She had a handyman for every kind of emergency and 3 or 4 back-ups listed in descending order of efficiency.

When she retired for the day, she'd often paint. Her studies of horses claimed every open space that a book did not. And she loved westerns- the old ones with cowboy stars like Gary Cooper, Randolph Scott, Audie Murphy, James Drury, John Wayne, Kirk Douglas, Adam Fuller... "Real men," she called them, but nevertheless, she was quick to address those lacking in equestrian skills.

Aunt Vickie, a tiny, indomitable combination (she was only 5' tall) of dynamic energy and pure grace and brick wall- not one to cross. She took a shotgun to a man caught sneaking into her barn. What the dogs missed she would have finished off if the guy hadn't been lucky enough to make it across the road and fall into the lake with her in hot pursuit.

She never revealed personal details, kept her own counsel, wasn't afraid to tell it like it was, never sugar-coated the truth.

Men admired her. What else could they do? She never expected anything from anyone, other than the animals duly respected and treated well. Rarely did she ask for anything.

Determined. I once heard a farmer call her 'the last of the old workhorses' and by the tone of his voice he meant it as a supreme compliment.

She never married and I didn't ask why. It was not a question you'd ask her. All of her love was lavished on the horses and the barnyard critters.

Did she love me? We worked well together and I soaked up her knowledge like a forlorn desert. I was extremely grateful to be with her. As for love... I, too, loved the horses and dogs, cats and assorted other creatures.

When I turned 15, she gave me the option- a car, or a horse of my own to work with. I already had the sketch tucked away. For me, there was no choice.

We'd traveled 270 miles to a Trakehner stable. Aunt Vickie had seen an ad on the internet from a breeder she thought well of. Weanlings and yearlings for sale. She'd scanned pictures and studied videos of the sale stock and of the stallion and mares, pointing out to me the benefits of shoulder and other conformational angles, and how heads correctly fit into necks into withers into backs into hips- allowing a horse to produce the desired gaits for dressage.

She taught me about the best leg construction and how it related to a horse holding up without putting undue stress on any particular joint or tendon. With all that in mind, she cautioned me that a horse with heart might toss most of this out the window. Heart counted for a lot in her book.

With her picks in mind, she stood circumspect as the handler brought them out one by one and gauged my reaction to each one in accordance with her own held-close-to-the-vest thoughts. Partial to geldings, I knew she leaned toward a black colt with a white star- his only marking, but the choice was mine to make.

Before a deal could be struck, I was called to a neighboring pasture by a snorting, prancing fireball of energy. Distended nostrils took up the entire muzzle.

IOU A HORSE

The artistic, gray head was thrust high in the air as if to catch a scent, or simply to display an overabundance of pride.

A squeal. Rear. Pirouette. Passage... Ah! There she is!

Aunt Vickie didn't quibble. "Arabians aren't especially renowned for their dressage talent as a rule. But life is about your creating. A special bond with a horse will earn you more than ribbons."

And so the magic led me to Sirocco.

7

On my 21st birthday, shortly before my life took a spin on a mind-searing whirlwind, Aunt Vickie presented me with an extraordinary gift. She was not one to indulge in gift-giving and I was completely taken unaware.

As an instructor and competitor, she'd honed her powers of observation to supra-normal heights. Catching a whiff of my interest in Celtic mythology and the megalithic stone formations from a book I'd dropped as I staggered into the house one night bearing grocery bags, dry-cleaned show shirts and jackets, keys and books... Step-savers were a rule at Creekside Stables- get organized and make do with one trip- step-savers.

"You need to see a bit of the world outside this one to determine if your place is really here," she simply stated.

To which I vigorously protested. How could she doubt my. . .the only home I cared to recall?

Shaking her head and pursing her lips in her usual manner she handed me a round-trip ticket to Ireland, 1000 euros, my passport and a credit card with my name on it. So that's why she'd encouraged me to keep an updated passport, not some business about showing internationally. I had three days to research a week's route, obtain an international driving permit, re-schedule my students and pack.

Not an auspicious beginning- my first day in Ireland. Landing in Dublin, I was not alarmed at the chill or the rain. Springtime was notorious for liquid sunshine and the weather forecast for the entire week's trip stipulated 'damp'. Lots of it.

IOU A HORSE

Emulating my Aunt Vickie, who never let weather get in the way, I had the necessary Outback coat and matching oiled-cotton, brimmed hat, a wool liner and an extra wool sweater, my waterproof paddock boots and winter riding breeches, as well as rain pants.

The rental agency had lost my reservation, but thankfully, they had one Ford Focus and one GPS left. Unfortunately, all my B&B's and ancient sites were identified by GPS coordinates and not a soul at the rental agency could tell me how to plug the coordinates in. At home we used maps- 'use your own brain' Aunt Vickie dictated, so I was rather out of my element.

"Ah, well, your first stop is Newgrange. Right. That's on the list of attractions. Easy. There you go," the inundated-with-customers agent touted as he hit a few buttons. "Ah, right. You'll be needin' to know how to return the car. Right. See, I've keyed in ENTERPRISE as home. Off you go. Safe trip."

Dumbfounded, I watched him scuttle away- a sea creature caught in the tide of impatiently waiting, drowning humanity. I numbly put my backpack inside the Ford. Panic is not part of my make-up. Perhaps it stems from my unanswered cries as a baby? I don't know. Irrelevant information. One deals with what is, and being upset is 'counter-productive'- Aunt Vickie's words. Growing up self-sufficient, indifferent to strangers, I mumbled to myself, "Where there's a will there's a way."

Aunt Vickie had explained the entire system of driving on the 'wrong' side of the road with, 'Keep your body next to the center line.' "Right," I snickered, in imitation of the rental agent. I set off.

While my fellow tourists at Newgrange shivered outside the enormous mound listening to our guide, I drily, warmly, was engaged in the scenery.

If ever a country was blessed for horses, it was Ireland. Drenched in green. Lush, greener-than-green grass stretching down to the river below. Enthralled with the setting, I turned my attention to the huge stone-ringed chamber-mound perched high on the hill.

White walls that would have glistened if the sun had deigned to toss a ray or two in their direction, banded the man-made mound. This alone, other than the enormous size of the structure, would strike with awe folk approaching from miles around.

Upon seeing the inside construction with all of its perfectly placed rocks of all sizes, the small side chambers, the astonishing corbelled roof, I was amazed at what had been built before heavy construction equipment came on the scene. The guide expressly made it a point to say that no one knew for sure what Newgrange and its surrounding, sister mound-chambers, were all about.

"Make up your own story," she smiled. I liked that- her encouraging folks to think creatively- it hinted of magic.

When she simulated the winter solstice sun beaming into the chamber's thin, black-as-night aisle-way by use of the only source of inside light- her flashlight, I was totally beguiled. As were the others. An experience of resurrection? From complete cave-dark to the enrapturing entrance of sunlight. Definitely something to think about.

"Do you need some help?"

Caught off guard trying to decipher the recalcitrant GPS, I jumped at the approach of a young couple. With the gadget in hand, I hesitated. I'd still not discovered how to use the darn thing and if I didn't head out to Tara soon the whole day would be off kilter. But, talking to strangers...

"My name is Bonnie," a tawny-crowned girl extended an introduction and hand, complete with a serene, amiable smile. "My husband, Riordan, is a wizard with any technical gizmo."

She snuggled into the t-shirt clad chest of a tall, mysterious figure. T-shirt, in this damp cold? His disarrayed long hair-streaks of blonde, auburn and black strands around his ears, tumbled rain drops. He seemed impervious to the weather, but a grin conspiratorially hoisted the corner of his mouth as he leaned down to his wife and gently gripped her ear.

The young couple moved in tandem like well-orchestrated ballroom dancers- graceful, agile, cat-like. So very young, obviously in love, but not crawling all over each other with x-rated PDA's.

IOU A HORSE

I scanned the other visitors hastily heading to their cars. Bonnie and Riordan patiently waited me out. I sensed only good intentions from them, though I remained alert. Old lessons.

"Thank you," relieved, I handed the small, black box to the man. His expressive brows framed thickly-lashed golden eyes. I glanced to his wife- all her attention fully on him. Pert, pretty blonde. She, at least, wore a flannel shirt that seemed to be...dry? In the perpetual Irish shower?

The unsettling feeling that they were very different, in an indescribable way, and even more surreal- that they knew everything about me, inched into my thoughts. Nonsense. I mentally kicked myself.

"I... My destinations are," I withheld most of my coordinates, except I showed him the numbers for the Hill of Tara- the ancestral crowning site of the ancient Irish High Kings, and my B&B for the night in Trim.

"You're missing a number, but this will get you real close. Ask someone when it says you've reached your destination even if you don't see it. See this," he guided me through his fingers' ministrations, "This is the format site." Slowly and patiently, he retraced his steps, and I ardently studied every move.

"Voila! Got it?"

"Yes, yes, I do. Thank you. How simple. Now why couldn't the rental car agency provide me with this information?"

"There's a good question," he chuckled and returned his arm to his wife's waist.

"Have a nice trip," Bonnie cheerily waved as I slid into the rental car.

"Riordan, that's amazing! She's awfully young and alone," I concernedly nudged my husband, knowing he was already privy to my mind.

"Young, eh?" He gave me one of his lifted brow chuckles. "I know her other destinations, though she tried to hide them. Maybe we'd best keep an eye out. Wouldn't want my Wife to worry." Riordan's tantalizing lips drew closer and closer until contact suspended my breath.

"You know you're creating a stir by wearing only a t-shirt in this chill?"

"As long as I stir you..."

I was glad the GPS lady talked my route to me- and kindly repeated her instructions when I wavered incorrectly. With the narrow lanes of the Irish country roads, blind curves, rock walls, constant brush of brush against the passenger door and the winding way- beautiful, but unnerving, I wondered how there could possibly be a single vehicle with an unblemished left side.

After a while, I quit cringing at the threatened passenger side with every scraping sound. I munched on almonds pleased the rain had finally given me a respite, although the clouds portended more to come.

I slipped up the Hill of Tara, touched the Stone of Destiny- said to shout for the rightful heir to Ireland's High Crown when he touched the king-size stone. The exhibit of the hostage site was closed, but off to the right twin trees decorated with colorful bits of cloth and ribbons drew me.

Fairy trees. Magic. I'd brought my sketch pad and lots of pencils. When the muse spoke, I wanted to be prepared. But the rain drops decided to cancel my sketching for the moment, so I stood spell-bound by the myriad, colorful gifts which petitioners to the otherworld denizens had tied to the branches.

Did I feel compelled to leave one of my own? No. The magic had other ways of opening communication with me. I took a few photos, and carefully made my way to a quaint book store at the base of the Hill, next to a souvenir and snack shop.

IOU A HORSE

The tiny, stone cottage was jam-packed with tomes old and new- a veritable library of Irish knowledge. I put my new credit card to good use obtaining a book on the ancient Celtic, Brehon law structure which gave women more rights than any other culture of that time. Before Romanized Christianity came and devastated the equality.

Mr. Slavin, the proprietor, had written a book on the Hill of Tara which he kindly signed for me. I could have stayed there for hours perusing the books, but I was beginning to wind down and still had miles to go.

Overnight was spent in a warm, comfortable B&B in Trim-The White Lodge, after touring what remained of Trim castle and feasting on a delicious steak served on a hot stone. I fell asleep the instant my head hit the pillow.

The Hill of Uisneach was preparing for the spring festival of Beltaine- an ancient celebration in hopes of fertility of soil and couplings. One of the set-up personnel, as early to the site as I was, kindly offered to give me a tour through a cow-pattied pasture leading up to the top of the Hill where the ancient fires were once lit on Beltaine night to signal fire celebrations all over Ireland.

Indeed, he pointed out to me, while we overlooked the Irish countryside, where the other fire sites had waited Uisneach's initial flames' signal. As if the imminence of Beltaine prodded it, the sun joined in our perambulations, causing me to delightedly shed my coat.

"Do you know where the Cat Stone is?" I asked Christian, my impromptu, but amicable guide. Ireland seemed to deny my usual circumspection- the people were downright friendly and seemed genuinely interested in talking with me. If I were here, I might as well learn and see all I could, and that involved speaking to strangers. Somehow, here, it didn't seem possible for anyone to be a stranger.

Christian ran his hand through his hair causing spikes to form and falter.

"It's one of those places that I've never been able to find," he ruefully admitted.

"Really? Does the huge pile of boulders left by nature in the heart of Ireland really resemble a cat's head?"

As it was something I wished to see and I hoped the magic was so inclined, I'd sketched a small drawing of it at my sumptuous breakfast- the Irish do nothing by halves- and I was stuffed.

"That's the Cat Stone," my B&B host had exclaimed, peering over my shoulder. "It delineates, supposedly, the ancient kingdoms of Ireland- Ulster, Mide, Connaught, Leinster and Muenster, as well as being the burial place or portal to Tir n' Nog of a Tuatha d' da Naan goddess."

"I'm going to see it today," I'd spouted, assuredly.

"Well," Christian grinned, shrugging, "Let's give it a go, shall we?" With me in tow, he set off.

Watching my step and the curious eyes of the mottled, black and white cattle spying us in turn, we'd just skirted some brush when I spied a familiar couple striding away.

"There it is!" Christian jubilantly hailed, arms soaring heavenward. "I can't believe it! Wow! We actually found it!"

Except for the retreating tall man and his petite wife, I was not surprised. I could almost feel the sense of wondrous magic that the ancients must have tuned in to at various sites in this lush green land. Had to be coincidence seeing Bonnie and Riordan here too, didn't it? Studiously, I walked around the Cat Stone, not seeing the cat.

"I think you have to see it from a distance to get the jist of a cat's head," Christian frowned, empathetically.

The week went much too fast. I spent a day on Clare Island-home of Granuaile, the Irish pirate queen who'd had a private audience with Queen Elizabeth.

IOU A HORSE

With the skills of a monkey, I managed to climb the derelict castle's walls to reach the floorless second story and view the blue bay beneath. Sun continued to light my way as I walked the island, loving the feel of the thick grass underfoot, the sight of gamboling lambs and foals, a wall-sitting border collie and the overall, reigning sense of peace.

Inside a tiny, stone church, I stopped at Granuaile's burial marker, reading her epitaph- STRONG BY LAND AND SEA- replaying in my head her life's adventures. I could picture Aunt Vickie in the role of that adventurous woman in a male-dominated era. I thoroughly relished seeing things I'd spent so many hours reading about over the years- thank you, Aunt Vickie!

Lunch was a loaf of bread I'd bought at a bakery and a thick slice of cheese from the island's small grocery shop as I sat on a bench and admired the glistening, sun-teased ocean.

A day on the isle of Inishmore with its overabundance of rock and superb fresh fish and chips was next. Every night I went to bed equably exhausted from my explorations.

The largest, stone circle in Ireland is at Lough Gur. Unlike Avebury and Stonehenge, it is set in the remote countryside. Farmland. Quiet. I arrived well before cockcrow, hoping to see a Beltaine dawn light the entry of the circle. If only there'd been a sunrise.

The rain had returned, but I was undeterred. More than any other site, this one drew me and I was rainproof. Pungent green enveloped me inside the circle of tremendous stones set up by ancient peoples as... To me, it represented a happy place of celebration, despite the tendrils of fog snaking about in an eerie, dragon-like manner, and the pitter patter of relentless raindrops.

Leafed-out trees of tremendous proportion seemed to take on different shapes in the misty air as their branches hovered over the stones. One of them turned into a lazy, speculative, stretched-out cat. Watching me? Long, thick roots alternated guises between vigilant, green-mossed crocodiles and slithering serpents.

What a fantastical place for imagination to flow! For magic to attend.

Stepping back in time by thousands of years, I walked from the processional entryway clockwise around the inside of the circle, touching each stone, hoping for something otherworldly- something more concrete than my imagination configuring cats and serpents from the sentinel-like massive trees.

I felt the moss patrolling the sides of the dark gray boulders. Diminutive pink and mauve and white flowers bloomed in the rocks' crevices. At one point, I stopped and peered across the wide circular expanse.

For a second, I thought a horse had escaped its fenced pasture. But I blinked away raindrops and... Nothing. Only me and my run-away, fanciful imagination.

By rights, a single female should probably have felt warily concerned about being alone in a deserted, ancient site. I did not. Fear did not come naturally to me, not that I considered myself foolhardy- I just did not live in fear. My early lessons had forged my armor.

I sensed no harm inside the megalithic circle. Leaning against one of the stones which towered over me, I kept my eyes on a thick-trunked tree whose branches spread out protectively above two guardians.

All at once, a peculiar chill swept along my arms. My heart began to pound. The flight or fight instinct of an adrenalin-rush battled for recognition and supremacy of action.

Someone was watching me! That same place where I thought I'd seen the horse! Perceptive people can feel when they are in the spotlight of another's eyes. My parents had unwittingly instilled this in me along with the advisability of invisibility. My training with the horses, and my solitary nature, propounded a heightened awareness, an intense observational skill.

Who? No cars. No traffic. No noise. Nothing moving. And yet, someone was there, I wholeheartedly knew it. I fingered the mace in my pocket, but whoever the gaze belonged to, I didn't feel unsafe, just...

Mind made up, I sprinted across the circle's expanse straight for the hiding place of...

IOU A HORSE

No one. No horse. Nothing. No hurried sounds of exit. I moved between the two stones that conspired to hide what or whoever. My eyes hastily swept all around, to no avail. I fingered the bark of the tree there. Gnarly. Drenched lichens. Only a tree, I blanched to think, but my gut's intuition had been so strong!

The ghost of a cloud drifted into my soft, wide-angle vision- a foggy obscure streak that bunched, thinned and galloped off. Magic? Or simply a coincidental fog-leftover from the vaporous morning? Hmmm...

I stumbled over a long drawn out root as I turned. In happening to glance down, I caught a glimmer of glass. Glass shouldn't litter this awesome place.

Squatting, I picked at it carefully to free it from the splattered mud and sodden grass. To clean the mud off, I swiped it on the wet grass. Curious and curiouser.

A two-inch long crystal. Six sides. Without a single blemish. It retained a warmth as if someone had just dropped it. Except, it wasn't mine and I was the only one around.

"Who's there?" I questioned the ancient spirits that undoubtedly continued to linger. Not a hint of a response.

I fingered the beautiful crystal. "Do I leave you here? Or are you a gift of the magic?"

A whisper caused me to gasp. The ghostly cloud reappeared, hovered across the way. My throat went dry. Believing in the magic of my sketch book was one thing, but confronting magic in the mysterious Lough Gur stone circle was another. I felt as if I'd ventured too close to a portal introducing another world- whether into reality or fantasy or momentary insanity, I couldn't tell.

I closed my eyes and whispered, not feeling the least bit foolish- "Is the crystal for me?"

Possibly I was mistaken, perhaps it was the trick of a brash breeze slashing renewed rain in my face and whipping a slight branch at my back, but I thought I heard a grunt.

When I opened my eyes, the ghost cloud had vanished, as had the rain and the sun peeked through lingering murky clouds. Time to go.

At my farmstead B&B that night, my hands itched for my sketch pad. Ensconced in a wingback chair inside a bay window, I paged through, barely noticing my pencil drawings of Newgrange, the Hill of Tara, the Hill of Uisneach, Rothcroghan, Granuaile's castle, Dun Aenghus, Bunratty Castle, St. Brighid's Well and the watchtower in the cathedral graveyard at Kildare.

Impatiently, my hand flipped to a blank page. The pencil flowed sub-consciously over the page- my hand a mere adjunct. Lough Gur's stone circle hastened to life.

Shading for the moss on the stones. The lead tip then went vertical placing the trees in their remembered positions. Except for the one where I'd felt something or someone had covertly watched me.

At that moment, the crystal rolled across the page, and there, beside the watcher's tree trunk, a head peered over the monolith- courtesy of the magic-imbued pencil.

IOU A HORSE

8

Aunt Vickie reserved her infrequent smiles, which made her downright pretty, for the antics of her critters (her collective expression for animals: horses, dogs, cats, squirrels, birds etc. "I've got to feed my critters; check on the critters.")

A stray kitten pleading to be picked up, a dog joyously rolling in fresh manure, a dawning understanding between her and the horse she was working with, the mutual comprehension of a student and her horse- all evoked a satisfied smile on Aunt Vickie's face. Otherwise, her facial poise ranged from poker plain to implacable pursed lips to verbal explosions with compressed brows if a critter was not being properly addressed.

"Fifteen minutes cool-down, not 14½," she'd raise her voice. This without checking a watch.

She never shared personal information or stories; she never seemed to take anyone into her confidence, other than teaching me to use my intuition around horses during my wondrous education at her hands. With people, she was at her best when in teaching mode and conversely, at a distinct loss with idle conversation. No personal friends- human ones, but she was utterly respected, admired, and men treated her as they would a lady.

I never saw her cry until... If she were in pain- rarely, she'd get out the arnica-infused horse liniment and douse herself. Hydrogen peroxide was always at hand for any skin-piercing injuries and aloe for burns. Not once did she ever seek a human doctor.

Although veterinarians were allowed on the farm, at times she'd dismiss or argue over their proscribed treatments- poor Dr. K; but to give him credit, as she was much older, he did hear her out and I believe he happily absorbed her vast lifetime's worth of experiences.

"Young know-it-alls! Fresh out of their books," I'd hear her grumble after Dr. K drove off- she never saw his smiling face.

Because he could immediately verify his diagnosis by pointing out reactions to acupressure points, Dr. L, a veterinarian, chiropractor and acupuncturist, was accepted full on with only polite questions.

Her world contained a lifetime's well-earned, intuitive and practical knowledge which she freely granted to me along with an ever increasing number of riding students.

She never bandied with others in a superior frame of mind. In an emergency, she remained absolutely clear-headed and calm.

"Panic is a waste of time. A cool head is paramount to productive thinking and action."

Affection was not for humans, me included. All her love was destined for animals. But I never minded. I'd grown my first five years with an inkling of self-sufficiency and being mostly ignored. Aunt Vickie completed my course on resourceful independence. And of course, I loved the animals, too.

"Teach, be organized, take care of the critters and the farm."

Only once did I see her cry.

She'd not come into breakfast as she regularly did. Thinking something had to be wrong, I rushed to the barn.

I found her kneeling at Marshall's head, softly stroking his closed eyes and still body, tears saturating her face, dropping onto his ears. After thirty-some years of beautiful togetherness, he'd moved on.

Beauty of his caliber has to have another dimension to thrive on. Though I never attended religious services, I believed in the Kind Man. There was a heaven for the Marshalls of the world and those who loved them. There had to be.

Tentatively, I rested my hand on her shoulder. My heart choked for her pain and a familiar creeping numbness taunted me as my tears unabashedly fell in torrents.

The very fabric that stabilized my world was shucked from under me, for within hours I dissolved, crying again- relentless buckets- for Aunt Vickie left me to join Marshall that very night. In her favorite western chair. With a smile on her face.

IOU A HORSE

9

"Riordan, look," Bonnie unnecessarily tipped her chin in the direction of horse and rider.

"I am looking," his double entendre was not lost on Bonnie Lance CatSkill. Her husband's deep whisper stirred the tendrils that lay against her sweating cheek. If his teeth settled on her ear the distraction would be too much. But that was another story.

"Riordan," she ignored her rippling senses- all of them. "Please."

As the beleaguered horse show husband, Riordan turned his attention from looking at his wife's neck to looking through her eyes. That way he could admire two things at once.

"Cheater," she murmured, delightedly. "Watch her ride. You always say Handsome and I have something special..."

Riordan snorted, "Bonnie, you're the only human I've ever met who can accurately speak with animals- on all levels."

With their shared supra-natural ability of seeing through each other's eyes, he checked out #17. "Familiar," he agreed.

The weather had doused the USDF show with heat and humidity teasingly bordering on showers. Nearly every rider had succumbed to the energy-sapping combination of 98 degrees and 90% humidity- some with canceled classes, some with fraying tempers, almost all with dazed expressions.

Waived black jackets had all competitors nearly sporting R-rated gear in sweat-drenched, white show shirts. The requisite white breeches weren't faring much better. And the tall, black boots looked torturous.

The Prix St. George class under the brilliant sun had severely tested the contenders- horses and riders. Paramedics had escorted one rider away and warned others to get out of the sun and stay hydrated.

Veterinarians raced by in air-conditioned carts, keeping close tabs on the equine contingent and administering electrolyte paste in weary Warmbloods' mouths.

The audience had dwindled to Bonnie, Riordan, and a handful of others sipping cold drinks and hiding under umbrellas. No other riders prepared for the class. The perfect #17 was the last competitor.

A normal couple wouldn't have been in such intimate contact as the CatSkills, even under the dusty, drooping oak tree. But that, too, was another story.

"Aren't they wonderful," Bonnie enthused, her eyes and therefore, Riordan's too, ardently watched every step of the complicated pattern #17 performed.

Collected, cadenced trot into an impossibly, air-borne extended trot and transition back without a second's hesitation. Flawless canter half-pirouettes and half passes and flying lead changes. And something rarely seen- a totally relaxed, extended walk that moved out, covering ground with alacrity.

"She's in complete harmony with her horse. An Arabian, Riordan- few of that breed make it so far. That gray mare is superb and she knows it. Going up against the big boys and girls. She's having as much fun as her rider. Look how her tail swings rhythmically. See the smile on the girl's face. And only the tiniest of spurs- probably because they are required. You know, in general, the spur of choice at these shows seems to be rowel spurs- a toned down version of cowboy's rowels. It's incongruous to breed a horse for supposed lightness and then ride him in rowels."

"One of Handsome's pet peeves, as I recall," Riordan offered.

Bonnie giggled. "You were so funny that day, perched up in that tree, ringside, in starling feathers, eavesdropping and issuing warnings."

"Until you cut me off! Make no mistake, Wife, if that beast of a stallion had made one untoward movement, he'd be dog, er, cat food," Riordan reminded her, in all sincerity.

IOU A HORSE

Bonnie leaned into her tall mate's chest, tipped her head back to catch the curl of his lips.

"We have to see her. Something is going on with her."

"Hmmm, can we eat first? I'd scale that tree for a cookie-one of yours," Riordan's lips twitched.

Ignoring her husband's attempts at levity, Bonnie checked her program as the Arabian floated across the diagonal in a last extended trot, went through a spate of perfectly timed flying lead changes, a true extended canter, collected up and blithely paraded down center line into a perfectly square halt. All without visible aids.

"No wonder she smiles," Bonnie sighed, happily. "Can you imagine, someday I might compete Handsome against her?"

Riordan's exceptionally dramatic brows rose. They clapped and whistled as the familiar-looking girl, #17, lovingly stroked her mare's silver mane-draped neck, loosed the reins, stopped at the judge's booth for congratulatory remarks and exited the sand ring.

"You know," Riordan finished his thoughts, "Handsome will probably act the gentleman and lose to her, don't you think? Even though he'd ordinarily stand on his head for you?"

Riordan momentarily reflected on how gallant Bonnie's stallion could be...

"Courtly, like Leicester must have been in Elizabeth's queenly court," Bonnie read his mind. "What a pair they'd make!"

Riordan was on instant alert. "Bonnie, I know you're not thinking of that mare and Handsome?"

"Mmmm....," she murmured.

"Bonnie?"

"Cloud."

"You've got to be kidding!" But Riordan knew she wasn't.

"Riordan, look how well it worked out for Wolf Walker and Dangir..."

"And another one bites the dust..." Riordan began singing an old rock tune by Queen. "As I remember," he broke off, "Wolf Walker wanted a mate. Wanted you, in fact."

"And you also knew that was impossible. You are the image from my dreams. You are the answer- the beat of my heart," she turned in his arms.

A passerby clicked in dismay while her young male companion chortled, "Get a room before you burst into flames."

Riordan intensely perused his wife's reminisces as they floated across the stage of her face.

"Wife, all the past is past. What are you thinking about, Cloud and...?" He'd graciously accepted that when Bonnie schemed it was hopeless to stand in the way.

"Dove Gray," Bonnie responded, wondering about the sadness behind the smile on #17's face.

"Seriously? What is it today with women and these strange names? Dangir Llyn was bad enough," he groused.

"Riordan, wouldn't it be nice for Cloud to meet her? She understands horses..."

"Like you do. Maybe she talks to animals, too."

"I...I sense something is wrong, something sad but also magical, and it's not just the combination of her and her Arabian mare," Bonnie tried to explain, knowing her husband instantaneously understood.

"Hmmm... You say she understands horses, but what about Cloud?"

10

A less than valiant breeze failed to stimulate the flag atop the announcer's booth. The score board which posted the rider's scores as soon as the judge delivered them to the scribe was nothing more than a washed out piece of technology lost in the late afternoon haze. A prophecy of rain taunted the show grounds as the awards ceremony began.

"Do we have to stay for this, Wife?" Riordan grudgingly asked.

"Riordan, I'll be showing soon and I want to..."

"To see how you'll accept your blue ribbon, I know."

"Uh," Bonnie hedged.

"Wife, you know that beast of yours will do hand stands if you ask," Riordan's lips twitched.

"He is good, isn't he, Riordan? And we really should see her..."

"I'll give him his props," he hastily broke off.

In reverse order, the announcer called the ribbons for #17's class.

"Riordan?"

"Be ready, Wife."

All Bonnie's senses opened; she knew her husband had an innate sense for reading situations. This had greatly served him many times. Sure enough, the Dutch Warmblood called forward, reluctantly promenaded to the ribbon presenter. His tail swished in aggravation and he threw in several bucks.

"You can't get through to him, Bonnie?"

"He won't respond- he's that upset!"

The huge, disgruntled horse was spurred forward by his rider as the announcer proceeded to summon Dove Gray and Sirocco- winner of the Prix St. George class.

Miss Gray maintained an energy-saving medium walk to the lackluster, linen-clad woman handing out ribbons and the Arabian's winning trophy. Sirocco's tail was flagged in victory; her ears twirled ahead to the smattering of applause in the stands and then, back to her rider. Dove Gray's lips moved in constant compliments to her mare.

As Miss Gray's hand accepted the long-trailing blue rosette, the Dutch Warmblood, victimized further by an avid horsefly added on top of the rest of the day's hardships, had had enough. He exploded, and his rider could not maintain her balance on what looked like a rodeo contender of the worst kind bucking out his every qualm. She toppled. Gray whirled her mare around to try and reach a safe distance, but the violence of the Warmblood dervish's hind feet caught the mare's right hindquarter.

"Riordan!"

"Got it, Wife," and the tall, lithe man easily vaulted over the rail and raced across the sand. Right behind him, Bonnie trailed in his wake, continuously sending out telepathic calming energies, desperately trying to break through to the pitching iron-shod malefactor.

The distant four other riders managed to escape the fallout unharmed as grooms surged forward to contain the loose cannon. But the damage had already been wreaked on Sirocco.

The flying hooves had grazed, knife-like, the length of the Arabian's hindquarter and had smacked into the much slighter horse's stifle and hock. In a slow motion horrific descent, horse and rider went down.

Someone grabbed the frothing Warmblood's bridle and fought to guide him away. Riordan's arms snuck under the Arab's side and with supra-human effort lifted just enough for Bonnie to pull Gray's pinned leg free.

"Easy, Sheer, easy girl," Gray slumped at her mare's head and continually, calmly whispered her mantra. Her fingers gently stroked the profile of the stunned Arabian's dished face.

'Riordan, see to the mare, I'll check Dove,' Bonnie silently communicated to her husband.

IOU A HORSE

A racing go-cart slid to a stop nearby, delivering a veterinarian, but Riordan had his hands on the injuries. Feeling Dove was mostly shocked and that her ankle could wait, Bonnie opened the gates of her own shamanic healing expertise to join with her husband's- the mare's injuries were the first priority.

"Get out of the way!" The doctor in blue coveralls tried to brush Riordan aside.

But nothing could dislodge Riordan CatSkill if he were not so inclined.

'Riordan?' Unwilling to cause a scene, Bonnie silently sent a question. He solemnly rose to his feet, his eyes and shamanic ability intent on the mare.

'Bonnie, talk to the mare, keep her calm,' he replied silently.

But her efforts were unnecessary. Dove Gray had crawled into a fetal position around the finely chiseled head and cooed softly as she stroked the Arab's head and situated the forelock.

"We'll have to put her down- the leg's broke," the vet delivered his diagnosis after a precursory examination.

"The leg is not broke," Riordan firmly announced.

The exasperated equine professional turned an affronted smirk on Riordan, "Just who the hell are you?"

"The leg is not broke; her hip is intact, too, though I believe it's shifted."

Riordan's stern expression and inviolable stance fended off the rest of the doctor's retorts and prognosis for future use.

"She'll be all right. Please tend to her as best you can," Gray's pale, stricken face appealed to all; her eyes never left her friend.

Out poured pain killers, thick bandages, saline solutions, condolences... Dove's own ankle ached and throbbed but could not swell inside the black leather case of her riding boot and she refused to give in to her own needs.

Other than the single order she gave the vet, she continued to croon to her mare. Unbelievably, the Arabian seemed to be as imperturbable as the CatSkills who were standing by and sending out their specialty healing frequencies.

Teary-eyed bystanders shuffled, holding onto programs, cell phones, each other.

"I'm sorry, so sorry," the rider of the loose cannon approached. Dove nodded without looking up. All her attention was for her best friend.

"It's all right, Sheer; it's all right," she murmured as if she could magically make it so.

The linen-clad woman who'd presented the awards picked up the crumpled blue from the sand and put it with the elaborate trophy. Another competitor said something to her, accepted the ribbon and trophy and crouched by Dove.

'Riordan, can we finish the healing, follow her home?' Bonnie moved into her husband's embrace, her own eyes misty with barely restrained tears. 'She has, Dove has...'

'I know, Wife. An injured heart and a wounded soul. The horse...'

'Will live, but her movement...might not be able to show again...'

'Up to the spirits. Miracles happen, Kitten. We'll follow her home, work at a distance. But I'm beginning to think your first idea was better.' Their conversation was inaudible to the bystanders as the means of communication...had a magic all its own.

IOU A HORSE

11

I staved off capitulating to the creeping numbness on the laborious drive home to Creekside Stables- a slow 2 hour drive from the Columbus show grounds. Must keep Sheer upright and as comfortable as possible in the trailer. Dear God- Sheer...

The young couple- the CatSkills, were determined to follow me home, as I'd attended the show alone. They refused to take no for an answer. I don't know how the man lifted Sheer or how Bonnie, as small as she is, pulled me from under Sheer's left side. I wouldn't have thought it possible, but there'd been no time to dwell on it. I had to keep Sheer calm and rein myself in. My stoic Sheer seemed to take it all in stride- how could I do otherwise?

Stride... The violence of her injuries- the massive tear in her hindquarter muscles running down below her stifle, her hock... Something about her hip, someone said... Would Sheer heal enough to love her life like...before?

"You might want to consider putting her down," the circumspect vet advised. This was the same vet who'd fought against Riordan CatSkill's insistence that the leg was not broken.

All the attention. All the sympathy in the murmurings around us. My Sheer... Aunt Vickie, Marshall and now, Sheer...

Where was the magic? I couldn't even sketch in the sand I'd sunk into. My fingers could only stroke Sheer's head and whisper encouragement.

"If she can stand, you'll know," Bonnie had knelt by me and supportably murmured.

After the vet's administrations, with Bonnie's helping hand I struggled to my feet. My tremulous left ankle- nothing compared to my best friend's injuries.

Sheer's head lifted as I stood with her lead line loosely held in my hand. Someone had thoughtfully supplied her soft, emerald green halter to replace the bridle.

"Try," I whispered encouragement. There wasn't an ounce of panic in her eye, simply the trust imbued in our friendship.

Bonnie's husband closed on her hindquarters while the vet readied another syringe. Sheer lurched, fell back, sighed and my heart cracked.

Her body trembled momentarily as she seemed to take stock of the circumstances. I glanced at the CatSkills and saw only placid hope. Familiar. Not until much later would I realize it was the young couple who'd helped me in Ireland. Perhaps that was magic of some sort- a magic I'd not thought of. How strange...

Bonnie smiled supportively. "Try, Sheer," I emboldened again.

The tall man squatted, hands under her left hip. Bonnie, at his side, placed her hands near his. Sheer seemed to find confidence in their deus ex machina.

With a tiny nicker and flip of her head at me, she lurched again. Front legs pulling, her left hindquarter supported by the CatSkills, she struggled up. Her right hind leg quivered and shudders ran through her body. Immediately, the CatSkills were there, blocking the vet for an instant as they applied their hands above the violated skin.

The vet watched as Sheer steadied, shook his head and replaced the syringe in an ice pack bearing container for me to use later.

Bonnie gently pulled the saddle off and stood waiting. I eyed the bandages the vet had applied to the torn right leg- above and below the hock. The sight of Sheer's blood and sundered skin were anathema to my soul. I felt faint, but I must control myself for her, I must... Would she walk? Could she...get in the trailer?

A tingling, not of sweat, zipped along my spine. Something beyond my ability to describe or fully comprehend palpably plied the air. Magic? The whoops and applause as Sheer tentatively set her right hind foot on the ground blocked the crackling in my heart from continuing.

IOU A HORSE

The CatSkills pulled my truck and trailer as close to Sheer as possible and Riordan, with Bonnie's help, supported her into the conveyance. He insisted on riding in the trailer with her and- legal or not- no one dared to argue with the implacable, young man.

I don't know how I'd have managed without their help. As it was, I used all my will power not to crumble. Not then.

At home, the nickers of the other horses seemed to ask 'what's happened?' Animals have those instincts- those we humans have mostly lost, unfortunately. The dogs and cats empathetically stood by as Sheer slowly backed out, and then they followed us to her stall.

Riordan rigged a sling for the night from equipment Aunt Vickie had used once before for a boarder's horse recuperating from a fractured leg. It would give Sheer better balance and support through the night- the first 24 hours generally being the worst.

Sheer refused a carrot, but I filled a hay net and hung it and a bucket of water within her reach. She was alert, but exhausted. I gently slathered arnica on the undamaged areas of her hindquarter, covering bruised muscles, and dissolved several tiny tablets in water and with a syringe shot them in her mouth. The vet had supplied me with plenty of pain meds and had put a call into Dr. K to schedule a visit early the next morning.

"Good choice," Riordan applauded my use of arnica.

"Indians have used arnica for centuries," Bonnie interjected. Such congenial voices in the turbulent silence.

"You need to attend to your ankle," she cautioned. I nodded and thanked them. She offered a business card, "Please let us know how she does," and I hobbled off. Nothing more I could do at the barn.

My sketch pad lay on a chest at the foot of my bed. I flipped to a blank page, took up a pencil. With ease, I drew a quick scene of Sirocco in a flawless collected canter in her favorite pasture. Pencil stroked paper depicting Sheer in her incomparable extended trot- completely airborne, tail proudly, gloriously flagged.

But then the magic took over. My hand, not of its own accord, drew an unfamiliar horse, head facing me, shaded legs, and mane and tail of extreme length. A bay. Why?

The magic wasn't finished- other views of the same horse appeared, portraying strange scars prominent on chest and shoulders, eyes that dwelled in a dimension beyond what was available to artists with pencil and paper.

Inside those eyes, other eyes. Magic eyes, supra-normal eyes spotlighted me. Almost as if I were looking at myself in one of those forever mirrors.

The pencil took over again as my puppet-self watched, spellbound. Thoughts of my throbbing ankle had long faded. On the page appeared the head I'd drawn in Lough Gur. Long black hair, black eyes, impressive brows, high set cheek bones, prominent nose, wide mouth, strong imperious chin- the kind that could block a punch and taunt for more. A face that exuded mystery and tremendous strength.

The lead pencil tip continued to a neck with a leather thong around it, bare shoulders, and suddenly the magic stopped. Was this the person I felt watching me inside the stone circle? Surely not- there'd been no one anywhere, but I flipped back to the page from Ireland- yes, I'd drawn a shadowed head over- looking one of the huge stones. Overactive imagination reveling in an ancient site? As for the scarred horse...

Completely enervated, my fingers trembled. The magic ended and my ankle begged attention in its stead. Locating a boot jack, stifling cries of pain, I somehow removed the old show boots, dug up Aunt Vickie's liniment, doused my swelling ankle, applied ice packs, set the alarm to check on Sheer during the night, felt the dogs and cats take up their respective positions in bed and let the numbness take me.

I choked on a flood of tears, my chest heaving. Aunt Vickie had left just days before. The familiar horror of mind-shattering sadness began with Sheer's injury, and like dominoes cascading rearwards, hit me with Aunt Vickie's and Marshall's passing and continued on back to other areas I never wished to relive.

IOU A HORSE

With my aunt's and the gentle giant's help, I'd learned the necessary high level movements to perform with Sheer, but my mind would not fasten on those rapturous moments. No. The whirlpool spiral cast me to bedlam. Other injured creatures, deaths, curses, slaps, cold, alone... Sad. Alone.

Somehow, I cried myself into oblivion.

12

Murphy's law. For three days following the accident at the show, I barely slept, shooting up at alarmed intervals to check on Sheer.

The first night she mostly ignored my presence at midnight and 3 am- like she was trying to tell me to quit fretting. Sheer loved to be admired, but not worried over. I administered more arnica and replaced cold wraps. And hoped.

The Creekside critters eyed me with curious speculation. Dogs, cats, horses- all extended their noses and empathetic barks, whiffles, snorts, whines and meows.

A different mist washed my bleary eyes when at 7 am Sheer's vocal cry for breakfast trumpeted as I exited my back door. As quick as a peg-leg pirate, I jubilantly hobbled to her stall- the first one in line.

I topped her breakfast with love and compliments and soft strokes on her neck. Crossing my fingers, I released the sling and she stood resolutely. Munching stopped for half a second as she tested herself, found nothing wanting and dug back in to her porridge.

Upon finishing, she tentatively stepped to the section of her stall reserved for manure placement.

"Easy Sheer, easy, wonderful, wonderful girl," I reassured her and poured on more endearments. Sheer expected and basked in compliments. She'd trained me in that regard and I was more than happy to comply.

I flushed a carrot from a pocket. The sound of it breaking had her ears flicking and her muzzle thrusting out. Her eyes betrayed the status of her hurting, but her stoic self was not surrendering.

"It's going to be all right, Sheer. Take your time," I left her with, as the rest of the menagerie yelled for their waitress.

IOU A HORSE

Dr. K eyed the injuries without much expression. Not a vet of the doom and gloom variety, he was more of a wait and see person. "I've seen cases where you'd swear there was no hope and darned if the animal didn't prove us wrong. We'll look to stave off infection and wait and see." He mentioned that infected tendon sheaths would mean trouble- keep a careful watch for any changes.

I put in a call to Dr. L to cover all bases- I so appreciated his expertise as had my aunt. In fact, the alternative specialties kept him so busy he'd given up regular veterinary office calls. He counseled giving Sheer a few days and then he'd stop by and try an acupuncture session. Chiropractics would have to wait a bit longer.

I kept myself in check during the day and rode out the storm of my draining nights. I would not break down in front of others. My misery was my own and I'd not burden anyone else.

With Aunt Vickie barely a week gone, I was sure health professionals would caution I'd not yet finished the grieving process, let alone begun such, but the complete management of Creekside rested solely on my shoulders, and my best friend had serious injuries that I must tend to while appearing to be in calm, if not exactly good, spirits.

I refused to cancel lessons with my students- being busy was indeed the only medicine for me. Bearing their sympathetic looks and condolences- that was terribly difficult. Nodding my thanks, I rushed to fill time with anything that remotely needed attention. And I was relieved and grateful when boarders and students and others left for the day.

Sundays had always been reserved as potential days off. It rarely worked that way, but the idea was good. When it worked.

By late Sunday afternoon, my blood sugar low from lack of feeding myself as well as I did the critters, I drank cold tomato soup from a jar against the sweltering weather and headed for the shower. My sticky hair needed attention.

Balancing against the shower stall wall, I shampooed my hair and reflected on the past week. I'd been railed at by Dr. K and Dr. L and a few tremulous, daring boarders for not taking care of myself, or asking for help- not to mention the vociferous tirade from Sierra,-being stared at by students as I hobbled, hopped and dragged myself from arena to stalls to the house.

Shoring myself up during the day, I collapsed into bed each night, too tired to distinguish exhaustion from the numbness of the downward mental spiral. The accompanying visual images ran together with the demands of my livelihood. Supply lists and lesson plans were fruitlessly propped up as shields against flashes of memories best not dwelled on. Cards recommended I remember the good times- why wouldn't that work for me? I had to get a better grip as I was starting to forget necessary daily needs- like putting up the fans. Lists, I needed more lists...

Ruminating had me not minding the shampoo. Suds escaped into an eye; I nearly lost my balance with the sting, adjusted the shower head for help and...

Bzzz! Bzzz!

Captain's heralding bark resounded. Someone was at the door. Who in the world? Had I missed an appointment? A dreadful thought, as I rigorously fought to never be late.

Bosun and Mate- Aunt Vickie's names. Why the nautical references? She never said.- added to the security system clamor.

"Coming," I shouted foolishly. Who'd hear me?

Knowing the process was inadequate, I hastily rinsed my hair, carefully stepped over the tub walls, half-heartedly dried and pulled on a thick house coat- much more modest covering than anyone wore on such a warm day.

"Coming!" I shouted again as I tried to hurry to the side door while the doorbell complained continuously, caught my hip on the corner of a chest, nearly collapsed with the pain, and finally flung open the door to an improbable sight. Murphy's Law, indeed!

A middle-aged man, sun-burnt face, scant graying brown hair, dressed in jeans and a polo shirt advertising a construction company, halted his next assault on my door bell. He was not above displaying his impatience and he confronted me as Captain took up guard position.

"Hello, finally," he grouched.

IOU A HORSE

My right eye still watering from soap, I wiped at it with my sleeve and called for Bosun and Mate to quiet. In the drive was an old, red stock trailer I recognized. Pulled by an overly lighted 4x4 pick-up. Ray Donner's outfit.

Next to the wiry, small frame of Ray Donner, a little girl, 6 or 7 years old, jumped up and down clapping her hands.

"Get him out! Get him out!" she screeched in a high-pitched voice, over and over like a broken machine, to the impervious horse trader.

"My name's Walt Thurman. You're Miss Gray, right?" The uncalled for visitor was not at all shy about interrupting a hard-working woman's shower.

I nodded, eyeing Ray whose eyes didn't meet mine.

"Have I missed something? Did you have an appointment?" I racked my brains.

Bosun and Mate stood half-crouching, keeping a decided distance from the screeching child. Creekside was a quiet venue and this child in her pink shorts, sneakers, tank top and flapping curls, with her irrepressible antics, was definitely out of their ordinary.

"Mr?"

"Thurman," he offered his thickly calloused hand- probably his construction company flaunted on the polo shirt. Ignoring my question about appointments, he proceeded, "I just bought my daughter this horse and Donner said you were the trainer for the job."

"Oh," I looked with growing skepticism at the situation transpiring in my drive.

This visitor had no qualms at all about barging in on someone unannounced. Didn't construction workers believe in appointments?

"Yeah. He said, uh, you were one of them horse whisperers, whatever that means. Well, Tilda picked out this horse and uh, here we are."

Murphy's law, cubed.

Obviously this man knew nothing about horses or etiquette-such as phoning ahead.

"Would you mind waiting here while I get dressed?" I asked and struggled to put my wits back together from an affronted jigsaw formation. "Perhaps you could quiet the child. Tilda?"

I patted Captain's head and closed the door. Pulling on jeans, I remembered other situations Donner had foisted off on me. Aunt Vickie would have nothing to do with the man and I was relegated to either helping him or waving good-by.

For instance, an elderly man wanted to own a horse before he died, and learn to ride it. Donner had sold him an arthritic quarter horse with navicular. Luckily, the gentleman- Tim Holt, had the patience and understanding of a saint. He not only loved that dear, old ailing horse, he seemed to comprehend just what kind of care the animal needed.

He told me after I'd advised him of all the ins and outs, "I reckon that's OK. I need the same kind of supplements. Both of us have been around. What I'd like to know is can you help us?"

Mr. Holt and Buddy were still with us...me. Good days and bad days they spent together, joyfully commiserating. But on the really good days, Mr. Holt carefully saddled the patient, grateful Buddy and they rode the trails through the woods and practiced large patterns in the covered sand ring.

Then, there was the control freak who had purchased a flighty, off-the-track Thoroughbred from Donner. It took a full 6 months and her broken nose before I had her finally realize this was not the best match for her.

My friend Sierra located a 4-H horse whose owner had gone to college. Perfect for Ms. Control-It-All. One of my better students bought the Thoroughbred and was doing well with him.

There were other instances that had involved a lot of time, patience and good luck. Aunt Vickie would shake her head every time Ray Donner called and hand the phone to me.

With greatly earned misgivings, I hobbled out to the trailer-ankle protesting all the way. "What is it this time, Ray?"

IOU A HORSE

The Thurmans, herded by the dogs, were examining the arena which gave me a few minutes alone with Donner. He was not my favorite person, as he didn't care what he sold to whom.

His excuse was, "Hey, this is what they wanted." And he sung my praises to the poor sods who bought what he sold- hook, line and sinker.

"Want me to bring him out?" A loaded question as it was a pretty sure bet if the animal came out it would invariably not get back in.

I looked through the slats of the stock trailer. Exceedingly long black mane, head hanging. The tell-tale symptoms.

"How much ace you give him?"

Donner cracked a smile, spit off to the side. "Now, Miss Dove..."

Everyone I dealt with titled me the way they'd addressed Aunt Vickie- Miss Dove. I looked at him expectantly. I knew his tricks and he knew I knew them.

"All right," he grunted.

"Hurry up, tell me. They're coming back," I urged. I needed some information I could use.

"All I could give him without killing him. This is one bad ass..."

"And you sold him to a kid!"

"Hey," he shrugged, "the kid insisted and her daddy can't say no to the little darlin'." At least, Donner and I had gained the same sort of conjecture regarding the Thurmans.

"You gonna get him out?" Thurman asked. His daughter began hopping around and clapping and shrilly singing.

What was her name? Tilda. "Tilda, you must be quiet around horses. It isn't safe to jump and scream. You might cause the horse to spook and hurt himself or you. Do you understand?"

Feeling myself the image of not-to-be-brooked Aunt Vickie, I donned my instructor's cap. It was really the only way I was comfortable conversing with anyone.

Her father crossed his arms, leaving it all up to me, while the child frowned, thinking over my words. She began kicking at the grass. An over-active little girl. One without parental supervision or guiding parameters. Great. Thanks, Murphy.

"We will not unload this horse until you are very still." There I'd done it. Opened the door to God only knows what.

I perched nonchalant on the trailer fender, easing the weight off my overlooked and loudly lamenting, injured ankle. And waited, feeling leftover soap drying in my hair. Mr. Thurman was absolutely no help at all.

"All right," she groused.

I lifted a brow at Donner. He released the back door with a metal squeal, dropped the ramp, entered and untied the hanging head. The horse refused to back out. Probably too drugged to believe he could actually, safely move, especially in that direction.

Donner went for a whip. Typical. Drug 'em and/or beat 'em. A surge of anger gripped me.

"Wait a minute," I interrupted. The last thing I'd stand by and witness in my lifetime was a horse being whipped.

Bad enough the poor animal was drugged to the hilt.

"Give me the lead line." I hoisted myself into the reeking, fly-full trailer. Did he never clean the thing out? Old and fresh manure piles defiled my clean paddock boots.

"Watch it, Miss," Donner whispered a warning. How kind of him! "You'll want to be very careful."

"Right," I retorted, furious with him and this entire impossible scenario.

I moved to the horse's head. Lustrous mane, clean face. Lack-luster eyes briefly registered my presence with a fraction of curiosity.

"I know you don't feel well," I began speaking to him in my most soothing voice- the one I reserved for the most put-upon creatures. "I want to help you, but I'll need you to try."

For a loaded minute nothing happened. Then, slowly, his eye never leaving mine, his head rose slightly. He blinked and a shudder raced through him.

IOU A HORSE

"I'm sorry," I placed my conciliatory hand, on his neck. "Will you try?"

With each guarded movement backward, he attempted to feel his way. Slowly, slowly, he staggered back and I thanked the powers that be that the damned trailer was at least a ramp load.

Once out, the head dropped again. Until Donner approached. Suddenly, fiercely, his head shot up. Ears flattened, teeth bared, the horse tried to lunge at the dealer. His unsteady legs brought him up short, but I'd not give odds on Donner's life if he came close.

"Whoa!" Shocked, the horse trader cursed and stumbled in retreat, whip flashing.

"What's wrong with him?" Thurman, the horse-ignorant, asked, and proceeded to thrust more questions at me.
His daughter added her piercing cries, "My horse! My horse!"

With the tone of voice I reserved for recalcitrant animals and the rare student who dared to say 'I can't', I rounded on Tilda.

"Do you remember what I said about noise and horses?"

Like a bucket of water tossed on a pair of fighting dogs, she instantly shut up. I found that particular vocal mannerism extremely useful when chaos struck. Like right then. No raising of voice, but it was a deep, serious-toned warning.

"Would you mind giving me a minute alone with Mr. Donner?"

Thurman frowned, started to object. Not used to a female calling the shots, I presumed. Thinking better of it, he kept his peace and stepped away, Tilda in tow. I'd really expected an argument. Perhaps my tone of voice had caused him to decide he'd rather not be on the same receiving end as his daughter.

"I want a paper from you detailing everything you know about this..."

I took a full, long look at the bay with its black legs and bronze body. An unusual shade. And...

And, "Oh, my!" Angrily, I turned on Donner. "He's a stallion! Are you crazy?" I almost shouted.

Donner simply shrugged. Why not? He'd taken their money and unloaded the problem on me. By rights, I should tell him to reload the stud and leave me out of it.

Except... The stallion's head remained high and alert-strangely alert for such a drugged animal. A lengthy lock of mane rose from his shoulder with the stir of a breeze. Something caught my eye- behind his shoulder. Mystery indentations, white hairs. Weirdly placed puckered scars. I walked around him. One patch atop each shoulder. Equal pairs on his chest.

Barbed wire accident? Something told me, no. But, how?

My face flushed and my heart quickened. The horse from my sketch pad! The unusual markings the magic had used my hand to create in place. Funny, inadvertently or not, the magic had forgotten to draw the sex of the sketched horse!

IOU A HORSE

13

After Donner provided me with a signed statement listing the drugs administered, the sex of the horse, a brief explanation of how the horse turned up in a lot that he'd bought at auction- no registration papers, the purchase price of $500 and- I had to fight him on this, how the horse attacked him, I felt as if I'd at least covered the initial bases to keep me out of court. In the event of an accident.

The stallion had not stirred or offered his teeth to me. This did not mean I'd shuffled my misgivings under a stall mat, but I was certainly curious.

Now, where to put him. Creekside had one small paddock with a run-in shelter. The fences weren't high enough to discourage a stallion bent on mayhem, but I had to start somewhere. He needed solitary quarters and that was the best I had to offer.

"Donner, I'll need you to move Pippin and Sam Mule to the left pasture." The covered sand ring separated the solitary paddock from the barn and pastures.

"I gotta get," he protested and walked toward the truck.

"Unless, you want to hold the stallion? Because you're not going anywhere until I get this situation under control." I used the same tone I'd used on Tilda.

He glanced at my injured ankle, "Heard about your accident, bad piece of luck." And he did an about-face, trekking to the curious Pippin and Sam Mule.

The stallion could not have cared less as Donner moved the two school horses. He didn't offer an instant's interest in the other horses nosily peering from their Dutch doors- just remained completely impervious to their equine queries.

Not until Sheer demanded attention did a single ear flick. Sheer, the flirt, would certainly gain the notice of a full-blooded male.

"Good luck," Donner nodded, walking purposefully to his truck- hell bent on leaving.

I waved over the pacing Thurman.

"So what's going on? Can you do something with him or not?" The construction boss held sway in his demeanor now that I was the only authority figure around.

Tilda started to skip, heading for the rear of the horse. "Watch out! Tilda, you must never run up behind a horse." And I fruitlessly explained the mechanics of a horse's eyesight.

Save me, would this day never end? My blood sugar levels were protesting and my head and body felt too light to continue this scenario.

Fingering the lead line, I considered the proposal I would make.

"I'll take him over," Thurman reached to take the lead from me and in a flash the stallion swung his head and lifted the man off his feet.

Thurman landed hard, knocked the breath right out of him.

"Son of a bitch," he thundered to his feet, arm ready to swing- the battle-cry of an affronted male.

I put myself in front of the horse, my back to him. Not smart.

"I wouldn't do that if I were you. You have no idea what this animal is capable of," I calmly stated while my mind revolutionized all my senses.

That took most of the wind out of his sails, but his face reddened beyond the sun's diatribe, with barely banked anger. He was not used to being told what to do.

"Daddy, you're funny," Tilda added fuel to the fire with her giggling.

"Mind yourself, missy," he rounded on her, hawked and spit a brazen, manly exhibition.

I had to defuse this situation in a hurry. "Listen, I'll keep him here for a week. Give him enough time for the drugs to wear off..."

"Drugs?"

IOU A HORSE

"Yes. He may have seemed docile to you at first. I assure you he has been drugged. I'll have my vet take a look at him. I need to do a thorough eval..."

"How much is this gonna cost?" The true macho construction boss seeing down to brass tacks.

I rejected explaining how the purchase price of a horse is often a drop in the bucket compared with the follow-up costs- waste of time on this...person.

"$210 for the week. That includes board and my fee."

It should have been more. I could almost hear Sierra telling me I was bonkers, with a few choice expletives thrown in. And spying on me from heaven, Aunt Vickie had that pursed-lip look, pursuant to shaking her head.

As Thurman had no choice with Donner high-tailed home, not that he'd have had one if Donner had stayed, recalling how the stallion reacted to the unethical horse trader and to him, he folded and called it quits.

"All right," he blustered, not the least bit happy. "I just wanted to buy my daughter a horse."

"In advance, please," I held out my hand. This was only good business sense. Sierra and Aunt Vickie applauded inside my head, but Thurman was less than pleased.

"I'm sure you pay for your materials upon arrival," I began to explain although I was pretty sure he did not.

He foisted a wad of money into my hand.

"So, do you think he'll be ride-able?"

I'd not give a snowballs chance.

"I want to ride now," Tilda stomped her foot and whined. "My horse, my horse," she kept the decibel level down but snidely checked me for a reaction.

She managed to escape her father's hand and rush under the nose of 'her horse'. The stallion chose this opportune time to exhale a large dose of snot all over her upturned face. Finally, something discouraged her. She scrambled behind her father and wiped the viscous substance on the back of his shirt. Which thrilled him even more.

I turned over Donner's statement. "You'll write a sentence giving me the care and custody of this animal and releasing me from all responsibility for any injuries."

"Injuries?" I think it began to further dawn on him that said horse was not only going to be expensive, but also potentially dangerous- a ball game he was not familiar with.

We exchanged phone numbers and I was never so glad to see the exit of anyone as Thurman and Tilda.

I was nearly happy about the stallion being under the influence as I hobbled and coaxed him to the paddock. If he'd been full of himself, I'd have been in trouble.

The small field had been adequate for Pippin and Sam Mule's antics. As with all fencing on a farm there were always posts and rails that needed replacing or shoring up, but I'd run out of steam hours ago.

Previously, it had not been a top priority. The stallion's entre changed all that. I adjusted his halter after leading him inside the gate- decided it was best to keep it on. Water and hay and several patches of grass were available.

I don't know what I expected when I unhooked the lead line, but he surprised me by dropping his head and in complete apathy, just stood.

"Right, then. There you go. Try to behave." Like Aunt Vickie, I always talked to the 'critters'. A co-dependent condition of being without human conversation the majority of time? Who knows? Or cares?

I retrieved the solar-powered electric fence strapping and rods. My ankle and soap-sodden scalp lamenting all the way, I rigged a further safety measure to the turn-out area and hobbled painfully back to the shower.

IOU A HORSE

14

"Are you out of your f****** mind?" Sierra exploded when I called two days later to tell her the news. I didn't get my words in edgewise as she perched on her podium and railed at me.

Sierra Sorenson, a 6' tall, Nordic blonde with Olympian shoulders, lived a mile down the road on a 1000 acre farm. Think Quarter horses and cows.

Alternately, she intrigued and scared the hell out of most men. Women, too. We'd formed an incongruous friendship when meeting by accident. Literally.

At the local feed store, I was flattened by a 50lb. sack of grain slipping off the shelf. With one hand, she picked up the bag and with the other hoisted me to my feet.

My Vetericyn purchase suffered the worst as the plastic bottle had burst and I slid precariously in the wound gel.

"Hey, Kid, you all right?"

Kid. Ever after she called me Kid. Was it because she was at least ten years my senior or because she dwarfed me?

"You don't weigh much more than this f**** bag." She had several favorite words. Sailors terms, I think they are referred to. Darned if she didn't mention a stint in the navy. The f-word was the top pick. I'll not mention the others.

"Dove Gray," I offered my thanks for the lift and a hand to shake.

"Sierra Sorenson. We're neighbors. Miss V is the shit!" She saw me wince and smiled broadly.

"Don't know 'bout you, but it's lunchtime in my book. C'mon!" It would be hard, if not downright dangerous, to refuse a Sierra-extended suggestion.

"Hey, Buck! This kid's taking a case of Vetericyn. Keep you out of court. Best watch whoever's stacking those bags." And she bowled past the manager, case in hand.

I had the distinct impression fire would separate and nobly allow her a safe, courtly corridor. Her wake propelled me along as if we were magnetized.

Over Frisch's fish sandwiches, fries and extra tartar sauce on the side for dipping, we made inroads into a state of friendship- totally out of character for me, but Sierra is not one to be deterred.

She was nosy and not shy about admitting it. Wanted to know everything. Yesterday. My reticence didn't dissuade her and she fired questions about my interests, boyfriends, girl friends, sex, beer... But she also equably accepted I was not to be the most verbose of her acquaintances.

Her forte in the horse world was cowboy mounted shooting and barrel racing. She was also a 4-H advisor to the largest group of children in the state of Ohio. Kids considered her a walking legend.

There were enough stories to back up her legendary notoriety. One involved a judge who made Sierra's 6-year old student cry, saying her horse was unsuitable. Apparently, Sierra not only told him he was a f**** moron and asshole without a shred of suitability to call his own in front of a crowd, but when he had the nerve to argue with her and point his finger at her chest- grazing a breast mind you, she decked him. Flat out. Bet he never pointed a finger at a woman's chest again or made a little girl cry insulting her horse.

Sierra had a separate no-nonsense yet fun way of coaching her kids and another irreverent style for most adults- "Get your ass in that saddle and glue it there!"

Aunt Vickie was not one to spread the news so Sierra asked how I came to be at Creekside.

"Everybody for miles around was shocked as shit when Miss V took in a waif," she dunked a French fry three times in tartar sauce and raised her brows for clarification.

"My parents died in a drunk-driving accident- my father being the drunk." I was not hesitant about this. Aunt Vickie waited until I was 12 to give me the details the kind woman had abstained from divulging to a 5-year old. "85 miles per hour and a concrete wall provided the accident."

"Hmmm," she reflected. "Probably for the best. Looks like you're doing all right. I hear you're as good with horses as Miss V?"

A compliment with a question mark at the end? I felt my face burn. Compliments were something I didn't know what to do with. I had the same difficult time with questions too, outside the schooling ring.

"I'll have to come by and watch you sometime," she chuckled at my flustered lack of response.

Turned out Sierra loved old western re-runs as much as Aunt Vickie and me. Wednesday nights turned into a threesome.

Of course, she had to watch certain expletives and the number of beers she consumed, but otherwise Aunt Vickie admired her. Even took a class in mounted shooting. Not on Marshall, though.

Sierra provided Aunt Vickie and me with two sound and ready horses, plugs in their ears- Quarter horses, and we were instructed to ride- walking, the line of poles and aim for the balloons attached and quivering in the breeze.

My aunt had some experience of firearms so walk was out of the question. She put her eager horse into a lope and attacked as Sierra cheered. Eight out of ten balloons popped on the first go. She got the remaining two after rolling back her mount and retracing the route at a thunderous pace. I clapped along with Sierra. Without any experience in shooting, which my aunt later remedied, I was quite a different story and needed lots of help.

"Kid, you need a f****** pistol and target practice," was Sierra's advice.

After two days surreptitiously and then, studiously, eyeing the stallion, I called Dr. K.

"He seems despondent," was the only way to describe him. "He stands with his head down most of the time."

"I'll be around this afternoon. It still might be the drugs," Dr. K shook his head over the phone.

I'd given the stallion two days of peace to let him settle in. Hay and water were refilled. At least, he was eating.

I warily approached him once as his head hung over his water bucket and softly asked, "You all right?" If the stud turned mean, I'd be in a world of hurt. No way to outrun him; I'd have to duck around the lean-to and hope.

Pointless thinking. He'd not once made an untoward move in my direction. Nevertheless, my attitude was one of cautious respect.

Oddly enough, in the two days since his arrival, my ankle had completely healed. What a relief to be able to move again! If only Sheer healed as fast. Dr. K would check out the heat I'd discovered the previous night- please don't let it be infection in the tendon sheath. He'd already warned me they were murder to deal with.

It was difficult to tend her wounds without my heart cringing. To see her in this condition... But Sheer didn't fold to her injuries; she tried to drag me out of her stall when most horses would not be the least inclined. And she demanded the newcomer's attention, as was her due.

The stallion ignored me and her. Ignored the hand I placed on his shoulder. This was not what I expected. Bugling at Sheer's flirtatious whinnies or at least showing some mettle would have been more like it.

"Can you catch him?" Dr. K asked that afternoon.

A leftover student, an early one, and Mr. Holt stood in the nearby shade and watched. Dr. K had examined Sheer first. The heat I'd felt the night before was thankfully gone and she fretted at being cooped up in her stall.

"Get her out for short intervals of walking. She's balanced, but take it slow. Let her tell you what she wants," he'd advised. Grass, I thought. Grass was good medicine.

IOU A HORSE

"Yeah, I can catch him," I said. There was no catch to it. Sierra was probably right, though. This was a crazy risk. Pictures of the stud attacking Donner and upending Thurman without any warning flickered like caution lights in my brain.

"Wait here, I'll bring him." My sixth sense told me to leave Dr. K on the safe side of the fence.

"Hello, there," I calmly announced myself. Without a single qualm on his part, I clipped on the lead as the strangely-colored, red-bronze bay seemed to doze in the afternoon sun.

"I was hoping you might let my vet take a look at you." An ear flicked as the only sign of pique, and he quietly walked by my side. All 16'2 hands and 1000 pounds of him.

He didn't push his way past me. I could swear he was purposely stepping in sync with me, making an expected allowance for the way I'd moved when he first came. I frowned at my thoughts.

Developing a rapport with horses was tantamount to working harmoniously with them and even though I tried to refrain from attributing human traits to them, all too often I discovered horses had a gamut of traits humans should be proud to have.

The closer we got to the gate, the higher the stallion's head rose. Dr. K opened the gate and all at once a different creature was on the end of the line.

Long, thick forelock was flung back as his head revolted. He didn't pull the line completely from my hand but it slid to a new length, and he was cavorting in place, snorting, nostrils wide, eyes brilliantly afire.

"Easy, there, easy," but my voice did not hinder his eruption.

Dr. K continued his approach, speaking in low tones. When the vet reached four feet from the stallion, the revolution took a turn for the worse. His head shot out, ears flat back, teeth bared, intent on Dr. K.

Half sitting on his haunches, he roared his intention and struck out. I fed out the line as he reared high above me.

"Hey, there, stop that," Dr. K yelled. "Give him a tug on that line, Dove!"

"Get out, Dr. K! Please," I ordered. Luckily, I found myself in a relatively secure position at the stud's side.

"Should have a chain across his nose," Dr. K seethed as he hastily backpedaled to the gate held open by my 1:00 student.

With the vet's exit, the stallion instantly settled. No more prancing. All four feet solidly planted on the ground. No more snorting or challenging cries. As if he'd never exploded.

Like a flash of light in utmost dark, I had it, "You don't like men, do you?"

My fingers stroked the scars on his shoulders, ran down the arch of his bronze neck. Not a sign of distress. Weird to go from rebellious to completely placid instantaneously.

I walked with him closer to the gate to talk to Dr. K without shouting. This seemed to be OK with the stallion.

"What would you like me to do? Obviously, if I'm to examine him he'll need to be tranquilized. Kind of defeats the purpose, but let's see." Dr. K put out a hand and the stallion bared his teeth again. However, he seemed to recognize the barrier between him and the vet and stood his ground.

"Dove, I'm afraid this one's probably been man-handled- the way he reacts just to my presence and what you describe happened with that Donner and the new owner. What exactly do you want me to do? He seems fine now, but I have to warn you. Fight or flight is part of a horse's make-up- this one would rather fight. You could be putting yourself in a potentially dangerous situation."

"Would you mind writing that up for me to give to the owner? The name's Thurman and he's totally ignorant where horses are concerned."

"He's going to get a mega-dose of what he'd rather not hear, then. You say he bought this for his daughter?"

"Yes, an overactive 6-year old named Tilda."

"Barking up the wrong fence. The kid needs a pony that's been around. You should call Sierra."

"That's a great idea," I mused, picturing just the one.

"What do you intend to do with this guy?" Dr. K asked.

IOU A HORSE

Tim Holt sauntered to the gate. The stallion's head swung in his direction.

"Watch out, Tim," I cautioned.

The elderly man nodded and smiled mysteriously. "Met a few bad 'uns, didn't you, boy?" Tim addressed the stud in a friendly manner.

Ears flicked in Tim's direction. You would have thought Tim won a gold medal when the stallion's muzzle slowly rested atop the gate near Tim's hand. Misty eyes betrayed the gentleman's emotion as the stallion gently stepped toward Tim and nuzzled his shoulder.

"Well," Dr. K kept well away from this scene. "He doesn't hate all men. Wonder what his history is."

"Donner didn't know or really care to find out. Quick turnaround is all he's interested in," I said.

"I'll write up a report that'll give Thurman a lot to think about. You know, you'll probably end up with this guy," Dr. K shrugged. "You could always geld him."

The bay's head gently rose from Tim's shoulder and fastened a piercing rebuke on Dr. K. 'You could try,' sounded clearly in my head in a deep, masculine voice.

I frowned, wondering if I'd heard what I thought I had.

"Did you say something, Tim?"

"No, Miss Dove. Have a good night," Tim smiled at the stallion and walked off.

15

"I'm coming over," Sierra closed her cell phone against my protests and I prepared myself for further remonstrances.

Dr. K had left; my 1:00 lesson was saddling up. I'd not had any lunch and although I knew I wasn't taking care of myself, I couldn't summon hunger. It seems I'd not been hungry for a very long time.

Something nagged me as I headed to the covered sand ring. What was it? I felt eyes watching me. Stopping, I turned. There. The stallion's eyes were glued on me. What was going on? Was I losing it?

Dr. K had suggested gelding and...something inside my head...words- 'You could try!'

Not Tim. Not Dr. K who had a slight drawl and was busy writing. Who? Along with not eating, I'd not been sleeping well and now... Was I hearing things? Was I slipping?

No time to think about it. My lesson waited. Better not think anyway. Nights waited for that tedious process. And that particular thought had me clutching my gut. Since Aunt Vickie left and Sheer's accident every night was torture.

The lesson had just finished on a great note when Sierra's dually rumbled up the drive. Clara, my student, had worked hard on lightening her inside rein when asking for canter. Finally, she found the correct, diplomatic tact and her horse 3 Time Charm rewarded her with a beautiful three-beat canter which precipitated a beaming, 'eureka' smile on Clara's face.

I was amazed to find myself trotting to meet Sierra. How could my ankle have healed in three days?

"Well, you're moving pretty damned good," Sierra gave me a hard going-over. "You look thin and..."

I waved off her less-than-genteel admonishments and nodded at the stallion peacefully standing in the paddock.

IOU A HORSE

"Let's have a look at the beast," her long strides had me doing double time to keep up.

The strangely colored bay had moved as far from the gate as possible, his hindquarters turned to us. Absolutely no interest at all. So unusual. Most horses exhibited some form of curiosity- at the very least, a perked ear. Unless turning his butt to us was his idea of proclaiming- 'bug off'. Hmmm...

Sierra let out a long, piercing whistle. Every equine head on the place tuned in. The dogs howled a bit and retreated. Sierra's whistle had that effect on sensitive ears. Thankfully, I saw it coming as her fingers traveled to her lips- I knew to hold my ears against her onslaught of the air waves.

But the stallion- not a hint of movement. Too darn strange. His head hung, completely disinterested. Not even a swipe at the patch of green under his nose. But I'd witnessed his split-second explosions, all without any warning.

"Does he hang around like this all the time?"

"Pretty much so, unless he takes a dislike to someone and then..." I hitched my bewildered shoulders.

"Yeah, you already described his treatment of that f****** Donner and whats-his-name. Could be this guy's smarter than a lot of people. I'd like to see him close up. Nice color- brushed bronze real striking against all that black framework. Almost freaky," Sierra studied the stallion.

"Miss Dove?" Tina, my next student, approached leading her leggy, chestnut Thoroughbred.

"Yes," I twisted to face her.

"Could you look at...?"

I heard the gate open behind me and I hurriedly swung around. "Sierra, wait!"

Just who does this brash, manly female think she is?

With a fierce sense of alarm riddling my spine I cut off Tina's question and raced inside the paddock.

"Sierra, wait!" I hurried to catch up with her, but the stallion beat me to it. His head snaked around, teeth bared, ears flat. He half-lunged at Sierra- a distinct warning for her to keep her distance. Determinedly, she snapped a lead line at him.

So you want to play, huh?

Swinging the lead like a lariat, Sierra donned her cowboy mien.

"This old boy just needs to learn a little respect," she grinned, self-confidently, and continued toward the stud- now, a completely different horse- talk about Jeckle and Hyde turnabout.

Head rising higher and higher, he snorted a challenge, bellowed admonishments.

"Sierra, stop, please," I begged, hastening closer to play mediator.

Ignoring me, she tossed out the line again looking to make the stud move off- trying to establish her authority.

But as Dr. K cautioned, this horse was more inclined to fight than flee. The line hit his front legs and the stallion fumed, screaming as he reared and advanced on his hind legs. His front legs shot out like a boxer throwing punches.

"STOP IT," I yelled at Sierra.

But she fired the line with one hand and reached for her ever-present pistol with the other. Not one of her cowboy mounted shooting pistols with its blanks, but one with live rounds.

Sierra stood her ground and raised her hand, sighting.

IOU A HORSE

Damn! How could things get out of hand so fast? Without a second's hesitation, I moved in front of her, the pistol at my head, the stallion at my back.

"Get out of the way! Are you f****** nuts? This f***** is dog meat," she glared at me.

I could feel the air bristle with the nearness of the stud's flailing feet behind me.

"Sierra, GET OUT! NOW!"

Her eyes widened; her face paled. What did she see? My potential death going down? Local trainer mauled by deranged stallion?

All of a sudden, Sierra didn't seem so sure of herself. I heard the stallion come to ground as she backed away, but I refused to turn until she stepped through the gate. When I did turn, the stallion was whisper-close, and we stared at each other, eye to lowered eye.

The manly woman begins to fear. The injured one knows no fear.

"Well," I took a deep breath. To gain a semblance of reality, I checked my previously injured ankle by moving it in circles. Absolutely no repercussions. The stallion merely studied me, shook his head, mane floundering, as if coming to grips with something, and idled off.

What else had the magic not sketched when the stallion appeared under my pencil-wielding fingers?

I joined Sierra. Tina's jaws remained dropped in shock.

"It's OK, Tina," I calmly said. "I'll check on him later. He's moving fine," I called to their retreating figures.

"What the hell was that all about?" Sierra rounded on me.

"You should have waited for me. Of all the people he's encountered since Sunday night, I'm the only constant that he's not tried to destroy." And Tim, I thought. Weird.

"Kid, you better get him outta here. Major safety issue with a capital M, and this pen here is not enough to waylay a dangerous f****** stallion." Her tone of voice belied the state of her nerves.

For want of a breather, I scrutinized the fence. The electric part was good, but it was attached to posts and rails that needed attention. As in yesterday.

I'd have to tend to the repairs. Soon. But I needed to get Sierra off my back, so I explained to her what I had in mind.

"You're out of your f****** mind, Kid," she recovered quickly.

"Maybe," I hedged.

"Maybe? Look at you! You look like hell, and you've got this whole place to run by yourself, and you'll do it if it f****** kills you! You don't need that," she thrust her middle finger at the oblivious stallion.

"Will you just think about my idea?"

Sierra holstered her pistol in the small of her back under her vest, draped the lead over the gate and crossed her arms, thoughtfully.

"What did you see before you stepped back?" I recalled the inexplicable look in her eyes, not exactly fear, but...

Frowning, she finally responded, "I've never seen a horse do what that one did. Your head was so close to being squished like a bombed melon when you moved between us. In a complete rear, he moved back one step at a time. I'd never have believed a circus horse could do that. I mean, I know those Lippizzans at the riding school in Vienna can propel themselves into the air using their hind legs while rearing like a hopping f****** rabbit, but this... This f****** freak actually took one step at a time, backwards...in a full rear," she let out a string of choice words, obviously at-odds all over again.

IOU A HORSE

If I hadn't wanted to shoot him so f****** bad, I would have taken a video on my cell. Most amazing thing I've ever seen a horse do. Like...nah, couldn't be, could it? It's as if h...he wouldn't hurt you for anything. But he'd not spin off and run either. F*****!"

I had felt the stallion's all-too-close mobilized mass. Why I wasn't shaking, I didn't know, except, I'd never been one to panic. The thought of my own death never consciously weighed on me.

"He's got the biggest feet," Sierra snidely remarked.

Of course, she'd got a firsthand look at his hooves. I hadn't even brushed him yet, or picked his feet.

"You know what they say about guys with big feet, dontcha, Kid?"

"Good foundation," I replied. A horse needed good feet.

"Nah, big feet big...," her brows rose provocatively, her hand brushed her zipper. "But I can't say it always holds true. I'm dating this guy, 6'4". Wears size 15 shoes but he's kind of lacking in the..."

"Sierra!" My face flamed. Was she actually comparing the stallion's equipment to her current boyfriend's?

"Lighten up, Kid. You need to get a life aside from horses and work. I'm just saying that beast has got one helluva package!"

I squirmed- there were enough things requiring my attention without standing around comparing sex organs of men and horses.

She gave up the ghost, seeing how discomfited I was- smacked of her still feeling out-of-sorts.

"Get some rest, Kid. I'll think about your plan. Maybe, I'll see you tomorrow. Thurman's coming around 2?"

I nodded, feeling almost faint with relief. The gravity of the episode caught up with me- blindsided me really. Sierra was still alive, thank God!

"But if I hear that f***** has so much as stepped on your little toe, I'll shoot the SOB."

16

Peace and quiet had descended on Creekside. The horrible early heat that had disparaged the show finally submitted to a typically pleasurable, late spring evening. But like the extended forecast of brutal heat to come, my inner mindset see-sawed in a state of turmoil I could not escape. My lists of things to do were inadequate. More needed doing than what registered on the tablet pages in front of me, but I couldn't dredge up what I'd missed. What was wrong with me?

I managed to swallow bites of turkey sandwich and cranberry juice- all without tasting. Not only my inadequacy in attending to all the requirements of the farm bothered me, but now I was hearing voices. Shake it off, Dove, I mentally berated myself, and get busy- not that I'd been idle by any means.

Sheer was up for a short walk; so, empathizing with her stilted gait and yet trying to curtail my fussing- she hated fussing- I became her puppet as she brought me out of her stall and practically dragged me to the lush clover in the side yard. Her compromised hind leg would not dare stand in the way of getting to choice grass.

The x-rays, true to CatSkill's surmise, showed no fractures, but tendon and muscle damage and bone bruising, the sundered skin... My fingers lovingly ran through her long, silvery mane. I bit my lip to refrain from tears, but my heart cried with every stilted step Sheer took. No matter what, I must keep up my spirits for her, even if she congenially took it all in stride- God, how could I come up with a pun in a situation like this?

"You're wonderful, Sheer. Wonderful girl," I chanted. Her ears swiveled like tiny satellites at my praise. She knew she was wonderful, but her courtier's plaudits were always welcome. And expected.

IOU A HORSE

After an hour of grazing, she unwillingly followed me towards her stall, stopping to pick another tasty tidbit with the ruse of 'I need to scratch my fetlock'. That's Sheer- way too smart.

As we neared the barn, I happened to glance over at the stallion. Sheer's head mirrored mine. The stallion nickered, winningly, and Sheer's muzzle basted the sky as she accepted his admiration. Her body trembled. Being the only mare in the place- this had the potential to get very interesting once she came in season.

"C'mon, Sheer. You can talk to him from your stall," I cut into their mutual communiqué.

For a moment she blocked me, her concentration solely on the stud. And suddenly, I got a wondrous taste of something else the stallion was capable of.

From a magnificent potentially volcanic standstill, he arched his perfectly placed neck and began to dance- the male trying to attract the female with his elegant performance. A sweet piaffe with lowered quarters and tremendous hocks reaching underneath his body- lifting in impeccable sync with their diagonal foreleg mates.

The dance in place dreamily floated. Moved forward effortlessly, halted. Danced, wind borne cloud-like in place again and then proudly strutted onward in passage.

Dear heaven! Aunt Vickie, wherever you are, look at the ground he's covering! Breathtaking! From the ethereal passage he drew out his gait into an extended trot that rivaled the finest Olympians, back to passage- one had the distinct sense he could soar over the fence effortlessly- not a good thing. Buoyant! Volatile! Absolutely beautiful! I was spellbound.

Sheer, however, was not impressed. She nuzzled me as if to say- hey, I can do that. Snorting, she tugged on the line for my attention. She was never one to accept the sharing of my regard- after all SHE was IT and she knew it. Time for snacks- she eagerly headed for her stall, taking me with her, giving the strutting stallion the brush-off.

I walked along, but my eyes swept back to the show in the paddock. To feel that kind of energy underneath me...

Sheer and I had achieved the miraculous, ballroom-dance partnership that equine aficionados pined for- we were that in sync. I'd earned my bronze, (and silver, too, come to think of it) medal with her- one of the awards offered by the United States Dressage Foundation. Our scores had been consistently in the high 60's; occasionally we reached 70's, once into the eighties, but her Arabian conformation didn't regularly earn 70's- it didn't matter to me. Hang the scores! All those covert taunts from fellow competitors when I rode in on an Arabian were abruptly silenced once they observed her ambitious, queenly performance.

And to Sheer, with her highly developed sense of pride, it was all a show. As long as I told her she was wonderful, she was game to try. Sheer's mind never caught a whiff of 'it's impossible', and I was overwhelmed with love for her. Aunt Vickie had nailed it when she spoke of the bond formed when you work with a horse rather than against. The ribbons- they were simply icing on the cake.

Watching the stud had me remembering the sight of Edward Gall on Moorland's Totilas at the World Equestrian Games in Lexington, Kentucky. That pair had sent chills up my spine as I watched their Grand Prix test. Pristine harmony and happiness in their work together.

The stallion had the movements... Sheer grabbed the lead from me, returning me to the present and her desires. After all, she was the Queen and I a mere servant, albeit a loved one.

Rising extra early the following morning after another restless night- I was coming to hate going to bed- I scrambled eggs, added a bit of ham, onion, cheese and ate most of it. Feeling somewhat fortified, I decided to spend some time grooming the stallion after making the morning feed rounds and before the late morning lessons and the dreaded arrival of Thurman and Tilda.

As per his norm, the stallion stood resolutely still and indifferent as I clipped the lead line to his halter and let it fall to the ground in front of him.

IOU A HORSE

"You're tied," I said. Every horse I worked with learned the words tied, stand, wait and halt as part of their initial repertoire. Countless times, these had come in handy.

Once, a young trainee had wrestled the lunge line from me as we worked at a trot on a circle in the sand arena. Inadvertently, the exiting rider had not latched the gate and the young gelding decided to high-tail a detour.

"HALT!" I belted in a deep and adamant tone. Without a pause, the youngster stopped dead, long enough for me to grab the line and shut the gate. That boy received multiple praises.

Eyeing the clean state of the stallion's coat, the perfection of his trimmed feet, I was struck- unbelievable! There was not a speck of dust on him; not a single chip on any hoof. I left the curry and stiff brush in the grooming kit and brought out a soft rubber-tipped implement for massage purposes.

With Sheer, I'd normally undertake a running dialogue: How do you feel today? What should we work on? How about grass? But the stallion seemed impervious to my presence; I almost felt childish speaking to him.

However, there were some topics that needed to be addressed. Thankfully, he was not immune to my gentle ministrations with the massage curry and he completely surprised me by turning his head to watch me make the clockwise, circular palpitations on his back muscles.

Cautiously, I minded him as I continued. Wouldn't do to get nipped. Or worse.

Strangely enough, as soon as I thought this he snorted and nuzzled the right side of my spine as I tended his. Astonished, I nearly dropped the massager. For an instant, time stopped and then his muzzle urged me to go on.

"I... All right," I agreed. Swallowing my foolish thoughts, I decided on another course of conversation. "We need to talk about something. You know you're not the best match for Tilda, right?"

I moved to his other side and he attended me likewise. At the mention of Tilda, he snorted and stomped, irritated.

"You know, I get the feeling you understand everything I say." Did I actually say that aloud?

Another snort- an harrumph?

"When the Thurmans come today, it might be a good idea if you put on a wild act. Quietly standing around could give them the impression they are up to owning you and..."

Flecks of snot spattered my shirt. A purposeful blow-out? Hmmm...

"Did you happen to uh, say something when Dr. K advised me to geld you?" I quickly, ridiculously spit out.

A tail swished across the back of my head.

"I believe you have a perverse sense of humor," I stated, checking the backlash of hair in my face. No response. I finished up by running a soft brush over his gleaming bronze coat. Not an ounce of dust! How is it possible for a horse to be so clean?

Gently, I touched the strange scars on shoulder blades and chest, but he tensed, moved away, as if guarding his privacy. How had he come by such marks? I was certainly puzzled to explain their origins, but I knew horses were overly adept at getting into trouble.

On safer terrain, my fingers ran through his mane. The black hair ran down his shoulders to his forearms, his forelock to his nostrils- silky, yet thick. "You are rather amazing," I complimented him and stepped away as his nostrils flared and his head rocked from side to side.

I ran my hand down his leg preparatory to asking him to lift a foot for me to pick out. But he refused to allow me the privilege. Time was running short; I figured I'd come back and deal with the issue later.

Gathering the grooming kit, I unhooked the lead, offered a peppermint snack especially designed for horses. I'd never had a horse turn up his nose at one. Until this one.

He simply looked at me as if to say, would you eat that? Feeling as if I'd been caught lacking, I re-pocketed the snack. I'd have to try something else, I guessed.

IOU A HORSE

"I need to call you something," I looked around for inspiration. A lovely blue sky with huge puffs of white and sunrise-tinted clouds lodged lazily above.

"What shall I call you?" Names like Cavalier, Cuchulain and Vanguard ran through my head. The stud nudged me to earth and lifted his head to the sky.

"What?" I peered up. Had I missed something? "Sky?"

He snorted, disgruntled, shook his head. A raven flew over, carousing on a draft, cawing raucously, as if privy to some private joke.

"Raven?" That didn't sound right. His nose rose to the sky and he held it there, giraffe-like.

Directly above, a white cloud billowed like a ship's sails fretted with tremendous draught. "Cloud?"

That couldn't be right. Not for such a magnificent animal. But his eyes came back to mine.

"Seriously? Cloud?" Liquid eyes bore into mine. I... It seemed too mundane. What in the world did clouds have to do with...?

A large foot stomped, rattling my inane perambulations. I refused to countenance Sierra's remarks about guys' feet, and I forcefully kept my eyes from investigating certain parts.

"How about Cloud Dancing?" I attempted to brighten the all-too-plain christening of Cloud, but received a distinct snort of disapproval for my efforts.

"Just, Cloud?" I swear a flicker of frustration crossed his thinking gaze.

"All right then, Cloud." Conceding to his wishes, I picked up the grooming kit, ready to leave. Time to get my riding gear on. Get ready for the day's lessons.

Before I reached the gate, that same deep masculine voice sounded in my head.

'I've been told I have no sense of humor.'

I stopped dead, tripped, managed to catch myself before the grooming kit contents and I hit the dirt. Goose-bumps raced along my arms. Swinging around, I half-hoped to see someone- anyone. But there was no one. No one, but Cloud. And me.

IOU A HORSE

17

The stage was nearly set. Stacey cooled off her horse while I went to greet Sierra who had unloaded the Pony of the Americas I had in mind.

Spot, he was called. Spots would have been more appropriate as he was a downsized version of a leopard Appaloosa. His coat truly looked like a Dalmatian dog's. The pony's face was so mottled with spots that at a distance, it looked all dark, instead of white with numerous black spots. A gray and white mane and tail completed his darling, God-given physique.

It was in his personality that Spot really portrayed the utmost in excellence. Spot loved children and he innately knew how to handle them. Fun-loving kids could hop on bareback and head off safer than with a contingent of babysitters. Crying children were nuzzled and licked until giggles replaced tears.

Spot had been known to tickle a hard-nosed bully until the errant child capitulated, rolling on the ground with Spot's nose sunk into the most ticklish spots- muzzle fervently at work.

With the fearful, Spot was an angel of patience, not a move did he make until he felt his person was OK. Truly, a pony worth his weight in gold. And Sierra owned two more POA's bent on imitating Spot's ingenuity. No child could resist Spot.

"Mr. Thurman, Tilda, my friend Sierra Sorenson," I introduced the major players.

Sierra had left Spot to his own devices, so he ambled along with his lead line slung over his back.

Thurman eyed Sierra with overt speculation. Used to rude appraisals, she waited it out with unabashed bravado.

"Damn, you're tall," he flirted and gripped her hand a second too long.

To which Sierra politely smiled, curled her long fingers around his and gripped harder.

Thurman flushed, caught out, until, in her own good time Sierra's hand relinquished his- with a feminine smile to boot. Maybe she didn't scare the hell out of him, but he'd certainly gained a newfound respect.

A roar of...distaste?- interrupted the little guinea play. Cloud had taken off in a bucking spree worthy of the bull Bodacious.

The fence, I thought! Please do not hit the fence, I prayed, as his hind feet shot high above the top rail. Fishtailing, he whirled, raced across the small expanse of the paddock and his body slunk to the ground only to rocket up- all four feet in the air.

A gurgle of a laugh bubbled up from inside my chest. I stifled it with a coughing fit. Cloud had come through in a vibrant, violent show of derring-do.

"Jesus!" Thurman whistled. "He been like that all the while?"

"Beast almost killed me yesterday," Sierra faithfully told the truth. "Nearly shot him. That one's an insurance man's nightmare."

I rolled my eyes at her on the sly. The bit about insurance, however, was something I'd not thought of. Great, more slippage on my part!

A spate of childish laughter dissolved our interest in Cloud's shenanigans. Spot had latched onto Tilda and vice-versa.

"Daddy, look! Spots!" Tilda laughed and threw her arms around the pony's neck. Spot, the ultimate charmer, nuzzled her jeans.

"That's his name, Spot," Sierra took over in her advisory 4-H role. "He loves kids. You want to ride him?"

That sealed it. A high-pitched "Yes," rent our ears.

"Now, we have to watch how we talk around horses," Sierra showed Tilda how to sit on Spot's back after giving her a leg up.

My turn. "Mr. Thurman, I have an evaluation from Dr. K concerning the stallion, as well as a statement from Mr. Donner and my own advice, which you've paid me for. I would suggest the stallion is not your best choice for your daughter's well-being. Along those lines, my friend Sierra has a proposition for you involving Spot."

"What am I supposed to do with him?" The construction boss grimly huffed. Cloud conveniently tossed his head, ears flattened, teeth exposed.

I steadied myself. "I'll give you what you paid for him. That will give you the funds to..."

Sierra was ten feet from us, all ears.

"I'll take a $1000," the macho Thurman stated, thinking he had a gullible fish on his line.

"Nah, Kid, tell him to get lost. Nobody will take a murderous horse for $1000. Not even the canners," Sierra tossed in.

"Daddy, I want Spot! I want Spot!" Tilda screeched a chorus until Sierra gave her a quiet wave. She toned down the pitch but kept up the refrain, "I want Spot!"

"You won't even find anybody to haul that..." Sierra directed none-too-fondly at Cloud, "away. I know. The horse-world grapevine already knows that monster is dangerous."

"I want Spot! I want Spot..."

"Now, the best plan for your daughter, and I'm sure you're thinking only of her well-being and enjoyment, is for her to join my 4-H group with other kids her own age. We'll work out a lease agreement and Tilda can ride Spot." Sierra left the ball idling in Thurman's court.

He wasn't entirely sure, but a woman might be putting one over on him.

"And what exactly are you going to do with him?" He smirked, all macho on display.

"Give him a home for a start," I shrugged and lifted five $100 bills from the zippered pocket of my riding breeches.

Hands on his hips, he gave a final once-over at Cloud. The stallion seemed to issue a last rebuke and vaulted for the gate, sliding into a stop inches from the poor old entry, bugling loudly.

I didn't feel sorry for Thurman, but I did think it was difficult for some men to walk away from a challenge. Even one they didn't stand a chance of winning.

"Where do I sign?" Thurman finally conceded, accepted the bill of sale, and I left him to discuss details with Sierra.

Horses generally involve a lot of money aside from the purchase price. Thurman would not be pleased, but if he really had his daughter's interests at heart, Spot was his best option. Spot obviously thought so; he and Tilda were pleasantly discoursing.

I made it through the single afternoon lesson, did the afternoon feed, double checked all the critters and waved at Tim, astride Buddy, returning from a trail ride through the woods.

A forceful gust of relief had me weak at the knees. Another horse... Not enough stalls... But Cloud was safe.

I sank to the ground outside his paddock and crossed my arms around my knees, drawing them close to my chest. My breath felt ragged. My heart quirky. Why had this outcome meant so much to me?

I tried recalling when I'd first sketched this mystic horse- with the magic's help. Was it in Ireland? The night of Sheer's accident? All of my drawings had dates- since I'd arrived at Creekside. I'd have to check.

Cloud advanced to the gate. Unfathomable eyes bored into mine. A sudden chill. I felt exposed- like he'd seen right through to my core. The stuff I kept to myself. Unnerving.

We engaged in a stare-down.

"Who are you?" I whispered. No reply. Where had that deep voice come from? The one that had clearly trespassed inside my head?

Sierra complained continuously that I looked awful. I'd caught the surreptitious, empathetic glances boarders and others tried to hide when they saw me coming.

Sleep evaded me. I wasn't exactly worried, just...lost? The numbness ruthlessly belabored me into a downward spiral I was helpless to stop. I didn't want to relive anymore sadness. I didn't want to recall my being a child and all that entailed. Why didn't the daily tasks wear me out completely? Why didn't I collapse into bed immune to anything but a deep, exhausted sleep?

"You need time to grieve. To heal. Talk to God," one of my more spiritual boarders had written a note to me.

Grieve. Heal. I broke the stare-down first and rested my forehead on my arms.

The Kind Man. The magic. Was Cloud here because of...?

"Miss Dove? Miss Dove?" A shadow blacked the late afternoon sun from me.

"Uh, Tim, is everything OK?" Looking up, I prepared myself to bound up, ready to address any need. At the same time I was ready to... What?

"I was about to ask you, are you all right?"

"Some might question my sanity," I tried to grin. "I seem to have bought the stallion. I... I call him Cloud."

Actually, he calls himself Cloud, but if I said that I knew for sure I'd receive an even more intense look of concern.

"Hmmm... He's a special boy," Tim mysteriously averred.

Special. That's not what Sierra parted with.

"Look, Kid. You're supposed to be smart enough to know this isn't Disney World. That beast..."

"Cloud. His name is Cloud," I was compelled to say.

"F***** is as far from a cloud as shit can be. You just remember I've got a bullet reserved for him. You keep safe."

18

"I can't make him move," Martine wailed in frustration.

"You are absolutely correct. You cannot make him move," I assured her.

Martine was a P&G executive with her mind awhirl considering the next mountain to climb. Though it made her a great exec, it was much harder for her to excel in the dressage world of harmony via relaxation.

Her previous riding experience involved trail horses with a basic pull on the reins to stop and kicking to go. She had the desire and the money to back her up, so after watching a clip of Olympic dressage champions, she'd decided that that was how she wanted to ride. Not necessarily for the Olympics, but she'd set herself a goal and would not back down. I believed she would have been a great general in some historic age.

For a month, I'd kept her on the lunge line with either Pippin or Sam Mule. No reins- Aunt Vickie's program, which I wholeheartedly agreed with- seat perfected first before trusting a horse's delicate mouth to hands.

As Martine was a person who always exerted control over every situation, not having the reins in her hand harkened red flags in all her sensibilities- "What if he runs away?"

I convinced her I had control of him, and that all my beginners had been safely and correctly started on Pippin and/or Sam Mule.

"Martine, do you carry a purse on your right shoulder?"

"How did you know that?" Her eyes pinned me, fascinated. "My chiropractor badgers me to ditch the purse."

"Your right shoulder is hitched up as if to hold something there. This creates a tension in the right side of your body and actually," I walked behind her, "puts you crooked in the saddle, makes it difficult for you to get the right seat position. You know what tension does- a crooked body will mirror itself in your horse and cause you to compensate horribly. For right now, roll your right shoulder clockwise and counterclockwise. Do the same with your left shoulder. Now, the right one again. Feel any release?"

She concentrated so hard on feeling, I wasn't sure if she would or not. Her eyes flew wide.

"I...I think I do. I'm tossing that Michael Kors," she declared with a snort.

I assumed that was a designer's name. "I'll remind you about your shoulder until it returns to its God-given place." And all the other factors involved in her achieving balance in the saddle.

Three times a week she'd arrived punctually, absolutely determined to conquer trust issues, fear issues and control issues- not to mention her body's physical issues. By the end of the month the changes were extraordinary. Mind over matter? Where there's a will there's a way?

I congratulated her on leaving her other life behind once she stepped into the stirrup, and so I should not have been completely surprised when she presented me with pictures and video clips of several prospects- Martine wanted a horse of her own. Oh, and could she board with me and continue lessons?

"We'll work something out," my mind raced with the slight problem of not enough stalls at the moment, let alone bringing in another horse, securing Cloud's paddock and a multitude of other listed and possibly not-yet-listed necessities.

"Let's get you working more on your own before we..."

"Look, I'll do whatever it takes. I can continue the three lessons a week and maybe add another one if you're up for it. You can ride my horse until you think I'm ready, but," she seemed embarrassed at what she was about to reveal. "Coming out here is the best thing I've ever done for myself. There's so much peace here. I hate to leave even when my lesson is over."

Her words made perfect sense to me. The only peace I whole-heartedly experienced was when mounted on a horse. Didn't matter if the horse was in training, already there, or doubly intransigent. For some reason, I was 'at home' once my right leg swung over a horse's back.

Nothing else in my life gave me that sense of serenity or of truly belonging. Teaching lessons was a part of the ballpark. Suddenly, it struck me hard- in a way, I was more like Martine than I cared to admit.

How had Aunt Vickie managed with all the constant demands on her? Was she happy in her every day routine? Alone? With the passing of Marshall had she given up? Was he her only source of peace...happiness?

All of her personal emotions were hidden from me and everyone else. No affectionate displays between us- at the most a congratulatory remark upon my accomplishing a particularly difficult task, but never an exchange of confidences.

Would she have passed on if I were still a child? For a second, a cinder of anger flared. Now, why should I be angry? Hadn't she left me her monumental legacy, magic-induced or not?

Was this introspection part of the grieving process? Feelings of abandonment? And anger? The hint of losing control?

Stop it, Dove, I chastised myself. You have a great home, loving critters...

Aunt Vickie is gone. Sheer is...disabled...

STOP IT! I couldn't afford the mental descent during the day. Concentrate on Martine; she's trying to decipher...

I shook myself out of it.

"Remember, Martine, if you retain tension anywhere Sam Mule will shut you out."

Sam Mule, a grade chestnut gelding could give a lesson better than I could. If his rider were not correct, he developed a semi-meditative state and would not move. Firecrackers under his feet wouldn't move him if the rider was tense and gripping. If the rider leaned or the inside rein turned into a roadblock and violated harmonious communication, he'd quickly stall. Shades of his namesake.

IOU A HORSE

Aunt Vickie's favorite saying came to mind- "Never discourage a horse's optimism. If you can't deal with it, get off. At least one of you should enjoy what you're doing."

I thought I had an inkling of how long-married couples followed each other to the other side. Marshall was her other half. I bit my lower lip to keep from tears.

"I'm not tense," Martine's voice betrayed the whole notion.

"You're hands are saying no and your legs are saying go," I cautioned her. "How should you be holding hands with him?"

Sam Mule was off in equine LaLa Land, waiting for the correct release.

"What are you thinking of right now, other than Sam Mule?" Her face developed a scowling mien under her certified helmet.

Just as I thought. "Tell me," I sighed.

"Damn!" she cursed in a loud exhale. "The conference tomorrow, picking up my presentation papers, dinner tonight."

"OK. Now that you realize where your head is, what do you expect this poor boy to do?" I ruffled the chestnut's flaxen mane.

Not one to win a conformation class, Sam Mule transformed from ugly duckling to magnificent swan when his rider allowed it.

"Will you show me?" Martine winced.

I'd not been on a horse since Sheer's accident. For one thing, my ankle had initially presented strenuous objections. But no longer; it felt great- miraculously fast healing!

Why hadn't I sought the peace of Pippin or Sam Mule or Venezia's back?

Venezia was the black gelding with a single white star marking- the original Trakhener horse Aunt Vickie had picked out for me. She'd decided he was too good a price to pass up and he'd come home along with Sheer.

The gelding had never shown Sirocco's pride of place. Although he could perform all the movements with ease, he was on the unenthused side of the fence.

Aunt Vickie had named him Venezia, saying he reminded

her of a Venetian gondola- his arched black neck like a gondola's prow. Perhaps he should have been a gondolier- languidly plying the Venetian canal waters.

"All right," I agreed. I adjusted the stirrup down two holes for my longer leg position.

Ned, my teenage stall mucker and working student, seeing the exchange, brought my helmet to me and lingered by the four foot wall of the arena to watch.

"OK, Sam Mule, sorry it's been awhile," I softly stroked his neck.

My legs sunk down and very gently clasped his barrel as if I were his second skin. I felt my seat key into the saddle like a plug into an electric socket- ready for the ignition of and prospective dance of two species' with compatible energy. My fingers threaded the reins between ring finger and little finger until I had a diplomatic feel of Sam Mule's mouth via the snaffle bit.

With the slightest whisper of my seat through a deep breath, gentle caress of leg and accepting hands, Sam Mule gathered himself. His neck arched into the feel of my hands as he left his meditative state and moved off with gusto.

I had to smile- a genuine smile that lit up my entire body. To be one with another living creature- how precious! Unfortunately, Sheer had also seen the change of rider and was whinnying her extreme discontent.

"Hold on Sheer, we'll go out later," I called. Which mollified her fractionally. Sam Mule, however, was undeterred.

"You make it look so easy," Martine applauded after I took Sam Mule for a brief trot and canter and halted by her side.

"If it's hard, you're doing it wrong and probably not breathing, either," I admitted as I dismounted. "There is a timing of communication- the application of aids, which is effortless."

My passion must have seeped into her, for Martine gleefully, hopefully, readjusted her stirrups and carefully mounted. The rest of the lesson loosed a smile on her normally taut face and her eyes misted at the gelding's response to her 'allowance of the dance'. I'd always thought compatible work between horse and rider mimicked ballroom dancing.

Sam Mule accepted his due of an organic apple afterwards as she walked him out, brushed him and told him how amazing he was. Of course, Sam Mule cordially agreed.

Before she left, Martine brought me three pictures of Warmbloods to look at- horses bred specifically for dressage.

"Please, would you go with me Sunday? I've signed up for Tai Chi classes to help myself get pliably supple and to help with my breathing. I'll follow you to the letter. I just can't wait to get started- if you think any of these are appropriate. Please?"

This woman, old enough to be my mother, was appealing to me to help her with a goal- one I felt would be very beneficial to her. I would not destroy her budding confidence and desire for an equine companion.

"You've already started. I'll go with you, but I'm going to be pretty picky. You're safety is my number #1 concern."

To my great surprise, she threw her arms around me and hugged me fiercely. "Thank you! Thank you!"

Hugs and emotional displays were never part of my world. Aunt Vickie reserved affection for her critters- not humans. Perhaps I mirrored her all too well in this, as well as my longing for equine company over humans.

When Martine released me I blushed, ill at ease. Not knowing how to respond I simply patted her arm, opened the distance between us, sought for anything to gain my attention, to rescue me from the chill shock of contact.

"You did a nice job today," I happened to glance at Cloud's paddock. He seemed to exude an intense interest. Once more I felt his thorough scrutiny- unnerving, as if I were bared naked before him.

19

6am wake-up alarm call. Not that it was necessary. Since Aunt Vickie...had left, and Sheer's accident, I slept in fits and bouts. More tired rising than when I turned in.

The alarm clock was a redundancy anyway. With the doggy door in the kitchen and my bedroom door open, various dogs and cats traipsed upon or neared my chest, checking my breathing, and upped the ante if I were actually sleeping by barking or meowing or racing over me- must not miss the breakfasts!

Aunt Vickie's handgun now resided on my bedside table, cozied up to the alarm clock. I wasn't afraid- not with all the critters, but it was a useful tool in certain situations, as my aunt always touted. Had she ever felt afraid? Lonely? So much information went with her. And if I'd asked? I'm sure only pursed lips would have replied.

She had maintained her distance with humans outside of the mechanics of business. One of her first remarks, "I don't do family," came readily to mind.

Aunt Vickie did you have to go? Was...death the only answer? Such a simple answer. She'd be on my case right now for dawdling. Too much to do. I gritted my teeth and agreed. That 'too much to do' was my only welcome, saving respite.

But something was definitely amiss with me. I felt so 'off', even though I uncomplainingly dragged myself out of bed instead of my previous eager risings. The critters- my guardians, hastened their herding me to the kitchen. Priorities...

Grinding flax seed, I mixed the fibrous powder into cranberry juice and water, sucked it down, rinsed the cup, placed it in the dish strainer, vaguely recalled the morning a raccoon sat up in this same sink, and I had to play referee with the dogs and cats while my aunt calmly opened the back door and said, "Get out, please." Not even a raccoon would dare disregard my aunt's ultimatum. I wondered how the lost creature might respond to me, in my current state.

Get your act in gear, I griped to myself. Inane thinking won't get anything done.

The next part of my morning routine involved a series of stretches with Aunt Vickie's admonition ringing in my ears, 'If you're not supple, don't expect your horse to be.'

7am, feed the critters. Thoroughly check each horse. Wheelbarrow hay to Cloud. Check the automatic waterers. Turn out Venezia, Buddy, Game Version, 3 Time Charm, My Ox- an off the track Thoroughbred, Regal Rogue- another off the track Thoroughbred, and No Surrender- an Irish draft cross. All into their respective pastures and paddocks. Sam and Pippin remained in the indoor arena, in lieu of the paddock Cloud now occupied, until it was needed for lessons.

Walk Sheer- who violently protested the others going out first- for ten minutes, and then place her in her mobile, solar-powered electric-fence paddock. Every other day I had to move it as she mowed the grass inside.

8:30. Breakfast- my own, if I could summon an appetite. Lately, like other pertinent details, this also eluded me. Lists of things needing mending: Cloud's paddock, leaky run-in, the boards No Surrender had kindly displaced...

I'd driven nails back in to hold the side wall together, but more TLC was in order- pronto. The bathroom sink had developed a leak...and there were more things requiring immediate attention, I was sure of it. I needed to make a list and call Allen- the first-choice handyman.

Check over the week's lessons, supplies, quarterly taxes, bills, water and rake the arena after it was cleaned of Sam Mule and Pippin's leftovers from the night before, ride Venezia, set up the car port for Sam Mule and Pippin- they couldn't continue to occupy the covered arena, ready Marshall's stall for Martine, call Gary Stern, our farrier. With his superb persona around horses and those who loved them, he patiently never argued with my aunt.

She trusted him beyond all other farriers and would wait for him no matter his schedule. Gary always made it a point to get to Creekside as soon after her call as he possibly could- he was another of her admirers. If an emergency transpired she'd do what she could rather than call anyone else- the admiration ran both ways. And...

Both of us had ridden the three prospects she'd selected. Used to the lightness of Sheer, the big boys were not my cup of tea, but I had to evaluate them for Martine's use, not mine.

I wanted to gauge each one's reaction to something completely out of their realm. Who was flighty. Who was curious enough to stay and investigate whatever monster I'd selected for the test.

Before riding, I'd blown up balloons and calmly walked toward the saddled, waiting horse with the balloons wavering in my hand. Martine stood at a safe distance, fingers crossed, as I tested the huge Warmbloods.

A leggy bay tried to bolt. One of the chestnuts quivered and danced with wild eyes. The last one's eyes grew large, but he stood his ground and his nose slowly stretched out. Needless to say which one I'd recommend.

"This is the one," Martine buoyantly announced after dismounting a copper-colored chestnut with white diagonal stockings- the curious stalwart.

I stood, non-committal, hoping she'd elaborate.

"He reminds me of Sam Mule. Did you see? My mind wondered and my seat got tight and he moped around. When I checked myself... I love how you put it, Dove- (she never called me Miss Dove) 'if you want automatic pilot take flying lessons; a partnership involves two'," Martine gushed. Her description left me more than satisfied as I'd come to the very same conclusion.

IOU A HORSE

"Any chance of a 30-day trial?" I asked the breeder. He eyed me with a sympathetic look. Not knowing what to do with sympathy, I dipped my head and scanned the immaculate premises.

Wynn Graeter knew of Creekside. Knew about Sheer, as did the entire equine grapevine. I'd competed against him, as had Aunt Vickie. It was worth a try to get the opportunity for a trial; many things could still come to light over that time period, but I didn't want him to feel he had to do it because of my recent losses.

"Sorry about your trouble. Is he staying at Creekside?" I answered in the affirmative. "For you, I'll do it." Silently, I sighed, uncomfortable and eager to leave, to escape what I read in his eyes.

Martine pulled out her checkbook. And Mr. Graeter turned his attention to her.

"Down-payment now; after he passes your vet check, I'll take half. The balance after 30 days. I'll expect you to carry insurance to cover his full value," he explained to Martine. So Copper was coming, soon.

Lunch time at various times, if at all. Work it in around the lessons, most of which were trailered in. Return phone calls, talk to Sierra about cutting our 60 acres of hay- our year's healthy supply, pray for suitable hay-cutting weather, check the status of other supplies- grain, meds... Clean tack, afternoon lessons, sort show bills with my students in mind, walk Sheer...

At some point, I fully realized her scores in Columbus had finished our requirements for the USDF silver medal. My hands shook as I filled out the paperwork. Sirocco. Sheer.

Biscuits, Dove, get a grip!

Late afternoon. Walk Sheer, check wound for signs of infection, call Dr. K, Dr. L, what am I going to do with Cloud?, run-in and temporary paddocks needed manure pick-up. As did the pastures... Speak to Ned...

"Miss Dove, could you take a look at Sir?" No Surrender. "I think he's picked up a thorn in his frog."

Nothing new for Mr. Big Foot. A slap happy giggle threatened. Sierra and her big feet. That reminded me- sheath cleaning time, though lately I'd read such was not always the best option. How would Cloud react to my attention on his private parts?

Supper. Not at set times for me. 4:00 for the critters. They'd learned patience with our routine. Coming in from pasture, anyone trying to push their way through me had an abrupt reawakening of their manners. One thing Aunt Vickie did not tolerate in horses was their crossing over into the handler's personal space. Ditto for me. Couldn't afford it.

Lists. Need a stall for Leopold- I'd forgotten about his arrival. I pulled my hair hoping to engage my brain. Where in the world was I going to put him? Creekside was outgrowing its original nine stalls by recent leaps and bounds.

"Hey, Kid," Sierra knew just the time to call. I refused to carry a cell phone and she caught me in the barn office/tack room. Answering machines were developed for a useful purpose and emergency phones- land lines, were in the barn and also in the covered arena. I'd not interrupt a student's lesson, or my own training time, to answer a phone precariously and noisily strutting at my side, nor did I allow my students to do so.

"Tonight's cowboy night, I'm coming over." Click. The irrepressible Sierra. Not since Aunt Vickie had we...

IOU A HORSE

"Kid, you look like hell," in lieu of a sociable hello. She then proceeded to foist a bowl of fried chicken into my hands and carted the apple pie and beer to the tiny living room.

Shuffling through old videos, she chose a John Wayne flick- RIO BRAVO. Before shoving it into the VCR, she gave me the full benefit of her fit-to-make-you-squirm glare, peering down at me from her great height.

"You do look like shit. You can't afford to lose more weight and you're not sleeping." She held up her hand to stave off my protests.

"Let me finish. You can't keep up the stoic act with me. I'm guessin' you're borderline depression what with missin' your aunt and Sheer's injury. I know. You need help. Here are three cards- counselors. Since you won't talk to me, your friend, maybe you'll consider talking to a stranger if you pay them. Insurance will cover it, Kid."

My mouth opened fruitlessly- a Venus fly trap without flies.

"I loved Miss V, but I don't want you to continue in her shoes, controlling every second. If you held Sheer with the same tight rein you hold yourself, she'd have revolted long ago. Species need species f****** specific conversation. The only time Miss V seemed happy was on a horse. The only time you lighten up is when you are on a horse. F***! You're twenty years old for f**** sake, not 70-something. As the friend I'd like to be to you, get some f****** help. Please. Let's eat," she shoved the video in and turned up the volume.

20

"Miss Dove, what are you doing?"

"Oh, hi, Tim. Is everything OK?" Anxiously, I stood up. Why was my first response to someone's question always an assumption that something might be wrong?

Tim Holt seemed ultra-comfortable in his worn jeans and long sleeved, western plaid shirt. His stilted gait never kept him from enjoying Buddy, and he visited every day, brushing and fussing over the chestnut gelding, with or without an accompanying trail ride.

With ease, he seemed to have shed his career uniform of suit and tie. I recalled he'd been an architect on major construction jobs before retiring, and he'd mentioned taking on a job or two if he found it of particular interest.

I thought of Sierra's words regarding species specific communication. Maybe she was right. How much did I know about boarders and students other than checks coming on time and their own personal quirks in the saddle? My communication skills, like Aunt Vickie's, were stuck in teaching mode rather than social niceties. Except for Sierra, who'd dig and pick relentlessly until she received an inkling of a response, however minute.

"I'm setting up a temporary run-in for Pippin and Sam. To get them out of the arena," I replied to my audience.

The car port would have to do in a pinch. The forecast for the long-run... Well, I'd think about that tomorrow. Seems I'd heard that expression somewhere.

I'd parked the car in front of the house. The truck and trailer were under an eave of the covered ring. Car port to equine run-in- it would work.

"Need some help? I used to be pretty good with my hands," he grinned, rubbing his hands together and hitching them in his pockets.

IOU A HORSE

I didn't see his face fall as I responded- "No, thanks Tim. Won't take me long." But I felt his concerned gaze linger on my back and a splinter ticked in my gut. Would it have hurt just to let him help place the rods for the solar-powered, temporary paddock?

My throat closed painfully. For some reason, asking for help gripped me in nonsensical talons. One of my earliest lessons in life- don't ask for anything, chafed me raw. So, why did I feel miserable for not taking Tim up on his offer?

Aunt Vickie never asked for help. She'd hire it, but...

'I don't want you to become like your aunt. You're too young to be 70 something,' Sierra had said. And some comment about a tight rein, too.

I bit my lip to keep my eyes dry. What's wrong with me? Was it simply a matter of depression, not that depression was simple? What did I know?

'A busy mind keeps one from being idle. But you must calm it when you're on a horse.' Another of my aunt's aphorisms. My mind certainly stayed busy during the course of the day, and if the day was especially trying, lists went down, defeated.

The old familiar numbness, the downward spiral to my early years would creep into the sidelines of my mind. Like a specter, it lingered on my skin, mingled with my sweat, seeking to smother me. The act of breathing might include a rush of anxiety.

The dreaded precursor that must not be surrendered to until...until night- when no one was about and the farm was put to rest. When no rest waited for me. The empathetic dogs and cats tried, and I appreciated their efforts to disengage the misery, but more often than not they were not successful and I...succumbed...to the past.

"Hey, Cloud," the gentleman rested his arms across the stock gate after dismantling the electric wire.

The stallion trotted over before Tim finished calling his name. Pulling out a baggie of chopped apples and orange slices, Tim offered one of each to Cloud. Promptly, the stallion devoured both and searched for more.

"Huh, you like oranges?" Tim picked out two more slices and rested his back against the gate.

Cloud's head soared over Tim's shoulder following the man's gaze, and patiently waited any more forthcoming snacks.

"I see you watching her- like Miss Dove's always in your peripheral vision," Tim stated.

Cloud ceased munching.

"You're not fooling me, son. You're here for a purpose. She doesn't know it yet, but we've gotta do something. That little lady's headed for a breakdown. I ought to know."

Grimly, Tim turned and stroked the stallion's jaw, deciding how to continue.

"Did I tell you I never married? Sixty years on this earth and I've no family. Not even a real friend until my heart attack ten years ago. Working isn't all there is to life. Took me near death to discover that.

Sold all the fancies I'd bought, except for one good suit- my burying clothes. Traveled around some. Got the feel of a happiness I'd never imagined while I was too busy making and investing money.

Opened myself up to meet people, learn some new things. Did I tell you I even went parasailing and skiing? After a stint on a dude ranch in Wyoming," he gave Cloud a pointed look, "I decided to come home, volunteer at various organizations that needed people. Discovered I liked trying to help others and," Tim scuffed his boot heel, "I bought myself a horse. God was watching out for me. That rascal Donner might have sold me an ailin' creature, but he also pointed me to Miss Dove.

Buddy is my best friend. I consider you a friend, but I've got human friends now, too."

IOU A HORSE

Tim wiped at his eyes. "So, what are you gonna do about Miss Dove? Me, I've got a few ideas in mind. She's gonna need both of us, I'm thinkin', and probably sooner than we think."

Cloud never gave a sign that he understood a single thing Tim said, but the elderly gentleman patted the black muzzle. Reaching up, he straightened the long, black forelock and turned to go.

"You're not foolin' me, son."

"Miss Dove," Ned nervously brushed at his riding breeches.

"Yes, Ned," I turned a real page in my planner- no tech device for me.

"I hope you don't mind, but what with the weekend forecast of high ninety degree weather and humidity, well, I," Ned hedged.

"Heat's returning already?" I closed my organizer.

"Yes, and I...I put up the fans. I mean I know how busy you've been... I hope you don't mind," Ned finished with a burst and avoided my eyes.

Heat. Humidity. The fans... Oh heavens, I'd forgot the stall fans! What else might I have forgotten?

Trying to cover-up my incompetence, I effusively thanked him and hastened to the house.

10pm- the before bedtime check on the critters. At the barn, toss more hay. Wheelbarrow some to Cloud, Pippin and Sam.

Leopold would be coming soon. Creekside needed another school horse and Leopold- a leopard Appaloosa, had been pointed out to me by Sierra- "Kid, he's an English horse, I'm tellin' you." And she was right. Now, where to put him?

The day had grown progressively hotter, extending into the night. Another drought year? Along with all the other farmers, I dearly hoped not.

"Sheesh, Sir! Not again!" With dismay, I eyed his dismantled stall. Damn! I forgot to call Allen. "I'll have to put you in Marshall's stall."

The big-footed beast had kicked loose my temporary fix. The 2x6 board hung into his stall, nails dangerously perked at odd angles. "How did I forget to call Allen?"

Lately, it seemed, I talked to myself as much as to the critters. For all the good it did me, sheesh!

"Good night, Sheer, my wonderful girl," I stepped into Sheer's stall and gave her a once-over, checking her wounds, looking for heat, new swelling...

Her nose ran down my arm, drawing my attention, stopped at my pockets. I smiled all the while, feeling more like crying even though I was so extremely grateful she was still with me and had all her prima donna attitude intact. Acceptance of the now- horses were good at that.

"Here you go," I gave her the carrot I'd brought and scratched under her chin. "With this heat, you're going to have to go out at night."

'No sense roasting your horse, if you have an option,' I heard Aunt Vickie clearly.

"Good night everybody," I called to the heads poking out of their stalls. Many nickered in response prior to delving into their hay.

The dogs shepherded me to the house. Until a sudden squeal of alarm rent the still night air.

Captain, Bosun and Mate raced off toward the road. "What in...?"

No time for speculation. Cloud reared high, dropped and catapulted to the fence line, set to...

I sprinted toward him. "NO! CLOUD, NO!" I screamed and waved my arms as he prepared to launch over the fence.

For some reason, he stopped dead, but he bugled and thrust his head in the direction of the road. The dogs!

I heard their distressed, clamorous barking. Flashlight in hand, I raced to see what dilemma was in the works. The long, gravel drive... I tried to run as fast as I could while protecting my newly-healed ankle from turning on the uneven footing.

Captain, Mate and Bosun were in the road, desperately whining.

"Get out of the road, Captain, Bosun, Mate! Come!" I ordered in vain. They weren't moving. I flashed my light at an oncoming car. The driver swerved to avoid the dogs, but the wheels must have been close enough to send a box scuttling.

"What...?" I hurried to the nosy dogs. A tiny wail of distress. Another.

"Oh, no, please, no," I whispered. Grabbing and cradling the box, I rushed to the safety of Creekside's drive, dogs acting as my personal guard.

Originally, the box had held a pair of hiking boots. Now duct tape wound around it. The dogs urgently encouraging me, I fought to pull off the sticky tape.

Opening the lid exposed four tiny kittens. Two tabbies, one calico, one golden... Was that blood? Two were very still. I didn't need to see more. Dr. K. I had to get to Dr. K!

Carefully, trying not to jostle the tiny bodies further, I hurried with the scared bundle close to my heart. I knew these little ones were too young to be away from their mother.

I desperately wanted to curse. Sierra's favorite words came to my lips and died. Creekside never had to go looking for a dog or cat. Our farm was a prime drop-off site for unwanted animals.

But to drop a taped-shut box of tiny kittens! Throw it out on the road!

In my wish-to-murder-semi-fog, I heard Cloud scream.

"Please, let them be all right," I prayed.

'BRING THEM HERE,' a resolute command in that deep, male voice sundered my distress.

Who?

Cloud was stomping at the gate, flinging his head. I had to get to the vet, but the dogs were inexorably pushing me toward the stallion, holding me against the gate.

His neck arched for all he was worth, Cloud's muzzle carefully investigated the tiny bodies in the box I held.

"I think two are seriously hurt," I murmured, feeling tears threatening. "I have to get to Dr. K..."

But Cloud's teeth clamped on the box and the huddled dogs forced me to stay put.   For an instant, I shut-up, and felt...something.

The magic was loose- without benefit of pencil and paper. The same magic that had conjured the stallion...

I must be dreaming.

'All right, now. Hungry,' the voice dictated. As if waking with a sudden start, I looked into the box. Cloud backed away.

Four tiny kittens that would fit into the palms of my small hands- all four of them pinned their blue eyes on me and I recognized the piteous cries for mother and milk. This was familiar territory.

They're alive, I chanted with teary relief, heading to the house. Alive, thank you... I set the box on the kitchen floor with the three babysitting dogs for company and pulled the kitten-survival kit from the pantry, along with a wooden box and a small baking pan for a litter pan- too soon for these kittens, my thinking brain took over.

Dry powder to mix up milk, kitten bottles, flannel blankets... The cries were approaching crescendo stage.

"Easy, little ones; I need six extra hands, don't I?"

Gently, I picked up the gold one, whetted the tiny rubber nipple with the special kitten milk replacer and the little tiger gripped on while its siblings caterwauled their distress.

"Patience," I crooned. The dogs collapsed around the box and commiserated.

Patient, intrigued, the shadowed man watched the proceedings. Time was no longer an issue in his life. Not like...

IOU A HORSE

Peering into the kitchen window, he studied the girl on her knees, lovingly feeding the kittens one by one.

Night after night, he'd entered the small house. Windows were excellent portals, but no door or lock could forestall him. The dogs and cats sensed an odd, but kindred spirit, and never protested his presence other than to flick an eye or ear open and then return to sleep.

The girl, however, was a different story; she tossed and turned, sometimes violently, at night. Writhed amidst the covers. Threw them off. Strangled cries. Tears. What demons pursued her? One so young...

When she did fall to sleep, the shadowed man moved through her bedroom. Atop her dresser... There it was. Long fingers pulled at the thong about his throat, missing its pendant.

With a shadow's stealth, he'd investigated the books on the shelves- art, history, horses, MYSTIC WARRIORS- a book on the Plains Indians- hmmm... More books on horses.

All was tidy in the old-fashioned room- everything in its place. The artwork on sections of walls throughout the house- the same artist- not the girl's hand. His eyes easily detected the similar strokes of brush.

A sketch pad rested on the cedar chest at the foot of her bed. Slowly, quietly, pages turned. The shadowed man hesitated, astonished at the drawings on the last pages. At the dates.

He scrutinized the still, female figure- her hair loose, disheveled from her turmoil. The long nightshirt had ridden high up her legs. An eerie ripple undulated in his chest.

Eyes returned to the sketches. A horse with scars of white hair on chest, shoulders. Long, black forelock. And the other startling drawing- a man's face. Imperturbable black eyes, high, wide cheek bones, long nose, hardened jaw, thin lips, wide mouth, long black hair down a bare chest, thong at throat, vague marks on the pectoral muscles, impassive visage. Friend or foe?

"Every few hours you'll need to eat," the girl crooned to the kittens now lying atop each other in the soft bed of flannel.

She set the timer on the stove and her head drooped to her chest. Tremors ran through her body. She curled up next to the kittens' bed, pulled a towel under her neck and cried, "God, I...I need...need some help."

'Finally,' the shadowed man exhaled. 'Finally.'

Long fingers picked up the discarded box- the kitten's would-be coffin. The dogs tilted their head at him and he nodded to them in silent communication.

He couldn't track the perpetrator, but he knew who could.

"CatSkill," the shadowed man thankfully greeted another, handed over the duct-taped box.

With a single whiff, golden eyes flared, "Kittens."

Another deep inhalation and eyes turned to the house- "Alive and well. Thank you," CatSkill approved. "You've made my night. I will so enjoy tracking and teaching this miserable piece of dung a lesson. Later."

The shadowed man would not know how the perpetrator would be dealt with, but it was a sure bet there would be a comeuppance in accord with the crime.

Nearly time. Something new. He'd never bottle-fed kittens before, but the girl would sleep tonight, he'd make sure of it.

As a last gesture, he put the threaded crystal pendant around her neck. Later, he'd hoist his tool belt and...

IOU A HORSE

21

I stretched, disrupting a phalanx of live bodies and striking hard wood. Where was I? On the kitchen floor? Sunlight peeped in at the window, scaling the African violets. In a foggy slow-motion recall, I slowly sat up, further dislodging two dogs and three cats. Cats...

The box next to me. Four, tiny sleeping beauties- all quiet. What was the time?

My hand fondled an incongruous something smooth and cold upon my chest. The crystal I'd found in the Lough Gur stone circle and... How in the world did it get here, around my neck? I'd left it on my dresser- not sure what I was going to do with it; I just loved the idea that the mystical Irish stones had gifted it to me.

The pointed end of the crystal was notched into a soft, russet suede, and extremely thin leather wrappings encircled the crystal, tied off in intricate knots. The leather extended into a loop about my neck. This necklace business was mysteriously, disconcertingly new. Had I sleepwalked and created it?

With a chill jolt, my head swung round. Had someone been here? While I slept? All quiet. Too quiet. What time was it?

I rose, the crystal slightly swinging on my chest. The kittens slept on. 6am- surely they'd not slept all night? Not at this age. But, I... I couldn't remember waking and mixing the milk, couldn't remember feeding, other than the first meal around midnight. What a queer feeling- this loss of memory.

I stumbled over the dogs, reflecting on how stiff I'd be from sleeping on the floor, but odd as the rest of the morning's beginning, my joints responded with elasticity.

My fingers cradled the crystal pendant on its leather thong. For some reason, the idea of a gift presented itself anew. The point rested near my heart. Why? And maybe more importantly, how in the world did it get there? I wasn't one for jewelry, except for a watch, but as I made to remove it a cool sense of bereft warning had me leaving it in place.

"Why didn't you wake me?" The dogs innocently peered up at me and the kittens picked that moment, while I abstractedly wondered, to make their needs known. Frowning, I looked around as if I'd just been dropped into the midst of a jigsaw puzzle.

No time to think. Four extra hungry mouths demanded breakfast and the invasive trill of a phone joined the noisy fray. At 6:30am?

"Dove, you remembered, right?"

Who was this?

"I'm sorry to call so early, but I know you're an early riser. You didn't forget, did you?"

Apparently, I'd not only forgotten whatever, but my brain cells weren't even spitting up the name of the person on the other end of the line.

"I'm..."

"Copper's coming today!" an excited voice bubbled.

Copper? I held the phone under my jaw and placed the nipple into the first, tiny creature's mouth. Its paws rested on the bottle, kneading encouragement to the flow of milk.

What day was it? I turned to look at the large block calendar on the refrigerator.

"Today?"

"Yes, it's Friday. He'll be there around 11. That's still OK, isn't it?" A note of worry immediately suffused the voice.

Friday. Copper. Martine. The cogs tumbled into place in my usually coherent brain.

"Yes, Martine, that will be fine. I'll see you then," I replaced the receiver on her good-byes. Stall must be ready. Call Allen. The mental list irritatingly scrolled in my head.

"Miss Dove? Miss Dove?"

IOU A HORSE

I felt as if I were walking in some kind of surreal dream. I tried to pin down in some order the events of the previous night's escapade. I remembered Cloud about to tackle the fence, the dogs racing to the road, finding the taped box with the kittens inside, but after that...a blank slate stared me in the face as if from a great distance- like a mirage wavering just beyond my reach and comprehension.

My fingers massaged my temples. For the first time since Aunt Vickie's passing, I'd been able to sleep. Perhaps I'd accumulated enough exhaustion that I'd dropped into a coma?

Hadn't at least one of the kittens been injured? Something about blood? But the box and its duct tape residue were nowhere to be found. And for the life of me, I couldn't say why?

"Miss Dove, are you all right?" A voice broached the mental haze that imprisoned me.

"Yes? Oh, Ned... Stalls all done?" I donned a semblance of my old self and gave the tall teenager my full attention.

"Just finished up. Night turn-out soon?"

"Good idea," I glanced at my watch. An early lesson waited. Allen was inspecting my work orders. Martine was due soon. I had to feed the kittens. Too bad Captain couldn't make the formula and hold the bottle, as he'd remained by the kitten's bedside playing adoring father. Bosun and Mate didn't quite share his fascination, and they wandered in and out- hopefully giving Captain a potty break.

"Miss Dove, you sure you're all right?"

Needed to check with Gary Stern, didn't one of the boarders have a loose shoe? Their horse, I meant...

My attention was suddenly, inexorably drawn to Cloud's paddock. The stallion was at the fence, huge black eyes fully trained on me.

"Miss Dove?" the worried Ned persisted.

"I...I'm sorry, Ned. I was up late with a box of discarded kittens." Had I just offered an excuse for my inattention? A sure sign of my being disconcerted or of 'slipping' into... When was the last time I'd not heard and promptly answered a query?

"Somebody dropped off more kittens? What's wrong with people? It's getting to be as much a cattery as a horse farm," Ned ruefully shook his head and picked up a tabby arching his back along his legs.

Glancing around, I easily counted ten cats sitting on various posts, Dutch doors, and even one on No Surrender's back. No surprise there. The big galoot loved cats, and when it was really cold you'd find his entire back lined up with curled cats.

"These were much too young to leave their mother," I refrained from the missing details.

"Miss Dove, I'm sorry to bother you..."

I returned to Cloud, but he broke our stare down, flung his head and meandered off.

"What is it, Ned?" I checked my student's warm-up before answering him.

"I was hoping you'd look at a horse with me." Ned, a high school senior, had learned most of Sam Mule's lessons and I'd recently decided to try him out on Venezia. His runner's build, fluid athleticism, ego-less, yet graceful pride of self, zeal to learn, avid listening and ability to ask thought-provoking questions made him a joy to work with.

He was a teenage, horse-loving girl's dream boy and the girls watched him religiously- an attractive, responsible and hard-working young man. Friendly to a fault, he'd inadvertently pulled everyone- critters, too, into his sphere. One couldn't help but like Ned, and I considered myself extremely lucky to have him at Creekside.

I loved introducing all my students to the keys of communicating with their mounts, but Ned was my favorite. And of course, after five years of working and learning, he'd want his own horse.

"Your parents?"

"I've been careful with my money." Ned not only worked cleaning stalls, spreading manure and assorted other odd jobs at Creekside, he also worked part-time at a tennis club, giving lessons.

"My parents said they'd wait your OK, and only if I keep her here. If you approve?"

Here. I'd run out of stalls three horses ago. Leopold was also on the way and Ned keyed into my misgivings.

"I'll build a run-in and put up extra fence. She could stay in one of the fields or..." Nervously, he brushed his sandy hair back and appealed to me for a solution.

"Hey, there, Ned, did you say something about building a run-in? I can help with that."

I'd been out-flanked by Tim Holt. The grinning gentleman swiped his ball cap from his crew-cut and looked innocently at me. Innocent? Anything but, I'd almost bet.

"Miss Dove, if you don't mind my saying so," he pulled out a sketch from his jean's back pocket. "Creekside needs a few more stalls and it would be easy as pie to extend the barn to the front," he pointed out an architect's design with a pen from his plaid shirt pocket's pen holder.

"Cool!" Ned enthused.

Money, I thought.

"I'm not sure how big I want Creekside to become. I don't want more than I can handle." Why did I feel like a bully bursting their balloon? And realistically, hadn't I already bit off more than I could chew?

"I know just what you mean," Tim agreed. "I've got a friend owes me a huge favor. The three of us- Ned, myself, and Jim, could extend the stalls, say four of them in this direction."

"Tim, I appreciate you thinking of this, but..."

"You're worried about money, right? No problem, I'll bankroll you. Give you the best deal you've ever had. I can afford it. You won't be able to say no. Besides, Ned here, needs a stall and..." Tim blushed fiercely.

"And?" Why did I have the feeling another bomb was about to drop?

"I bought another horse," he chuckled.

"My goodness!" Blindsided on all sides! Horses coming out of the woodwork! An odd something gurgled deep within me and I didn't think it was panic- slap happy?

"We'll talk about it over dinner tonight, OK?" I've brought a grill and some steaks. Ned and I will check out another paddock site with the potential for a run-in. Don't want to be too far from the barn, but have to keep a distance from the stallion."

Why did I feel like a tiny substance caught up in a monstrous snowball rolling hell bent for leather down a mountain?

"Miss Dove?" Ned raced to me as I finished my lesson and went to feed the kittens. Luckily, horse and rider had inspired something within my fugue to force me to be of some use. Student and horse walked off gratified, whereas I could not exactly pin down what we'd worked on. I had to get a grip...
"The mare I was telling you about..."

Mare, I missed the part where he mentioned 'her'. "When do you want me to go with you?"

"Uh, I know you're awfully busy- would Sunday be OK?"

"Could we do it inside two hours, I'm mothering kittens now?"

"Sure thing, it's not far. I'll pick you up at noon," he beamed.

Pick me up? Almost like a date. No boy had ever said those words to me. An odd constriction in my throat. I'd avoided dates, but in retrospect, I'd kept so much to myself that no boy had been given the chance to ask.

With the persona of my father ingrained in me and no other male figure to admire other than the Kind Man- and he was a picture- while growing up, I'd not been inclined to let a boy get close to me. Besides, there were the horses...

Ned wasn't thinking along those lines, I knew. This was just another piece of the puzzle of me pricking at my sanity. Did it add to whatever resided in me that I felt was unraveling?

IOU A HORSE

Allen, the beefy handyman, seemed puzzled. I'd held Cloud, who had no interest at all in Allen, while he investigated the sturdiness of Cloud's fence and the state of the lean-to's roof.

"Weeell," he drew out, "there ain't nothing wrong with this here fence. I mean, I found one post a fly's ass shy of good and tight, but the rest are fine and dandy."

My turn to be confounded.

"Somebody musta beat me to the job. Oh, and that stall you had me take a look at- weeell, that board is as solidly nailed as a rock. Ain't nothin' I can improve on," he scratched his neck as if to say: you foolin' with me?

But, that's impossible, I almost blurted. I know I moved Sir to Marshall's stall. That board had been hanging... Was the magic about? I'd not had time to sketch repaired stalls or paddocks... Or had I imagined everything? The inordinate confusion left me struggling in a mental quagmire.

"You mentioned a bathroom sink?" Dejected about missing a full day's work, Allen's brows rose with a modicum of hope.

He followed me into the kitchen, peeked at the just waking kittens and the overseer, Captain, and headed for the bathroom. Was I amazed or relieved to find the faucet leaking?

"All right, Cloud," I felt utterly ridiculous. "No one here, but the two of us. Who or what are you?" Finishing my supernumerary brushing of his immaculate bronze coat, I turned up a bucket, sat down, and held the lead line in an effort to keep his head facing mine.

His stand-offish act was well in place. "What happened last night? I thought I...felt something, uh, with you and uh...the kittens." I glanced around just in case someone had sneaked back on the farm. I must be crazy venturing on this tack.

"Did you heal...the injured kittens?" To my ears, this sounded patently absurd, crazy.

An impassive horse face studied me for half a second and then snorted. Great globs of green gook! I rocketed off the bucket backwards and when I gained my feet, Cloud's nose was airborne in a perfect imitation of Mr. Ed's laughing lips.

Tim did present me with an offer I could not refuse.

"Miss Dove, I'm not as crippled as my legs might have you think. I can help out around here," he forestalled my protest. "I want to; I'm not ready to die. I've done all the traveling I want to. I love horses, and I want to spend my days here, not at home in front of a TV or computer screen. Please?" His sincere, ruddy face entreated me.

Earlier, Ned and Tim had worked out construction details. My trust attorney would provide me with pro and con advice. If it came down to it, I could handle four more stalls. With horses on the way, I didn't have much choice.

I clasped my crystal before climbing into bed. Sleep sat on the sidelines while I continued to contemplate the events of the past 24 hours- never mind I had to get up in two hours to feed kittens.

How did those repairs get...repaired? Without any sound of hammering or the requisite construction work curse? Or had my comatose sleep hindered my ears? But the dogs would have heard and wakened me, right? Who could have done it? Tim? Or had a fairy godmother come to call?

Was I a 21st century Cinderella? And when was the ball and where was my ball gown? I had a crystal- not a slipper, but a crystal pendant. Or did it simply boil down to I had a secret admirer? If so, who? Ned and Tim were the only regular men on the property. Imagine me and a Prince Charming... What a load of nonsense!

Mentally, I scanned the mended fence and stall. Near midnight, I abdicated my cool bed. The early spring heat seemed disposed to stay and torment and I'd turned on the window a/c unit.

IOU A HORSE

Disregarding pulling on pants- my night shirt covered me to my knees- I quietly sprinted through the house, out the kitchen door. Surprised, Sam Mule and Pippin eyed each other and me before re-tucking into their shared hay pile.

Across the night-dampened grass, my eyes turned to Cloud's gate. Unbelievably, he was there as if waiting for me. Perhaps I was sleepwalking or dreaming. If I rolled over, would I land upon something hard enough to wake me?

The moon glowed with its watery aura. Too many thoughts erratically spit along the current of my brain waves.

Manners, manners were an important part of Aunt Vickie's life and of the magic. I always remembered to thank the magic. So, I put my face up to the bluish-white moon and imagined a face receptive to gratitude.

"Thank you," I whispered.

And that deep, mysterious male voice unnerved me without benefit of viable sound, except for what reverberated inside my head, 'You're welcome.'

22

My sleep, better interpreted as non-sleep, returned after my all-too-brief stint in the twilight zone. I woke agitated, and the radio's forecast of hot and humid only added to the atlas weights balanced precariously on my shoulders. My heart cramped- relentlessly gripped in the prison-constriction of my chest.

I forced myself to get a move on- too much to do to sit around scrutinizing, introspecting, and fruitlessly trying to destruct the psychological impediments battering me. Even breaking them down into manageable pieces would take too much time- if such were possible.

Not one to dream at night, I thought I remembered thanking the moon- only something else answered. Too insane to believe the moon was talking to me. Too insane to think about the words clearly pronounced in my head. Must not dwell on the consequences of prodigal thinking...

Feed rounds, beginning with mewling kittens, dogs, cats, horses...

"Miss Dove, I'm afraid My Ox sprained a suspensory. Would you show me how to wrap him? Do you have spare wraps?"

Put a check on the tack room chart- loaned out leg wraps, arnica. Note to myself to check the wraps daily as Jeanna, My Ox's owner, was leaving for a week.

"Miss Dove, Sir stepped on his lead line and broke it. Could you possibly loan me another? We're headed out to a show and..."

More checks on the tack room chart. My morning agitation had turned to irritation and it was all I could do to keep myself in check as the day progressed. I'd never felt like this before- all was simply in keeping with the ordinary day-to-day running of the stable. Perhaps I needed a swift kick in the breeches to snap out of

IOU A HORSE

it. A loud snort from across the way did nothing to amuse me. That Cloud- if he was reading my thoughts...

Ned's lesson on Venezia ran over as the gelding consistently threw Ned's seat to the left to avoid working his right hind. And Ned, not having experienced this particular trick, had the dickens of a time recognizing and correcting his position. But patience paid off.

"Thanks, Miss Dove. Wow! That was really something," he grinned boyishly, softly stroking the black gelding's arched neck. "I really get it now- if your seat isn't correctly placed nothing else works- the whole bit about compromising isn't proper riding. Great lesson, can't wait for the next one!"

I nodded, my mind already fixated on the kittens' feed schedule and what else was on the list? A frantic gurgle burped inside my chest.

And the day rolled on in the same vein. Buddy's eye watered and Tim over-worried- Dr. K was called. 3 Time Charm's owner, Tina, had to go out of town unexpectedly- could I ride Charm at least three times?

Pippin got stung and rubbed his haunch on a miniscule sharp extension on the carport stanchion. Minor wound care and Flys- Off application. In taking Sheer out to her daily grass ring, I examined her wounds as I did several times a day. Abnormal heat below the hock? Oh, no... Infection of the tendon? Dr. K would make the call. I prayed not; I hated giving penicillin shots- she'd been doing so well.

Martine's first scheduled lesson on Copper... I guzzled electrolyte-spritzed water and mouthed an organic peanut butter sandwich on sprouted grain bread. Tasteless. Focus, Dove, I railed at myself.

I met Martine and the curious Copper in the covered ring. His coat resembled a polished copper penny- one of the old ones that actually had copper in it. Martine's face was blazing smiles as she lavished pets on his neck, adjusted her helmet on her head and moved to the mounting block.

"Martine, why don't you just walk him in hand around the ring- both directions, before mounting," I advised. I believed he'd not do anything idiotic, but best to allow a curious horse time to indulge his intellect- especially in a new place, patience being the key.

The lesson began well. Warm-up walk, a modicum of free rein- as much as Martine was comfortable with. Short stretches of leg yield, large circles with quarter arcs of shoulder fore, half voltes in trot. Canter on a 20meter circle...

"Martine, what are you think...?"

When accidents happen, everything seems to turn to slow motion. As an instructor, you're powerless to interfere with the inevitable once it's begun.

Copper's footfalls had become noticeably less energetic in his canter stride, but no sooner had I begun to ask...

I watched helplessly as if an undulating, invisible wall rose between Martine and me. Copper, lollygagging along with his unfocused rider, clipped his front foot with his hind, Martine jerked up on the reins, and he was unable to use his head and neck to rebalance.

Down into the soft sand his front descended and Martine tumbled over his left shoulder. Slightly taken aback, Copper, nevertheless, righted himself immediately. My trust in his stalwart personality was rewarded as he stood waiting for his rider with a peculiar look in his eyes, wondering- What are you doing down there?

I'd already grabbed the phone from the ring wall.

"Easy Copper. Easy Martine. Are you OK?" I calmly walked long strides, speaking soothingly.

To my great dismay, Martine made a gasping noise. "Martine?" I knelt at her side, prepared to dial 911. Ned had witnessed the scene and had taken Copper, moving him away.

"Martine?" She was...laughing. Laughing!

"Did you see?" She gasped and giggled. "Do you know what happened?"

"Well, yes. Definitely not a laughing matter in my book," I replied, flummoxed.

"You told me to get my head in the right place and damned if I wasn't thinking about..." she erupted, "my anniversary. I...I stopped riding... Just blipped out...and...and he did, too." Holding her left shoulder, she rocked, laughing and crying at the same time.

"Are you hurt?"

"I think I've knocked the hell out of my shoulder. Can I get back on?"

"We'd better get you to an emergency room," I placidly sanctioned even as my gut began to revolt over my hurried lunch.

"No, no I have to get back on first. Please, just to get on..."

I recognized that hard-headed look in her eyes. She may have pleaded, but that was simply a nicety. Martine was determined to get back on.

"Ned, bring Copper to the mounting block, please," I gave in against my better judgment.

With Ned's help and the resolute Copper standing stock-still, Martine remounted. I walked Copper and her in a circle and Ned helped her dismount.

"It's just like you said," she winced. "A horse will mirror its rider." Her face had resigned its laughter in favor of signs of pain.

"Let's get you to an emergency room," I said, wondering how I'd finish the rest of the day's responsibilities.

"I'll take you, if that's OK?" Tim, like a guardian angel, appeared.

Martine grimaced. "Take care of my boy. It wasn't his fault." She kissed the huge muzzle and supporting her arm, departed alongside Tim.

Ned took charge of Copper and I...had kittens to feed.

I barely registered the drive to Morning Sun. The ever-forming lists in my head and that irritating sense of...

Ned was fairly quiet on the drive- his hopes fervently pinned on the next hour. Right on Rt. 732. Right into a gravel drive, and we stopped near the entrance to a sizeable pole barn with extensive turn-outs harboring cliques of horses.

The facility exuded a caretaker's enthusiasm for immaculate upkeep- not a single weed sought the steel siding as a backdrop. As we exited Ned's car, a man pulled up on a John Deere Gator and waved at us.

"Billie's on her way," and he loaded up shovels and other tools from a storage shed and drove off.

"C'mon," highly anticipatory, Ned urged me on. I followed him into an equally pristine barn. Stalls lined each wall. A few equine heads peered out speculatively. What was bothersome, were the ones not exhibiting any curiosity whatsoever- their heads remained tucked into far corners.

"In here, Miss Dove," he took down a lead line from a bridle rack on the stall post. We walked through a 12x12 stall, out the open back doorway.

A dark bay stood at the far end of the turn-out, in the shade of an oak, hind foot cocked, eyes closed. The adjacent turn-outs were empty.

"The horses get alternate turn-out until they've had supervised time to adjust. Make sure everyone gets along," Ned explained.

"Chanson," he sing-songed.

"Song?" I whispered.

The mare's eyes opened, all four feet flattened on the ground, but she made no effort to join us.

"I... I talk to her in French," Ned blushingly displayed more than an iota of shyness at this admission. I had to wonder if he were the average run-of-the-mill teenage boy. Highly doubted it. "She seems to like it."

"I could see how she might. French sounds softer than English." What girl wouldn't like to be addressed in French?

"Chanson, ma petite," he took the requisite Creekside snacks- peppermints, from his jeans' pocket.

IOU A HORSE

The mare's delicately-formed head rose, ears perked, but she took her time reaching us. Warily, she refused to step any nearer than ten feet from where we stood.

"You're new to her," Ned blushed again.

"It's OK. Wait. Just wait." Aunt Vickie's words- 'Don't crowd a horse. Everyone has a personal space, animals included. Give them an opportunity to greet you. Don't sneak up; always let them know where you are. Remember, a horse is a prey animal and always mindful of potential predators. Having said that, try to get a horse to notice you if one seems disinclined- don't settle for hindquarters turned to you, but use caution. Give yourself and the horse a moment to tap into each other's souls.'

"Chanson, ma petite jeune fille," I spoke to her.

"You know French, Miss Dove?" Ned asked, amazed.

"Not much."

The mare's ears flicked forward and back. She returned our scrutiny and cautiously stepped closer. In a quiet tone, Ned revealed her story as she gently accepted peppermints with her neck fully extended.

"The owner thought she had hunter potential. Took her to a trainer. Ran out of money and I... I think the trainer took it out on her," Ned indicated whip marks on both hind legs, one on the left front and several on shoulders and haunches. I was distraught seeing the evidence of wound infection. Some trainer- horrible enough to whip her, but to let infection set in, too. Damn, the so-and-so.

"Chanson," I wanted to cry. If it were only possible to return those whip marks to that so-called 'trainer'- multiplied a thousand-fold. "Je suis desolate," I apologized for the worst side of humanity.

Being a mirror image of my aunt, an abused animal angered me as nothing else. My gut cringed with every story or picture, or as in Chanson's case, the living proof. The kittens came readily to mind, too. The futility of it all took me from anger to despair, but I checked myself from further descent. Focus on the present, I silently intoned.

Chanson seemed to accept my apology; she closed the distance further and accepted a peppermint from my outstretched hand.

Having run out of French words, I continued to whisper, "Pretty, pretty girl," and held my hand full of snacks low and close to my hip- an invitation for her to bridge the gap between us. I kept my breathing deep and regular to encourage relaxation.

Tears threatened when Chanson's head rested into my chest. Her muzzle delicately finished the proffered snacks, and she did not back away.

"Come va, Chanson," Ned slowly clipped the lead as the mare continued to trust her head fully into my chest. I felt a sharp protrusion near my breastbone- the mysteriously placed crystal. A bit of magic at work?

Chanson, Ned's name for her, had been at Peaceful Farm two weeks. Initially drugged to keep her calm enough to be safely approached for treatment of her oozing, infected wounds, it was discovered that as she was weaned from the ace coincident with her physical healing, no one could get near her, until Ned came to see about rescuing a horse. He was the only one she'd accepted and that acceptance had its caveats.

An arm raised above waist level with speed over a snail's pace sent her rocketing backward, eyes wild. This horse was not a fighter, but a scared creature begging for flight.

As Ned slowly stroked her neck, I did the same to her unblemished chest, moved to her withers and found a ticklish spot. She cocked her head and allowed me to move further along her side, continuing with my scratching fingers.

A thought came to me; I took a chestnut recently peeled from the inside of Sheer's leg, rubbed it in my hands and let Chanson sniff. She gave a shuddering sigh and seemed to dredge up long-buried trust. Thank you, Mrs. Crawford Contarini for that sweet piece of advice.

With exaggerated slow and deep breathing, I ever-so-gently massaged along her spine to her hips. A slight tremor of expectation...

IOU A HORSE

I returned to her head once more and offered another sniff of the shedding. "Chanson, Chanson," I quietly sung to her.

"She was mostly skin and bone when she came," Ned's voice quivered.

"She's got a ways to go," I murmured, eying ribs. I moved my hand slowly down her left front leg, mindful of the scabbed-over whip mark. "Chanson, pretty girl," deeply inhaling, I asked for her foot, my hand gently but firmly strolling down her tendon and fingering her fetlock joint.

To give her credit, she did not retreat, but seemed to truly mull over the safety of complying; I patiently continued my ministrations until she eventually sighed and responded. "Such nice feet," I complimented her as I released her hoof.

My hands ran down her neck, scratched her withers again, down the wasted musculature alongside her spine. Slowly over the croup. Over her hip, down to stifle- a tremor...

"Chanson, Chanson..."

"Miss Dove," Ned's voice had a cautionary note.

"Chanson," I slid my hand softly along her gaskin, back up to hip and then gently back down, skirting the wounds, but moving down to fetlock and asking for her hind foot- breathing slowly and deeply all the while.

Aunt Vickie's teachings- 'A horse needs to know you are completely at ease, calmly prepared to be the lead. He'll take his cue from you. So be careful of your body language.' My aunt never encountered a horse she couldn't get along with. I owed her a lifetime's worth of accumulated experience and loving fascination.

Chanson thought extra-long about the new request, but she eventually shifted her weight, gave me her hind foot for an instance and then snatched it back, trembling...expecting...

"Good, good girl," I praised her with soft enthusiasm- here was something to work with. The trainer hadn't destroyed her. "Thank you, Chanson."

I gently stroked her as I returned to a shocked Ned and an astonished, older woman.

"Chanson, ma petite, merci," I offered her a last peppermint.

"I...I'm Billie," the woman swallowed her evident surprise and offered her hand. "How did you do that?"

My turn to look puzzled.

"Miss Dove, no one's been able to touch her hindquarters, let alone her feet without..."

"It's OK, Ned," I scratched under her jaw. "Let's talk outside, shall we?"

Ned lovingly stroked the side of Chanson's face, unclipped the lead and we walked through the stall, exiting into the aisle-way. Chanson followed us to the door of the stall and would have accompanied us further.

"Ned told me you were good with horses. That mare has turned away every so-called horse whisperer... Wow! I wish, I... Nevermind, I'm sure you have enough to care for. My husband and I retired to the country, wanted to do something to make a difference. We'd always enjoyed riding together; somehow, we agreed this is what we wanted to do with our retirement," Billie hitched her thumbs in her pockets. I complimented her on how grand everything looked.

"I believe Chanson is an Anglo-Arab, a wonderful cross. This will not be an easy task, Ned. As much as you love her, she could still harbor and display dangerous tendencies- self-saving mechanisms she developed to deal with that other..." I so wanted to curse, but I maintained. "We'll work on a program, but you must promise me and we'll speak of it with your parents, that you will not attempt to work with her without my being present."

Ned brushed at his hair, swiped at his eyes, "Anything you say, Miss Dove. Anything." Chanson rested her head against the door, listening to her future?

On the return trip to Creekside, I tried not to kill Ned's optimism, but to put it in a healthy perspective. He assured me he understood. I felt like a caring parent- how could I? Good grief, I was only maybe three years Ned's senior.

IOU A HORSE

But, I felt so much older. In awkward silence, I sat, thinking.

"Miss Dove, I can't thank you enough for coming today. Uh, you look awful tired. Why don't you take a cat nap?"

Tit for tat on the parental scale. I pretended to nap while considering the rest of the day's activities. Although it was Sunday, I'd accepted two additional lessons- one at three and one at four- trailered in ones.

I had not only my contingent of students, but Aunt Vickie's also. A few of her upper level riders went to Russ Mahler who regularly worked with Grand Prix students. Even though I'd learned the movements on Marshall and was beginning them with Sheer, I did not have the experience, but Aunt Vickie claimed I had the eye and the instinct, and many of her students seemed to agree. I was indeed very lucky.

At five, I fed every creature but myself. No hunger pangs to direct me. No taste or craving for any kind of food. Instead, I saddled Copper and worked on basics- geometrical figures to supple him and gauge his aptitude for listening. Martine, unfortunately, would be ground-bound for a while.

Venezia had his exercise, too. Mostly, working on his response time- the lazy cuss. Discovering he couldn't put me off to the left, he balked at forward. I hated to don my swan-neck spurs, but his thick body consistently ignored my leg.

'Don't put up with that,' I could hear Aunt Vickie. Hear her... Everything had run so smoothly with her around- was I that deficient? A wave of misery tossed my heart- she'd counted on me.

With three successful tempi changes of lead, I ended the session- endeavoring to hold myself together. Thankfully, I was alone. I happened to glance over to the paddock only to find Cloud's surveillance ardently directed at me. Crazy, I thought.

I'd been cautioned to allow myself time to grieve. How? Did grieving involve crying until one became a human desert? What then? Put one foot in front of another until 'time healed all', when my chest ached interminably with restrictive pressure? I had no anger, just...

Later, eying lists, I eventually gave up on idly picking at a spinach salad and added it to the compost pile. Put the horses to bed. My last visit, as always, was with Sheer. My partner had never been shy about voicing her instant demand for my services. Her whiffling for me to hurry to her put a grinning mask on my face.

I administered the penicillin shot which she wasn't overly pleased with, checked the level of heat and swelling- gratefully noted improvement. Offered carrots, hugs and kisses.

I dropped off Cloud's hay and as I exited the gate, he nickered. Secretly pleased, I reflected I'd not spent hardly any time with him in the past days. With a sudden burst of energy, I raced to the barn, retrieved a grooming kit.

In trying to blank my mind, I concentrated on nothing but the sweep of the brush on his dustless hide, but the wave of misery that assaulted me earlier cannoned through me once more.

My chest convulsed with its tremendous ever-present weight, my heart choked, my throat closed. Shoulders? Cloud had huge shoulders. Massive, male shoulders. Imperviously still, he seemed to offer...a shoulder to cry on?

All of a sudden, I dissolved- surrendered to saturating pain. The brush fell, thumped to the ground and I leaned into him, only to encounter the mysterious scars. This magnificent creature had suffered, too!

Chanson's horrid treatment, the discarded kittens, Sheer's accident, Aunt Vickie's departure, Marshall, other...moments, my lonely aloneness stretching back to when I was three years old...

Tears burst from their confines, flowed heavily. My arms barely held me to his side. My fingers laced in his mane for support.

All the misery I'd not allowed Sheer to witness I poured, literally, onto Cloud. Barely aware of it, my knees buckled. Why didn't I simply despair/melt into the ground?

IOU A HORSE

Cloud's head swung around and held me. A completely alien experience for me- being cradled. I cried myself into oblivion.

23

The shadowed man gently laid the senseless girl on her bed, placed an afghan over her to ward off the chill of the air conditioning. Long fingers softly stroked her brow then stilled- she would assuredly sleep peacefully this night. Kitten duty awaited, a certain wound needed tending and then...

'Shaman,' a silent appeal rode across time and space.

The obnoxious buzzing of a horse fly whipped by the shadowed man's head and set down on his bare shoulder.

Irritated fingers brushed it off, none too gently.

"I thought it appropriate," CatSkill quipped as he lithely landed in his human guise.

"Huh," his protégé grunted.

"Was that a grunt of amusement?" CatSkill's lips turned up in delight.

"I believe so," the response didn't indicate the least bit of jollity. "Was it your idea or the Lady Shaman's- my coming here?"

"Does it matter?" CatSkill's lips twitched.

"Always the coyote teacher- answering a question with a question?" The protégé questioned.

"You might say Bonnie and I arrived at the same conclusion, but for different purposes. I've blocked your history from my Wife, privacy issues and all. By the way, Bonnie sends greetings and," CatSkill held up a bag, "since you don't care for sweets- corn fritters and turkey sandwiches."

An avid gleam flashed and died in the shadowed man's eyes, but did not disturb his impassive mien as he accepted the bag. "Please thank her."

"She wasn't too happy about being left behind..."

"Are your eyes open to her at this moment?"

IOU A HORSE

CatSkill shook his head, "I thought you'd not appreciate sharing our conversation. Any difficulties?"

CatSkill's acolyte struck a mute note for a second. "You knew- she's my mirror image. Tonight I witnessed her childhood. And all the rest up to this point. In her teaching others, she has no idea she is also a healer- addressing everyone's needs but her own."

"And what, may I ask, do you intend to do about it?" CatSkill smiled, highly gratified.

"Give her the ride of her life," the slow, thoughtful response.

The flushing out of the girl's short stint with inattentive parents brought flashbacks to the shadowed man. He let the scenes scroll by even as he believed they no longer held him prisoner.

All the years of beatings from his father, his mother's abandonment, the bottling of any show of emotion until implacability became a welcome guise- a second skin. CatSkill continually challenged him on this 'hindrance' as the shaman termed it.

At 14, he'd achieved a stature sufficient enough to strike back. The physical beatings ended. The boy took his strength out on others who crossed a line which only existed inside his cold, wounded psyche. On his own, he'd survived, physically, remaining alone and aloof. Except for... Until CatSkill.

Dreams. Dreams. Dreams invaded my nights. Beginning the night of my downpour on Cloud's stalwart shoulders. Not dreams of a longed-for serenity, but thought-provoking, search oneself, questioning experiences.

I found myself once more in Lough Gur. Only the weather had much improved. Alone, I stood inside the amazing, immense stone circle. Dew glistened on the lush grass underfoot and dripped from the leafed branches hanging like tentacles over the massive, mossy, rough stones.

Slowly, I turned clockwise, admiring the tiny flowers calling spring hellos while peeking from rocky crevices. The sun had just begun its stretch prior to rising and its red-gold burnished the dark and regally dismissed it.

The ancient stone-lined entry into the circle provided the red carpet promenade onto the stage of the day. Sun beams strolled along the route set up by star-watchers thousands of years ago, until I stood in a warm, golden spotlight- quite the opposite of my first visit.

With a sense of déjà vu, I was warned of another presence. Watching me. I heard hoofbeats in the distance. But nothing or no one stepped into view.

My eyes soared up into the shadows of a thick branch. Not one given to fanciful imaginings, I nevertheless spied what looked like the head of a lion-sized cat peering at me- just as in my first visit. In blinking, though, I determined it was all a trick of the light and shadows.

Or was it? Was the magic about? Something watched me... Someone...

"Who's there?" I called out and spun 360 degrees but my eyes were inexplicably drawn to six of the huge upright boulders to the left of the entry. Under the bough I thought I'd seen the cat. Near where I'd found the crystal pendant I'd at first mistaken for a tossed bit of glass.

"I know you're there. Are you hiding behind the stone?" My feet grew roots; I couldn't force myself to investigate. Although not fearful, I was not foolhardy either.

How odd- no intuitive alarm bells rattled at me! Only the shroud of adrenalin boosted my senses.

"I'm not afraid of you," I challenged. "Show yourself."

Near to conceding that it was all a fantasy, I searched for the rental car. None. How had I got there? Dreams apparently do not allow for ingress and egress. Patiently, I waited. What else could I do?

IOU A HORSE

Without prior knowledge of the workings of dreams and only a personal experience with magic via pencil and paper, I asked again.

"Who are you?"

A gasp escaped me as a figure emerged from behind the tree trunk. Taller than the stones, he sideways skirted between them and entered the circle to confront me.

Not a sign of expression on a sun-bronzed face. Long, black hair fell from a center part down and over bare bronzed shoulders- thick, stalwart shoulders. Black eyes. Imperious nose. Wide, high cheekbones. Square jaw. Thin lips, wide mouth.

At his throat, a leather thong bore a crystal. Inadvertently, my fingers sought my chest, feeling for the twin of his pendant. But it wasn't there! Suddenly, I wasn't sure I liked this dream.

A breeze stirred the long hair laden upon his sharply planed naked chest- great strength exuded from its splendor, and heavy scars were instantly revealed- forever foisted into his pectoral muscles. Idly, and eerily without a qualm, I studied this mysterious stranger. Worn, black jeans. Barefoot.

Hastily my eyes rose, returning to his poker face. A strange warmth, having nothing to do with the sun, spread out from my gut and rashly presented itself on my face.

His arms hung casually at his sides as he stopped six feet from me. A sliver of a breeze resettled several strands of black hair across his face- no visible effect registered. He certainly didn't swipe the hair away, perhaps he knew another breeze might come and do it for him.

"Who are you?" I asked.

"Why did you summon me?"

Puzzled, I stammered, "I...summoned you?"

"Why?"

This had to be the most bizarre conversation I'd ever had, not that I engaged in conversations, but one question followed by another? I returned his stare, unsure of what tact to use to continue. Conversations in my life were to be avoided unless they were part of a lesson I was giving.

In a mute stalemate, we stood regarding each other. Only, I felt he was gauging me on a level totally beyond my wherewithal. His eyes never left my face. Foolishly, I wondered what I wore...

"What do you want?" he initiated.

Questions again. "Who are you?"

"Don't you know?" he continued to ply me.

"I'm sorry, should I?"

"Tell me, what do you want?"

"You mean, other than to know who you are?" There had to be a way to bridge this very weird rabbit hole of a stalemate.

"What's in a name?"

I thought for half a second, "A means to an introduction?"

"You may call me Teacher," after what seemed a lifetime, he finally conceded.

"Dove Gray. Why are you here?" Should I offer my hand? This was Lough Gur in Ireland. Why was a...Plains Tribe Indian inside a stone circle in Ireland? I guessed dreams had no compunction about mixing extraneous details or cultures.

"What do you want?"

Want? Me? "N...nothing," I honestly answered.

To which he crossed his arms as if my reply were unacceptable and he intended to wait forever or at least, until I modified what I believed to be truthful.

The longer the silence, the more a burgeoning frustration opened inside me.

"What...do...you...want?" He phrased the question this time as if speaking to a language-impaired person.

I opened my mouth to repeat my original response, but a black brow rose provocatively- daring me.

What did I want? I'd stopped wanting or asking for anything when I was four years old. Learned to get it for myself.

What did I want? I had so much... A flicker of inspiration, "To be useful."

This didn't seem to satisfy him either.

IOU A HORSE

"If you think on it, I may return," he enigmatically stated, and with that singular good-bye, he turned and retraced his entrance- disappearing behind the tall lichen-adorned tree.

For a horrible moment, with my feet mired/glued to the ground, I experienced a tremendous despair.

"Wait," I called, unable to go after him. "Wait!"

But there was no waiting. No release, other than morning breaking, a cat staring me in the face, a dog pawing at the mattress.

Time to begin another day.

24

For days, at arbitrary times, I pondered the question from my dream. And for nights, too, as dreams deserted me. The longer the stretch of that mystifying Teacher's absence, the more I thought to brush the whole thing off as a coincidence of something I ate. What had I eaten that night? As near as I could remember, probably nothing.

But, I had drenched Cloud's shoulder with the sum total of my pitiful mewlings. Like a newborn kitten. Coming back down to earth, I donned my mantle of determination and tackled the daily routine.

The question, however, refused to be set aside. What did I want? I had everything, didn't I? A home, a career, horses to ride- thanks to Aunt Vickie and the magic.

Ashamed of my embarrassing, melting display, I purposely ignored Cloud- only to feel even more miserable. Why take it out on him? 'A sound horse should be worked,' I could hear my aunt tut-tutting.

"Miss Dove, what do you think about the new stalls?" I probably should have paid more attention to what the men were doing, but the trust attorney had assured me of the perfection of the architectural design, the ease of construction and the financial viability.

"Looks great. I'll be glad when the noise is over. Ned, would you pull out the round pen and set it up at A?" The covered sand ring had room enough for a standard dressage ring and extra space for a 40-meter circle's worth of warm-up space at the end of the arena.

Cloud, with his perverse work ethic, had blithely worked with me in hand for moments at a time and then suddenly, shut down. Absolutely intransigent- not to be budged. He'd made the decision easy for me. I'd lunge him, and the round pen would provide the safety factor as I'd not yet braved taking the stallion from his electric-boosted paddock.

A new agent from Creekside's insurance carrier made an impromptu visit.

"Josh Harris," he foisted/introduced himself and promptly wrote me off as too young for him to take seriously.

His arrogant attitude and wandering eyes, not to mention his death grip on a folder, led me to believe he was all book learning, no common sense and therefore- trouble.

"We heard you acquired a stallion..."

"Excuse me, where's Sam?"- my regular agent, who understood horses and farms and the people that went with them.

"He's on vacation."

"Then I'll wait and meet with him. Sorry you came all this way for nothing," I said. He'd had the gall to just drop in- like I had nothing better to do than entertain him.

"We may have to adjust your rates or even cancel your insurance..." he officiously tossed down the gauntlet.

"There are many stables that have stallions," I retorted, irritation flaring.

"I...we heard this one was dangerous and attacked..."

"Attacked?" Uh, oh. "Who is your informant?"

"That's not pertinent..."

"I beg to differ," I flatly rejoined.

"Uh...," he stumbled, taken aback by my not passively rolling up in his presence like a wrinkled door mat.

I felt my aunt at my back, 'Never let anyone walk all over you, especially on your own turf.'

Cloud had sauntered to the gate. Those eyes, glowering?

"If you'll excuse me, I've got work to do." Cloud nickered as Tim advanced. He whiffled at Tim's ball cap and Tim stroked under his jaws.

"Does that look like a dangerous stallion?" I rounded on the supercilious agent, wondering what busybody had fed him 'information'.

"No, but I'll need to make a report."

"Whatever. Have Sam call me. He's the one I'll speak to."
Sensing my disquiet with this ego-driven so and so, Captain, Bosun
and Mate protectively ringed me.

"I think I'll just check on..." the agent made to bypass me.

"You will do nothing as far as I'm concerned. You are
trespassing and either you leave or..."

"Any trouble, Miss Dove?" Tim called over as he dispensed
snacks to Cloud.

"This," I wanted to say idiot, but at least one of us should act
professionally, "person wants to cancel my insurance because of
Cloud."

"Hell, if he's that stupid, I know an insurance company that
would love to have your business," Tim- a man directly from and
comfortable in the suited business world, patted Cloud and
sauntered toward us.

"I...I didn't say that..." Josh Harris backpedaled; sweat
formed on his ruddy cheeks and promptly traced crevices.

"Once more, good day. You're not welcome," I turned my
back on him, knowing he'd be amply guarded either to his car or
pinned in the hot sun of the afternoon by the dogs. My ears
welcomed the sound of his car slowly striking dust from the
driveway. Add to the list: call Sam.

What do you want? That question popped in and bugged
me, like a relentless deer fly.

I fingered the crystal inside my shirt. My hand seemed to be
drawn to check it's reality at inadvertent times throughout the day.
Weird or magical? How had it left Teacher's neck and graced
mine? I seemed to be perched on a dividing line between what was
generally accepted as real, and fantasy- the magic?

Had it always been this way for me? If Teacher strode back
into my dreams, I'd certainly have more questions. Not that I really
expected he'd answer.

What did I want?

IOU A HORSE

I wanted Sheer all better and happy, although she didn't seem disturbed at her current condition. All of the extra attention, I supposed. Oddly enough, the heat below her hock had completely vanished- only a day after the dream and her first penicillin dose. But, if Teacher returned, I'd talk about Sheer.

Ned and I worked with Chanson five days a week- the other two he reserved strictly for grooming and giving her French lessons. Simple ground exercises- walk and trot in hand from both sides, halts, turn on the haunches and forehand along with introducing her to everything I'd want a youngster to accept without any qualms- a sort of monster training which induced trust between the two parties. Lunge work would follow in time. It was obvious her initial trainer had neglected the foundation of a good working partnership.

Luckily, Ned had as much patience as I did- he'd need it all. Loud noises, quick movements, raised hands and Chanson would tremble and attempt to fly out of Ned's hands. At times, she'd nervously stall out or push ahead, but Ned didn't tumble to frustration.

"We'll get it Ned. Takes time. Can't undo six months of that kind of training in a matter of days. Sheer has an interest in her. We'll try putting them fairly close together while grazing. Chanson can learn a lot from Sheer."

"I'm not worried, Miss Dove. I'm too happy she's mine and I'm in it for the long haul," Ned's gaze rested softly on his new love.

If I were a normal twenty year old and Ned was a little older... Where did that crazy idea come from?

"Care to watch Cloud's first lunge lesson?"

"I'd love to, but I promised mom I'd be home for a BBQ. Good luck!"

As it turned out, I was very glad Ned had gone home.

Cloud walked gentlemanly by my side as we entered the sand

ring and made our way to the round pen- no pushing to get ahead. No dawdling behind.

Aunt Vickie and I were not great fans of round pens, but when training young prospects or retraining others, a round pen could suffice for lack of a helper. In this type of ring, set up by interlocking stock panels, a horse could be encouraged forward without getting stuck in a corner or running out.

Once the trainee was settled on the circular path, the round pen came down and we'd advance to lung work in a section of the sand ring. After all, there were no round pens on show grounds.

As I brought Cloud to the center of the round pen, a pair of ravens settled on the top bar.

"Seems we have an audience," I mused aloud. Cloud gave them scant notice other than a simple snort.

Whatever form Cloud's manhandling had taken, he wasn't the least bit disturbed by dressage whips or lengthy lunge whips. When he wasn't exhibiting his impassive quirks and glaring at me with condescending eyes, he accepted my gently touching him with a whip as easily as the pressure of my hand.

I gave him a length of lunge line. "Walk," I smoothly instructed, lifting the lunge whip to the girth area, where my inside leg would reside at some point in the future- I hoped.

Snorting anew, and tossing his head at the ravens which seemed to cuddle as if at a drive-in movie, he promptly walked on.

"Good boy," I encouraged.

His ears flattened. Not a happy camper. I fed out more line, slightly lifted the whip and asked for a "TrrrOT." His back arched as his great hocks struck well under his body. For half of a circle, I drooled over a magnificent, airborne, extended trot.

"Beautiful, Cloud..." I verbally applauded.

At the end of the half circle, Cloud stopped dead and cocked his head- daring me?

"C'mon, you've got more than that in you," I grinned. "TrrrOT!"

He completely ignored me. I raised the whip fractionally higher, gave a subtle flick. Nothing.

IOU A HORSE

"TrrrOTT!" I flicked the whip on the ground- not wanting at this stage to actually touch him with it. Nothing. "Look, Mister, I know you can go on. Complete circles are not out of your realm."

I tried again. Nothing. I then let the flash of the whip tickle his ribs. Nothing. No response at all- not even an objection from his tail.

"Cloud," I remonstrated.

'Why?' The word clearly rang in my head.

My head spun. Who said that? Relentlessly, I scanned the premises. No one around. That same deep voice. Was I losing it? Had I eaten today?

Unlike my previously diligent self, I'd forgotten to return a few phone calls and had misplaced a check that should have been deposited. What was going on with me? Hearing voices... Did I only hear the deep male voice when I was with him? I tried to reflect on the conundrum, but my brain failed me.

'What do you want?' came to mind to add to my...whatever I was feeling- mostly inadequate.

Dare I explain dressage 101 aloud? Was this how Alice in Wonderland felt? Surreptitiously, I glanced around again, assuring myself of no human presence, and took a deep breath. In for a penny, in for a pound.

"This is strictly a training exercise. All young prospects begin this way." Boy, did I feel ridiculous.

With his huge, vibrant black eyes regarding me, I nearly convinced myself I was the student.

'I do not need to be trained.' The clear, masculine response sundered my senses.

Inexplicably, I heard a spate of giggles- not from my stunned self. The ravens cawed, fell off the top rail and flew away, somersaulting in the sky.

Trembling, I reeled Cloud in and deposited him back in his paddock without a backward glance. A pang scourged behind my eyes. Headaches were not part of my make-up. Maybe there was something physically wrong with me.

Hearing things, things that weren't...possible, was not a good sign. 'I do not need to be trained,' seriously?

What do you want? Right, hearing things and that damned question, too. I hurried to the house.

IOU A HORSE

25

I made an effort to swallow tasteless soup. No one could run on an empty tank, so I forced every drop, hoping for a surcease of the strange phenomenon that had entered my life and had me questioning my sanity.

Thankfully, the little kittens were now old enough to feed their own eager little bodies.

Eenie, Meenie, Minie and Mo scampered around my feet. I entered their joi d' vive with ribbon and felted wool balls with bells hidden inside. The faithful Captain nudged at the toys to enhance the playing field and allowed the kittens to crawl upon him. Playtime- how nice to grow up rollicking, being nourished and cared for, and for me there was a sweet sense of...familial happiness in playing with them.

Captain patiently waited the end of their mealtimes and my display of affection with the little ones. He loved to play mother 'possum.' One little one would claw its way to his indulgent back and pounce on the three still climbing. Ambush was a favorite game. The other cats that visited the house had important lessons to impart too, as in how best to sneak up on a culprit. These episodes were too much for Bosun and Mate, but Captain obligingly hung in there.

If it weren't for my uneasy psych making me restless, I'd spend more time with them. More time. Where would I get more time? Less time thinking about time might do it.

If it weren't for that insidious question constantly nagging me- What do you want? Like a child with birthday candles- something I'd never had, but had heard about- I clutched the crystal hanging between my breasts and made a wish.

I'd already sketched Sheer in her favorite extended trot, hoping the magic might heal her. Magic- miracle.

No Lough Gur. I stood on an endless expanse of prairie. Cloudless blue sky above. Prairie grass up to my waist. An assortment of brightly colored wildflowers strewn haphazardly about drew in an equal assortment of butterflies and humming bees.

And striding toward me as if he owned the entire plain... My breath caught. Unlike most people walking, his arms never swung the slightest bit, but remained quietly impervious at his sides, brushing the beaded heads of grass in his passing.

It almost seemed as if the prairie created a path for his approach to me. I half expected a royal red carpet to roll out before him, as regal certainly described his advance. I had ample time to admire and study him as he covered a lengthy stretch to reach me- a much longer walk than at Lough Gur.

Very tall- surely well over 6'. His eminent shoulders had flicks of long, black hair scuttling across them due to an ever-present breeze. Long, black brows. His black eyes didn't squint against the sun, nor did they bear any sign of greeting. I half-wondered if I were actually present. His mouth set callously- not an iota of welcome.

My eyes were drawn to the strange scars on his chest with lingering interest. I should research...research what? A figment of my imagination? Dreams, though, were supposed to mean something, weren't they?

No hellos. Simply, "What do you want?"

I tried to smile, surprised just how glad I was to see him, question or not. The smile slowly died as I realized he could not have cared less. But, I was ready.

"Other than world peace, no more abused animals." Or children, either, I thought.

Although he didn't show it- not a single sign of emotion (kind of like myself in a way, I unhappily reflected) I believed he was piqued with me.

"Why did you summon me?"

IOU A HORSE

"Summon you? I don't know you, nor was I aware that you even existed." Frustration- there was an emotion that was becoming all too familiar.

What was happening to the tight self-control I usually exhibited? Some consideration- at least I hadn't fallen apart on Tim's or worse, Ned's shoulders.

"You drew me to you."

Drew him? Literally? Paper and pencil? The magic...

"My drawings?" I searched the files in my brain. The drawings of Lough Gur? That eerie feeling of being watched sidled from the corners of memory. I had drawn...

"It's you!" Astounded, I threw etiquette out the window and stared intently up at him.

He crossed his jean-clad legs and settled into the indented throne of prairie grass he'd stood upon. Feeling absurd standing alone, I joined him, supple enough to do it with equal grace.

A flicker in his eyes had me checking myself. Blushing, I found I was in my night shirt. Sitting cross-legged was therefore out of the question. I folded my legs to the side, pulling my shirt as far down as it would go, dilatorily giving my face the chance to shed the errant flames in my cheeks.

"Why?" He asked.

Why, indeed? His image was one of the magical moments when the pencil and paper united in creating...something that I needed?

My forehead crinkled, I was honestly bewildered. "I don't know. I..." Dare I explain how the magic had helped me in the past?

Black orbs of infinite depth crossed an invisible threshold into my soul- not a chilly trespass. Nearer magical- spell binding. Who was this mysterious figure?

"You're not exactly a can of chicken soup," I blurted.

His lips never moved, but he closed his eyes as if to hide and turned his head. Lifting his hand he attracted a butterfly. I had an awkward, empathetic sense of what that butterfly was about.

Teacher. This strange Indian/psychologist was definitely a far cry from chicken soup. Unless- I remembered a book I'd once got at the library. CHICKEN SOUP FOR THE PET LOVER'S SOUL or something like that.

What was the magic up to? Addressing a need I was unaware of? What kind of need? This close-mouthed Adonis of the Plains...

"Why are your drawings so minute? Detailed, but in miniature?"

"How do you know about my drawings?" A race of chills up my back and arms. My face burned again at the intimate, surreal TWILIGHT ZONE I'd entered. He ignored me for a loaded three seconds.

"I know everything about you," he simply, impassively replied as if discussing a totally innocuous topic rather than my life.

Contrary or not to his design, that did not put me at ease. I could only think of one way he'd seen my sketch book and equally astounding, had I been sleeping when he was there? And, should anyone know everything about another?

I'd made it a matter of self-preservation to keep myself to myself. From an early age, I'd learned to do so. I opened my mouth, stopped short. If all of this was magic, then surely he'd understand. Wouldn't he?

His glare...challenged my thinking? Something inside me bristled. One of his brows rose, expectant.

He said he knew everything. If so, why did he keep questioning me? I avoided the intensity of his black eyes and a smart comeback which would only get me... What? Did I think he'd harm me?

Embarrassed, I tried to explain, "As a kid and...I guess I thought...think...maybe the magic is only invested in that particular sketch pad and..."

The cover of the drawing tablet still held its place. I'd been extremely careful. Blank pages remained. Enough for my lifetime? Was I foolish enough to believe that? Obviously, yes.

IOU A HORSE

But maybe not. He'd...manifested? There had to be a reason. I started to explain about being hungry, but his hand stopped me. A long, sun-bronzed finger stilled my lips.

"I know," he said. His touch filled me with a strange sense of serenity. My eyes misted, betraying me.

"If...if you know...everything about me, why don't you answer the question you keep asking me?" Flushing with my temerity, I tossed the entire game in his court.

Teacher's eyes flared and I could almost swear his lips twitched as if a fly scorned to disturb them. He was statue-still, tranquil, yet powerful- ambiguously alluring, like the perfect dream you wanted to keep dreaming over and over again.

As if he'd been privy to my every thought, he indifferently grunted and my whole body blushed.

"How can I help you if I answer the question for you?"

Ah, a recurrence of questions in a merry-go-round worthy of some incomprehensible psychological dream, or was it just shy of a nightmare?

"What do you want?"
The hopeful placidity he'd initially imbued in me fled. I squirmed- the worm on the hook. I'd drawn, but...

"I want Sheer to be perfectly healed, like she was before the acci..."

A flicker in Teacher's infinite twin pools. If it were up to me, certain aspects of the dream could go on and on.

"Everything that exists has a path. Sometimes...there is no interference." I detected a modicum of resigned sadness in the issued tenant.

"Then, why do you continue asking me what I want, if it doesn't matter? If I have no choice?" Could I really not help Sheer? Would the magic conjure such a perverse outcome for something so incredibly important to me?

My eyes were near tears, but I would not cry in front of him. I would not. "If you can't help me, why are you here?"

"How about an easy question? What do you need?"

"Appropriately timed meals along with hunger so I actually eat, and water," I deceptively coughed to stave off dissembling or screaming in aggravation.

"Do you find this amusing?"

"I find it frustrating; I don't know what answers you expect me to give you. Sheer..."

"I know you don't, Dove Gray," he murmured.

"How do you?"

"Everyone has intrinsic requirements, wants and needs. They may be pretty much the same. When you're ready to confront and express your own wants and needs... Perhaps, this will help."

How had I not noticed my crystal pendant dangling at his throat? My hand felt for the resting place on my breastbone. Not there!

Teacher pulled the leather thong from his neck and placed it over my head.

"I...I found this at Lough Gur. I wear it..." confusion flooded me.

"A gift is better if presented as a gift," his unfathomable reply.

In one swift move, he rose, extended his hand to me. As our hands united and he pulled me up, I had an instant flash of tremendous, other-worldly power, and the sensitivity behind his implacable façade defied magic.

"Your homework- ask another what he wants."

I have an inkling of what a trial I'd been to CatSkill when he found me hunting, by means of a snare, for sustenance.

"Your soul is far hungrier than your physical body," he had startled me with. Later, I considered his remark quite thought-provoking. Much later.

IOU A HORSE

It took years, but not once had CatSkill exhibited the least bit of impatience. What better means to extol your mentor than to try to emulate him? Unfortunately, I lack the patience of the cat.

I watch her sleep, something I can do without compromising the path she needs to find. Sleep is healing. Rest is endemic to all.

Dove, a lovely name for one who desperately needs, but lacks, peace; she continues to lose weight. Not good. The sooner she attains a resolution, the more her body will demand sustenance and she'll not be able to deny it.

A cap of swirling, sun-streaked crescents... I prefer she let her hair lengthen. I prefer? A twinge crackles inside of me. No turning back.

Part of my 'becoming' involved listening. At the moment of our touching hands, our hearts synchronized. I no longer question what might transpire. The spirits are always ahead. But I am thoughtful.

CatSkill mentioned different purposes. I know of his mindset- aid one who'd built a similar defense as mine.

The girl, though she bears an injured heart and incomplete soul, does have a daily routine. I'd lacked even that, but as for the rest- like looking into a placid lake of concealed currents.

What was the Lady Shaman's purpose? CatSkill and his woman are a perfect union. I believe that gave me a sense of her intention.

Quietly, I page through the sketch book. 14 x 17. Creased cover. The dogs idly glance my way. The kittens have curled into her fetal sleeping position as if she is their mother.

A can of chicken soup, my heart revolts. What young child draws a can of chicken soup? A hungry one.

Hungers lay banked deep within her- I know them.

Her lone soul had turned to pencil and paper, but no stick figures of mother, father and child. She'd expanded her world to include mostly animals and the woman who had donned the walls with her own equine art. Magic, Dove thinks. Why not? At least, it is something to believe in.

I can work with that.

26

"Ned," I hesitated. Conversation outside my teaching role was anathema to my nature. Hadn't my growing up years verified quiet, unobtrusive...? How did Sierra cope with me? I was definitely outside the species specific role she'd advised me of and the only way to pursue it was to jump right in, right? Taking a deep breath, I urged myself to jump.

We'd started a course of 'monster' training with Chanson, using Sheer as an example. Chanson's female, part-Arab blood interested Sheer. In a stable full of males, my partner was no longer the sole minority, though she reigned supreme and always would. Within a week of Sheer's grazing next to Chanson's turn-out area, the two girls had developed a friendship- talking girly things? Talking about Cloud?

Why had Sheer found it easy to talk with another while I struggled so horribly? Was I an anomaly- against the nature of things? Teacher might understand, but he would not put up with any excuse from me- this I was sure of. I had to try or, get suspended?

In waiting for Sheer to mature to riding age, I'd introduced her to an inordinate number of interesting brain-teasers: balls, umbrellas, balloons, skates, pistols- water and otherwise, tarpaulins, teeter-totters, bicycles, mazes- I couldn't remember them all.

While playing those 'games', we formed a trusting partnership, and had lots of fun to boot. Any new obstacle that came afterwards, well, all I had to say was, "Check it out" and whether I was mounted or not, Sheer accepted my encouraging "I've got you, check it out" without any qualms. I'd be willing to bet if a pink elephant landed, she'd listen for my lead cue before making up her mind. I envisioned the same for Ned and Chanson.

Granted, Chanson was not a yearling, but a bond struck was a bond forged. We began with a soccer ball. I led Sheer to the arena and began to slowly move the ball around her feet. Though her movement was curtailed, her eyes lit up, her neck arched. Sheer loved to play. She knew snacks were also involved, but even without one, she was game.

I had Ned bring Chanson into our sphere. She skittered as she entered the ring, but her attention soon focused on Sheer and our antics as Ned soothed her and walked her closer.

"Get it, Sheer," I challenged and Sheer put her nose to the black and white ball and pushed. As the ball rolled away, Chanson's head reared back, eyes frantic. She danced a bit and Ned gave her room to move.

Sheer ignored her friend's upset. I tossed the lead line over her back and she sauntered to the ball and returned it to me. The more we played, the more Chanson settled and exhibited inquisitiveness- her ears flicked, her eyes gentled and her body relaxed.

Sheer upped the ante when she gently pushed the ball to Chanson. And her new friend agreeably sniffed the ball; inadvertently huffing at it, the ball rolled slightly and Chanson, fascinated, boldly held her place, and then stepped forward, mimicking Sheer's going after the ball.

"Ned, I think we've got the makings of an equine soccer team."

"Ah, Chanson, magnifique!" Ned produced a peppermint as Chanson moved to investigate the ball again.

"Try to present the most frightening monsters you can dream up. Take your time and introduce her to a new one every day, provided you get a positive response from the previous one- similar to police horse training. If one startles her, don't quit. Just be patient and make sure I'm near, at least for a little while longer."

Ned wiped at his eyes, "She's going to be all right, Miss Dove."

"Of course she is; this is what a partnership is all about." My heart tickled joyfully for Ned and his 'amour'. "That's enough for today."

I had to literally rescue the ball from Sheer as she diligently continued to pursue it.

"Ned," I broke into his admiration of Chanson's passing her first 'monster' class with flying colors via Sheer's tutelage and his patient heart. Here goes, "What do you want?"

His immediate response, "Short term or long term?"

Startled, I tried to think of how Teacher might respond if I asked this. He'd probably expire in amazement and gratitude.

"Uh, both."

"Long term, to go to the Olympics," he promptly answered. No trouble voicing his wants.

"With her?" I was dubious.

"Not necessarily, but you'll help me decide that. Short term- to gain her trust, ride her and have her happy about it," he appealed to me with raised brows.

"Let's keep up monster training. I've a feeling it won't be long."

"Thanks, Miss Dove."

"Thank you, Ned." I hastened away; that hadn't been that difficult, but I needed to think.

Lessons at 11, 1, 2, 3. Two horses to ride. Not much time to ponder.

"Miss Dove," Tim hailed me as I left my 11:00 student to cool off her mount and load up.

"Yes, Tim," I had a thought I wished to pursue, but it slithered away with Tim's advance.

"Join me for lunch?" he held up a cooler.

Flustered, I looked for an outlet. Tim was having none of it. "You have to eat," he settled a concerned parental smile on me. At least, I assumed it was one.

"C'mon, I love to cook. In my travels I've discovered some awesome recipes. You can pretend to be a guinea pig."

He'd already unfolded a small table with white linen table cloth and a vase of carnations in the shade of the pin oak near Cloud's paddock. Grinning, he gallantly pulled out a chair for me.

Chicken salad dosed with fresh herbs on a flaky croissant, pineapple-orange tarts... For the first time in such a long time, my taste buds sputtered to life. To my chagrin, I was starving.

Delighted, Tim replenished my china plate and poured fresh squeezed lemonade.

"Tim, this is delicious. Thank you," I blushed, scooping crumbs from the corner of my mouth.

"It pleases me to share," he said. Now, why wasn't he married? Nice looking, not that old...

Ask another...but not that one. "Tim, what do you want?"

He sipped at his lemonade; kindly, thoughtfully, he studied me. My mind raced, thinking of Tim's new horse, a black and white paint Tennessee Walker. This new boy gave Tim a chance to really move out without his arthritic body suffering much discomfort.

I worked with Tim regularly twice a week, and on Sunday I'd arranged for time to trail ride with him. The Walker's gaits were lovely- pure, smooth and fluid, especially when he accelerated. I found myself eagerly waiting Tim's answer.

"Why, to stay healthy and have fun, I guess." Answering didn't seem to disconcert him and had come easily to mind- the same with Ned. At least these two men didn't consider it an invasion of privacy to talk about themselves. So, what was my problem?

"What do you want, Miss Dove?"

Want? I knew what I didn't want- one more person asking me what I wanted!

Saved by an unfamiliar Jaguar dusting my gravel drive.

"Now, who is that?" I checked my watch. Fifteen minutes before my next lesson.

IOU A HORSE

A man exuding wealthy elegance exited the Jag and offered his hand to the canine greeters for an introductory sniff. At home with animals- a good sign.

His eyes swept Creekside and he curtly nodded with obvious approval. Extra seconds were dedicated to Cloud who studiously ignored the perusal, and then an extra, loaded moment for Sheer. My mare gave him a cursory going-over and returned to grazing the quickly depleting grass. The summer drought played havoc with forage.

"Can I help you?" The visitor swiped at his graying hair and adjusted his glasses. Immaculately attired in a designer polo shirt of butter cream and stone-colored Dockers, the gentleman- as perfectly in shape as his apparel, offered his hand.

"I'm sorry. I've waited over-long in coming to see you, Miss Gray. Please forgive me. I'm Tribune Thorne."
Politely, I shook his hand. The name didn't register, immediately.

"Mr. Thorne?" My confusion increased his unease.

"The accident... It was my horse...that injured your mare. How is she doing?"

A flashback blindsided me- desperately pirouetting Sheer away and lying beneath her as she buckled in the wake of the Warmblood's outburst. The blood drained from my senses, my knees weakened.

Captain nuzzled me, Cloud screamed and Tim's hand was at my shoulder. "Miss Dove, you all right?"

"Y...yes," I managed, biting the inside of my lip to regain my aplomb, and introduced Tim to Mr. Thorne.

"Miss Gray, I'm terribly sorry for your suffering. I watched you ride- it was absolutely beautiful, most inspiring." His shoulders sagged; his lips thinned, his expression haunted grim.

"Why don't the two of you get out of the sun?" Tim suggested.

I asked him if he'd apologize to my student and tell her I might be a little late.

"I should have insisted that my trainer refrain from the

awards ceremony. I knew Jock was not himself, but I let him override me. 'The ribbons are important,' the professional claimed. Important? God help me, I'm so sorry." Thorne wiped at his sweated face with an initial-embroidered handkerchief.

His distress and sorrow soulfully apparent, I shuffled my feet, eying the grass, equally discomfited. What could I say? Why had he come- to ask forgiveness? Accidents...happened. I didn't blame anyone. I was just...heartsick. Buck up, Dove, you've got lessons.

"Mr. Thorne, I appreciate your coming; I'm sorry if it seems as if I'm hurrying you, but I've a full afternoon of lessons."

Anxious to put it behind me, I knew I probably sounded abrupt, but he was a business man. He'd just admitted his horse should have been pulled from the awards ceremony. If only it had.

With reddened cheeks indicating his embarrassment and the awkwardness of his position, he cleared his throat, pulled an envelope from his pocket, laid it on the clothed table and reset the vase on it. As if a breeze- what breeze?- would displace the pristine missive.

"Jock had to be put down a week after the show- a bad colic. Also, his system was riddled with ulcers. I'd already dismissed the trainer..." he floundered, eyes watering.

"I'm so very sorry," it was my turn to apologize and feel horrible for his loss. We were two commiserating horse-lovers, only he had lost his friend.

"Miss Gray, I have a proposition for you. My daughter needs lessons if she's to progress with her riding..."

I thought to protest.

"Please," he fended me off. "Please, would you at least hear me out?"

I nodded, glancing at the covered ring.

"Jock's full sister- she's three years younger. I bred both of them. She has the potential- I believe, but I'd like your opinion- to be an Olympic contender. My daughter, Corrina, has her own horse which she's comfortable with. She has no desire to go on the road to international competition.

This mare, well suffice it to say, my ex-trainer did not get along with her, at all. The sky is the limit as far as what I'll pay to give this mare the opportunity to advance to her full capabilities.

Her gaits are extraordinary. I'm asking you to take on my daughter and Jacqueline- Jock's sister. I bred both," he repeated, wiping his eyes, "and they were and are, extremely important to me."

Folding his hands on the table he waited, hopefully.

"Mr. Thorne, I've a pretty full schedule..."

An idea flitted and I immediately changed course. Ned. Ned had expressed a desire to compete in the Olympics. Was the magic at work? For some inexplicable reason, my eyes flew to Cloud.

"A magnificent stallion. What is his breeding?"

"I don't know. He's pretty much a wild card," I murmured. "Mr. Thorne, let me check my schedule. Obviously, it would be best for me if Jacqueline were here, but my stalls are... Let me see what I can arrange, and then schedule a time to come and meet her and your daughter, too."

"If it would help, I could set up a temporary stall- similar to those used at the Kentucky Horse Park," he suggested, the gleam of buoyant spirit enlivening his eyes.

"You know, of course, there are eminently more experienced trainers for your goals?" I had to tell him that, although he certainly had to be aware of my limitations.

"I figure it's pretty much up to Jacqueline. You've been highly recommended as the best starting point for this mare."

Was this a red flag? "Hmmm..." I mused, knowing there were those who preferred not to deal with mares. "I'll call you, tonight?"

"Thank you," he smiled in tremendous, conspicuous relief, warmly shook my hand, and rose to leave.

I glanced at my watch. Had time taken a breather? I wasn't late, yet.

"Mr. Thorne," I called after him. "You left this," I held up the envelope.

"For you," he waved me off. "It's not a bribe."

Not a bribe? Now, what was that about?

IOU A HORSE

27

Luckily, I did not open the envelope until after my lessons were over. My focus might have been compromised.

A short note was enclosed: Please accept my insurance settlement to keep Sirocco comfortable and for all of her veterinary needs. The check was for $45,000!

I was still staring at it when Sierra burst into the house.

"I hope you're hungry, Kid. I'm sick of seeing your skinny ass getting skinnier while mine heads the other way." She side-stepped me, hop-scotched over four racing kittens and set a scent-full box on the kitchen table.

"Meatloaf, courtesy of Schoe, my au'gratin potatoes and Schoe's famous green beans," she boasted.

Schoemaker Sorenson, named for a famous jockey- Willie Shoemaker, was Sierra's older, taller brother. As Schoe looked less like a jockey than a giraffe, the name really stuck with me. Perhaps his parents had won money on Mr. Shoemaker.

Schoe, Sierra, and their crew maintained the neighboring farm in immaculate splendor and took care of Creekside's hay needs, too. Her brother had a special talent for meatloaf, BBQ ribs and green beans, and he was the polar opposite of his sister- being quiet and quite curse-less.

"What's up, Kid?" Sierra leaned down and examined every pore of my face. "Been sleeping lately, huh?"

I had, too, ever since my falling apart on Cloud's shoulders and the advent of counseling sessions in my sleep via a bare-chested Indian psychologist... How magically weird my nights had become!

No longer did I cry myself to sleep, and I woke up refreshed as if I'd actually slept deeply- despite the question that hung inside my brain like a feisty, irritating termite.

"What's that?" Sierra snatched the note and check from my hands. Nothing was sacred to Sierra.

"F****** A!" she gasped.

"I'll have to return it," I countered, my ears ringing from the loud expletive.

"You are f****** kidding, right, Kid? I've heard of this guy. He's extremely f****** well off. Cash the f****** check and take me out to eat. Speaking of eat, c'mon, let's eat before ptomaine or salmonella or something similarly nasty gets to it first." She eyed the sniffing kittens scampering toward the table.

I couldn't make her understand about the check or the dinner, having overindulged in chicken salad for lunch. She kindly stocked my refrigerator with all the leftovers- enough for me for a week and told me to just cash the f*** check. If he wanted me to have it, well...

For the third time, as she pried the climbing Eenie and Meanie from her jeans, she gave me an odd look.

"Did you happen to see the news about a month ago?"

News? I cannot tolerate the news. My aunt didn't care for it either. Just how alike were we? I guess I'd never fully understand with her passing on.

Certain news headlines triggered the spiral down, as did unwanted and abused animals. I'd met and adopted so many over the years that I...I could almost fend off the numb dissembling- until night. Something about night or maybe it was only finding the privacy to fall apart in. The sole exception was my incident with Cloud.

"I don't watch the news."

"That's right, you don't. Shit, Kid, you would have loved this story, I think. Some f****** asshole was found with his hands and feet duct-taped, gagged, and duct-taped inside a cardboard washing machine box alongside I-75. The box was so close to the fast lane he cried thinking he was a goner every time a semi barreled by, not to mention the state of his pants. I guess some trucker called in about the potential for an accident involving the huge box.

Get, this. When the cops asked him how the f****** hell he got there, the f****** moron admitted he'd tossed a duct-taped box of kittens in the road, and the next thing he knew this huge monster with vampire fangs- can you f****** believe it?- grabbed him by the scruff of his neck, taped him up and tossed him in that box and told him he better never do it again or something worse would befall his sorry, f****** ass. ASPCA is after his ass, now."

She continued to weigh me as if I were on trial. Perhaps I hadn't dreamed Cloud's calling me to bring the box of kittens to him. It had been a duct-taped shoe box, hadn't it? One of the kittens really had been bleeding, right? Maybe, dead? The evidence had disappeared over night... Magical things seemed to be in the works since... Since when? I shuddered under Sierra's scrutiny.

"Well, you don't think I did it, do you?"

"Nah, he was a great f****** blubber boy, and it's not your style, Kid. But I sure wish I'd got a piece of him," she smirked.

Sierra proceeded to push me through old re-runs of LARAMIE, LAWMAN and LANCER, and gigged me repeatedly about my plans for the stallion.

"I've got a couple mares I'd like to send to him," she loudly hinted.

"Could we hold off on that for a while?" I managed to discourage her- for the moment. By 9:00, I was yawning to beat the band and I still had night check to do.

"Get your sleep, Kid. Catch you later. You gonna keep all these kittens?"

By this time, they were all abed on my lap. At 3 am it would be a different story. Somehow I managed to sleep on as they raced across the bed, playing kitten games. I trusted Captain, on guard, as always, to make sure nothing was destroyed while I slept. There was enough to do without repairing kitten-tornado damages.

"I reckon so. Good night, Sierra, and thanks."

The prairie seemed to be his office of choice. We never returned to Lough Gur. I didn't mind. Lough Gur was mysterious and suited his aura, but the plains were more in keeping with his heritage. Of course, he'd look awesome anywhere, if perhaps slightly out of place with his sartorial choice.

Before he could ask- "I did as you recommended, I asked Ned and Tim what they wanted."

This did not forestall the inevitable, "What do you want?" That magnetic gaze of his felt like a Superman x-ray and I was laid bare. Ridiculously, a thought popped into my head- I wouldn't bet on Kryptonite to dispel Teacher.

"Won't you tell me about...yourself?" I dared to ask, hoping for a reprieve.

An imperceptible shake of his head and he dismissively turned away. Leaving? He couldn't go already!

"Wait," even I heard the pathos in my call. "Teacher?"

Not bothering to turn, his head proudly held high as the ever-present wind batted his long locks, he reiterated, "What do you want?"

In dire straits to forestall his exit, an idea bounded into my pathetic mind. Could it be as simple as that? Except it wasn't simple, not for me.

"I..." my eyes scrambled for purchase on anything except him, but I caught the movement as he shifted his stance, interest engaged. Why was it so unbelievably hard?

"Because you've had your lifetime to practice," he gently resolved my dilemma.

My heart tripped. I forgot to breathe. The last time I'd expressed a want, I was told to get it myself. But, I was grown up now. I had no needs. Nothing I could not provide for myself. Was this some kind of a test? How could one be tested inside a dream? Wasn't sleep supposed to be about peace and rest?

Teacher shrugged and began walking away.

"Teacher, I...I...want," shivers ran under my night shirt. "I want to talk...for us to talk."

Abruptly, he turned on his heel. I felt as if I'd been richly rewarded. His lips deigned a unique sort-of-a-grin which suited him, and was quite a welcome respite from his usual unforgiving, dour mien. Almost, bearably...friendly?

"Care to join me?" He sat cross-legged in the grass.

"S...sure," I stammered, relieved, and self-consciously flustered.

"What would you like to talk about?"

My goodness, I was being given a choice? "Will you tell me something about you? I mean I still don't understand how you are here."

"This is my home," he indicated the wide open prairie.

"I mean, inside my head, my dreams," I tried to explain.

He grunted, "Humor."

"Oh," he'd tried to be funny! "Sorry, I didn't catch that," I squirmed; apparently humor was not de rigueur for either of us. "What tribe are you?" I hoped that was the politically correct way to ask.

"Lakota." Silence.

"Talking involves at least two participants, I think." I guess if he knew all about me...well, reciprocity would be nice. "Where were you...?"

"The past is...past."

"OK," be glad for any response shy of a question, I congratulated myself. "Uh, how old are you?"

"Mid-twenties or so," the man of few words allowed after a moment's silence.

"What do you do? Or, I mean do you just visit people in their dreams?" My lack of communication skills had me sounding quite inane, to my ears, anyway.

"I come to you because you...drew me to you."

Here we go again. "So, you can't explain that, either?"

Did he never blink? Those black eyes of his made me glad I didn't sleep in...

His lips curled up.

"Can you read my mind?" My entire body burned at the prospect.

"Not difficult. You are uncomfortable in this apparel and setting," his eyes dropped to my chest and lower. "Why do you hold yourself from others?"

Protesting, "I don't. I...give lessons to people and work with horses."

His eyes finally closed and I was lost- I'd disappointed him again.

Sensing he was ready to rise and go, "Please," my fingers grazed his knee, causing his nostrils to flare and his eyes to glare. "Sorry," I repented.

"If a student touched you by surprise..."

"Are you saying we're the same?" A ray of something vital- hope, maybe, flitted through my gut.

"We used to be," he murmured.

"Won't you please expound on that?" I realized it had become exceedingly important to me...to know him.

"Say it aloud," he commanded.

My body fired with shock and embarrassment, but I pinned him with every ounce of audacity I could muster. "I want to know you." A great sense of solace baptized me.

Grunting, he nodded. A grunt in lieu of a chuckle?

"Yes," he answered my unspoken question. "I've yet to improve in the 'laughter' department."

I found this pretty amusing- I could surely empathize, and shyly grinned at him. Hard to believe he lacked in any department. I happened to glance at his feet. Dear God! I needed to watch my thoughts. Drat that Sierra!

Teacher threw back his head and barked at my predicament. Oh, no! He knew what... I suffered a turbulent, blistering heat which manifested in an overwhelming blush. Oh for a place to hide, but where could one hide inside a dream? Especially one I apparently drew?

"You're not an ordinary man," I blurted, wanting to kick myself.

"No."

"I...want you to tell me," I managed to pull myself together- just barely.

"Do you? You're not afraid?"

"I'm never afraid," maybe backwards, but not afraid.

IOU A HORSE

"I am a shaman. For your homework," his eyes glinted, "You will break the barrier you put up between yourself and others."

"What is a shaman?"

Stubborn, uncompromising silence his rejoinder. Get on with it, Dove, before he leaves, I warned myself. "I don't know what you mean. Do you want me to just continue talking with people? Outside lessons?"

"You tell me, Miss Dove." And our nightly session ended.

28

Today was the day- I intended to ride Cloud. A good idea? I was positive he'd tell me. And therein lay the creepy part.

After he steadfastly refused to lunge, I'd retreated to gather my scattered wits and reconnoiter the weird situation I'd been inducted into.

Being the non-confrontational sort, I most assuredly did not intend to beat him- though part of me half-wondered how that might go over with him. An idiotic scene of Cloud wielding a lunge whip and ordering me to 'trrott' flashed before my eyes. The more intellectually-active section of my brain refused to entertain any thought of force and Cloud in the same picture. Or the ramifications.

The...words I'd heard clearly inside my head- 'I do not need to be trained' and the other incidents of my hearing things, whirled me in a puzzling, playing field. Coupled with not always eating right, perhaps I'd neared half a bubble off plumb.

Once the lessons were over for the day... Is it possible to look forward to something and not at the same time?

"Miss Dove, I'm so excited!" Martine effervesced toward me, eyes afire. She was the only student who arbitrarily prefixed my name with Miss, I mused, while thanking the Kind Man that the injury to her shoulder hadn't been as serious as it could have been.

She practically danced in place with her gleaming black boots, pristine taupe breeches and a sleeveless, light blue polo shirt ardently tucked in with a designer belt clasping a lithe waist- her appearance was par for the course, but her dancing- totally new.

My visual scan of her- no spot would dare inflict itself upon Martine- did not forestall the list of the day's activities rapidly forming in my head. Until...

174

IOU A HORSE

'ASK!' A deep, familiar male voice resoundingly demanded. Silently? Not to me. The voice was for my ears only- they rattled with the ferocity- and a chill seeped through my attire.

Cloud banged on his gate, tossing his black-crowned head. 'ASK!'

"Are you all right, Dove?"

I tried to ignore Martine's concern- I was immersed in enough of my own. "I...I'm fine. Uh, Cloud seemed bothered by something. Probably just a B-52 horse fly," I grasped at any interjection.

A monumental horse snort and a final bang on the gate. Ask, I'd been commanded. By Cloud, or did Teacher watch me throughout the day? Ridiculous, a dream did not step out of a dream into reality. But then, how could I ask such a question when the magic often stepped from paper and pencil?

"What were you saying, Martine? You were excited ab...?"

I partially listened to her vivid description of attending a horse show...

'LISTEN!'

Leaning into the ridge of an arena beam proved to me I was awake, forced my backbone to shore up a semblance of sanity, and my attention promptly, at least 9/10's of it, swung to her.

"I want to show Copper. Will you help me? Do you think we could show this year? Next month, maybe?"

I broke into her irrepressible list of spewing questions. "I think if that is what you'd like to do, then, of course, I'll help you. The judges will like Copper. He's steady and built for the job. I'll acquire a test booklet for you..."

"I've already got one- I joined USDF at the show," she pulled out a fistful of catalogs from an LL Bean bag resting at her feet- one of them being the Calendar of Competitions which contained all the show test patterns from introductory to Grand Prix, and other pertinent information.

"I so wanted to buy show clothes, but I thought I'd best get your advice. I did find this beautiful brow band," she held up a black band inset with large rhinestone crystals which sent rainbows flying as it caught the sunlight.

"That's beautiful!" I attempted to indulge in unfamiliar social enthusiasm, just in case Teacher was grading me. "I think we should practice our riding..."

"Oh, my lesson! Sorry, Miss Dove, I got carried away." I could have sworn the patient Copper rolled his eyes. And a snort of disappointment(?) from Cloud's paddock battered my conscious.

"Uh, Martine," I remembered my lesson of the previous night and I had an inkling of what it might mean. "Just Dove, please. No Miss. If that's all right?"

Why did I feel like a piece of myself dropped away? Or that I was shoved under a disapproving spotlight? Aunt Vickie had everyone address her as Miss, and when she began turning lessons over to me, she instituted the whole Miss Dove thing. I'd not considered it odd at the time, even though many of my students were older than me.

"Dove, thanks," and Martine joyfully threw her arms around me. Copper stood steadfast as catalogs slid along the ground at his feet. Martine did manage to keep a hold of the reins, I saw, as I blushed and tried to refrain from squirming like a captured bird.

"Hey, Miss Dove, you up for smoked salmon today?" Tim presented me with the lunch menu. He was doing his best to make sure I had at least one good meal a day, bless him. "I've got plenty if you want to join us," he called after Martine.

She stopped, model-like, eyed Tim speculatively for a loaded second, "I'd love to."

I recalled how she'd been terribly excited about her anniversary, before abruptly descending from Copper. From somewhere in my filing system, I also remembered an odd explanation she'd delivered at some point- she celebrated the anniversaries of her divorce. With grand fanfare. Martine was not shy about the end of her marriage and how it 'totally released' her, as she put it. Hmmm, Tim and Martine?

IOU A HORSE

Tim winked at me- "Miss Dove, if I were 20 years younger, I'd make a beeline for you, but..." He avidly inspected Martine's backside as she mounted Copper.

Abashed once more, I rubbed my hands together, knocked my back against the beam's ridge and scrambled for a list to eschew my embarrassment. A list to hide behind. Barriers. Distance from others.

"Tim, why don't you just call me Dove," I astounded the air waves.

"Why thanks, I'll do that," and he ambled off to join Buddy and Tennerife. His whole manner of movement had improved remarkably since... Since when?

Dr. K had remarked last week that Sheer's progress was nothing short of miraculous. She might not compete again (this was not ingrained in stone), but she certainly was moving with gusto.

And me? I was having nightly counseling sessions with a Native American in my dreams. And looking forward to them, well, looking forward to seeing him and hopefully learning more about him and that 'shaman' business. His striding into my dreams seemed to have stultified the downward spiraling to my childhood distresses and the ensuing crying jags.

Except for that voice inside my head and that damned pesky question of 'what do you want?' I almost felt...like I was a different person playing me?

"Martine, deep breaths from your diaphragm promote relaxation in you and Copper and loosen your lower back. The energy you usually exude is great for sleeping convention-goers, but maybe a little too much for your ride," I advised.

I knew Sheer's saddle was a possibility, but Marshall's saddle, I believed would work better. If another trainer confided in me what I intended to do- here and alone, I'd have concerns about his sanity, certainly his safety. And I'd already experienced enough incidents to have me questioning my own psychological state.

But I was not dissuaded. Placing Marshall's dressage saddle atop the covered ring's 4' rail along with a Woolback saddle pad and several bridles, I took a deep breath. Tim remained somewhere on the property so I wasn't totally alone. Alone, something about that word was unsettling, though I'd be the first to admit, we- alone and I- had always been compatibly on the same team.

I brought Cloud out of his paddock, gave him a good, but unnecessary brushing- how could a horse stay so clean?- and checked his big feet. Sierra and her big feet- would I ever get that image out of my mind?

Cloud stood the perfect gentleman with his lead line dropped in front of him. Ground-tied- the cowboys certainly had a winner with the notion a horse should remain in place if the rein dropped to the ground.

"You sleepy, Cloud?" His eyes betrayed no interest whatsoever in the horses across the ring, but their heads poked out, curing their curiosity about him and the imminent, out-of-the-ordinary proceedings regarding the newcomer.

I'd already been personally apprised that the stallion had a most interesting way about him; I wondered if he'd ever been ridden. It's not like he was a yearling. Around 6 or 7 years old was my best guess.

Finishing up with a soft brush on his face, I straightened the lengthy forelock between his huge, black eyes- so long it hung between large, placid, black nostrils. Something made me think he was feigning a nap or boredom.

"I believe I'll saddle you and see what you think about that," I ruminated aloud.

'I don't believe so,' that clear, deep male voice sundered my peace quotient.

Weak at the knees, I leaned back on the rail, massaged my temples and refrained from biting my lower lip, barely. A breeze flicked through. There was always a breeze across the ring- very gratifying in our 90-plus, muggy heat wave.

Deciding to pretend I'd not heard a thing- like as not, I hadn't anyway- I placed the saddle pad upon Cloud's substantial back and reached for the saddle.

Only to turn back to him and find the pad not only lying in the sand, but a well-placed, large hoof directly atop it.

"I've seen this trick before, nothing new. Are you a circus horse? Worked with clowns, perhaps?"

I didn't expect an answer from Mr. Smart Aleck. And I sincerely hoped I'd not be privy to one.

'Clowns!' followed by a snort that speckled my long sleeve white shirt.

"All right! Who the devil are you? Who's speaking?" I wheeled around in overheated frustration.

Had Tim taken up ventriloquism? No, Tim wouldn't play that kind of a joke. But someone had taught the stallion how to disrobe. Cloud and the funhouse had come to Creekside- what would keep me out of the madhouse?

"All right, then. You don't want a pad under the saddle, I can live with that." I wasn't about to retrieve it and try to replace it. Let him stand on the damn pad til the cows came home!

I lifted the saddle from the top rail. Cloud was certainly as tall as Marshall and I had to tip toe to reach. As I tried to lower the dressage saddle upon his back, Cloud side-passed away and repeated the chicanery as I persevered, saddle in hand. I'd become part of a comedic routine- shades of Francis, the talking mule, with me as the flabbergasted Donald O'Connor.

Marshall's saddle is not light. Three times you're out. I put the saddle back on the rail with weary arms and a whirling dervish brain. I could do bareback...

"You think you are going to win this bout, too, don't you?" Beleaguered, I dared question his motives. "The only one who stands to lose is you." Did I really say that?

He turned his head from the bridle I offered and thrust his muzzle way up, well beyond my reach. Blast!

"If you snort one more time, I'll...I'll..." I felt a headache coming on. I never get headaches.

'I'll make a deal with you,' the voice trespassed on me.

Turning over a bucket, I sat down, enervated, dispirited, and feeling like a cuckoo struck asunder from its clock. The stallion, how else could I explain it, had access to the inside of my head.

I'd always conversed with the horses I worked with, but not on such a 'supernatural' level. How did the Cloud-inspired tete-a-tete fit in with Sierra's species specific conversation? What if I dialed her up and turned him over to her? The madhouse loomed large.

Sheer had a vocabulary a professor might envy, otherwise, I used vocal tones to calm or call single commands to or to praise a horse, in conjunction with my body language. Riding was a fusion of two different species as far as I was concerned- harmony the requisite goal. Should I face some surreal music and respond to Cloud's challenge?

"Who or what are you?"

'Cloud,' the immediate, stoic reply lambasted me. I was not amused.

"What are you?" I glanced around. It was enough that I was going crazy, no one else needed to witness the proceedings.

A snort of derision, 'A horse.'

Save me! For some reason the crackbrained conversation reminded me of another one. I shook myself back to the present. To retreat would bother me no end. I'd never considered myself a quitter.

"What is the deal?" I sighed in resigned exasperation.

'You ride my way first, I'll consider yours.'

I must be dreaming. Seriously?

'You're not,' he whiffled my hair as I dropped my head in my hands.

I'm sure there's a sense of dread that interferes with a person's vital signs when confronted with something completely and irrevocably over said person's head.

IOU A HORSE

Aunt Vickie had guided me through a widespread spectrum of equine 'episodes' over our years together and I'd continued to develop my repertoire of responses to equine 'surprises' when working alone. But in all of my learning, I'd never experienced the sensation of I'm-completely-out-of-my-element that Cloud presented me with.

'Comfortable?' Cloud congenially asked. I had to admit his bare back with its plenitude of muscle development along his spine suited me very well. Behind his great withers was a perfect spot for my seat without injury to private parts.

Bareback riding was nothing new to me, except I had no reins with the bridle-less Cloud, but there was a plethora of mane to grab and my helmet was securely fastened on my head.

I checked that not a single one of my muscles tightened; disregarded my inner qualms, cautioned myself to breathe. Whatever else he might be, Cloud was still a horse. Tight meant flight.

'Hold on,' he directed and from a standstill he shot off.

Inadvertently- hell, to save myself- I gripped with everything I had.

'Naughty, naughty,' I heard the clear corrective inside my brain. 'I thought you weren't afraid,' he taunted.

My breathing hesitated and my heart hammered as he flew around the sand ring like a trainee for the Kentucky Derby. Was I afraid? I'd have to be crazy to say no. Hearing voices inside my head probably already confirmed the idea of my being mentally unsound...

But my body, from years of education in the saddle, innately recognized how to sit, how to relax, how to be 'with' the incredible, single-minded, unbelievably balanced stallion.

'Good,' he complimented my getting with the program.

It had been a long time since I'd had a lesson- I needed to amend that. Every ride on a horse was a two-way lesson, but Cloud's idea of class...

I couldn't finish the thought.

'I'll not let you fall.'

"What? Oh, no!"

'Duck,' he called and sailed over the 4'rail of the sand ring, clearing the roof beams by... I didn't want to know.

At least my head remained attached to my body as I hunkered into the lustrous mane flicking from his neck and strewing upon my face. My fingers braided into long, black strands and Cloud, landing perfectly balanced, bolted off.

Horses called out behind us- the Derby audience, sans elegant chapeaus- as we ran Cloud's course, Cloud's way. Without competition.

Pasture gates and fences meant nothing to him. My body naturally inclined with the thrust of his hindquarters. Down to the creek at a more sensible pace. Splashing among the rocks, lunging up and over the bank on a Cloud-designed trail for two.

'Let go!'

Let go?

'What happens when a horse is kept under a tight rein?' Cloud asked.

"He revolts," came readily to my lips.

'The same for a human.'

Back up to speed, the fence posts and trees flew by as if a multi-colored curtain walled our path. The speed- I'd never felt such speed! The muggy air hit my eyes so forcefully, I unintentionally cried.

'LET GO!' Cloud commanded.

I sat up, barely registered the sun about to set. Was my body revolting? From what? From being the 'me' I'd become?

What would happen if I let go? A tumble wasn't completely out of the realm, but I doubted it, and there was the bigger question. I was perfectly in tune, at home, astride a horse. What about off the horse?

'LET GO!!!'

Without another second's hesitation my fingers released his long locks and with the rhythm of his great strides echoing in every cell of my body, I was no longer me. No longer a person at all.

IOU A HORSE

Simply at one with a horse, as all my rides aspired to be, only there...was so much more!

My arms rose. Wings to Cloud's body. Pegasus. I half-expected to be airborne and join his namesake high above.

Let go... Had I imprisoned myself?

I closed my eyes and let go.

"Son, I knew you had a plan of some sort," Tim leaned against Cloud's gate, wiped the sweat from his brow and replaced his John Deere cap. "But, Jimminy Christmas! You gotta warn an old man! When I saw you fly over that rail! Gee whillikers! Has to be 4', at the very least! And that little girl clinging to you like a tick on a hound... I...I thought my ticker might clock out! Jimminy Christmas!"

Tim sighed, enormously relieved, yet spellbound. "You don't do things by half, do you?"

To which Cloud simply nuzzled Tim's ear, displacing his ball cap.

29

I couldn't stifle the goofy, inane smile issuing forth from my exuberant face at Teacher's implacable approach. So totally unlike me- I nearly bounced with pleasure. Not even that insidious question of 'what do you want?' would ground me from the high of my ride on Cloud. Like a student who'd thought she'd done well, I guessed I expected to surprise him with my progress. After all, hadn't I been doing my homework?

But Teacher interrupted that notion, taking his customary cross-legged position, sinking to the thick prairie grass and indicating for me to follow suit, "What do you feel when you ride?"

Had he witnessed my fling into insanity? Galloping without any means of control upon a rogue stallion? And what had happened to the impersonal tone of that singularly irritating, 'what do you want?'

I regarded his tall, imperturbable figure, which did not wilt, as I was doing, while he reciprocated with an intense perusal of his own. The word arrogant came to mind, but I inherently knew that was incorrect. Deer in the headlights came to mind, too- describing me. I'm sure he never felt put on the spot.

My mind was on a foray of its own. If Teacher substituted leather leggings and breechclout, maybe added a feather and a little war paint, he'd be the living, mystic image of his long deceased ancestors- warriors of the plains.

Still as a marble statue, he waited. If he'd read my thoughts, which was quite likely- I blushed in realization, then I deserved whatever fallout was headed my way. He certainly was...attractively intriguing, in a most unusual fashion.

"You're sweaty tonight, been running?" I blurted. Question for question. The glistening sheen of sweat remarkably enhanced the hard planes of his chest muscles and drew my eyes to those mysterious scars which seemed almost artfully framed by his black hair- when those lengths deigned to shift. Something about...

IOU A HORSE

"Does my sweat offend you?" Did he growl at me?

"N...no, not at all," I stammered, flustered. I didn't know how to get out of the discomfiting mess I'd gotten myself into. Those scars, his defined abdomen- did they call that a 6-pack? Those lethal, feral black eyes... I couldn't hardly look around him at the prairie grass- wasn't it rude not to look at someone talking to you? I certainly could not look over him- he took up my full, vertical field of vision.

"It looks...n...nice on you." God did I feel like an idiot- ground hurry, open up and swallow me, please. How did girls talk to tantalizing men without seeming like raving nutcases?

Teacher grunted with no perceptible variance of his wide lips. I must have amused him with my wayward thoughts and loss-of-etiquette gaping as I entered bedlam.

"Are you going to answer me?" Patient reiteration.

Questions. Questions. Questions.

What did I feel when I rode? To answer that almost seemed like an invasion of my privacy. My communication with a horse was...for me and that horse. Yet, to inspire my students hadn't I tried to offer glimpses into that world?

His silence was an impalpable, irksome goad. But hey, wait a minute, it was only a dream after all, wasn't it? Confidentiality must prevail between dreamer and...dreamed?

"I...I feel like I belong," I bit my lower lip- the kid forced to answer when called upon and dead sure he had the wrong answer. Would he understand?

"Yes. That feeling of belonging should have taken hold when you developed in your mother's womb. It should have stayed with you always," Teacher quietly prompted.

He allowed me a full minute for the effect of his words to take root. His lips thinned, intriguing me- he was remembering something!

"You...know," I murmured, my eyes misting at this unlooked for connection becoming apparent. Of course, I'd never believed I was the only one with a messed-up childhood; I'd simply retreated into myself and not spoken to any potential compatriots.

"What do you feel when you teach?" He adroitly redirected me.

"Useful," I said. He nodded compassionately; his eyes scanned the horizon.

I plunged backwards. "How do you know about those feelings? I...w...want to know everything about you," I recognized that I honestly wanted that very much and he wished to know my wants...

"Do you tell your students everything?" Frustratingly, he'd cunningly sidestepped me once more.

"No," I agreed, "not until they are ready."

"And so it is."

The spiritual heights I'd felt with Cloud plummeted as silence seeped in, sizzling between us. That old familiar shroud of numbness struggled up to draw me down. Grasping for my gifted crystal, I closed my fist around it. Since its placement about my neck, I often touched it when I became annoyed or...

Teacher's long fingers touched the side of my face. The serene power of his butterfly wing flick of contact annihilated the downward spiral and immediately cast me into a magical realm. Ah, to always have instant access to wondrous peace!

"You have suffered. Enough. What do you feel outside of riding and teaching?"

Desperately, I wanted to lean into his hand, but I held...I held the reins tight.

"Keep control of myself," I spoke as if hypnotized. Perhaps I was. Sinking into infinity via the mirror of his eyes. Mirror?

"It is time to let go and create a different path. End the route that keeps you in check like an automaton left outside to play only once in a while. You make magic for others when you instruct them. Is this not creating? When alone, you shut the door on creating when you cry. The sad spiral down, back to your beginnings... Have done! No more suffering- control may work in another fashion and so induce liberation."

IOU A HORSE

An emanation of serenity like osmosis flowed into my cheek, as if a light sought every dark recess within me. I began to feel shucked from a husk, untethered, soaring but not giddy, nearly as free as when I let go with Cloud.

"I never thought of it as suffering- just coping, I guess, continuing... How do you know about my...crying? Do you watch me?"

Again, I saw myself reflected in the depths of his eyes. Black pools of magical mirrors. Not only did he watch me, but...

"You have suffered, too," I educed aloud.

Instantaneously, his eyes slammed shut; his hand dropped and I sensed I'd been recalled from heaven- found deficient in some way, cast into...

"What do you want?" Teacher tossed at me, rose and strode away, shoulders set defiantly, without giving me a chance to repeat- 'I want to know you.'

My want or need to know him seemed to unsettle him as much as his questions unsettled me. And I felt awful all over again.

I watch her sleep; thinking, always thinking- unless the numbing haunt steals through the tight self-control she cocoons herself with.

A revolver lies under a paperback book by the alarm clock. I have no fear she'll turn it on herself- her responsibilities are too great- and paradoxically, she loves them.

CatSkill, you knew exactly what you were doing opening this door for me. You and your lady. Were you in conjunction with the spirits or had the spirits planned it all along?

Her drawings drawing me to her. Her powers of intuition have truly shocked me. I must be careful, mustn't I? But if the spirits have designed it so...

The fine line between being drawn by her and to her seems to be dissolving into our drawing together. So much for opposites attract.   I   understand   now   about   Shadow   and   myself. Understanding engulfs me.

I was sure our cultural differences would stand...would be my personal impediment.   My people need me, but I am not supposed to be constrained, am I? CatSkill had proved otherwise-his half-Lakota lineage had not hindered the Lady Shaman and they are a powerful pair.

The imagined surety I had of our differences, Dove's and mine- if I were a laughing man, I'd howl. CatSkill knew- found gentle humor in the ways of spirit, but only in a loving desire for what's best. Still, I am not sure about everything, and just maybe, that is how it should be- for me. Time to withdraw and seek the spirits' guidance.

IOU A HORSE

30

"Ned, what are you doing Saturday?   I don't want to interrupt a date or anything..."

He'd loaded the manure spreader and was headed out.

"Heck, Miss Dove,"- he'd not taken me up on my offer of dropping the Miss- "The only girl on my mind is right there."

An enthusiastic smile fastened on the dark bay grazing in Sheer's shadow. Chanson was more than happy to bow to Sheer's 'I'm the boss' attitude and never outpaced her compromised gait. Like a courtier to a queen, Chanson knew her place, yet also acted the friendly cheerleader.

"What's up, Miss Dove?"

"I was thinking of checking out a potential Olympic mount," I explained.

"Mr. Thorne's mare? What time?"

I wished I might miraculously self-absorb his enthusiasm- too bad it wasn't contagious like the flu.

The last session with Teacher had ignited something. Intuition had lent me insight into my provocative professor; something about his past or present he did NOT want to share. Something important- that we apparently were mirrors for each other. He knew how difficult it was for me to... That was it! Oh, my, please let him come back, very soon.

"There she is, my Jacqueline," Mr. Thorne's head proudly inclined to a small paddock- all dirt, no grass. "Is this the young man thinking to go to the Olympics?"

I introduced Ned.   Mr. Thorne judged my student's handshake and eyes. Found neither lacking. Our attentions turned to the mare.

"Does she not graze?"

Beyond the 3-storey colonial mansion were acres and acres of lush green- the result of diligent field irrigation, no other possible explanation. In this summer drought, that particular color was a delightful shock to the eyes. I'd moved Sheer and Chanson to every last shaded spot harboring forage and increased the others hay as they depleted their pastures.

"Well... Oh, this is my daughter, Corrina, and her mount, Craft."

I shook hands with a female version of her father- runway elegance with a true horsemanship ken.

"I've heard a lot of good things about you and I'm looking forward to our lessons. If you'll excuse me, I need to cool off my boy," she patted a solid black gelding with one white near sock, nodded at Ned with one of those looks that comes naturally to some girls.

"Uh," Thorne hedged, "she's hard to catch." He obviously hated to admit this. "I...I'll get her. Joe, bring me some grain, please," he addressed an older man wielding a broom in the immaculate aisle of the barn.

Grain, I mused. Ned and I exchanged glances. No horse at Creekside avoided humans, none required bribes.

We followed the owner to the end of the small run where lounged Jacqueline, a leggy chestnut with a perfect topline and tremendous hindquarters. She deigned to flick an ear- barely acknowledging our existence, her self-absorption off the charts.

The grain didn't entice her to take a single step in our direction, and as Thorne moved toward her she sat down, reversed and cantered off- practically dancing on a dime- keeping her distance. With a condescending air she stood snorting, ready to do it again. You could almost hear her challenge- 'Just try me!'

"Isn't she beautiful?" Thorne enthused, completely avoiding the fact of the mare's intransigence. "Pretty girl," he glowed.

Pretty witch, I kept to myself. Spoiled and arrogant, but exhibiting exceptional talent. What a combination- if it could be tapped...

IOU A HORSE

"C'mon now, beautiful," Thorne sweet-talked her and shook the grain scoop. With a flourish of her great arched neck, she allowed him to approach, but at the last second, she pirouetted- her final taunt- just to let him know it was her game.

"Good girl," he patted her neck and gave her a handful of grain, clipping the lead line as she chewed. He led her away, tried to, but the mare wasn't having any of it.

"C'mon, now," he lowered his voice and gave a tug on the line. No effect.

"How does she respond to a whip?" I asked.

Flushed with annoyance at being made a fool of by a mare he thought the world of, Thorne equivocated.

"Uh, my old trainer never seemed to get along with her. If he brought out a whip," he eyed the dirt and shook his head, "Not a pretty sight, but he got her to move. Eventually."

"Has she been put under saddle?" Ned quietly observed, letting me ask the questions.

"She's been backed in her stall. Some lunge work...but then, our relationship ended," he hesitantly divulged.

"And she's four," I recalled. This mare could be a nightmare or a spitfire or an intriguing combination of both.

"Mr. Thorne, as I indicated before, I'm not on any list for the Olympics. You'd probably be better off with another trainer," I wanted him to remember my limitations.

"I hear what you're saying Miss Gray, but please give her a chance. Please."

Part of me was beginning to wonder how many other trainers had turned him down. I shrugged, asked for the lead and for Mr. Thorne to wait outside the gate with Ned.

Soft leather lead in gloved hands, I stood placidly next to the mare. To an observer, I'm sure I looked like a miniscule David next to a behemoth Goliath, but Aunt Vickie had ingrained in my head, 'It's not the physical stature, it's the mental one.'

I didn't say a word; pretty words weren't acknowledged by her- they were simply gobbled up- meant nothing, and she hadn't done anything to deserve them. We just stood, gauging each other.

I knew she expected me to try to lead her away and she would respond, as usual, in her dictatorial mindset, by avoiding/ignoring the human for a while, allow them a semblance of hope and then play mule games. Fine with me, we'd stand.

Her left front foot struck at the ground after two whole minutes and she set it forward of her right front. I nudged it back in line with the toe of my boot.

I knew Mr. Thorne was driving Ned crazy with whispered questions. Used to having his own way immediately, he found himself irritatingly stumped by a horse.

"What is she doing? Why is she just standing there?"

I also knew Ned would champion me with a 'wait and see,' politely couched.

"Walk on," I dictated to the mare and made a move to take a step. I'd gained a pretty good idea of her personality and that she had no respect for humans. Not mean in any fashion, just didn't see any need for reciprocal communication.

Jacqueline was an entity unto herself. The person who gained her respect might achieve wonders, because the mare was built to ascend the levels. Having no fear of anything, she would have been an ideal knight's mount- if she respected him. Spurs and whip wouldn't do it. She would fight, not flee- I'd bet on it, and I was not a betting person. The whole scenario was eerily similar to...

A slight hesitation when I asked her to move on, but ultimately she figured it wasn't worth her while. Make me, was her agenda.

In a flash, I turned her head to the left. Small or not, I had enough leverage to bring her stubborn head around with my finger pointing into her neck until she moved her left hind leg and crossed it over her right hind. Immediately, I brought her head facing front and asked her to "Walk on!"

This time she took two steps- surprising herself I imagined- and abruptly halted. Immediately, I swung her head right, foisting her off balance just enough.

Inherently, I knew she expected me to get riled like the

previous trainer, and go for a whip or harsh words, and I'd bet she'd heard every word Sierra could toss out.

I preferred the waiting game. Patience paid off in more cases than not, and I needed her respectful acquiescence if we were to work together. Deviating from her norm might get her thinking in a direction we could both live with.

"Walk on," I reiterated and the mare directly walked forward as if it had been her idea all along.

"There's a girl," I scratched her withers as we exited the gate to an open-mouthed Mr. Thorne and a grinning Ned.

"I'd like to see her move," I said to the dumbfounded owner and jubilant Ned. Had Mr. Thorne really expected me to descend like the wrath of God on this creature he'd lovingly named Jacqueline? I could think of more appropriate names- Amazon being foremost in my mind.

On an estate where money was no object, I turned her loose in a walnut-stained round pen complete with its own canopy and with gleaming brass edging topping the high rails.

Lunge whip in hand, I asked her to walk on to the left. She sauntered forward nose to the ground. Normally, I'd love to see that kind of stretch, but it had to be backed with forward-thinking strides.

"No pussyfooting," I murmured. "More," I called, raising the whip fractionally to catch her eye. No response. I gave a short, shrill whistle and flicked the whip, touching her rib cage. That got her attention.

Piqued at my calm, yet definitive action, her inside ear twitched, and she vaulted off with the trot of an Olympic contender. When I called canter and slightly raised the whip briefly above her girth's mid-section, she was already there, perfectly balanced- using the gifts she'd been born with. Her satellite ears twisted, listening for the next cue.

I took a deep breath, asked for trot and then walk. I had her. At least for today- horses are, after all, the greatest 'humilifiers'- Aunt Vicky's word. "Halt," I called with a light feel on the line, to which she responded with her great big eyes fully focused on me.

Walking toward her, "I think that deserves a snack."

"Isn't she a beaut! What about that trot!" Thorne's face beamed with an ebullient optimism I'm sure he'd not felt in quite a while.

"You should see Miss Dove riding Cloud- there's a trot to die for," Ned's first faux pas.

"Cloud?"

"The stallion," I divulged and rushed on, "She's a definite challenge, but I think, if I can perk her respectful interest, like today, we may develop a working relationship," I offered the Amazon a peppermint.

Queenly, she sought another. "You're welcome to bring her, if you're still interested. Ned and I will work with her at least five days a week. Learning to come will be one of our first lessons, as all my horses go out in large fields or extensive run-ins. If you find we're not to your satisfaction, please feel free to take her home, though I'd prefer if you spoke with me about any concerns, first."

Thorne, skipping all the necessary basics, had a single question, "Will Ned be ready in time?"

"Mr. Thorne, the more appropriate question is, will Jacqueline tow the line?- not every horse likes to show."

As it turned out, lucky me, Jacqueline loved to show. Off.

"Sorry about that quip," Ned apologized on the way home.

"Don't worry about it." I spent the ride back to Creekside reliving Cloud, instead of compiling training lists for the newcomer.

The stallion's endearing comments started as soon as I placed the saddle pad on his back.

Plop! Back on the ground.

"You are one perverse critter," I sighed.

'Critter?'

IOU A HORSE

"I thought you said you'd consider it?" Mind you, I made sure no one was within auditory distance. Without a chance of not hearing Mr. Ed in my head, I simply assumed...I was hearing things, and stopped fighting the notion I might...never mind.

'I did,' Cloud swung his head like an intransigent colt, but at least he did not stand on the clean white pad. 'I believe you enjoyed our night ride.'

I stroked his neck and the shoulders I'd fallen apart on. "It was one of the greatest experiences of my life. Thank you," I freely admitted.

'One of?'

"You never saw Sheer and me together," I choked and bit my lower lip for control.

'I can bear your sorrow,' Cloud empathetically nuzzled me.

"I'm sorry. I'm extremely grateful she's here and moving and she seems happy and I can still spend time with her..."

'You don't have to put up a front for her. She knows you worry and she wishes you'd stop. Do you miss the show ring?'

"Not especially, I do miss our working together and progressing as we tackle new movements. Sheer and I, we...are the epitome of partnership." What more could I say?

'All right,' Cloud exhaled loudly- just shy of a snort. 'Put the thing on,' he grunted, and grunted again when I girthed the saddle, even though I slowly and barely tightened it.

"Have you ever worn a saddle before?" Maybe...

'Have you?' His endearing manner returned.

Cloud balked at the bridle, and to my dismay Tim and Ned wandered over to the rail of the covered ring. I was pretty well immune to an audience, but I had to watch what I said, aloud.

"I'm known to have gentle hands. Please," I added, offering the bit.

I swear, if a horse could roll his eyes, Cloud succeeded with the most put-upon face, and snatched the bit from my hands. Leading Mr. Smarty Pants to the mounting block, I checked my helmet and mounted.

He stood stock-still as I settled lightly in Aunt Vickie's ultra-comfortable show saddle. Gentlemanly, he allowed me time to check my position and the feel of my legs relaxing on his sides.

An untoward notion suddenly knocked at my sensibilities. "Cloud, no racing around the ring this time, please?" Near begging, I appealed to his better nature. Better nature?

Another grunt. Something about that particular response... but he gave me no time to mull it over. He began to shake his head up and down.

"All right, all right." I gently gathered the reins and asked for a walk.

Cloud moved off like an aged barrel horse with no sign of barrels anywhere around. As if to say 'what's the point?'

My inside leg asked for more and my seat waltzed with the resultant fantastic impulsion. I dreamily pictured the over-stride.

Proceeding to gauge his reaction to my seat and legs with changes of direction earned me, 'Boring, boring,' clearly blaring inside my head.

Grinning, I softly closed my legs, picturing a working trot. And his crisp response profoundly bewitched me! Lightly, I posted, rising with his inside hind and gently re-touching saddle- no horse likes to be plopped down on.

'What are you doing?' railed silently in my head.

Did I hear that right? "Uh, posting," mindful of my audience, I quietly countered.

'I'm not a fence, sit down,' he growled. This time I felt like grunting. Of all the crazy weirdness since...Cloud's coming, this had to rank as the top oddity- bar none. Cloud had averred he didn't need training- I had to keep reminding myself.

I experimented with his patience and spiraling circles. His degree of suppleness was amazing. What an athlete! Surely, he'd been ridden before.

A resounding 'No' flashed in my brain.

I couldn't help it, I laughed aloud- my whole body sang with the gift of the moment and also for our previous nightly venture.

IOU A HORSE

I collected him in a corner and asked for more of a trot across the diagonal. Must be what it feels like to ride a trotter, I thought, as he sprinted over the expanse.

With a deep breath for my poor, jostled body and his abrupt re-collection, we approached the corner again. "How about if we try that again?"

'You want to go faster? Good!'

"No, no, I'd like a longer stride, if you think you can do that?"

'Why didn't you say so?' he fumed.

Bending into the corner, using a few steps of shoulder-in and... "WOW!"

His magnificent back arched under me and we sailed across the line- airborne- with no change in pace!

Applause from the ranks. "Magnificent," Ned hailed.

"Go for it, son," Tim hooted.

'Satisfied?' Cloud smugly queried.

"You are incredible!" I stroked the side of his withers, collected him again and asked for canter. I adjusted my position for half-pass after experimenting with extended and collected canter.

"How about tempi changes?" I dared push the envelope.

'I don't speak foreign languages.'

"Oh." Think, Dove. "It's a change of lead every so many strides," I translated.

'How many strides, or do I read your mind, or simply choose for myself?'

"Will you?" A horse that would read my mind! But he'd already indicated being inside my head, hadn't he? Animal communicators trained students to picture-talk with animals... Really, what did I expect from him? He'd never been ridden. Might the riding masters of Vienna achieve heaven without a horse having any previous riding experience?

A derisive snort. 'Show me in your head.'

I pictured lead changes every three strides. He rose to the occasion with clear, collected changes of lead, and thankfully, my seat was supple enough not to be unseated with his incredible thrusts.

Approaching the next diagonal, I pictured changes of lead every stride. Sheer had loved them, considered it fun.

Boom! Boom! Boom! Not to say he was heavy in any way- I wished I could see what I'd ridden! If Pegasus existed, I knew exactly how it would feel to ride the legend. Like a dream... Dream? Vigorous cheering from our audience of two brought me quickly back to reality.

My mind conveyed a free rein walk with exceptional over-stride. Every cell in my body tingled with energetic resonance to the point I nearly trembled. Never before had I ridden a horse with such fantastic scope and natural talent. Moorlands Totilas couldn't come close to competing with Cloud!

'Who?' Cloud startled my reverie.

I 'showed' him the famous dressage horse and his congenial rider. My head whirled with the dream- to ride a horse who agreed with your concept of a working partnership- one you needn't push or cajole, but a horse who took pride in his movement- the absolute height of riding!

Sheer and I had it together- that 'aura' of ballroom dancing. Cloud had all the natural built-in talent. Could I show Cloud?

IOU A HORSE

31

After two nights without my enigmatic teacher wandering in, I despairingly fought for sleep. Fitfully, I tossed, wondering where he was...and with whom. Could one fall in love with someone in a dream? Or was the notion simply another symptom of a nervous breakdown of sorts? Had my dreams become enablers? An idiotic giggle gurgled, sought escape.

I'd lie awake with the crystal cradled in my right hand. Why had he given it to me? And how did it get from Lough Gur to me to a dream and then back to me? Tangling with reality? Crossing dimensions?

In entertaining those questions, I seemed to gain a modicum of peace, if no veritable answers- which didn't make sense, either. But somehow, I rolled to my right side, displacing four kittens, checked the clock- 3am, curled into a fetal position and closed my eyes, praying he'd return. A dream is better than nothing.

"Dove, that was great! I feel like Copper and I are really getting it together," Martine unlatched her helmet, hugged the big chestnut and bounded toward me.

"You are, Martine. There was only a single instance when you rode your pattern..."

"I know, I know. I forgot to think one quarter of the circle at a time and ended up with an odd-shaped second half. But I'm getting there. Could we do two lessons a week?" She effervesced all over me; I could not sidestep her energy or arms.

"I'm not giving you enough homework?" I puzzled; every student left his lesson with what I considered to be just the right amount of assignments to be carried out on their own. I didn't believe in 24/7 coaching. At some point, I expected my students to be able to inherently comprehend what I'd tried to instill in them, and act accordingly. None of my students should feel abandoned-I'd be there to condone, criticize and add more to the mix in whatever fashion it took until they fully 'got it'.

"Oh, I can't complain about that. I just...I love our lessons. You've done so much for my relaxation level while keeping me focused on Copper. I don't think you realize what a gem you are," she confronted me with the executive-in-charge look on her face.

My eyes avoided her steadfast intensity. "Uh, I'm glad you're pleased," I sidestepped the compliment.

"Dove, you give great lessons, I'm not kidding. Your students, including horses, all seem to enjoy themselves with you. I think you're wonderful," Martine wasn't shy at all with my shyness.

'Say thank you,' rang in my ears. Was that darned Cloud spotlighting me, too?

"Thank you," I murmured.

"What about two lessons a week?"

"I'm afraid my schedule is rather over-full, right now..."

"Yeah, since you brought in that big, hulking mare," Martine smirked.

"The Amazon?"

"That's the right name for her. Jacqueline- who in the world came up with such a pretty name for that beast? A Jacqueline Onassis fan?"

"I suppose Mr. Thorne did. If it's OK with you, I'll call if anyone cancels," I offered.

"Perfect, please do," Martine threw an arm over my shoulders, again.

I thought about my lessons with Teacher and breaking barriers. Tried not to think about his absence.

"Martine, what do you want?"

That got her started.

"To win my classes at the show, to be the best damn rider and owner and buddy Copper could hope for, to make you proud of me and..." she peered down the aisle, "to knock the socks off a certain gentleman."

IOU A HORSE

She began to unsaddle Copper and I was amazed and intrigued enough to the point I had to ask, "Who?" Had to be someone she'd met recently at work.

"Why, Tim, of course. I don't think he's as old as he lets on, at least, I hope not, cuz if I'm going to light his fire I want reciprocity. Did you know he'd been diagnosed with fibromyalgia several years ago? That he felt like he'd been turned into a cripple- the pain would get so unbearable?"

"Really?" Heartily dismayed, I reflected, I didn't know that important information. I saw Tim in my head. The way he moved lately- didn't seem possible that it was the same man Martine described. I blushed at the thought of Tim and Martine together.

"He said you and Creekside were the miracle he hadn't a hope of finding and didn't know he was looking for. Something about this place," Martine shook her head.

"Churchill claimed the outside of a horse is good for the inside of a man," I patted Copper's sweaty shoulder.

"It's not just the horses, Dove. It's you, and Creekside, all the dogs and cats... It's the whole package. This place is a bit of heaven right here on earth. And all of us who come here, whether we say it or not, are extremely grateful," Martine pinned me.

Mist fogged my eyes. "I...thank you," and I scurried away. Not until later did it come to me again- Martine and Tim.

Tim had made it part of his day to bring me lunch- a gourmet lunch, no less. Even if there were times he couldn't stay, he'd leave a cooler under the pin oak.

Sunday with no afternoon lessons, I leisurely finished off a Caesar salad with chopped chicken breast. Tim and Martine had gone off together trail riding, without me.

"You won't be offended Dove, if an old man plays the field?"

"Old man, my foot," Martine provocatively smirked, tapping her foot.

"Have fun," I'd called after them, feeling a sense of...something nameless irritatingly niggling me.

Peace and quiet all about. Ned had taken Chanson out for a walk. Our work together with the Amazon was progressing nicely. The idea of her challenging us to come up with ever new, interesting puzzles appealed to me and kept Ned and I on our toes. The mare reveled in games- she'd be a perfect tank of a polo pony, and she zealously destroyed the monsters we built for her.

I expected to have her under saddle for Mr. Thorne in the coming week. Surprisingly, Chanson wasn't the only one who kindled to the sound of the French tongue. Jacqueline vociferously demanded Ned's attention when she spied him with Chanson. Talk about playing the field- Ned had to sneak out to his dark bay, hoping to foil the Amazon.

He was not always successful. If a strident bugling hit the air waves, it wasn't Cloud, but Jacqueline trumpeting for her due. Shades of Sheer, only my girl had no cause for concern.

Sheer and I worked in the woods, in and out of the creek rather than limiting her exercise to flat ground. Her hindquarter muscles, as Dr. K predicted, had healed unbelievably well and in record time. The idea of her tendon sheath being compromised with infection must have been a lucky misdiagnosis- one day she was in pain and the next, no heat or pain. No more penicillin shots, thank goodness!

Something healing about this place, Tim had told Martine. And it wasn't solely healing. I couldn't recall the last time anything broke down. The fences, the stalls- if something was amiss, I never knew of it, and I was always on the lookout for things needing mending. How odd was that?

Perhaps Tim was using his skills, though I never caught him out, and he'd surely not admit it. He certainly spent a great deal of his time at Creekside and had mentioned buying a nearby ranch house to save on driving time.

At times, I did catch him with a weed-eater in-hand when the regular maintenance man couldn't make it, and he refused to speak of money.

IOU A HORSE

"Dove, I don't need money; I need to be of some use and besides, it makes me happy," Tim boyishly grinned.

Useful. If Teacher- no, when Teacher returned, I'd have to ask him why being useful wasn't enough. Conveniently, I skipped over the happy part.

I refused to countenance the prospect of Teacher's not being in my dream- of not seeing his mysterious form striding across the prairie.

My gaze alternated between Sheer dozing in the late afternoon sun and Cloud studiously ignoring my watching him.

As my eyes focused intently on his sun-bronzed shoulder, the one I'd cried on, burnished with its strange scar, the horse disappeared and I experienced what I could only believe was a vision!

A young boy in a disheveled, dirty room. A broken-backed wood chair and an old, scarred kitchen table. I felt his hunger gripping my stomach. Empty shelves.

My heart beat escalated with a flood of memories. I bit my lower lip hoping to stave off the nasty, familiar spiral.

The boy, maybe 10 or 12, wore thread-bare jeans which were too short, no shirt, shoulder-length black hair. The door knob to the side door of the kitchen rattled and turned. A sense of impending doom assailed me to the point I fought nausea.

The boy sought to contain bile rising in his throat. Why did I feel it? Nowhere to hide, nowhere to run to in the single room hut with a dirty cot tucked in the corner.

Slamming open, the door convulsed at its moorings and in staggered a thin man, all the worse for wear, with his bloodshot eyes and dried spittle at the corner of his mouth. In his hand a switch tapped at his thigh.

Never dropping his eyes, the boy seemed resigned, yet almost defiant, and the man grasped him by the arm, turned him over the table with the boy's arm bent up backwards and laid the switch across his emaciated ribcage and arm. The man jerked at the boy's jeans and lashed away.

Blood flecks. Blisters. Old wounds- the boy never made a sound; the vile, determined malefactor ran out of energy, mid-swing, he passed out.

I'd wrapped my arms around myself, shaking, wanting to kill anyone who'd treat a child so horrifically.

Slowly, the boy righted himself, pulled up his jeans and edged away from the man crumpled on the floor.

Dry eyes. Deep black implacable pools. With distinct unease, my heart quaked and my gut revolted- I knew those eyes.

IOU A HORSE

32

The prairie sky abounded with expressive clouds- white and blue gray and every hue in between- as if it couldn't make up its mind to be a happy or stormy day. A brisk wind battered the tremendous puff balls and jostled butterflies in their windward tasks of seeking nourishment.

From which direction would he come? I circled like a child's wind toy, anxious and anticipating. Surely, my dreams would not have opened on the prairie splendor unless Teacher was imminent.

As a general practitioner of the non-descript facial expression myself, I wondered at the unfamiliar tug of muscles when my lips curled and at the lightening of my heart- actually it thudded like a John Phillips Souza band number- as Teacher strode through the waving, tall grasses which nearly hid me. In the summer heat, which the prairie loved so well, I was astounded at the growth over such a short time.

I managed to refrain from any further eager outbursts such as jumping up and down, but the effect he had on me- well, I was astounded by all the hoopla engaging my every cell. What was going on with me?

His long hair was driven across his face by a playful draft. Not a hand lifted to clear his eyes. Walking blind came to mind as he never wavered in his advance.

Surrendering to my impatience, I didn't wait for him to stop and begin our typical impasse with 'What do you want?'

"I missed you," I shamelessly spouted.

No sign of recognition, no sign of anything on that poker face and my breath caught. Was he angry with me?

A weighty tightness seemed to bear on his shoulders and his mouth was more than usually grim-set. A moment of silence descended like a guillotine, cutting off my eudemonia, and I felt like a fool. Stupid kid, I could hear my father declare before the ensuing slap sharpened the sting of his rebuke.

"My people needed me," Teacher said without inflection.

Although his hair curtained most of his eyes' boring into me, I knew what an unsightly specimen must feel like caught in the light of a laboratory's microscope.

His people needed him. Of course they did, and I received the whiplash of his reply like a bucket of ice water cast upon a warm, unsuspecting body.

Imperceptible ice crystals invaded my chest, fracturing my heart and lungs. Cold contractions were the result, and my breathing was stifled.

"I...I'm sorry...sorry that...my drawing you here is against your will. I...I didn't know...about..." I stumbled through my apology. I thought he understood about the magic- it wasn't my fault.

"What do you want?"

"I..." My teeth clamped on the inside of my mouth, tasted blood- I would not cry. I would not- it was not an option. "I just want...to talk with you."

Those inflexible thin lips in his tightly clenched jaw grimaced with...disgust? With my wrong answer? Again? What a disappointing student I was.

Suddenly, my head bucked in revolt- "Why don't you just go then? Stop coming. If you're so strong, refuse whatever brings you here! I...I don't need anything. I don't need you," I stormed all the while my gut betrayed every spoken word.

She whirls, striding obdurately away, but I can feel the quaking of her injured heart. All too familiar. Defiant, yet doing its best to rebuff defeat. Her slight figure is dwarfed in my native grasses, thin shoulders curl into her chest.

Worse than a slap across my face, the spirits hiss with utmost displeasure. I am not worthy...

IOU A HORSE

"Dove," I reach for her- for the first time I call her by her lovely name- a name significant of peace. Let there be peace between us, I pray. My fingers close, endeavoring to be gentle, around her elbow.

Stiff resolve outside, crumbling inside, but she is going to fight. That's fine; I've been there, too.

The night CatSkill held me as I struggled and eventually fell into his engulfing serenity, let go and cried over my...life? Spirits, help me, I plead.

"Dove," I gently turn her and she staggers awkwardly.

Against my own volition, I was enveloped in a massive warmth. My eyes had already begun their betrayal. I had to get away. To be alone...

Fruitlessly, I pummeled- cotton against rock- my fists against his chest, until I could struggle no more. I cried out my last breath, choking, trembling, and suddenly I felt a magical captivation. Serenity, like a drug inside my veins, swept through me- further loosening the tight rein I harnessed myself with, quelling my...self-denial? Soothing my rebellion. Forcing my surrender without the hindrance of pain.

"You do not have to continue in the prison of your past. Let go," he murmured into my hair.

Slowly, I unclenched my fists, tentatively returned his embrace as he repeated commandingly, "LET GO!" A vague familiarity flickered and fled as I melted into him.

The following day I retreated into myself once more, rehearsing his combatant attitude, my weak defense and ultimate surrender. Or had we both experienced surrender, a truce of sorts? If he never returned, how would I feel? The answer to that was quite simple- absolutely, off-the-chart miserable.

He was there ahead of me. Waiting. Patient. Thank you, I whispered to the powers that be. Thank you.

The prairie was wet- the clouds of the night before had correctly presaged the winds of a storm mirroring the storm inside of me.

His eyes searched me, gauging the state of my nerves, I guessed. I returned his nod, shy about my theatrics of the previous dream.

"There is nothing to be shy of," he soothingly informed me. "Please forgive my abrupt and ill-mannered self." His tone reflected honest sincerity.

Teacher was apologizing? To me?

Crossing his legs, unmindful of the wet ground, he gracefully settled and indicated for me to join him.

Relieved he wasn't angry with me, I did likewise. Dying for shame, too late I realized I only wore a night shirt and my underwear.

"It's all right. You need have no fear of me," a twitch at the corner of his mouth.

It wasn't fear, but modesty, that had me arranging my lap to the side. Had I done this before? I'd wear shorts to bed tomorrow, I thought and every night, for heaven's sake. A resounding grunt from Teacher had me blushing relentlessly.

Think of something else... A safe topic.

He'd told me to work on destructing barriers which I assumed meant opening up lines of communication, so...

"Why were you so sweaty the other night?"

Another twitch at the corner of his wide mouth. His strongly defined square jaw dipped slightly, "I love to run."

Run? Running was good- a hobby- Teacher had a hobby. How nicely normal! I plowed ahead as he didn't seem willing to hold up his end of the communication line.

IOU A HORSE

"Why isn't it correct to...simply want to be useful?" I peered at him, blushed and looked away, and peered back- there was no resisting the effect he had on me.

"Who said it was incorrect?"

"You acted as if I gave you the wrong answer..." When was it that we'd had that question and answer session?

"Woman, you are still ignoring or..." There, her puzzled expression- she is totally in the dark. "Everything you give to others is unequal to what you allow yourself to receive."

I must have been quite a trial for CatSkill. How to get her to admit she is a person in her own right with needs and wants and that she is entitled to them.

"You are a part of everything, and everything whispers for you to accept this- be part of the 'now', similar to when you are with horses. Everything that exists has needs and desires." How do I break through to her?

I knew he was trying to impart something he felt was vitally important for me to understand. The passivity on his face was replaced with the definite concern a teacher feels when his student lingers a step behind. Hadn't I felt the same in some of the lessons I'd given?

His ardency, and remembering the way he'd held me, and that essence of peace he'd imbued me with- my eyes grew misty. Needs and desires... Dear heaven, I knew what my body inferred as I blushed to deny it. I wanted him to be real and more...

I sensed his patience running thin as I speculated along fantasy lines he'd not be amused with. He was near to leaving- leaving me to ponder in misshapen circles.

I caught at his hand as he moved to rise, "Please."

"What do you want?"

"Please, I want you to stay and talk...with me," I foolishly pleaded with a dream. A body would think it should have more control of its dreams, wouldn't it?

He gazed at my hand on his. Why would a Lakota shaman care to help a whiter-than-white girl? I wasn't even much to look at.

A grunt. "You know little of yourself. Very well, we will talk."

Silence.

Think, Dove. Right, I had to initiate our talk and with my limited conversational repertoire- hmmm...

"Uh, I...I know conversations are difficult...for you, too," I began.

Black eyes narrowed, questioning. Inherently, intuitively, I knew my vision had been of Teacher when he was a young boy. Our pasts had probably given us some shared traits. Lack of conversational skills came quickly to mind. In our personal stretches of aloneness...

"You told me you are a shaman, what does that mean? I...I believe your past and mine have...some...connection," I lamely offered. "Do you...barricade yourself...away from others?"

"The student seeks to teach?" One lengthy black brow rose.

"No, sorry," I quickly backed down. "Could you tell me about being a shaman?"

"You haven't looked it up in one of your many books?"

We're back to question-v-question. Damn't!

"I...I... Books are not always correct. Why shouldn't I ask at the source?" I refused to flinch under his ardent glare.

As the only person who'd ever held me and offered comfort, magic or not, he must have come to help me. "I would like to learn. From you."

A deep breath portrayed the muscles of his chest to greater effect than those grotesque, oiled contestants in body building competitions. The blatant scars over his pectorals stood out and then resignedly flattened somewhat as he exhaled. I was eager to learn about what had caused them.

IOU A HORSE

"Among my people, I am a teacher. An oral keeper of our history and our ceremonies as in olden times- before white men came," he gauged my reaction to his use of 'white men'.

I nodded my understanding, "I'm sorry."

"What have you to be sorry for?" He tersely fired.

I shrugged awkwardly, "I'm sorry history is rarely just." That pretty much summed it up.

Shrewdly, he stalled over my response.

Why had I gained an ability to see a vision of his past and then think I could comprehend him- never mind the lack of expression that was his normal visage? Were all Native Americans like him? Taciturn?

"Do you expect 'all' to fall neatly into some category?"

He read me! "No. Aunt Vickie and I visited Crazy Horse's monument- it seems so long ago. Many of the people there were friendly and willing to talk and answer questions. I met Mr. Ed McGaa and purchased several of his books. I believe he really wanted to help visitors understand things- things not taught in schools. Do you know him?"

"I've heard the name," Teacher said. "Crazy Horse would not be pleased at being made a spectacle of," he added after a moment's reflection.

"Maybe not, but he belongs there more so than the heads of presidents, and people are going there to learn," I attempted to point out another view.

"Perhaps you are right," he agreed.

I flushed under what I deemed a compliment- from Teacher!

"Will you tell me more of being a shaman?" I so wanted to keep the talking ball rolling. Keep him there, if only in my dream.

"Shamans are healers, spiritual guides and advisors. We help with the ceremonies and rituals of our people," he hedged.

I pretty well figured there was much he'd not relate. But if we had similar past experiences...

If he didn't preface his visits with that thought-provoking question, he issued it in lieu of good-by. Otherwise, there were no more confrontational attitudes. Together, we'd learned the art of companionable silence strewn randomly amidst moments of discourse.

IOU A HORSE

33

Unlike Sierra's usual announcement of her impending visit, i.e.- the constant rattling of the phone until a human took the message to personally relay to me- 'tell the kid I'm comin' over,' I found my irreverent friend seated in a chair, its front legs airborne as she leaned it back against the pin oak.

She seemed quite intent on Cloud who impolitely ignored her. A 6-pack resting at her feet, she slugged the beer in her hand with abandon.

"Sierra?" Supper chores finished, I was glad to see her- maybe my chance to ask her what she wanted. I'd been getting fairly comfortable with asking those around me.

"That is one hunk of manly grace," she slurred as Cloud danced a few steps upon my approach. "F****** males!"

Something in the tone of her voice didn't smack of the norm. The ubiquitous F word was there but...

I pulled up a chair and regarded her; she avoided my concerned perusal, ducked under a Stetson and took another long pull on her beer.

"You ride that f**** yet?"

"Sierra, what's wrong?"

"Just tell me Kid, you been on him?"

"Yes," I replied, all the while wondering what had instigated the over-imbibing- by the acrid scent she was pretty far gone. And she'd been driving- Sierra never drank and drove.

An underlying edge of violence rent her speech, "What's it like to have Mr. F****** Universe under you?"

"Sierra, what is wrong?" Since she wouldn't look at me, I rose and squatted before her, moving the 6-pack out of her reach. I'd never seen her in such condition- not the indomitable Sierra. "Sierra, tell me."

Her thick white blonde hair, unkempt under the cowboy hat, hid her features. Undeterred, I tapped at her knee with increasing vigor. "Tell me," I almost cursed from frustration-something I never did.

"F***!" she bellowed and vehemently tossed her beer can which skidded and spewed froth across the sun-burnt grass, hung her head in her hands and bawled.

Sierra, crying? Her shoulders trembled and it was hard to tell if her main purpose was crying or laughing. A lot of both vied for preeminence. I couldn't think of a single thing that would influence her this way- Sierra always had a handle on everything.

"Is Shoe all right?"

A snort for a reply.

"Is that a yes?"

Another snort. This conversation smacked of a recent venture with Cloud. Thankfully, Sierra was not snorting beer on me.

"C'mon Sierra, tell me what's going on," I took a lesson from Cloud and put demand in my voice. Speaking of Cloud, he'd ambled to the fence to watch people TV.

"Kid, I think I've gone and done it."

Finally, she lifted her head. Bloodshot eyes, dark circles... What? When was the last time I'd seen Sierra? A week? Two?

"Done what?" I pulled a chair in front of her and sat down, grimly wondering what she could possibly have done to merit tortured drama.

She wiped her wet face against her sleeve. "Timberman."

"Yeeesss," I drug out. Was this going to be another round of Twenty Questions- I'd become rather adept at that particular game lately. My personal life had broken down to questions tossed at me and my own attempts to decipher the art of conversation by means of returning questions. Perhaps my experience was going to come in handy?

"Kid, what am I going to do?"

"You're asking me?" I was further caught off kilter. Sierra never asked for advice. Certainly not from me, I mean what did I know, other than horses?

"F***!" She pulled at her hair with both hands, sent the Stetson tumbling. "Where's my beer?"

"What...Is...Wrong?" I expressly emphasized each word, hoping to get through to her.

"I think I love the big galoot. SHIT!"

Wow! As far as I knew, Sierra, now in her thirties, had never married. She had a few choice words for many of the guys she went out with. Remarks about feet came readily to mind. The word LOVE, never.

"What's the problem with falling in love with Timberman?" Didn't most women aspire to falling in love?

'What about you?' rang clearly inside my head, startling me on another front. My head swung from Sierra. Cloud was obviously eavesdropping. A horse querying me about love?

Oh, brother! I gave him an imperceptible shake of my head. To which he snorted, tossing his head. A slight fallout caught an errant breeze and snot hit my face. But I had no time to remonstrate with him. Venturing into ventriloquism in a 3-way conversation was beyond me.

"Can you see me in love? Married? You are the only one who accepts me the way I am. Others laugh behind my back- not that I give a shit. They know I can take on any of them. If I wanted to," she threw back her head, shook it and ran her fingers through her hair to sweep it out of her steamed, tear-tracked face.

"F***! I'm a mess! F****** men!"

"Sierra, I...I don't understand. Why aren't you having this talk with him? With Timberman? Love is about trust and truth, isn't it?" I mean what the heck did I know? "You've been seeing him pretty steady for how many months?"

"What if he doesn't love me? What if he laughs?" Her weary eyes engaged me in her personal pathos.

In another dimension this might seem funny to both of us- Sierra asking me about love, or life, for that matter.

"Well," I thoughtfully balked, please let me say the right thing. "You could always deck him," my hand flew to my mouth. Had I really said that?

Cloud rocketed off, bugling and bucking. In hilarity? And Sierra, Sierra fell off her chair, clutching her stomach and howled. Feeling like an over-fermented fruitcake, I joined in.

Once she recovered her aplomb, and I realized how good it felt to out and out laugh, she righted her chair, plopped down and studied me.

"Kid, there's something different about you," her eyes narrowed in her exam.

"Uh," I looked around the farm. Surely something needed tending... I wasn't crazy enough to tell her about hearing voices, my own dreams of a certain Teacher, my thrilling and adventurous rides on Cloud... Best not give any detailed information.

The stallion had returned to the fence, ears twitching. Wait until later, I telepathically warned him, doubting if he would get it. Never discount the improbable, I thought, as he thrust his nose in the air and curled his lip back.

"Can't quite put my finger on it, except..." her calloused fingers snared my errant chin and forced me to face her. Older sis to younger? She could nearly be my mother.

I gulped.

"That 'do not disturb' sign you always carry outside your lessons or when you're riding, seems to be fading. You've gained some weight back, looks like you're sleeping. Hmmm..."

I forced myself not to squirm when she released me.

"That big beast have anything to do with it?"

"I...I don't know what you're talking about. What are you going to say to Timberman?" I responded in imitation of Teacher- question to question.

"Is he grand to ride?" A snide smile took the place of her scrunched-up bawling features.

I wasn't sure which visage I preferred- not caring to be imprisoned in the smirking spotlight she fixed on me, yet not wishing to see her suffer, either.

IOU A HORSE

"He's amazing!" There, turn the attention on Cloud. "The local dressage organization has hit me up to stage their quarterly clinic. Their usual facility is under quarantine, so I've leased my ring on Sunday and Monday of Labor Day weekend. I also get two free rides. I'm thinking of taking Cloud in the clinic. Come and watch," I offered a neutral topic.

Cloud cocked his head- I'd not yet broached the subject with him. Oh, boy, I might be in trouble. He much preferred our moonlit rides, but I thought he'd begun to enjoy the higher level dressage movements.

"Hmmm..." Sierra mused. "Go on a double date with me and Timberman," she blindsided me with.

"Uh, a...double...date?" I blushed and Cloud's ears struck a forward pose.

"Sure. Hell, you never been on a f****** date? Don't you like guys? Human guys?" This from the one who had just sobbed over a 'human' guy.

Throughout school it had been easy to avoid being asked on a date. Keep my head down, keep to myself. I'm sure I was considered not worth the attention. And that was fine with me.

I had books to read, horses to ride, and the relentless picture of my father in my head. "Stupid, kid," he'd yell at me when I couldn't tell him the time on the clock. No matter I was only four years old.

No, dating was not worth the risk of being on the end of cruel remarks or actions. I'd studiously avoided making friends with girls, too. The first girl I tried to talk to ended up committing suicide. Not that I thought it was my fault, but it left me with more reasons to keep to myself. Alone, no one could disavow me of my ingrained notions. No one could breast the fortress I sealed myself within.

"C'mon, I'll be with you every second. Pig roast at The Oasis, Saturday night. You got a dress?"

I almost blurted Hell, No! All to no avail.

34

Saturday night. Me in a red and white checked dress. Peasant blouse type bodice with short sleeves, mid-thigh length, full skirt which flared if I turned too fast. And white sneakers. My attire was compliments of Sierra's dragging me kicking and screaming- almost literally, to a dress shop. Feeling as out of place as a whale in my sand riding ring.

The craziest thing I'd ever done. My initial ride with Cloud ranked tame next to this. How had Sierra talked me into it? The shopping episode, the pedicure and manicure, and waiting for a blind date? My stomach sparked the beginnings of a full-blown revolution.

Two cars pulled up. One was Sierra's 4-wheel drive Jeep and the other, a BMW sports car- in flaming red. Talk about red flags. I should have listened to the burgeoning civil war alarming my senses. Stupid kid, indeed.

I left off ruminating over my misgivings to Cloud, and forcing myself to don manners, walked over to greet guests.

"Hey, Kid," Sierra wore a short jean skirt and sparkly tank top- with cowboy boots, a new Stetson, and Timberman draped across her shoulders, nuzzling at her ear.

"Hi, Dove, I'd like you to meet Troy Saxon," Timberman introduced a brawny, bleach-blonde, well-tanned construction worker who'd exited the BMW.

"Hellooo, Dove." Tight jeans, expensive, intricately-designed boots and a custom-fitted, white dress shirt tucked in, with too many buttons unbuttoned. Troy had removed his sunglasses, smiled wide enough to show off perfect teeth, winked a blue eye at me, and offered his hand.

"Troy as in Troy-built. Pleased to meet you," he fondled my hand before I quickly pulled it away.

IOU A HORSE

Sierra rolled her eyes, and the dogs barked, ringing me closely like my own personal security guard. For some odd reason, Cloud was staunchly still.

"Ready to go and have some fun, Dove?" Fun and Troy did not fit in the same world as far as I was concerned. My inner senses clamored- renege! Renege!

Sierra realized I was on the verge of doing just that.

"Troy, get a load of that stallion- there's a f****** hunk of manhood," Sierra pointed Troy in the direction of Cloud's enclosure, giving her beau a loaded look.

Leaving the human males to Cloud with a direct warning not to go inside the paddock, she ushered me into the house. Timberman leaned against the Jeep, kicking his heels and ruing the mess he'd instigated.

"You're one big son-of-a-bitch, ain't you? Been getting any lately?"

Cloud's nostrils flared, and he started to pace the fence line, gauging the newcomer, all senses alert and agitated.

"Sorry about your luck, old son, stuck behind that fence. Now me, I'm gonna get me a sweet piece of meat tonight. Maybe I'll tell you about it, later," Troy chuckled at the stallion and sauntered away.

Cloud bucked his disapproval and screamed a challenge which only made Troy's smile widen.

"Look, Kid, he's a GGW, but remember I'm not leaving you alone with him," Sierra desperately tried to convince me not to back out.

"Two cars?"

"The GGW's idea, but..."

"What is a GGW?" What in the world had I got myself into?

"God's gift to women- only in his own eyes. Timberman originally had Larry going with us- he's nice, a little on the quiet side, absolutely trustworthy. But his dad was rushed to the hospital and... C'mon, I swear I'll deck him if he misbehaves," Sierra vowed, showing me her fist.

She would, too, and happily relish the delivered punch which would most assuredly put the GGW on his pristine butt.

"Promise not to leave me alone with him?" Idiotically, I surrendered to her pleading.

The Oasis' parking lot fanned out across neighbors' yards and an adjacent farmer's vacant field. Apparently, Labor Day weekend pig roast was a huge drawing card.

I'd always resisted Sierra's attempts to drag me along to her favorite functions. Strangely, she'd pleaded 'love's vulnerability', and thus ensnared me. She thought Timberman was close to popping the question, especially after she'd taken my advice and spilled her guts. In tears, over the phone, she'd told me he'd calmly picked them up- her guts, kissed them and kindly replaced them with his own rejoinder of love.

Sierra and I rode together, which hadn't pleased the GGW one whit. In an aside to Sierra, but within my earshot, once we arrived at The Oasis and Troy had gone off to the rest room, Timberman expressed his own misgivings concerning Troy.

"You think," Sierra playfully/seriously punched him.

By way of apology, the big, flustered galoot leaned down and kissed her. "You sure look good, Baby," which caused Sierra to uncharacteristically blush.

In her short skirt and top which left not much to anyone's imagination, Sierra line-danced on cloud nine. In reappearing, Troy tried to escort me through the crowd with his hand possessively at my waist. Hemmed in on all sides by the hordes of partiers, I failed to elude his touch, and I shuddered at the contact. My every cell raised cane.

IOU A HORSE

Friends of Sierra's and Timberman's hailed us on our path to a picnic table laden with chips, pretzels and pitchers of beer.

Three huge smoker grills- their attendants removing the pork, slicing and pulling meat from the bones, created an audience of appreciative, hungry onlookers. An intrepid taste-tester ventured to sneak a slice of the succulent pork before the bell rang to encourage the line-up of salivating patrons. His drooling lips and rolling eyes verified the delicacy.

There were baked beans, potato salad, buns, rye and white bread, cole slaw, hot slaw, and an assortment of home-baked desserts supplied by the regulars.

But my taste buds had taken a sabbatical and any semblance of hunger died sudden death. Troy continually leaned in, whispering, offering beer or a mixed drink, and laughed when I asked only for water. All the while, he deeply inhaled close enough to cause my hair to tickle my cheeks. I felt like throwing up when he proffered a pretzel to my lips- one which he'd already bitten half off.

Sierra couldn't babysit me every moment; I'd have to endure some of the fiasco on my own. Where was my backbone? Why did I feel like a lost kid all over again?

"Tell me about that stallion of yours?" Troy finished off the pretzel, and tried distractedly conversing with me as his eyes reconnoitered every likely female attendant prior to sidling smugly back to me.

It's hard enough for me to indulge in conversation without trying to speak to someone whose eyes are eagerly judging every piece of female flesh including mine. Once, to my disgust, he patted my knee, obliviously hearing-impaired to my explanation of Cloud's coming to Creekside. I shoved his hand off and slid further down the picnic table bench, hoping to escape his further chortling proximity.

Sighing in relief when he excused himself to say hello to some friends, I watched him walk, wondering how he managed to carry such a load of pride bound up in his tight apparel. How utterly distasteful!

Everyone but me seemed to be enjoying the cacophonous shin-dig. Sierra and Timberman shared their food with lingering fingers at each other's mouths. The audience and the dancers' laughter vied with the staged band's overly-loud country music, performed rambunctiously under a vibrantly-striped shade awning. Jeans, t-shirts, flashy flesh-revealing dresses, southwestern jewelry, colorful boots... Some of the dancers clung much too close in their public displays of affection, in my opinion- I half expected the movie raters to step in and rate the whole scene an R. Quite uncomfortable, I averted my eyes. But mine was a sheltered existence, my world revolved around the barn- maybe all the posturing was normal when one went on a date. I was determined never to learn more.

I just wanted to go home, but it wouldn't be fair to interfere with Sierra's fun. Not so soon.

Friends of Sierra's that I'd met at her ranch stopped by and asked after me and Cloud. I answered amiably, but they weren't interested in specifics, not when a party was going on in full swing. A date, a beer in hand, and a song calling them to the dance floor were foremost in their minds. I didn't blame them, outsider that I was.

What little I managed to eat sat heavy in my stomach. I just wanted to go home.

For some reason, my thoughts turned to Teacher and my fingers sought the comfort of my crystal. Although he'd look as out of place here as I felt, he'd be a most welcome addition- to me. To roll over in my pet-overburdened bed and have the unwelcome pig roast party disappear and have Teacher walk toward me...

"Let's dance, Dove, c'mon," not waiting for an answer, Troy pulled me to me feet and into his chest. My cells' strident clamoring nearly had me vomiting on his overly perfumed shirt- I stifled a gag reflex at the stench. "Let's go," he hustled me in the direction of the other dancers.

IOU A HORSE

There. She envisions me. I'd nearly called CatSkill to track her whereabouts. I am powerless to go to her without her opening her eyes and thinking of me.

My senses know that scented poppycock bodes ill for my student. Through her eyes I see and frown at the crowd and its antics. The uninvited hands...

What exactly is this territoriality assailing me? Mere solicitude for a student? Or will I open myself to admit more? A distinct whisper of an harrumph sizzles the air- the spirits are impatient with me and make it known.

"Get your f****** hands off her! Are you f****** blind?" Sierra had unwrapped herself from Timberman and violently kicked Troy. Her grabbing at his shirt in conjunction with her cowboy boot's making headway had him instantly releasing me, and my repugnant look told him he was in dire straits with the head female.

"Hey, sorry, geez... Dove, I'm sorry. I...I thought you might like to dance," he stammered, attempting to defuse the situation with all the charm of his practiced GGW expertise. Since when did dancing involve dragging a girl across the floor? Why hadn't I fought him off? Shades of being a little girl, punished...

Not wanting to extend the knock-down-drag-out Sierra was intent on escalating, I sucked in air and simply stuttered, "I...I'd rather not...dance. Thank you."

"OK. Hey, Sierra," he rubbed his shin, "My bad. Why don't we sit and watch then?"

Feeling like a big baby, I crawled into my shell. I really didn't want to ruin the party for my friend.

"Kid, you OK?"

"I'm fine, Sierra. I didn't mean to cause such a fuss," I found myself apologizing to her and Troy and Timberman as I struggled to hide the level of my disquiet.

"I'll be watching," she leaned down, whispered assurance in my ear and bestowed a vehement glare, fraught with the potential of impending doomsday, on Troy.

Dumbly, I nodded, feeling like one of those nodding toys in a backseat window. Soon, it would end soon, please hurry...

Upon returning to our picnic table, I inadvertently knocked my water over. Troy rushed off to do the 'dately' thing- acquire napkins, I guessed, while I succumbed to misery, alone in the midst of a whirl of activity, which brought to mind the gist of being stuck in a nightmare windstorm without the right apparel and no likely shelter in sight.

I wished I were in my bed, sleeping, in order to invite dreams. Dreams including Teacher. Talking to Teacher. I'd been in his arms, comfortably embraced, and I wished to be there again. If he asked me to dance...

How ludicrous! Teacher line-dancing at a pig roast! With his indomitable, oh-so-conspicuous heritage. Some idiot might cross the line with him, but I knew Teacher would not be on the losing end of any skirmish- verbal or otherwise. One of his implacable stares would quell anyone harboring an ounce of common sense. But, what about the drunks, the ones with pickled, senseless brain cells?

I also had the feeling, if he wanted to, he'd put all the dancers to shame- he had that inherent grace of movement. And foolishly, I longed to feel that in his arms. Inane thinking.

"Yes, sir," Troy readjusted a wayward, blonde hair. "I'll just sneak a few of these into Little Miss Muffet's drink and then, we'll go and inspect her tuffet," he cackled to himself. His eager eyes never wavered from the mottled mirror- his own countenance too good to cease admiring.

IOU A HORSE

"Hey," a young cowboy wannabe drifted toward Troy from the urinal, not minding his own appearance in the mirror as Troy steadfastly hogged the space. "Aren't you with Sierra and her friend, Dove?"

"What of it, cowboy?" Troy drove his shirt into his jeans, smoothed his hand down his chest and turned sideways to admire his profile.

"I heard some of what you were saying. Best watch it, Sierra thinks of Dove as her little sister and she will..."

"What Sierra doesn't know won't hurt her," Troy smiled cunningly. "See these, and I'll give you some if you want, Little Miss Muffet will simply get a little sleepy and I'll offer to take her home. After a few more..."

"Better not," the young man warned, shaking his head.

Troy pushed his jaw into the nosy man's face, "You a snitch, cowboy?"

The sudden flick of a knife as it snapped open had the interloper stumbling in retreat, hands flailing in white flag mode.

"Hey, not my business," the guy staggered out, door swinging violently in his wake, leaving the room to Troy, and a shadow.

A wedge surreptitiously slipped under the door.

"You like to prey on the defenseless?"

An incredibly strong vise gripped Troy by the back of his neck and the next thing he knew he was lifted from the ground. Eyes wide, he stared down into the mirror to gain a semblance of his antagonist. But his nose suddenly slammed into the glass, splintering it and buckling cartilage, causing a howl of pain which was abruptly cut off as Troy's face was shoved into the breakage again.

The GGW had no idea what held him, but his blade was still open. Ignoring his bleeding face, and the fallout of shards of glass piercing his formerly snow-white shirt, he turned the knife...

A low grunt in his ear, and the knife was expertly reversed- it plunged into a scrap of stricken mirror, bored into the corkboard behind it.

"Now, take out your packet of pills and swallow them," the disembodied voice demanded.

On the horns of a frightful dilemma, struggling to breathe, Troy hesitated, thinking fast and hard, but coming up empty-handed.

"Every one, and I'll know if you miss one. Believe me, I'll know," the growl had shivers recoiling under the custom-made shirt.

"S...sure," Troy trembled, completely out of his league. Taking his time, he desperately hoped someone, anyone, would come through the door.

Outside, footsteps finally did approach. A hammer on the door, but it didn't budge. Troy opened his mouth to call and the vise unbelievably clamped harder, nearly causing the GGW to pass out.

Footsteps receded. Guys didn't need a rest room, anyway-no help from that quarter.

"Swallow."

Blood trickled into his mouth; utterly dismayed, Troy's fingers fumbled, and the pills trickled to the floor.

"Uh..."

"Good idea!" And the vise pushed Troy's bloody face into the heavy, stinking grime of the floor.

"Lick them up," the command was followed by a warning shove. The potential of further damage had Troy's tongue lapping at the floor, swallowing his own blood, the pills and assorted other unmentionables.

"Damn, Sierra, I'm awfully sorry," Timberman fell all over himself apologizing as a young man told them what he'd overheard in the bathroom.

"He...he...was...going to d...drug me?" As if the night couldn't get any worse, a fainting spell loomed.

IOU A HORSE

"C'mon Kid, I'm taking you home," she put her arm around me to keep me on my feet. "You coming, or are you going to clean up the shit?" Sierra fumed at Timberman.

Numbness, like a haunting wraith, stole over me as Sierra drove me home.

"Kid, don't waste any time thinking about that bastard. F***, don't waste a second, you hear me? Believe me that SOB will get his. I'd like to trade off with Timberman, punch for punch until all those f****** bleached teeth have gone down his f****** throat!"

But I barely heard her, barely registered anything as I locked myself in the house, refusing to allow her to stay a moment longer. Tim had offered to do the 10 pm hay time; I was gratefully alone, except for the commiserating critters attempting to draw me out with wet noses, extended paws, woofs, meows. Their antics went unheeded as...

No comprising lists ventured to guide me onto a safe tack. Nothing for me to do. Nothing to keep me from...

I fled to the bathroom, just lifted the toilet lid when everything erupted- every horrible second of the evening, every horrible flashback memory of long ago. Every speck of that greasy pork gagging me...

I watch in the shadows as defeat tortures her. Spilling nightmares, memories, remorse...

I recognize every sordid scene as it gushes from her heaving body. Once the expulsions slacken, she curls into herself, rocking, crying and shuddering.

Four kittens station about her; sensing her distress, yet too young to know how to help, they mewl their solicitude and paw helplessly at her body. Captain, the gallant, settles at her feet, nudging her leg. This is nothing new to him.

Unleashing every resonant healing frequency I am capable of mustering by the spirit's good grace, I induce her to sleep- a deep, quiet slumber.

"No dreams tonight, Dove. Only peace," I murmur.

Gently, I wash her arms which she'd used to hold herself together. With a warm wash cloth I bathe her face, remove the vomit-splattered dress, flush the toilet and open the window to air the bathroom.

Some of the vomit had penetrated the dress- her bra retained the odor. As I unhook the garment, my fingers discover...

I had known they were there, but contact with the fractured flesh summons obdurate anger, sears my soul. How could anyone defile something so innocently beautiful? If he were still alive...

Tracing the old scars of cigarette burns on her back, I will myself and Dove to find serenity.

My heart heavy with the emotion I also deny, I diligently watch her eyelids and their long, dark shutters of lashes; her nostrils flutter as she breathes, her lips are quiet in slumber.

I know every ray of color in her gray-green eyes, every freckle. Perhaps she'd be surprised to know how ardently I've studied her. My fingers catch in the swirl of tawny curls. To my deep satisfaction, her hair is lengthening- she'd not cut it.

Lifting her body, weightless to me, I carry her to her bed, turn on the window fan, remove her sneakers and gently cover her.

Do I desire her?

Foolishly, I'd once thought myself in love with Shadow. It took a while for me to understand Shadow's qualities are not in accord with my needs. Nor mine with hers. And this selfless waif- not one of my people, but most assuredly she is of my spirit... Soon, I must decide.

"Sierra," Timberman's voice.

"Hmmm..."

"You remember that story about the jerk they found in a duct-taped box?"

Sierra slowly sat up, "Why?"

IOU A HORSE

"The damndest thing. Troy isn't light you know, but he swears some monster picked him up by the scruff of his neck. He's got massive bruises on his neck to show for it, not to mention..."

"He better hope he never crosses my path or he'll be missing teeth to show for it, that f*****!"

"Easy, Baby, I'm really sorry. He's in the hospital right now; they're uh...pumping his stomach, fixing his nose."

"I'm glad that monster-angel, whoever he is, is out there. Poor Dove- you have no idea."

Timberman hung his head, "Will she be OK?"

"She better be- she'd been doing so well too... Now, just how sorry are you?"

35

As if the alarm had clanged 1000 times more powerfully than it was capable of, I bolted upright, totally befuddled.

What day was it? What time?

The clock- 6 am. The clinic! And heaven help me, I hadn't told Cloud!

I took time with the morning's stretch, perplexed, amazed and grateful at how relaxed my mind was- especially after...

Had I ever slept that well?

A lingering scent of the pig roast remains harkened- don't think of it or I'll gag. Except, I did wonder about my lovely, restful sleep. No drugs, never- I'd not swallowed anything but water once I'd arrived home. Drugs...what that GGW wanted to... Don't think about it. Done and over. Never again. The only thing I wistfully regretted was that sleep had come without dreams, I'd missed Teacher.

I could not even recall undressing myself. Sleeping in just my underwear- that was not like me. I'd taken the time to rinse out my dress? But, no more time to dwell on it. What would Cloud say? Heaven help me!

"Cloud, I'm sorry, I know I should have told you- excuse me, I should have asked you." Did anyone else talk this way to a horse?

No response. And my Sunday ride was at 9 am- the first rider of the clinic, and auditors were arriving. Thinking of our moonlight rides, I reflected that maybe Cloud was not a morning horse. Boy, the path of my ruminating!

"I could always ride Venezia," I gloomily suggested.

Tribune Thorne had paid for a session with me riding the Amazon- there was no way I could refer to her as Jacqueline,- and

IOU A HORSE

Venezia was groomed and ready- as I'd given myself a back-up plan and called Ned, asking him to prepare the gelding as soon as he arrived. But, I was scheduled for two free rides...

Glancing over the rail, I watched Ned, Martine and Tim directing auditors- droves of auditors. Cloud blatantly indicated he could not have cared less. The numbers didn't bother me, I just...really wanted to ride Cloud. How to make it up to him?

He stood gentlemanly as always. Only, without his offhand way of registering his opinions rankling in my head, I might be in serious- with a capital S- trouble if I did pursue riding him. Fifteen minutes to decide.

Horses were the great 'humilifiers'- Aunt Vicky's word. As soon as you thought you had one figured out- well, surprises were certainly never out of the equine realm.

The decision was silently taken from me as Cloud took the white Woolback pad from my tentative fingers and slung it on his back. I nearly cried for joy.

"Hey, Kid," I looked up. Sierra, Timberman and Schoe had stationed themselves on the rail. "You OK?"

Beaming as if I'd won a great prize, and Cloud's acquiescence certainly qualified as such, I happily nodded. I might have expected Sierra's support this morning as she'd hated to leave me the previous night, but Timberman? And Schoe?- a tall, slightly younger version of Sierra, minus her grammatical idiosyncrasies.

Schoe was into cattle- longhorn cattle, and he herded them on horseback in his cowboy regalia. Also competing in roping and penning, he looked every inch the real McCoy working a genuine ranch in Ohio. And I was all too glad of their proximity and skills.

"Cattle can eat what a horse can't," he'd say, as often he'd bale our hay first with his eye tuned in on the weather and the state of the ripening grasses. Schoe made sure to gather the best hay for our horses- baling once the grasses reached their optimum nutrient level. Kind of on the quiet side- who could get a word in with Sierra around?- he always tipped his Stetson to me and had treated Aunt Vickie likewise. In his distinctive garb, he was always a welcome addition.

'Coming for the show?' Cloud's first words rang in my head.

"Cloud, I promise I'll make it up to you," I whispered. Why hadn't I asked him beforehand? Why did I think to simply spring it on him? What possessed me to think I might revert to some non-existent powers of persuasion to induce his cooperation? What had I been thinking?

A disgruntled grunt greeted my meandering mind. "Sorry," I apologized again, not caring if I were heard or not by anyone.

He ran his muzzle softly up my legs, arms, up to my hair which I'd pinned up and enclosed in a small snood. My hair had grown considerably, surprising me with its wavy fullness.

Guess it's time for a haircut, I thought. Somehow that had missed my lists, lately.

'Don't cut it,' Cloud commanded.

With no time to wonder why he had an opinion on my hair length, I quickly cautioned myself to watch any further conversing aloud with him. Time to face the music. I swallowed hard- what had I gotten the two of us into?

Talk about really strange- the essence of my life lately- I'd not had a lesson since...Aunt Vickie- months ago, unless you gave credence to Cloud's nitpicking volubility while I was aboard. My heart clenched in sadness, heralding teary eyes, thinking of her, but no time for that either.

The German clinician, with his rather militaristic bearing, unsmilingly spied left and right as he made his way to my arena. Dressed in highly polished riding boots- which he probably used as mirrors, perfect crew-cut gray hair, taupe breeches, spotless long sleeve white shirt...

For a second, I pictured Cloud snorting all over that haughty splendor. Where had that come from? I nearly giggled-relief blessedly took up residence within. Breathe, Dove, same as whenever you ride, I coached myself.

Cloud silently scanned the environs, but ignored me. I gently stationed his head to face me, looked up, smiled, fingered his lengthy forelock, engaged his huge eyes bounded by the sheen of bronze. It would be just like this opinionated stallion to pull off some grand unexpected gesture.

What transpired in me? The previous night I'd been a basket case, and clinic day I was shamelessly beguiled by the prospect of one of Cloud's potential antics- God knew when! Astonishing what a good night's sleep did for a person's attitude.

"Dove, I'd like to present Herr Burgemeir," Stacey, the clinic coordinator, introduced the instructor.

He inclined his head, but gave me scant notice as she continued to deliver my competition record and relate my ownership of Creekside.

"Breeding?" The ruddy-faced, gray haired man rudely cut in while conducting an intense examination of Cloud. His demeanor spoke obvious distaste at the unbraided mane, unwrapped legs, but I was not perturbed as I'd never braided or wrapped Sheer. To me she was God-gifted perfect, and so was Cloud.

"I don't know," I honestly replied, but I could have told him some things that...

A frown of disbelief tossed my way, "You have a stallion and you do not know his breeding?"

"Cloud arrived here in a rather unlooked for and dramatic manner," I stated, beginning to acquire a bad taste at this so-called instructor's lack of manners- talk about breeding.

Smiling, Ned handed me my helmet with a 'have a good ride.' All along the rail my boarders and...friends waited. Sierra, Timberman's arm draped over her, gave me a thumbs-up.

"Age? Training?" The questions thundered like assault weapons.

"He knows the movements." I responded with the facts I could relay without appearing to be endorsed by the ranks of lunacy.

"My dear young lady, they all know the movements," he smirked.

"Name?"

"Cloud."

"Cloud," he grimaced, sure he'd not heard correctly. "Cloud?"

Thinking he didn't know that particular word in English, the coordinator pointed to the gathered puffballs in the sky.

"Absurd," the Herr haughtily sniffed.

To which Cloud promptly picked up one of his large feet.

"Cloud," I shook my head. And that wonderfully perverse sense of humor had Cloud putting his foot down close enough to that polished boot that the Herr registered another emotion. Oh, boy, I thought, here we go; in for a penny, in for a pound.

Once I was in the saddle, the Herr wasted no time at all and loudly barked gruff orders. All followed by, "More! More! Contact!"

Granted, I did not have international experience, but I thought the man was either putting on a show for the auditors, or I had really missed something- what, I hadn't a clue.

I pictured Aunt Vickie about to put her foot down- she'd not countenance that sort of militaristic training. 'No one knows your horse better than you do, don't let anyone try and tell you different. Follow your instincts, above all else.'

Cloud's transitions were flawless, his collected gaits beautifully cadenced, light. I'd never felt so much like dancing as his great supple back arched under my seat, via his great hind legs easily reaching under. Ned, bless him, was taping the session; I couldn't wait to see the airborne extensions and all the rest. See myself transported into heaven by... For a second I pictured Sheer and I blissfully together. Even though she lacked some of Cloud's physical prowess, we'd danced...

"Piaffe to passage and return!"

'Speak English!' Cloud grumbled inside my head.

"Piaffe, NOW!"

I pictured the ultimate collective dance of piaffe and then, passage. Cloud arched and swung into it.

"Beautiful Cloud! Beautiful!" I radiantly whispered.

'Drop those damn reins,' Cloud instructed.

IOU A HORSE

Although I much preferred his orders, I balked- I'd not brought out the double bridle... "Cloud, I don't want to be a showoff."

'Contrary to my nature, I'll be the showoff. Let go!'

I hastily contrived a knot so the reins wouldn't hang too low, took a deep breath, checked my softly draped legs on his sides and lifted my arms out to my sides. I closed my eyes and in perfect communion Cloud danced his piaffe, passage, collected canter, pirouettes, and for good measure tempi changes every stride. The auditors erupted with whistles, clapping, stamping...

"CONTACT!" screamed the affronted man with the microphone at his loss of control of the situation, and he included an unfriendly-sounding German word to boot.

Applause from the crowd gradually turned to murmurs of disapproval as the Herr continued to bark orders. Which I ignored. After all, Cloud had the reins and woe betide anyone ignoring his orders!

"Let's walk," I finally asked Cloud as the Herr was wearing on my parade; I directed my confusion to the flushed instructor, "I don't understand what you want."

"Obviously," he drolly seethed.

"I do, er, did have contact. Isn't he doing the movements correctly?"

"If you wish to show on the international level, you must have contact and submission. This is not a circus, and this one is playing with you," he retorted spitefully.

Cloud playing? Well, why shouldn't he? Why shouldn't he have fun, too? Of course, I didn't ask that particular question.

'Maybe you should,' Cloud offered, helpfully.

"Too light. You American women... You're light, too light. You must drive him up and feel... Let me show you." He indicated for me to dismount.

"I don't think that's a good idea," I unwittingly battered his ego. "He's been manhandled."

"I'm sure I've ridden worse," the clinician cynically rejoined.

"Cloud?"

'Let him ride.'

"You won't kill him?" I played ventriloquist.

'We'll see.'

"Cloud?" I pictured the headlines: Stallion Drowns Trainer In Snot After Throwing Him Three Ways To Sunday.

'I won't kill him,' Cloud grunted.

With misgivings, I asked Ned to bring a release form.

"Release? What is this release?"

The coordinator flushed- the entire scenario had slithered beyond her pay grade. "Uh, it's required by her insurance company. Right, Dove?"

"Absolutely," I affirmed.

With an elaborate flourish, the Herr signed his name without reading a word.

"Your helmet?" I cautioned. "And you will please remove your spurs, too." No one would dare mark the gorgeous Cloud ever again, not as long as I lived!

"Bah!" but he complied and accepted a helmet from the organizer whose brows worriedly wrinkled. I figured she'd most likely heard of Cloud's arrival; even the audience seemed to hold their collective breath.

Cloud stood as if dozing- a volcano on standby. Oh, boy, I thought- hang onto your hats, folks!

'Something was mentioned about a show?' were his last words, right before...

The Herr had just mounted, after adjusting the stirrup length. Mine were much too short for his regal bearing. He took up the reins in one of those crushing hand shake maneuvers. Nothing light about him.

The following seconds' activity 'tornadoed' through the ring faster than the human eye could comprehend. The Herr drove with seat and leg into his heavy hands and Cloud shifted into Mount Vesuvius run amok. There had to be disasters a body would find preferable to experiencing a Cloud-eruption in all its glorious fury. Pompeii came to mind.

IOU A HORSE

Only the recording, as my friends and I watched later, slowed down as far as the digital recorder would allow, showed an interplay of rodeo movements of shocking brilliance. I had no idea of the names of the maneuvers Cloud pulled off- a rodeo professional would have to be consulted, and like as not he'd be stunned, too!

The Herr, to give him credit, sat the first fish tail, but Cloud unsettled him with a great burst of all four feet off the ground, followed by a tremendous rear and all-out bucking bravado- hind feet barely gracing the beam above. My dear heaven!

With his back impossibly arched- talk about supple- Cloud whirled like a dervish on speed- the drug- and sent the Herr ignobly flying. True inspiration for one of those dramatic amusement park rides!

My heart pattering its own rodeo, I was sincerely glad of the ring's soft footing, as the Herr landed plop on his butt. And bounced!

The international clinician slowly got to his feet with grim determination and menacingly advanced on Cloud, but I stepped between the duelists. Nothing like a testosterone test between species!

"He doesn't care for your...ideas," I stated rather mildly, though I really wanted to reprimand him and laugh in his face. But, the clinician had to continue, and he'd been severely put in his place. Bravo, Cloud!

"I'm excusing us from the remainder of the session," I slipped the reins over Cloud's bowed head. Did he actually take a bow? Right before I led him away, a great snort of derision, or pleasure, sprayed the Herr's dusty shirt and splattered his ruddy complexion.

'He was disrespectful, and certainly in need of a lesson,' Cloud grunted as I un-tacked him. My hands were shaking something fierce, as was the rest of me- the saddle nearly slid from my grasp.

'Are you all right?' he concernedly asked, further discombobulating me.

I leaned into his neck, relished our privacy, and giggled for all I was worth into his thick mane.

He arched his neck around me, gently holding me. Tears to giggles on his massive shoulders...

"You are absolutely magnificent," I extolled his praises. "I wish Aunt Vickie could see you. Marshall couldn't have performed with more brilliance."

'Was he good at bucking, too?' Cloud innocently queried, and I laughed until my sides hurt. A definite first for me.

I was most assuredly not looking forward to riding the Amazon, or Venezia later on, but Mr. Thorne had paid a substantial amount of money for the clinic. He'd missed the Cloud episode, but everyone quickly filled him in on the sly.

Under the not-at-all subtle scrutiny of the Herr, I walked the prima donna, Jacqueline, into the ring. I noticed he'd changed his shirt over the lunch break, and he walked a bit more gingerly.

Microphone in hand, he totally caught me off guard in front of the auditors with, "Miss Gray, I wish to apologize for my lack of manners earlier. Please accept my regrets," Herr Burgemeir bowed to me. "I took advantage of your youth- like an old fool. Your stallion saw right through me," he offered his hand, which in stark amazement, I gratefully accepted.

Not willing to push his luck with another of my horses, he declined to ride the Amazon. But she behaved as if the whole enterprise was her personal show, and she lapped up the applause as she strutted her stuff.

Ned avidly, intently, watched. I'd brought Jacqueline along to the point where it was time for him to try her out- I knew the partnership would be successful.

Later, once the clinic was wrapped up, I had a question for the star of the event.

"Why Cloud, Cloud?" The name certainly did not do him justice.

'Born under a dark cloud,' he replied and snatched half of my tomato sandwich. Nothing more would he divulge as to his enigmatic revelation. Hmmm...

IOU A HORSE

36

"Why did you react the way you did?" Teacher further analyzed after probing me for all the sordid details regarding the pig roast fiasco. Confused at his insistent analysis, I puzzled anew over my superb night's sleep after my near demise, and sat opposite him in prolonged silence. What was I supposed to say?

"Your friend, Sierra, what was her response?"

An easy question, finally, I exhaled in relief, "She wanted to annihilate the GGW."

"GGW? I do not know this term," his normally taciturn expression mused thoughtfully with furrowed brow.

"God's gift to women," I murmured.

"Abhorrent!" he exclaimed.

Something we were in accord over- a night of firsts?

"Why weren't you angry instead of...dissolving?"

"I..." A very interesting question. Why wasn't I mad as hell? Anger and I had never been on speaking terms. Even when I found the kittens it was only sadness and the imminent sense of spiraling to depths best left alone, except, I somehow could not escape. Had I ever delved into downright, madder-than-a-wet-cat fury?

"Do you consider yourself a worthy friend?" Teacher steamrolled over my introspection.

Worthy? "I...I'm a good listener."

"There is no denying your past affects you, the course of that effect is up to you. This overruling sadness...the past imprisons you. Being a good listener is not all there is to friendship. Sharing is also a component," Teacher advised.

"Have you ever had an adverse reaction to a situation?" I recalled my vision of a young, defiant, battered Teacher, and as if he read my mind his brows drew together for an incendiary second, his nostrils flared- oh, heavens- he'd seen- he knew I knew!

"I do not cry," impassivity quickly re-established, he left no doubt of dry eyes. Of course he didn't. I couldn't fathom what might make Teacher shed a tear. Being beaten regularly as a kid hadn't done it.

What might make you cry? I almost dared ask.

But he persisted, "Do you believe you are deserving of love, worthy of friends?"

My unspoken question scuttled to a dark recess in my mind and therefore would not stand a chance of recognition, let alone an answer; but I was not the teacher, not in his presence. Was I afraid to ask something so personal? My head ached as if it were about to split, but he pushed on.

"What do you want?"

Silence. All of a sudden the wondrous heights evaporated and I slipped into a state of complete enervation. And hence, back to square one, like a nightmare board game.

"Do you know what we need here?" Martine studied a blank wall space on the center aisle of the barn.

Sure she'd provide enlightenment I stared alongside of her, patiently waiting. Sensing no resistance, she spread her hands on the space in question.

"One of those big block calendars you can mark on. Everyone can check off birthdays- horses', their own... Celebration times- I love celebrations! What do you think?" I knew her bubbling enthusiasm would not suffer containment, but...

She was pushing the ultimate in invisibility- me, to step outside and..join the world.

'Share!' Teacher's advice battered my hesitation.

"Where can I get one?" Shocked at my immediate positive surrender, Martine threw her arms around me- in celebration, I assumed. I believed I was her pet project, as I seemed to be on the end of many of her exuberant hugs.

IOU A HORSE

"We'll definitely have to mark a day to celebrate Cloud. What an astounding horse! You have no idea how blessed I feel to be here and to have you help me and to watch you work. You should have heard those auditors talking about you and that jackass, Herr Whatsisname- throwing his weight around. "CONTACT!!!" she imitated him, strutting around with her jaw thrust out.

"And you were so calm! Wow! I do love to watch you ride- it's like you're half horse. And you're Johnny-on-the-spot to compliment the slightest improvements in me, in the horses- I'm sooo glad I found you for my instructor."

"Thanks, Martine," the betraying blush I associated with compliments paraded across my face. What would a friend do?

'Share!' How did Teacher know what I was doing? What I was speaking of? 'Share!' he repeated.

"It certainly ranked as one of my more memorable rides." Dare I tell her about...? "I've ridden him bareback, without reins," I startled myself by blurting out. "He...he seemed very mindful of my safety."

Did I say that right? Martine gave me an odd look. I felt a chill- that's what happens when you share, I guess. I turned with an excuse about doing something or other.

"Dove, wait. You...just surprised me, that's all. You actually admitted that you really feel safe...with him? Without any means of control?" Her corporate mind whirled.

"I do," I unequivocally answered.

"I can't think of any horse I'd get on without reins," she deliberated, astounded. "The two of you seem like...a perfect marriage- like I assume one would be. You and Cloud, sitting in a tree....," she began to sing. "Wait a minute- that certainly wouldn't work!"

Her forehead wrinkled for a moment, cleared, and she changed the subject, leaving me to wonder what her little ditty was all about. Me and Cloud, sitting in a tree?

"Did Tim tell you he bought the house across the street?" An unexpected tidbit.

"Really? I...I haven't seen him as much the past couple of days," I recalled Tim's unusual absence and my missing his gourmet lunches.

"He's packing and supervising paint parties. He can't wait to be close to his horses and to start gardening on his own acreage. Why don't you come trail riding with us Sunday?"

"Oh, I...I wouldn't want to be...uh, in the way," I wondered about their new friendship, but was too shy to ask about 'knocking his socks off.'

"You would never be in the way. Our trail ride is...kind of like... Nevermind. Come this Sunday," she pleaded.

Part of me prayed I wasn't to be put in a mediator position, as with Sierra and the possibility of Timberman's proposing at the pig roast. But there would be no GGW's on the ride- I nearly giggled recalling Teacher's response to the term.

"Maybe I'll ride the Amazon," I stepped up to the invitation. With Tim's laid back buddies under saddle as company, it might be a suitable introduction for the Amazon to enjoy something outside of a ring.

"There you go," Martine applauded. "I hope to take Copper out someday, but..."

Listening stood me in good stead. She had concerns and I could belay them- "I'll take Pippin out if you want to try Copper on a trail ride. Pippin is bomb-proof and Copper likes him."

"Really? When?" She buoyantly glowed.

"Teacher, are we...friends?"

Black pools studied me, and I rejoiced inside as he ultimately, but curtly, nodded.

"Would you share something from your past? Something...good?" After all, I'd been a witness to his personal horrors.

IOU A HORSE

He took an audible, deep breath, and I instinctively knew he'd refuse. But, friends shared and listened to each other, right? A twitch at the corner of his mouth served to tell me he'd gleaned where I headed.

"When I was fourteen, my father trapped a wild horse and brought her...home. As he was fond of lashing out, the mare suffered a few beatings." He paused, reflecting.

I felt sadness descending, not sure I wanted to hear that particular story. Teacher had a weird definition of 'something good.'

"I empathized with the mare- she was young, feisty, and refused to concede the battle," his jaw clenched in memory; my heart grew fiercely protective and wow- in a flash I knew exactly what true unadulterated anger consisted of!

A rush of emotion assailed me. Anger for the boy and the horse. Anger for the state of innocents suffering. Teacher's comments about feeling worthy... All creatures were worthy of being safe- and why hadn't I ever thought that included me? How did the Kind Man deal with humanity?

He slightly inclined his head- infinite, dark eyes read my Eureka moment, and after a profound silence, he continued. "My father preferred to whip...when no one watched. So it was the aftereffects I witnessed two days running. I promised the mare it would not happen again while I tended her wounds after he drank himself into oblivion.

Hiding out on the third day- I had already seen just how many bottles he needed to consume before the whip appeared- and I was prepared. I'd dug up an old, discarded axe handle and when he raised the whip I was right behind him. The last I saw of him, he was lying in the dirt.

The mare's right foreleg had been compromised, but I slowly led her away- both of us left. For good. She hobbled next to me- two souls seeking..." he broke off, peered into and curtained the scene.

Every ounce of his pain was mine and I wanted to take it all away. There should be a place to store or, better yet, destroy all past, present and future pain. If the Kind Man left me in charge of that task, I'd find a way to accomplish it. No more suffering- but, then we'd be in heaven, wouldn't we? And what was wrong with that?

Shyly, my fingers empathetically touched his knee. A spark in the depths of his eyes acknowledged my effort- whether with gratitude or not, the jury remained out.

"Once I found a safe location, I cared for her until she was sound. Eventually, she joined with another wild band a friend of mine watches over.

Sometimes I visit, just to watch her. She's free and a paradigm of wonder- she may remember the whip, but it does not confuse or hinder her life."

Teacher seemed neither happy nor sad- he'd merely escaped the nightmare of his childhood and helped a friend along the way. Were he and the mare so alike? Did the past hinder Teacher? I so longed to ask certain questions, but feared his rebuke.

"Your turn," he startled me.

Oh, boy- well, I'd asked for this. Inhaling the cool prairie air, it came to me. Share something good. Simple.

"The magic. I don't know if you really understand about it. I know I don't, but I'll try to explain."

"The life force inside you attempts to guide you, to aid you. If you are still, you may hear and receive...a helping hand. Your magic fits in that direction," Teacher's eyes grew warm, for a change.

The magic as a helping hand- it certainly had helped me and charmed me and gave me...intermittent solace and...hope? The pencil's taking over- always when I was still, and generally, when in need. Hmmm...

"Whenever I'm still?"

Teacher's mouth betrayed him- he was not without feelings, despite his usual intractable mannerism. How enchanting he seemed with that tiny concession brooking his taciturnity!

IOU A HORSE

"Do you realize you are rarely still? Completely quiet? Not moving? Not thinking? Your mind fills with lists, endless lists. When you draw, your mind is hushed- open to the spirits. The same when you ride. You become one with the horse and open yourself up with soft eyes to all about you- similar to a prey animal's intuitive attention to its surrounds, yet not overwrought, not reactive, unless it is required to maintain life. The realization of the 'now'. Magic."

"Hmmm... Like a meditation?"

Teacher must have been pleased. We'd talked more than in all the other dreams put together. And so amicably, too.

"What do you want?"

For the first time, it didn't irk me as such an intrusive query. "For us to be friends," I replied immediately.

Teacher took my hands in his. A warmth and peace emanated from our contact- let me never wake from this, I prayed. In his eyes I capitulated, eager to be lost.

A flickering in those dark pools. "Friends," he murmured.

The best part of my day was always Sheer time- every morning and evening. Our quality time together, beginning with massages, a host of various brushing techniques, always involved two-way communication- her soft whiffles and my voiced admiration of her awesome beauty.

The injured muscles of her hindquarters had gone from raw hamburger to uneven, yet healed tissue, with some scarring, which I did my utmost to stave off with appropriate, consistent manipulations- per Dr. L's instructions. His acupuncture sessions I was sure had aided her healing, but even he was amazed at how fast her recovery was.

To me it seemed miraculous. Dr. K said he'd seen muscle injuries he'd not bet on a positive outcome, heal up unbelievably, but he, too, thought Sheer's recovery a case for the books.

Her hock was a different matter. Stiffness and a slight shortness of stride lingered. Chiropractic and acupuncture sessions were regularly scheduled with Dr. L, who also loved working on Sheer. He considered her his best patient as she was perfectly amenable to particular acupuncture applications he recommended that other horses dramatically objected to.

We engaged in physical therapy walks in the woods which Sheer enjoyed, especially once autumn arrived and the vile heat and irritating bugs had bowed out. I cheered her and clung to the ranks of optimism- she would keep improving.

I let her dictate how far, how long, and which trail we'd take- called it 'letting her drive'. I'd tell her about Cloud and his idea of humor, the clinic, about Teacher and my burgeoning new outlook on life- my own physical, er, mental therapy and recovery, so to speak. So easy to talk to her.

As a friend, I listened to her. Though she spoke differently than Cloud, she was never shy about making her desires known. I watched the plants she selected to forage and her hunt for hedge apples- was it the color or the scent or both that had her at the appropriate place to find those fragrant, yellow-green, softball-sized fruits?

Dr. K and Dr. L had encouraged me to start riding again- very lightly, and see how things progressed. Until then, we'd enjoyed each other as we had before she was mature enough to ride. When she'd stop to indulge in a particular patch of green, I'd untangle her Rastafarian knots, which she'd relentlessly shake into her long mane, and tell her how wonderful she was.

Wonderful Sheer. At times, when she'd turn her great, white-lashed dark eyes on me, I was sure she knew everything I never said. And if I got too quiet, which was generally a sign of my regressive list-making, she'd purposely bump me back to the present- Teacher's concept of 'now', and her attention- right now! Usually, asking for a pocket snack was included.

My wonderful friend, Sheer.

IOU A HORSE

37

I reviewed the clinic tapes of the Amazon and Cloud, agreeing and disagreeing with various points the Herr tried to impress upon us. To me, Cloud was infallible. However, the Herr wished to step up the Amazon's curriculum. In his enthusiasm, I believe he'd forgotten that she was only four years old.

I'd probably have to fend off Mr. Thorne- if he trusted the Herr was correct. He'd witnessed mine and Ned's work with the big chestnut mare well before the clinic came to Creekside, and it was good solid work, laying down the basics- 'the basement', Aunt Vickie had termed initial ground work. 'Getting into the saddle should be anti-climactic', she'd instructed regarding my early training with Sheer and others.

Only time would tell if Thorne's showy mare would meet his high expectations, but I had no reservations. The thought of the Amazon storming the dressage world and loving every minute of it was quite believable. Magic? Perhaps.

An unexpected guest caught me off guard after my makeshift dinner al fresco at Cloud's paddock. I'd declined Martine and Tim's offer to 'celebrate' the clinic and their moving efforts by dining out with them. Directly upon bowing out, I almost ran after them, having changed my mind- feeling like I'd been wrong not to have accepted their invitation. But I didn't.

"Hi, Schoe," I rose from my favorite post under the pin oak where I'd been watching Cloud and the rest of the gang.

The dogs lurched to their feet from snoring slumbers to investigate a friend. Captain had succumbed to a well-deserved nap after interminable kitten sitting- the blessed martyr endured multiple sharp teeth gnawing his ears, clawed sundry other body parts, and all around general kitten badgering.

The lithe, masculine rancher waved, exiting his blue dually, thumbs hitched in his jeans' pockets. He ambled over slowly, patting Captain, Mate and Bosun as they warmly greeted him by pushing against his legs. It was quite evident he was gauging something as his subtly head shifted left and right in his approach.

I reseated myself as he pulled up a chair, shyly smiled and turned to admire Cloud's sauntering to the gate. An awkward silence ensued.

Unlike Sierra, Schoe was the essence of mannerly reserve and had a much easier-on-the-ear vocabulary when he did speak. Withering under his surreptitious scrutiny of me, I kicked myself to break the impasse.

"Is everything OK, Schoe?"

He merely nodded, discomfited, as was I, and focused his attention on Cloud. Expressing curiosity for once, Cloud trotted a series of shoulders-in along the fence line. All the better to hear, I nearly said aloud. Ever the opinionated, his rejoining snort let me know what he thought of my would-be remark.

"He's a beaut," Schoe whistled praise.

I noticed a tic at the corner of my unexpected visitor's left eye. His fingers were tapping a silent rhythm on his thigh. Schoe, nervous? Whatever for? He cleared his throat and leaned slightly toward me. Uh oh...

"I heard about the pig roast incident," he sundered the silent impasse with.

I shrugged it off; with all the attendants- most of them friends, I assumed everyone knew about it. And I didn't want to go there, ever again.

"Sierra had no right to fix you up."

"It was supposed to be someone else, Larry, I think she said. Last minute emergency change-up," I leaped to her defense. Why? Because she was my friend and had been terribly distraught at the shenanigans.

"I should have asked you," Schoe reddened, brushing his tanned, calloused hand through his short, white-blonde hair.

IOU A HORSE

Awkwardness escalated. Having no idea what to say, I didn't say a word. Instead I, too, focused on Cloud- he'd delayed his perfect, lateral show-off movements, stationed his high-headed stance at the fence and stared at us. Did I expect Cloud to get me out of the stalemate?

"I'd be a good man for you, Dove. I'm older, but I'm reliable." The nervous tic at his eye moved to the corner of his mouth and accelerated, as did the tapping rhythm of his fingers.

"Uh," I stammered, feeling fire besiege my face. Was he asking me out or to get married? Was 'reliable' a sole requisite for either?

Schoe was younger than Sierra, but at least ten years older than me. Was he attractive? Yes, I suppose so, but I'd not thought of him in those terms. I'd not thought of any human male in those terms. Except, maybe for really old movie stars or deceased ones- Randolph Scott for one. James Drury for another, Adam Fuller. And Teacher- yes, certainly Teacher. God, how ludicrous! Safety in thinking of myself in impossible company? Welcome to my world of weird, I bit my lower lip to stave off insanity.

"Why don't you let me...uh,...take you to dinner one night? We could try...uh, like a date?"

Both of us in a pickle of a quandary, both of us dancing atop pins and needles- perturbed as all get-out. Cloud hadn't made a single move. What did he think? No snort, no flick of ear or toss of head, no nothing. Save me, I was on my own.

I gripped my hands together, held tight. "Schoe, I...I'm really not wanting to...date...uh, right now. That fix-up with Sierra was a fluke. She thought Timberman might pop the question that night and I guess she figured I'd provide support. Funny, huh?" It had turned out anything but amusing.

Schoe leaned back in his chair, let out a deep sigh. Of relief? Or had I hurt his feelings? What did I know of men, other than on the business side of things, as students, or in a strange dream, or at the end of a slap or worse?

He crossed a booted ankle over his knee. "He'll be good for her. He's strong enough not to get trampled on by her. Does this mean no?"

"Will you hate me if I say can we just be friends?"

"As long as you don't rule out the possibility at some point in the future." I think he surprised us both with that prospect. Even in the chill of dusk, I was sweating before he left- all too glad to see the end of that knotty experience.

'Let's go for a ride,' Cloud shouted in my head after Schoe's abbreviated quagmire of a visit.

Why did a tad of dread continue to lurk in my gut about turning Schoe down? Although glad he'd not stayed and/or pursued the matter, I was perplexed about Schoe's invitation. Felt like a potential mail-order bride with all that talk of reliability. Sheesh! What happened to small talk and romance?

'You exposed his vulnerability, but he'll be OK with it because you were honest. Just because he's possibly attracted to you and asked you out doesn't mean you have to reciprocate,' Cloud issued his sensible two cents.

How does a horse know words like 'reciprocate' and 'vulnerability'? Cloud had donned the mantle of a big brother or caring father- things I saw at times on old TV shows. Cloud advising me on men? Could life get any more convoluted?

'C'mon!' he trumpeted.

Why not? He'd performed so amazingly wonderful at the clinic and wow, I'd forgotten- he'd had me laughing, to boot, with his rodeo stunts and cute, cunning comebacks. It had felt astonishingly good, especially that belly-roiling laugh. If a night ride pleased him- in reciprocity, (I giggled) it would me, too.

IOU A HORSE

"Tell me more of being a shaman," I ventured into the conversational foray with my Teacher friend.

He gazed out at the drying prairie grass tantalized by a cool breeze. Silence was such a familiar wardrobe on him.

"I am a healer."

"Does that mean you can cure everything? All diseases?"

"Not everything," he ruefully stated, and I sensed immediately he'd not expound on that particular admission- which only intrigued me more.

Another topic. Hmmm...

"What of the shaman who taught you?"

"His story is not mine to tell." Cross off that subject, too, darn it. Mirror images, indeed. Difficult conversations were our specialty, I nearly snorted.

"Can you tell me about your rituals, the ceremonies you host? I...read of a yuwipi ceremony..."

He growled, "You want to see flashing lights- look in the sky! You want to hear animals- open your ears!"

It had been such a long time since I'd upset him, my spirits plummeted. How did normal people get to know each other, I wondered? Questions seemed like the ticket, but I constantly struck out.

"I'm...sorry I asked. I...I would just like to know more about you," I stammered. Did Sierra find it this difficult to talk to me?

Silence. So much for understanding shamans, and I'd been eager to learn from the source, but how? Dispirited, I searched for a less personal question.

"Have you been running lately?" Three strikes you're out, right? I figured that was surely an innocuous pitch.

"Run with me," he rose gracefully and caught me off guard by pulling me up with him.

"Run?" I hurriedly looked down at my shorts and night shirt and bare feet. Being pulled so close to him... Heavens above! Opposite shades of Schoe- boy, was I floundering in interesting waters. Safe topic, safe topic, I sought to ground myself as my heart raced off.

"I didn't bring any shoes," I eyed his bare feet- either had he. "Do you ever wear shoes? Don't your feet get cold or c...cut...up?" Sierra's notion of big feet struck me right then and I thought I'd perish from embarrassment. Where to look? Not at his feet, not anywhere on his person, certainly not at those enigmatic scars, not at those impervious eyes- God help me!

"I prefer bare feet, sometimes moccasins. I control my own body's temperature so I do not feel the cold. If my feet are pricked by thorns or cuts, I restore them."

My jaw dropped with the ramifications of his indulgent explanation. Healer, indeed! What a useful skill to take care of your personal physical well-being! But what about the mental aspect of healing, if you were a shaman? I refrained from asking, since we seemed to have reached a congenial footing and I wished to stay there.

"Wait here," he told me and walked into an undulating essence of a mirage- disappeared!

"Teacher," I called, just a dream side of frantic. He'd really disappeared! "Teacher!" I hit frantic with a higher pitch. Chills ran up and down my body- he'd not left me alone on the prairie before. Where had he gone? Would I be able to get back? To my bed? Oh for God's sake, Dove- dream, duh! Sheesh!

Waves in the air pulsed and darned if Teacher didn't walk to me with running shoes in hand. Escalated eccentricities, indeed!

"How did you do that?"

Ignoring my astounded inquiry, he merely said, "Put them on."

"But, how did you do that?" Silence and an impassive gaze. He wasn't going to explain the disappearing and reappearing Teacher business! I pictured a pit bull oddly ineffective in gripping and holding onto a swinging tire, sheesh!

IOU A HORSE

"They're not mine," absolutely frustrated, I nevertheless took the lightly worn shoes from him.

"I'll return them," he grunted.

Magic?

My first lesson in running involved a short, Teacher-like quip of instruction.

"In order to run efficiently, you must be at ease and breathe."

"Like riding a horse," I acknowledged.

"As in everything else in life," he added. I caught a glimpse of that precarious twitch at the corner of his mouth before he sprinted off.

"Are you a real person or only a figment of imagination in my dreams?" Lately, I found myself comparing Teacher to Schoe. To deceased movie stars. Attractive? Sans make-up and camera angles, and reality, I'd have to say a heartfelt yes. Without hesitation. Big, resounding YES.

Sun-bronzed skin reminded me of... Uh oh! The corner of his mouth was twitching. I abruptly ceased perambulating- he'd read me!

"As a shaman, I have greatly enhanced senses- spirit ordained; I also move along different dimensions," he succinctly stated.

It was Twilight Zone clear, but it gave me something to think about- as if I needed more homework.

"Do you live on a reservation? Out here?" Simple question, I thought.

"Do you wish to write me a letter?"

"Would you write back?" I shamelessly rejoined. Could a dream cross over into reality? If one of the participants was a shaman was it possible? If magic was involved?

"Why?"

"Why not?" I felt like I was getting pretty good with the question for question business, but then he threw in the ringer.

"What do you want?"

I didn't pause for breath, "You got those running shoes handy? Let's run!"

A flicker of surprise glinted in the depths of infinity- his black eyes, and a resultant grunt of amusement cheered my heart.

I'd enjoyed the delightful running bouts with him. No way could I keep up with him endurance-wise or with his long strides and speed, but I didn't complain. I loved the moving lessons- plus, I had no breath to speak anyway.

Teacher adjusted his stride to mine and I stuck with him. In a dream one might enhance one's prowess, right? Perhaps, I could pretend to be a shaman- someone worthy of him? The fronds of the prairie grasses' seeded heads gently slapped me along the way- to ground me or to lightly punish my intrepid thought?

On an endless expanse of bluestem, buffalo and Indian grasses pockmarked with purple coneflowers, many different sunflowers and ironweed thrown in, we ran in companionable silence. And for me, it was complete joy.

Teacher sensibly gauged my limit and slowed to a walk just as in our first day/night run. Night, because I was dreaming, and day, because it was always daylight where we met.

He waited for my breath to even. "Close your eyes. Tell me what you hear. Only in complete stillness within yourself will you receive," he softly murmured. If only my early schooling had been so...spiritual...so intuitive?

A new Teacher request, but I was game. "Bees, insects- I don't know all their names," I apologized.

"Continue," he encouraged.

"The wind moving the tall grasses- the rustle they make touching stem to stem." My head swiveled. "Birds, there," I pointed. "And a...a hawk on a mission."

With great intent, as I wished to please him, I diligently listened for all I was worth. "A rustle deep in the grass- a small creature," a smile formed.

IOU A HORSE

There were no lists in my head, but a wondrous, serene stillness.

"Your heart and your breathing," I whispered, awestruck.

Were we that close? I almost lifted a hand rather than open my eyes to this sweet, aural wonder.

"And yours?" he softly asked.

Reluctantly opening my eyes, I fell. Fell into hypnotic eyes mirroring me. The appropriate description is fell- 'fell in love'. Suddenly, I knew exactly what I wanted. Absolutely, not a single doubt.

I became weightless and giddy- sure I'd take flight. I slammed my eyes shut against black pools intent on me, against being read, against dismissal, against vertigo in my heart. I whirled, ready to run. Must not let him know. The power of a timeless moment? Magic? No, surely one could not draw this.

38

"What do you feel when you are the speaker at a conference in a new venue, full of people you don't know?"

I'd finished saddling Pippin and presented Martine with something to think about. My first 'real' introduction to riding whiffled for a bribe before we joined her and the patiently waiting Copper. The tall gelding nickered at his small friend.

"Easy, I own it. I know every expression and what it means, and I can attest to the veracity of every reaction. I know when I've got them and the moment before I'm losing them- very rare occurrence. Hell, I even know when someone has to go to the bathroom," she boasted.

"That same attitude of awareness and owning the situation carries over when you ride. Doubly so when you take a horse into unfamiliar territory. As a pack-designed prey animal, your horse needs to know who the leader is at all times. If you don't calmly fill that role every second or veer into a crooked position..." I had my teaching cap on.

"Horses are creatures of flight, and I might end up on an unscheduled flight- I've got it. I'm all right. Let's go," she teemed with flamboyant enthusiasm.

Side by side, Pippin totally at ease, and Copper following suit, we walked along the pastures' perimeters prior to entering the woods.

"This is soooo cool! Me on my own horse! I love riding Buddy with Tim, but Copper...Copper is mine," Martine smiled high wattage.

"I'm glad you're enjoying yourself. I am, too," I was forced to admit, aloud. Why did it feel so odd to say that I was having a good time with a friend on a trail ride? Years of steadily and studiously quietly keeping to myself had left me a true 'outsider' and I was beginning to understand just what that entailed- and what I'd missed.

IOU A HORSE

My trail rides were mostly solo ventures which I dearly loved, especially my recent rides on the opinionated Cloud, but Martine was laid back and wise and bubbling fun all at the same time.

With her flagrant exuberance and trim shape, she seemed more like a 20-year old than I did. Hadn't Sierra said something about my being a 70-year old twenty year old?

"I've got to reiterate, you are the finest teacher I've ever had, in my entire life- the way you help me understand how my body works in conjunction with Copper- horse language... Wow, what I've learned about myself! And you're so quick to catch the slightest improvement and compliment on it. For me, at least, this spurs me to do better. I know compliments make you nervous, but you'll just have to get used to it, because I'm not going to stop. I'm learning so much from you. Thank you," Martine laughed.

"Are you up for a trot in the woods?" I adroitly changed the subject.

"There you go, affirming what I just said," Martine shook her head. "Trot sounds great!"

Copper behaved himself with the innate trustworthiness I originally believed he naturally possessed- Martine was a different matter.

"You don't date, do you?" She startled me as we transitioned back to walk, negotiated the steep, rocky creek bank, and allowed the horses to relax and drink the clear, cool waters.

"Not interested."

"Father issues? Sorry, I'm naturally nosy. You don't have to answer, but if Ned were a bit older wouldn't you be interested? He's kinda cute. Looks nice on a horse. Nice ass..."

"Martine!"

Ned and Schoe- probably perfect choices for me according to Martine's idea of what I needed. I could not share that my heart belonged to a dream. Literally. Neither Martine nor Sierra would take that lying down. I could tell Cloud- hmmm...

I wondered if Aunt Vickie had ever fallen in love with the impossible. Was that why she never married? I think, just maybe,

I understood a little more about her. Or perhaps the love of her life was not impossible, but existed in Marshall.

William Marshall- the famous knight, counselor to kings and regent to a king... How could a person take the place of all that- all that Marshall, that great-hearted horse, meant to her? I pictured the two of them together, wherever one went when this life's plane ended. Piaffing and passaging on clouds.

I loved my life at Creekside, all its creatures, especially Sheer and Cloud, and I was learning about friendships with the people in my world. I supposed a special growth spurt had dawned- one I'd not imagined before...before when? Before Cloud? Teacher?

"Earth to Dove," Martine cut in on my reverie. "Ned?"

"Uh, no- Ned's interested in females of the equine persuasion. And no, anyway. What about you and Tim?"

Deftly, I changed the subject as we arrived back at the barn. Martine dismounted, twisting the reins with her fingers and took her time answering. That did not bode well.

"Martine?"

"Tim asked me to marry him," she mumbled.

"Wow!" Why was I not completely shocked? I had watched Tim crane his neck to keep her in his sight and vice versa. And something was said about 'knocking off Tim's socks'.

"Wow is right. I get the feeling we'd be right for each other, but..."

"But, what?" What could be the problem? Tim was a little older...

"Did you know his rheumatoid arthritis is...in remission?" Martine informed me.

"He's been moving like he's never had it," I reflected on Tim since he'd arrived at Creekside.

"It boils down to sex. Kind of strange discussing this with you, but you're very insightful, whether you think so or not. He wants to wait until we're married and I...I want a trial run. And I worry about him getting sick again. I mean, God, this is hard, I'd take care of him, of course, but I'm not the nursing sort of person, and I feel terrible for thinking along these lines," she drilled into me with misted eyes.

"Uh," I flushed. How should I respond? Shouldn't it simply boil down to love? Love, sure... Traveling on dimensions shouldn't matter. We shared a common past. Couldn't we share a future? Oh, wait- Teacher is...the product of a dream, right? But, I'd drawn him, or the magic had helped- would it ultimately betray me?

What if I broached this with Teacher? He'd probably grunt and disappear for good. Me falling in love with a dream teacher... The whole issue of reciprocity reared its head. Sheesh! I wasn't willing to roll the dice, was I? The very thought of his leaving for good started heart palpitations.

I cleared my throat. "Shouldn't you be telling Tim all of this?" Me, the chicken, offered.

"Yes, I should," she sighed. "Thanks for listening. Being around you gives me a better perspective."

I still could not believe it. Even as I sat next to the trust attorney in the county court house waiting for the judge. Courts were for wrongdoers, weren't they?

Sierra, Tim, Martine and Schoe were sitting behind me. And in the other corner- that all-too-full-of-his-own-importance Walt Thurman, the jerk with the high-pitched, out-of-control daughter.

Sierra had apologized repeatedly, but I quickly let her know it was not her fault and please not to take it out on 6-year old Corrina- not that Sierra would. I could see her pulling Thurman aside and decking him, though. To which, I'd definitely cheer.

Judge Newholt briskly stepped to her podium and took her seat, idly flipping through papers concerning the case. The door behind us opened, caught her attention. The plump, no-nonsense, female judge with her pursed lips and severely short brown hair glanced up.

"Willis?"

"I have a young couple here, flown in from Wyoming. They claim to have information pertinent to this case," the deputy said.

Newholt's hand rose to usher in the newcomers. Apprehensively, I glanced over my shoulder. The CatSkills! What in the world? Despite Bonnie's bestowing a sweet smile in my direction, her husband a thumbs-up at me and reserving a feral gaze for the instigator of the proceedings, butterflies somersaulted in my stomach. I'd never been to court.

"As I understand it, Mr. Thurman, you claim Miss Gray cheated you out of the value of a particular...stallion? Are you forgoing counsel, sir?"

"Yes, ma'am, your honor. It's a simple case," Thurman rose and tried to appear an honest, sincere citizen kowtowing to the judge. A new act for him, I felt sure. So secure in his self-righteous demeanor, he no doubt firmly believed he did not require counsel.

The judge's brows arched. "There are no simple cases, sir. But please, state the facts as you see them and your reason for this lawsuit."

Thurman stuck to the details of his impromptu arrival at Creekside, but he omitted the pertinent facts.

"You may take your seat. Miss Gray?"

My trust attorney rose, papers in hand. "Your honor, Mr. Thurman sought Miss Gray's expertise in judging the aptitude of a stallion he'd purchased for his 6-year old daughter."

Judge Newholt's brows arched to the point of meeting her hairline.

"Upon the unscheduled arrival of Mr. Thurman, his daughter and the stallion at Creekside, the horse not only attacked the transporter, but also Mr. Thurman. I have affidavits attesting to this..."

Mr. Thurman shot to his feet, blustering to catch the judge's attention.

"Sit down and do not interrupt my court again," she glared at him.

Abashed and red-faced, Thurman plopped into his chair.

IOU A HORSE

"Continue," the judge ordered.

"Mr. Thurman did not call Miss Gray beforehand to engage her services- he simply showed up and had the stallion unloaded. Miss Gray, with misgivings, agreed to board the stallion for a week in order to gain veterinary advice and observe the horse to offer her professional opinion as to its potential as a child's horse.

After the stallion attacked a friend of hers- a witness in this courtroom, Miss Gray offered an alternate plan. She agreed to purchase the stallion for the original sum paid, and presented Mr. Thurman with the opportunity to lease an experienced, child-friendly pony. Thurman asked for more money, but Miss Gray refused, stating that she doubted anyone would dare to haul the stallion away. I also have a statement from the horse trader which states that the horse was heavily drugged when Mr. Thurman bought it. And the veterinarian's statement that the horse exhibited dangerous tendencies upon his inspection."

"Mr. Thurman, did you seek professional advice before purchasing this horse?"

"No, ma'am," Thurman was visibly embarrassed to admit.

"And are you an equine specialist?"

"No, ma'am," Thurman squirmed.

"Why do you believe you should receive," she shuffled papers, "$10,000?" Shocked, she descended on Thurman, "For a horse described by professionals as dangerous?"

"It's like this- she's gonna stand him at stud- that's thousands of dollars per," he reddened and hurried on, "and show him, and maybe go to the Olympics," he huffed- the affronted, cheated innocent.

"And where did you come by this information, sir?"

"It's all over the internet, your honor," he sputtered.

"Do you have the receipt for purchasing this animal?"

"No, ma'am," he mumbled, to everyone's surprise. For a businessman to neglect this imperative detail...

The judge sipped from her water glass, eyeing Thurman with the fervor usually directed at an escaped rat.

"Yes?" she inspected Bonnie who'd bounded to her feet.

"Your honor, I'm Bonnie Lance CatSkill. My husband and I," she held up several pictures, "acquired this particular stallion months ago. He was running with a small band of mares on the high desert plains of Wyoming, near our home. We boxed the band in a canyon with the purpose of gentling and training the horses. But the stallion disappeared after two days. There are known rustlers in the area. I believe these pictures portray the stallion in question. He has very distinctive marks and a most unusual coat color."

Judge Newholt beckoned for the pictures and studied each one. "Is this the animal in question?" She had the deputy present the pictures to Thurman.

"Yes," he grimly admitted.

"So, we have the possibility of a stolen horse, a man who claims no expertise in the equine field yet also claims this stallion is worth $10,000, and this same man," she arched her confrontational brows at Thurman, "has no receipt indicating he purchased said stallion. Thurman, this is a frivolous case. You have misused my court's time. Miss Gray did not twist your arm to sell the horse in question. She does have a receipt. I'm fining you court costs and, Miss Gray, did you incur any expenses to attend this court?"

"I had to reschedule three lessons."

"And what is the total, please?"

"$225," hope bloomed within me- the butterflies were flying off, having happily reconnoitered a patch of worthier flowers.

"Thurman, I fine you $225, plus court costs." She discarded Thurman and turned to me. "Out of curiosity, Miss Gray, why did you decide to buy a horse which displayed such injurious tendencies? You don't have to answer," she politely added.

"I felt sorry for him. He'd been drugged and manhandled- he's scarred," I honestly appealed to her.

"Is he a danger to you?" her curiosity prevailed.

"I don't believe so." The judge's eyes flickered with interest.

"Case dismissed." The gavel fell.

IOU A HORSE

"I told you," Sierra tapped my shoulder.

Outside the courtroom, I received multiple congratulations and an ill-humored quick glimpse from Thurman as he hurriedly exited. Though I'd grown accustomed somewhat to Martine's 'celebratory' hugs- one came with every milestone she achieved in her riding- the effusive response of these friends overwhelmed me.

Bonnie's hand settled lightly on my forearm, and a profound sense of serenity emanated from her touch- it seemed to saturate my every cell. But it did not alleviate my questions.

"How did you know about this? I can't believe you came all this way!"

"Are you kidding? Your ride on Cloud- only the most fantastic ride I've ever seen- went viral on the internet. Can I please come for lessons and bring Handsome? You are internationally famous! Someone heard about the lawsuit, too, and it's on the internet," she gushed.

No privacy any longer, I reflected, but I was glad of the CatSkills' support and all their help with Sheer- it seemed ages ago.

"How is Sirocco?"

My eyes were dangerously close to tearing up, recalling that tragic day. I bit my lower lip for control. Riordan CatSkill stood back in all his wildly disarrayed hair and nodded encouragingly at me.

"She's doing great," I replied, "thank you."

"Wonderful," Bonnie beamed and slid into her husband's arms. They seemed so young, so right for each other and so totally in love. Riordan kissed the crown of her head as she practically danced in his embrace.

So young... Close to my age. I needed to stop thinking like a 70-year old, I berated myself.

"We have to catch...a plane. We're off to Venice. Riordan has to check on his Palazzo," Bonnie's eyes were alight with anticipation.

Tim perked up- he glanced lovingly at Martine who blushed under his intensity.

"A Palazzo, for real? On the Grand Canal?" Riordan CatSkill circumspectly assented. "Say, do you rent out any part of it? As an architect in a previous life, I'd love to see Venice with my new bride," he held up Martine's hand, kissed her palm and showed a sizeable diamond engagement ring foisting rainbows around the incongruous court hallway.

"Oh, Martine, Tim, how wonderful," I smiled and then bit harder on my lower lip, feeling inordinately warm. More congratulations cheered the quiet ambience of the courthouse.

A rush of happiness blustered about my heart for them- two very happy couples. An unfamiliar longing gripped me- one I had probably experienced as a tiny baby. One that had got lost somewhere on the roadside of growing up in self-imposed isolation.

"Let's celebrate over lunch. My treat," Martine crowed, as Tim's arms wrapped around her waist.

"We have to run, but congratulations to you. We wish you great happiness," Bonnie shook hands. "Riordan?"

Her husband drew a card out of his jeans and proffered it to Tim. "If you call this number, my secretary will gladly help you with your arrangements. As an aficionado of Venetian architecture, myself, I can wholeheartedly say- you're going to love it."

"Bonnie, those pictures," I indicated the pocket of her flannel shirt where she'd placed the photos. She flashed them quickly at me. For certain, it was Cloud.

"When we first acquired...Cloud," her husband averted his head; his shoulders trembled suspiciously like one desperately trying to contain laughter. Something about those pictures...

"Coming, Wife?" he drew Bonnie and her pictures into his chest. Towering over her, he swept her off her feet preparatory to leaving.

One of his black brows rose provocatively at Bonnie's chortling into his neck. If Teacher asked me what I wanted right now... Unequivocally, I'd tell him- a relationship like the CatSkills.

IOU A HORSE

39

"Ned, uh," what I had in my head was definitely on the weird scale, but... "Are you or Tim uh, fixing things on the sly?" There, I'd slipped out on the ice.

Ned stood mute, obviously puzzled. "I haven't found a loose fence board in, I don't know how long. Whew! What luck! Knock on wood!" He rapped the barn wall.

"How odd," I mused.

"Gee, Miss Dove, if something needed mending, I'd sure tell you and then be happy to take up a hammer. I bet Tim would, too."

"Hmmm..." One thing about having a stable is that something always required a handyman- fence posts, rails, overly-ambitious automatic waterers, shifting stall mats, numerous and constant pop-up need-immediate-attention tasks. But not at Creekside. Since when? Magic?

"I guess I'd best knock on wood, too." Which I promptly did with a silent thanks to...the powers that be.

True to her inexorable nature, Martine had posted a large block calendar inside the tack room and she'd filled in a few blocks: her birthday, Tim's, Copper's, Buddy's, Tenerife's. I shouldn't have been surprised to see she'd also blocked my birthday, Sheer's, Pippin's, Leopold's, Sam Mule's, Venezia's, Chanson's, Ned's, and a made-up date for Cloud. She had done her homework! There was even a doggie birthday marked and one for the kitties!

Creekside had gained a sense of 'hominess' and camaraderie unknown during Aunt Vickie's tenure. What would my aunt think of it all? As for me, along for the ride and un-protesting, I'd bought several boxes of cards and was busy thumbing through birthday and wedding selections- Sierra and Timberman were getting married on January 1- when a knock rattled the door.

Saturday night. 11 pm. Unheralded by the dogs... Who in the world?

I set aside the cards wondering why not a single dog barked, not a single cat made a move to scatter- very peculiar. Another knock. I considered getting my pistol, but if the dogs weren't concerned- the dogs always warned me.

"Captain?" Big brown eyes rolled up at me as his head barely rose in acknowledgement and then promptly dropped back onto his paws. "Didn't mean to disturb you," I apologized.

A knock registering distinct indignation shook the door.

"Coming," I hollered. Sweeping back the dead bolt without scanning the outside first, I opened the door to...

"Cloud?"

With his two black legs staunchly poised on the threshold my opening the door sent me right into his face.

'Surprise! Let's go for a ride,' he reversed a step, leaving me room to breathe.

"H...how did you get loose?" I was flabbergasted- actually, more like appalled, considering certain consequences inherent in a curious, loose stallion.

'Seriously?'

I could have sworn if he had a brow it would have risen in derision- shades of Judge Newholt.

"Oh God! The Amazon!" If he'd...

'Relax, she's not my type,' he quipped inside my head.

In another situation the very idea might be funny. My mind was having difficulty wrapping itself around this fantastic, wonderful...

'LET'S GO!' he bellowed.

With a strange sense of relief- a horse wouldn't lie, would he?- I gathered a jacket and slipped on my sweat pants against the cold.

'Harvest moon,' he stuck his nose high in the air. Indeed, a stupendous, expressive golden orb lit up Creekside as if it were a clandestine movie set.

IOU A HORSE

"How do you know about harvest moons?" Why was it so easy for me to speak with the perversely-humored Cloud and so onerous to try and converse with humans- although I was improving- and impossibly laborious to maintain a conversation with Teacher?

'In case you've forgotten, I live outside. Not much to do at night but look at the sky,' Cloud smirked aloud- er, in my head.

And why hadn't I thought of that? I walked alongside Cloud on the way to the barn. "I'd best get my helmet," I blissfully shook my head at the incongruity of this surreal scenario.

While I fished my helmet off a hook in the tack room, Cloud studiously ignored the curious eyes and nickers of the stalled horses. Sheer seemed to be the only one who enticed any response from him- a gentleman courting a lady?

Jacqueline got her knickers in a twist as Sheer and Cloud whiffled in the usual equine mode of male and female. How dare the Jack of Knaves not bow to the Amazon Queen! I could just hear her condescending disdain.

Chanson, the remaining mare, daintily nibbled her hay, strewing pieces outside of her open Dutch door, her eyes on Sheer- a true lady's maid. How fanciful I'd become!

"C'mon, Cloud, before the Amazon decides to put you in your place," I mounted from an upturned bucket.

'She's welcome to try,' he glibly retorted.

I giggled, allowed my legs to embrace his ample rib cage. Cloud made me feel...so awfully...young? Relaxing onto him with a light seat, I released another bout of giggles. Girly me- enchanted by... Skip the knight and give me the horse, I thought. Unless...unless Teacher...

'Speak with your mind,' he ordered. 'Fast or slow?'

In keeping with the magic of our relationship, I accepted his terms. 'Whatever you decide,' I telepathically turned it all over to him.

'Hmmm... Any apple orchards near?'

I laughed in delight. 'No, but I do know where a patch of

hedge apples have fallen,' I responded. Men and their stomachs. 'Don't I give you enough snacks?'

We walked together as one, me astride, under the auspices of the grand, gold moon. Such a marvel assuredly deserved a salute, and giddy, I complied, waving my right-handed admiration at the beaming wonder.

'I'm a horse and no, there are never enough snacks,' he snorted. 'Heads up!' And with that second's warning, we were flying.

I didn't bother to reach for his mane- just let the wind blow it back on me as Cloud surged from walk to full-out gallop. Whoosh! The incredible launch under me like a rocket blasting off- WOW, did I feel like a cannonball!!! And we soared over a pasture fence. Flying on!

I raised my arms in the open expanse of the field. Closed my eyes against the cold draft assaulting them. No matter how cold it got, I would continue these rides- my jaunt into a dance with the magic I'd drawn.

Or insanity, as a sane person might spitefully spout. Only, I didn't feel the least bit insane. Didn't I run my own business, successfully? Hadn't I made inroads to making friends? No more self-defeating introspection with its backlash suction to... Live in the magic of the moment!

My seat rhythmically melded with the dancing splurge of Cloud's massive engine and fluid limbs. I could be a horse. I could...

"I love you Cloud!" I shouted aloud. There. My first heralded admission of love into the magic world where I knew I belonged.

Only the most discerning eye might distinguish where the horse ended and the girl began. Even their auras merged in like colors.

IOU A HORSE

The stallion negotiated the rocky ledge leading down into the creek and playfully created massive waves as he splashed/pawed in a deep pool. Leafless boughs above provided a derelict umbrella-scant protection from the moonlight.

And no guard at all from the malevolent intentions of the intruder on the far bank who'd patiently tracked and waited.

Despite the chime laughter of the girl on the receiving end of the monumental splashing, the stallion should have been fully apprized of the trespasser's foul presence. But no one is perfect.

With the slightest of rent wind piercing the frequencies in the air, the stallion's head bolted upright, but too late.

A horrendous scream reviled the same frequencies as the swoosh abruptly ended upon its projectile's sinking into its chosen target. She'd never know what had hit her. The stallion, however, heard the raunchy cackle from the opposite side of the creek bank.

A shadowed man caught the slumped girl as she toppled, bleeding profusely.

At the same instant, the phone rang inside the house and the answering machine kicked in to the utter dissatisfaction of the caller.

"Now, where in the world is she? It's nearly midnight."

"Relax, Sierra, come to bed," Timberman slipped a calloused hand up a smooth thigh.

"Nah, I gotta ask her something about the wedding..."

"Let it wait 'til tomorrow. Surely, she's sleeping," he rained kisses on the same thigh.

"If she's out riding and gets hurt off that big-footed f****** beast..." Sierra replaced the phone on the bedside table as Timberman redirected her attention.

"Teacher," her stricken whisper assaults me. "I...hurt," her fluttering eyes plead for explanations and reassurance and the surcease of pain.

"I'll make it go away, love." My hands of their own shamanic healing accord douse her pain sensors with resonant energy, stemm the blood pouring from the...

"I'm here, brother. He's gone," my tall mentor with his incongruous wildly disarrayed hair appears at my side.

"CatSkill, I've not mended this kind of wound before," disconsolate, I regret being out of my depth.

"Break off the shaft, here." My mentor steadies the blasphemous arrow piercing her left shoulder and I snap off the tell-tale fletch, tear at her shirt to allow better access. The cackle was enough, but with grave remorse I fully concede- the particular feathers of the arrow do not lie.

"To contain the damage, because of its depth in her flesh, you must finish sending the arrowhead through, healing all in its wake. Understand?"

My jaw creaks with the force of my gritted teeth; I acknowledge his quiet instruction. I succeed in anesthetizing her from the worst of the pain, and now I watch a part of me, my long, slim fingers, melt into her bleeding wound as I finish driving the arrow's course. An undeniably spiritual experience- Dove, at one with the stallion, and now her body melding with my restorative fingers.

My right hand receives the point and the short remaining shaft, slick with her blood. As I eject the missile from her slight body, I close the wound with a slow, gradual retreat of my finger from the depth in her living tissue. I institute a cauterization effect- closing the blood circulators, repairing a nicked bone, mending tissue and closing the skin as if it had never been violently breached.

In minutes, the only signs of her assault are the holes in her blood-sodden clothes.

"She's lost too much blood."

"You can mend that, too. In case you've overlooked the spirits' sense of irony, your blood and hers are the same type," CatSkill enlightens me.

IOU A HORSE

"This procedure is also new to me," I bow to the wisdom inherent in his ages of healing experience. Thank the spirits for CatSkill, my friend and teacher.

"Join your wrist with her jugular vein. Open your heart and send. It's sort of a blood transfusion, only on another plane. The spirits will call to you when she's received what her body needs. Be mindful of replenishing yourself as you aid her, because your blood and mine are different," he chuckles.

The moon provides the unnecessary hospital light on the creek's emergency bedside bank. At length, I study her unconscious form. And gratefully bow to the spirits- her pale face exhibits not a sign of distress. Gently I move aside the leather thong of the crystal which hums with my close proximity. Does it sing to her when I am not present?

She curls into my wrist with her chin as I set my prominent wrist's veins against the pulsing lifeline in her neck. A chiming, like a joyous chant, accompanies what most assuredly is a sacred ceremony.

All the times she'd questioned me about our rituals and here, together, we are part of one not spoken of in any oral or written histories- yet it harkens beyond ancient times, to healing powers gifted to the chosen, shamans considered worthy by Spirit. I bow to a deep prayerful sense of awe regarding Spirit, for their having accepted me, for their gracefully bestowing such a tremendous benediction on me.

"We're going to need Bonnie," CatSkill hints, politely asking my permission. "The phone's been ringing on and off at the house. Could be an issue."

"Hello!" Bonnie stepped up her breathing and answered the phone to a disconcerted silence. "Oh, sorry, Creekside, hello," she amended her address.

"Who is this?" Bonnie recognized the voice- the tall blonde with the boisterous mannerisms.

"Bonnie Lance CatSkill. May I ask who's calling?"

"Sierra Sorenson. Where's the Kid...Dove?"

"Oh, she's out trail riding."

"At this hour? I've been calling for...quite some time. What are you doing there? I thought you were in Venice," Sierra blustered.

"Stopped off here on our way home. We were sitting outside enjoying the moon. I noticed the phone kept ringing and thought I'd better answer it just in case," Bonnie equably responded.

"How long has the Kid been out?"

A conundrum as Bonnie had no idea when Dove had left. 'Riordan?' she silently asked her husband.

'About an hour, Wife,' his instant silent reply.

"Around an hour, I guess," Bonnie spoke into the phone.

"That's pretty long isn't it?" the worried Sierra was not to be put off.

"Uh, I don't know, but it's so beautiful out tonight..."

"Will you tell her to call me when she gets back? If that f****** beast has dumped her, I'll shoot the..." the phone clicked off.

"Sierra, how would you feel if somebody said they'd shoot Ace if he dumped you into a barrel?" Timberman referred to Sierra's champion barrel racer. "Let's get some sleep, please?"

"Thank you for coming, Lady Shaman, CatSkill." Contrary to her offer, I clean the blood from my...student, gently dress her in her familiar night shirt and shorts- soft green flannel ones in keeping with the time of the year. My hands tremble slightly at the extraordinary implication of what I have managed to do with my mentor's and the spirits' aid.

An assorted audience of kittens and dogs patiently waits their opportunity to ascend to the bed and take up their respective slumber positions as I reluctantly release the sleeping girl from my arms. The Lady Shaman dallies with the youngsters, and assures all felines and canines of their beloved's well-being, while CatSkill idly strokes the patient Captain.

"She'll be tired tomorrow," the Lady Shaman places her own healing hands on Dove's shoulder. "Riordan, perhaps we might camp out tonight and help her tomorrow? I mean if Sierra confronts..."

"Just for tonight, Wife," CatSkill takes his lady in his arms- a perfect, yet truly unexpected pairing. One I'd not have believed possible and had, at first, been abhorred by.

"What about her clothes?"

Ah, yes, the evidence... "I can't mend them," I eye the bloody holes, "But, if I can get the blood out, I suppose I might enlarge the tears as if a branch had..." I shrug.

"What about the...other matter?" CatSkill needlessly reminds me.

The short window of reprieve I'd had with the arrival of the CatSkills and the subsequent healing of my student ends; the weight of an issue too long deferred strikes at my core.

"At times the spirits offer difficult lessons, remember?" CatSkill supportively adds.

"I remember, remember too much," I murmur. All the fury, the senseless abuse, the wasted youth... The spirits, no doubt, believed nothing was wasted; I'd not attained such sagacity- I was yet, quite a novice under their benevolence.

The malefactor would not have gone far. By now he probably lay curled in the cold with a bottle of his favorite poison. With the moonlight to see by and figuring the trajectory of the offending arrow, I'd soon have him- I'd not need CatSkill to track this offender.

"Ah, my son, the great shaman," the withered specter taunts me with cracked, drooling lips. "I hope she dies." The stench of his living-dead physique should sicken me. Certainly his words should.

"She won't."

"Maybe I'll be more successful next time," spit slides from his chortling mouth, dribbles down his filthy shirt.

"There won't be a next time." An inordinate sense of peace steals over me- compliments of the spirits, bless them. I'd not seen my father since a fourteen year old boy hit him with an axe handle, left him lying in the dirt in his own decaying fluids, and ran to escape, leading away the inebriate's latest scape goat. The mare had been my salvation.

In the long interim, I'd gone beyond the lone cast-off- gone well beyond any inkling of my former self. Nowhere to turn, I gave myself, a willing sacrifice, to the spirits. Chosen by horse spirit and thus guided, I vowed, let them do with me as they might.

"You took everything from me," the derelict squabbles. "My woman, my son..."

"I'm your son," I hear the spirits applaud- pluck at my supra-human senses with 'you are a healer.'

"You're nothing to me. Nothing..." Trails of tears glisten across the deep ravines of his mottled face. His thin frame rocks to and fro on the cold ground. What had kept him alive all the years since?

"I am a healer," I aver, as I break his bow and the remaining arrows across my knee, and gather the wounded soul to my chest.

IOU A HORSE

40

Gravity-less inside a palpable black pall. No feelings. No dreams. Nothing. Floating. A deep meditative state?

How did I get within? Was I...dead? Waiting for a tunnel of light to show me the way? I awaited Aunt Vicky and Marshall-hoping they'd come for me.

Suddenly, a bubble gurgled from within my...body. An errant last gasp of...what? An expectancy of...the picture show/light to begin or illuminate me, guide me to...? My last grip on life hastening away...

A brilliant, warm vista cajoled my eyes to open. I could see dry, hot, seared sage- the high desert? It was unlike Teacher's classroom, and therefore somewhat frightening, considering my 'state'.

Teacher, I tried to call, but I had no voice.

There- a boy, a young teenager. Much too thin. Torn t-shirt and ragged jeans. Dusty. Shoulder length black hair. Running barefoot alongside a red roan. Sprinting, galloping, soaring over deep ravines.

A dusty trail led up to a rock-strewn mesa with desiccated foliage and scattered tumble weeds; billowing clouds vied with each other dancing on a blue racing field high above. The mare jubilantly crested the rise first- the boy close behind, his chest heaving with his overdrawn lungs' exertion.

At the far end of the mesa, heads shot up. A band of four mares- two bays, one chestnut and a mottled chocolate brown one were guarded by a scarred, gray stallion. On instant alert, the stallion prepared to signal for flight.

The roan mare, the boy's companion, stopped and nickered. Tossing his head, the stallion pranced forward and neighed his welcoming summons. Without a backward glance, the roan mare tore off, pelting the boy in her wake with hoof-dispatched dust and pebbles.

"Wait," he called after her, raising a hand as he bent over, hands on his knees, seeking to steady himself against the inevitable, his breath on hold.

The mare skidded to a stop at the sound of his voice and flagrantly shook her head in the semblance of a decided farewell, pirouetted and raced away. The band enclosed her in its ranks with the equine version of a once-over, and as if one body, they flowed off in a heat haze.

Were they a mirage? The boy?

I watched as the boy, heart-broken and alone, collapsed, holding onto himself. Oh, how I recognized that feeling- desperately trying to keep from falling apart as sadness rendered you impotent.

The scene telescoped to black and then, rather like a working kaleidoscope slipped into another setting.

A tree-trunk pole set in the stomped earth. Its uppermost height bore a few leafy branches. Each leaf shuddered in the slightest of breezes. Heart shapes- cottonwood leaves. A cottonwood tree.

Colorful ties abounded- prayer ties similar to the ones left at sites in Ireland to beseech the spirits or the faeries, and what was the difference, anyway?

Tethered to the cottonwood trunk via long rawhide ropes pinned by means of thin, sharpened stakes through pierced flesh on each side of sun-bronzed breast was a man attired solely in the breech clout of his ancestors. Long, muscular, runner's legs, bare feet. His head was thrown back to the sun, eyes closed in prayer, supplication. Long black hair- "Teacher," I gasped.

Another vantage opened to me. The piercings were not only in his chest. From high up on his back near his shoulder blades, two thongs extended down, heavily-laden with bleached skulls, perhaps buffalo.

With palms open, he danced to the pole and back, repeatedly- a dance so far removed from the pig roast as to suggest otherworldly. Sweat streams gathering dust ran down his skin in a never ending outpour of life, gratitude, sacrifice.

IOU A HORSE

My eyes refused to absorb the background. They were indelibly fastened on Teacher to the point I felt the anguish of the piercings in my own chest and back and the struggle to breathe, to keep moving. Empathy pains? His weary state was my own. How long would he continue in the mystical rite of his people?

"No more pain," I whispered. "No more..." I prayed along with him. Aghast, I could only wonder about the outcome for the curtains abruptly folded and everything blackened, sending me adrift once more.

An alarm intrinsic to me woke me at 6am. Carefully dislodging warm critters, I slowly rose only to feel a terrible stiffness in my left shoulder and hear strange noises from outside my room. Rubbing the perplexing, muted pain, I stepped into the living room and...

"Bonnie?" I was in my house, wasn't I?

A friendly, albeit abashed, smile greeted me as Bonnie Lance CatSkill was reluctantly relinquished from her husband's arms.

"What...what are you doing here?" I didn't mean to sound ungracious, but confusion certainly reigned in my head.

"Don't you remember? Our flight was delayed and we called and you offered your spare room..." Bonnie's voice sank as I did not register any such recall.

"Oh," I frowned, rubbing my confounded shoulder. Maybe I'd hit it against the door jamb going to the bathroom in the middle of the night. I didn't remember...much of anything past...

Going for a ride. A fantastic golden moon. Flying across a field. Declaring my love for Cloud, actually shouting it to the world. I must have returned more exhausted than I imagined.

No meeting with Teacher last night, but strange dreams- like eavesdropping on a vision.

"You OK?" Bonnie asked with obvious concern. "Did you hurt your shoulder?" She glanced at her husband.

"I...I guess I slept the wrong way. Sometimes the animals are a mite greedy about superseding my place in my bed," I looked around for the guilty crew, but they all seemed terribly engaged in grooming activities.

"And that is why we have a king-sized bed," Riordan CatSkill unfolded from my way-too-small-for-him couch and quite catlike, proceeded to stretch all muscle groups.

"If you like, we brought provisions. I'll cook breakfast and Riordan will help you feed. Oh, by the way, Sierra called," Bonnie said.

"I'm yours to command," Riordan winked at his wife, saluted me. "I'm used to working in a barn."

"Thanks," I sincerely and graciously, yet still a bit mentally muddled, replied to their offers.

Sunday morning and I had company, very welcome unexpected company. Why was I so tired? I threw on sweats, looked for my jacket. How did I do that? I eyed the torn shoulder area dubiously. Another something I forgot? How remiss of me.

With Riordan CatSkill in tow, I headed to the barn, leaving Bonnie to fend for herself in the kitchen.

As if reading my mind, CatSkill declared, "Bonnie's completely at home in a kitchen. I hope you're hungry- she does nothing by bits and pieces and it's all great; come to think of it, I'm starving." A mysterious smile allowed a dimple to strut and he hesitated for a second as if listening to something only he could hear- leaving me to wonder anew.

Cloud nickered a good morning- equine style, and issued a more demanding summons as I tried to continue on with a wave of my hand.

'Come here!' rang inside my head.

"I'd best give him a snack or we'll not hear the end of it," I blushed as my assistant appeared to supernaturally gauge me. . "Dictatorial horse," I kept under my breath.

"No problem," CatSkill crossed his arms to wait at a distance, after disturbing his already wildly disarrayed tawny, auburn, black and every-shade-in-between hair.

IOU A HORSE

"How are you?" I offered Cloud a piece of carrot. Since hearing of his preference in the snack department, I amiably complied. "Some ride, huh? Under that glorious moon?"

Cloud, not one to recognize privacy issues, stuck his muzzle into my sore shoulder, artfully grazing my breast in the process.

"Ow," I winced. But as I stood there breaking off bits of carrot, his warm breath seemed to act as a healing balm. Within seconds, my shoulder lost its uncharacteristic stiffness and felt good as new.

Fervently, I kissed his soft muzzle and forgot all about whatever it was I forgot.

"She's taking a grand nap- you don't think she'll sleep through feed time, Riordan?" Teasingly, he ruffles my hair and then nibbles my ear.

"Are you kidding? With all the hungry mouths around here? I'm sure they'll be most insistent about sounding the alarm. Bonnie, Kitten, stop fretting. She's not your student..."

"No, but she is a friend," I hitch a shoulder.

"And look at the progress she's made since we first saw her trying to master a GPS in a foreign country," my dream cougar reminds me.

"Yes, she's lucky to be surrounded by good people and horses, dogs, kitties... It's just..."

"She reminds you of someone," Riordan murmurs as I tuck into his warm chest.

"She's much stronger than I was. At least, I knew my dad loved me from the very beginning."

"Wife, the strong rarely admit- even to themselves, how strong they truly are. I thank the spirits daily for bringing me to you. Let's hope she is as resilient as she is strong. The journey is not easy, but it is supposed to build you up. Brittle won't do, and her hardest test is coming. I assume you left her well-provisioned?" One of his glorious, expressive, black brows rises over a golden eye.

"Beef and noodles, chili, cookies..."

"Did you say cookies?" I giggle all the way home- a journey of seconds.

IOU A HORSE

41

"I saw you last night," I hailed my mentor.

Teacher strode into my dream, impassive head high, oblivious to the heightened breeze riling his long, black hair. My heart lightened at the sight of him and my fingers longed to challenge the wind for his hair, even as the logical part of me recognized that the prairie had changed, echoing the progression of the seasons in my everyday life. Magic...dreams...where did one begin and the other end? Shades of Celtic spirituality, there was no linearity.

Teacher imperceptibly paused at my remark and then re-veiled himself in his stoic implacability.

"I did not come to you last night. You slept...very weary. I did not wish to disturb you."

I hastened to fill the conundrum void I knew he sought to conceal. Not stopping to fathom his cryptic attitude, and no longer leery about being close to him or being rebuffed, I singularly invaded his personal space.

My fingers dared to graze the puckering scar tissue over each breast and his nostrils flared at my invasive touch. Hooded black eyes briefly closed and upon opening glared at me with emotion impossible to interpret. Aware of my disrupting his innate stoicism, I braced myself, refused to retreat. But my stomach lurched as I recalled the means that inflicted the wounds, even though it had been a ceremony sacred to Teacher- a ritual of utmost importance.

A current sizzled as my skin touched his- not a current to run from, but toward. He'd been so close-mouthed about explaining the rites of his people; I understood his love for the 'old' ways, and regarding his cultural heritage as private. Privacy, I comprehended very well.

Nevertheless, I had devoured Ed McGaa's books to gain a semblance of knowledge about what I'd envisioned. I desperately wished to comprehend, even if all the ramifications might be beyond me.

But, nothing in books explained this mysterious, magical connection I seemed to have with Teacher. It went beyond our pasts.

"I know how you received these." Unabashed, I boldly delved into his eyes. Mirrors, indeed, we were for each other. I expected him to growl or maybe simply vanish, tossing his persistent question of 'What do you want?' over his shoulder.

Instead, something much more shocking...

The empathy in her eyes...draws me in. Through those grey-green orbs I see what she has witnessed. Why? Why had the spirits given her a glimpse into my soul? My private experiences?

'Look to yourself,' whispers in my head.

Myself? I deeply inhale, open and ground myself with the spirits. Ah...

The transmission of my blood to her has opened a mystic portal of sorts. I can hear her blood- my blood, calling, skipping through the canals of her body, resonating as if I am confronted by part of my own body.

And more. She senses it, too. Although she has no idea of the... Or does she?

Is she more than a mirror of my being? Have I unwittingly gifted my crystal around her neck as an involuntary, proprietary symbol? And, now her body's acceptance of my blood seems spiritually satisfying and natural- forgetting the fact it had been an imperative lifesaver at the time. What are the odds we'd incur the necessity to share blood, to have the same type?

What do I feel for this young woman? It is nearly time to decide once and for all.

"What do you want?" My voice sounds overly grating even to my own ears. But she doesn't flinch.

IOU A HORSE

I was ready for him to be disagreeable. His nature compelled defensiveness if I closed in on something too close to his heart. Boy, did I know that feeling.

"These scars," my hand still rested over his pounding heart, "did not wipe out the earlier ones. It is up to us how our past affects us." I echoed his words back to him all the while expecting a backhand slap to put me in my place. My place?

Many people shared disheartening pasts, and yet lived productive lives. I did. I assumed he did, too. Could the sadness never be stemmed, though? Must it always lurk in a corner of our minds, ready at the slightest provocation to lay siege to our souls over and over again? Was a true happiness not allowed us? How did one tap into a seemingly unknown power within and use it to defeat painful beginnings forever? I wanted the spectral past haunting me to end.

"I want to be healed," I murmured to the shaman/healer, as I held his eyes captive and vaulted deeper into the world of magic. The surreal realm of our meeting was similar to Alice tumbling into her Wonderland- a magic that I'd come to believe originated from my pencil strictly for Teacher's and my benefit. One a fairy tale's author would approve of and most assuredly, envy.

Her hand on my chest...the immutable sensation of falling into her essence, being absorbed in something more...similar to the spirits enfolding me in their ranks. All those years believing, rationalizing my love was destined for Shadow... In all those years nothing as inexorable as...Dove, as this mirror of my injured soul.

"I want peace for you, Teacher," she clearly states, missing the greater point.

My question pertains to her needs, not mine. I make ready to protest, but a musical note trills in my veins. Our needs...the same?

"There is still a...tiny nook that needs a stitch. I think you know it, too," she continues in a surprising role reversal.

Her strength and compassion flow within me, emanating from her hand over my heart- an electrical musical stanza cresting on a potential wave of pure and joyous life.

"What do you want, Teacher?" She completely stuns me.

Aunt Vickie had not celebrated Christmas with her students or boarders, other than wishing all of them Happy Christmas and leaving the week between Christmas and New Year's lesson-free. She decorated a table-top Norfolk pine with tiny, red satin bows and we had a small ham for Christmas dinner- one already prepared as neither of us stayed in a kitchen long enough to work out recipes. The critters were our family and their needs were simple and always happily attended to- what they gave to us in return was incalculable.

Aunt Vickie had a polite way about her that discouraged gifts. We never shopped for each other- if something was needed that need was addressed at the specific time. No gifts.

Sierra, though, always presented me with a small present- a book, a set of drawing pencils, pastels... In turn, I'd offer a sketch of one of her equine students or of Sierra mounted and shooting or racing barrels. These were done from memory or a snap shot if I had a camera available. Her effusive gratitude always made me uncomfortable- the same way a compliment did.

But everything had turned on an invisible axis at Creekside. Martine and Tim were the great instigators for Creekside's first open house Christmas- a celebration for boarders, students and friends. And I was the willing, albeit clueless, hostess.

IOU A HORSE

With Tim helping me cook and Martine bustling here and there, we held my small home open for three hours on the day after Christmas.

"It's the old English Boxing Day," Martine chirped spiritedly, as she set up punch bowl, finger foods and party crackers- an English tradition, not the eating kind. Her enthusiasm was as usual, unbounded. She'd sold her house and was moving in with Tim across the street from Creekside. A tiny wedding ceremony was in the planning stages and thanks to the CatSkill's generosity, a honeymoon in Venice cordially loomed.

Funny enough, in thoroughly renovating his ranch house, taking advantage of a low-lying area and putting in a substantial pond, he'd discovered his bride-to-be loved to fish as much as he did. I guessed love was like that- soul mates surprisingly drawn to each other.

My awkward attempts to greet and wish my guests Merry Christmas were soon tempered by Martine into a display of warmth which I found contagious and ultimately very satisfying. Teacher should see me now, I reflected. Sighing, I wished he could be with us, for real, in my house. Why did I assume he could not? Only a hopeful dreamer teetering on the brink of insanity would think a dream might actually walk into her life. Or one who believed in magic the way kids wholeheartedly believed in Santa Claus? I giggled, thinking I should have written Santa a letter.

My boarders/students/friends enjoyed themselves and the numerous paintings Aunt Vicky had never displayed for anyone but Sierra, and no one minded the miniscule space. I wondered what my aunt would think of all the folks admiring her artwork, leaving small gifts under the red-bow trimmed table-top tree, laughingly bumping into each other, savoring the cakes I'd made and Tim's turkey and ham and Martine's fixings and punch.

Sierra minded her language- kept the gathering rated for general audiences. She loudly regaled everyone with her New Year's Eve wedding plans as Timberman made himself scarce with Schoe in a corner and discussed...manly things.

Ned brought his parents, and of course, everyone strolled out in the cold to see Cloud and the rest of the gang. The stallion engaged in the spirit of the season and made no un-gentlemanly advances, although Sierra maintained a remote stance, preferring not to tempt fate.

Sheer and the Amazon ate up all the attention. Sheer got snippy when someone mentioned her weight. I brushed off the remark with, 'hay belly from lack of proper work.' After the first of the year that would change; Sheer was going back to work- I'd developed a new rehab regime, harkening to our initial forays into dressage. Her hock, well, time would tell.

Nearly every night, but especially Christmas Eve and Christmas Day, I braved the cold, and Cloud and I ventured out on our nightly escapades. I attempted to explain about the holiday and to his credit, he listened- at least, no perverse rejoinders ransacked the air waves in my head. After a long companionable jaunt- no racing when the ground was slippery, I went to bed gift-wrapped in a lovely warm essence. Happy- and hoping Teacher would fill my dreams.

He'd warned me he'd be away for a time. His people. I never thought to ask him if he had a...girlfriend. Like a kid pinning all his hopes on his Santa letter, I yearned to place all my faith in the magic that had brought me this far, but I was still cautiously leery about daring to mix dreams and reality.

IOU A HORSE

42

As Sierra's maid of honor, I donned a brave face and allowed her to 'deck' me out in a cocktail-length, Christmas-red confection, which she chose. I had to refuse the stiletto heels in order to save my neck.

"Sierra, I have to work. I can't afford to break or sprain anything in a fall," I put my flat-soled foot down. Rolling her eyes, she sulkily gave in, and bought the red high heels to match the lingerie and garters she'd already purchased.

"Timberman will be in for a treat," she crooned.

Schoe, my escort, picked me up under hovering clouds rife with snow, which provided us with stoic rumination on how much of the stuff we'd receive. We indulged in other, vague topics of conversation during the short drive to the 1800's brick, country church. His offer of 'reliability' and the imminent wedding lingered like stale hay in the air between us. I couldn't wait for that unromantic notion to be completely exorcised and for the return of our previous, at-ease relationship.

Sierra and Timberman's ceremony was a simple affair with a few invited family members and close friends in attendance as Sierra, resplendent in a white, off-the-shoulders lace dress, exchanged vows with the head-above-hers Timberman.

Her voice hiccupped and she began to cry as she recited the words tying her to her beau. Behind her back, her hand sought mine and I grasped it and returned her squeeze, feeling a great tug of emotion bubble in my chest. I bit at my lower lip to contain the threat of my own tears.

All of my life I'd considered tears to be the enemy and a sign of defeat on my part. They were only to be accorded once I was alone. Why?

Upon reflection of Teacher's urgent endorsement, I realized I'd garnered a veritable fortress about me from the time I was very young- one that forbid putting myself in the slightest vulnerable position. But weren't all kids vulnerable? Weren't parents supposed to protect...? The sadness that rankled, threatening to drown me, the numbness that kept me from experiencing joy with other humans... Perhaps I'd really finally progressed, because at that moment, I did feel joy- an ecstasy for my human friend, Sierra.

The reception was an entirely different matter from the solemnity of the church service. A huge hall with loud country music blasting hosted hordes of people sporting everything from jeans and designer cowboy boots to New Year's Eve regalia of sequins and flesh-revealing dresses of sundry lengths and colors.

Schoe cautiously guided me around the dance floor. I had no experience with dancing and I could tell he would have preferred not to have to acknowledge his own two left feet. Considerately, he religiously watched his, hoping to keep my toes safe.

For the slow numbers, he tried to draw me close and forge a sway here and there- making us both feel like automatons minus batteries. Close proximity with Schoe, who hoped for an intimate relationship with me- believed, in fact, we should be together for nothing more than 'expedience' sake- though he wasn't ardently pursuing me, had me gently setting the boundary. If he had pursued me I'm sure our friendship would have suffered, perhaps irrevocably.

Incongruously and unfairly, I pictured Teacher in Schoe's place. Teacher. A circuit of rampant heat circumnavigated my system. To be this close to Teacher with music playing. At our own ceremony...

If anyone would have felt more out of place here than me, it would be Teacher. And not just because of his bare feet and in-your-face heritage. It had hurt when he mentioned 'his people'. Why couldn't it be all people?

IOU A HORSE

A giggly girl part hidden deep inside of me wondered what Teacher might look like clad in a double-breasted, custom-fitted black tux. I tripped into Schoe's arms and he considerately asked if I were all right.

No, I'm dreaming I'm in another's arms- my head resting on another's shoulder as we move artfully together, entranced by music. Dreaming...

What would Teacher speak of to these people- if he did speak? Our first meeting had been quite trying. Schoe and Timberman and Martine, Tim and Ned would be genuinely interested in meeting and getting to know him. Sierra might be considered 'pushy' by Teacher. As for the others, I shuddered physically and mentally. Thinking he'd stepped on my foot, Schoe escorted me to the bride's table with apologies and went to replenish my punch, leaving me to my reverie.

Those others, the impertinent ones, their questions would be intrusive to him- he was much too private an individual. If anyone dared- and it was a guarantee someone would- push into his space... Reality's recoil snapped at me. Would Teacher fight? There was no question in my mind that he would capably defend his rights, but would he? Would he simply walk away? Or would his shamanic ability have him naturally defusing the situation with an enigmatic, unfathomable look? Or would he provide an intangible shower of peace?

What future could there possibly be for...us? If the magic even deigned to allow one. Would Teacher remain a figment solely available via my dreams? Remain a teacher only? Could the magic brook this divide? Dare I believe in the absolute impossible?

My feet and heart were heavy and despite all the well-wishers and frivolity about me, I wished I were at home- in bed and dreaming.

At around 10 pm, I shucked my dress which made me feel like a discarded Christmas ornament and donned flannel-lined jeans. The temperature had dropped with great velocity so I gathered a thermal, long sleeved shirt and a wool sweater and my outback coat.

'Surprise!' Cloud was standing at my front door as I opened it. I practically fell into his face.

"I was just coming to get you!" We chimed together.

I laughed, my heart regaining its natural purr in his presence and he nickered, gently ruffling my hair with his great muzzle. And the first snowflakes let loose.

'Get on!' he commanded. 'Forget the helmet tonight.'

Bending his left leg, he bowed low enough for me to climb aboard.

"You're a regular circus horse," I complimented him aloud.

A loud snort scuttled a swathe of large snowflakes. 'Hang on! Nothing regular here,' he pirouetted and sprinted off.

Soaring over a fence into a blinding fall of snow, I closed my eyes. All my newfound trust, I light-heartedly, merrily gave to Cloud, and lived the magic-inspired moment.

When I opened them, I discovered it was hard to distinguish much of anything- the snow fell heavily. Momentarily, I hoped Sierra's plane got away- their honeymoon was in Hawaii.

But Cloud quickly regained my attention in the white wonderland.

'What's that funny word for prance?'

I laughed, swallowing a few snowflakes.

'Piaffe and passage,' I returned to speaking with my mind- wouldn't do to drown swallowing snowflakes.

'Right, what's wrong with English?' he quibbled as his legs danced under him and his body arched under me.

A ballroom dance I thoroughly approved of, thrilled to be led by such a perfect partner. I should be a horse, I thought, not for the first time, as I effortlessly became one with Cloud's transitions from piaffe to passage. Who needed a dance floor? Or music, for that matter?

Talk about dancing with the stars... Cloud was the star- a warm, snow-horse. Black-framed, sun-bronzed life frosted with

IOU A HORSE

lacy white.

If my hands had sought his mane I'd find the silken, black strands under a pelt of snow, but my arms were out- wing fashion.

'I wish I were a horse, Cloud, I'd marry you,' I sang my magical line in my magical role.

'Silly, right now you are a horse- part of one- same thing.'

My frost-breathing dragon snorted snow and we blended with the near-blizzard in our own fairy tale wonderland- total happiness. An overflow of gratitude simmered delightfully within me. What had I done to deserve this magnificence? And thank you to the magic for making it happen. Thank you. Thank you. Thank you.

There was no concept of time and I had no idea, nor did I care to know, how long we danced together. I had entered heaven without passing on and I never wanted to leave.

Eventually Cloud minded his steps as it became rather slippery.

'Cloud, what would you think about...showing? Riding these movements in competition?' I broached the subject as I slid off his back and escorted him inside his paddock.

His snow-flaked whiskers brushed against my neck. Warm breath found the veins there in a touch beyond intimate. What if I curled up in the hay with him? I didn't want the magical night to end. Ever.

'You're falling asleep,' Cloud quietly said.

'If I didn't think I'd wake up a Popsicle I'd sleep on your back," I replied with my fingers caressing his jaw.

Silence. No cute comeback?

"Cloud?"

'I'll be leaving you...Dove,' Cloud withdrew his muzzle and tossed the snowflakes covering his head, creating a magnified snowfall all about me.

"I guess that's my signal to let you go to bed, huh?" I threw my arms around his neck and breathed in the sweet scent of horse.

"I love you, Cloud. Thank you, thank you," I chimed as we parted- Cloud to his run-in and me to my bed.

43

New Year's Day. I woke at the usual 6 am, my ingrained alarm substantiated by Captain stretched out at my back, Bosun and Mate on both sides of my feet, Eenie on my head, Meenie and Mo curled atop each other under my chin, purring, and Minie within my arms, purring and kneading my chest- their stomachs ran by hunger clocks and were very regular. No way I could hope to oversleep.

A chill braced the air, though I was certainly warm as toast. As I lifted my head, the critters mirrored my movement. Must have got pretty cold overnight- two of the barn cats were under my covers.

"Rise and shine," I called, unnecessarily. The prospect of imminent breakfasts saved me from un-contorting myself- they raced for the kitchen.

Looking out the window as I stretched, it was plain the snowfall had continued in earnest and drifted at some point, followed by an icy frosting. Every branch, fence rail and other farm accouterment had been adorned in a thick layer of glistening crystal.

I leisurely doled out kitty and canine repasts while admiring the view and speculating on how deep the snow was. Pulling out my tall insulated boots to be safe, I also threw my Carhart insulated coveralls on before venturing forth. Wrestling with the door, which snow had drifted against, gave me an idea of what I had to plow through to get to the barn.

"Morning, Cloud," I hailed, watching my breath cloud in the crisp dawn.

Not a peep.

"Sissy," I murmured under my breath. I pictured him nibbling hay, warm and dry inside the run-in shed.

IOU A HORSE

The rest of the gang of critters was quite vocal as always. Hurry, they demanded as I greeted each one on my way to the feed room.

Scooping grain and supplements into feed bins, I eyed each individual. A horse could get up to an injury in a padded stall- every horse person would tell you that. But thankfully, per the norm, everyone was on all fours and eager for breakfast.

I wheeled hay around, making the over-achievers step back until I placed the flakes inside their stalls.

Odd, Cloud had not issued his standard good morning nicker. Sleeping in, eh?

He'd definitely worked harder than I had. Pirouetting in the snow, piaffing, passage... He'd even surprised me with a levade and had me discouraging his idea of courbette. A magnificent ride. I couldn't wait for tonight, but it might be too icy. Darn! If I could only talk him into the show ring...

I found myself smiling. It didn't matter- the show ring business, as long as I could enjoy him and his unique sense of humor. Sheer whinnied for further attention and morning peppermints, bringing me back to business.

"How's my girl?" I scratched under her jaw, under her mane and both sides of her withers. "Being out of work has certainly let you put on a hay belly, goodness!" In response, she nuzzled for another pocket snack.

Schoe had arrived in a rooster-tail of white as his snow plow took care of my driveway. I waved as I crushed through the snow to Cloud.

"Cloud," I called as I laboriously wheeled a bale of hay inside the gate. No response.

"Cloud?" A premonitory flicker of unease curdled in my gut.

Very odd. What if he were hurt? I dropped the barrow handles and clumsily ran in the deep snow to the run-in shed, slipping along the way. Into the dim stall. Empty!

"Playing hide and seek, Cloud?" That would be just like him, especially in the deep snow.

No response. Of course, the whole idea of hide and seek was not to give yourself away. But the only place to hide was behind the shelter.

I slipped along the walls of the shed. By now the sun had busily dispersed the nighttime shadows. No Cloud!

"Cloud!" That character, what if he'd gone walkabout? But he'd always been eager for breakfast.

"Cloud!" I yelled as loud as the cold would allow me. But a note of panic had crept into my voice.

The dogs paced the outside of the fence, by the gate. A burgeoning sense of despair gripped me and twisted my heart. What had he told me last night?

Cloud kisses, a hug... 'I'll be leaving you...'

NO!!! It was just a good night saying, wasn't it? Dear heaven! Cloud would not leave me, would he? I must have misunderstood. Yes, that was it. Cloud was only saying good night... But then, where was he?

Stolen? Mr. Thurman hadn't been too pleased at the court's verdict, but how would he have loaded Cloud? The stallion would not have gone without a fight! The dogs would have sounded the alarm...

What thieves would have gone out in last night's snowstorm?

"Dove? Dove, you all right?" Schoe coming inside the gate. Me standing, forlorn, numb, totally lost.

"Schoe, look out," I called out of habit.

Look out for what? Cloud wasn't... Oh God, Cloud wasn't there! My tortured soul screamed.

"Where's the stallion?" Schoe stomped through the snow which blanketed all in its innocent, pristine splendor- how dare it!

"I...I don't know," I managed, quivering inside and biting ruthlessly on my lower lip to quell a rush of sick emotion.

"Maybe a section of fence is..." he offered, surveying the paddock.

I shook my head, afraid to speak.

IOU A HORSE

"I'll check anyway. Here," he handed me his cell phone as I stood frozen in shock. Schoe was all alert, all business. "Call the police," he firmly ordered, breaking into my fog.

Without a hope, I dialed 911. The snow and humans would take precedence over a missing horse. Cloud was...gone.

Schoe returned to my side, solicitous and brainstorming.

"The depth of the snow would have covered any tracks. Hard to believe some idiot would try and steal a horse- especially this one- on a night like last night," he grimly stated, dumbfounded.

Dumbly numb, I nodded.

"Let's get you inside. I'll make breakfast. You call Tim and Martine and Sierra. We'll check out internet sites that help with lost horses, come on."

I didn't feel Schoe's guiding hand at my elbow. I didn't register the concern in his blue eyes. I had to hold it together. My mind scrolled through scape goats and began making lists. An oddly familiar, yet out-of-practice chore.

Tim and Martine bustled in within minutes. Luckily, Schoe had finished plowing the drive of its two feet of snow. He set a bowl of oats and a plate of toast and a glass of orange juice in front of me.

"Dove, eat, you'll need your strength," Martine's words could not pierce the ice gathering in my heart.

Strength, yes, I would need strength. At least until I was alone. At night. The day had just begun; I had to maintain for a while.

I refused to call Sierra and pleaded with Schoe not to bother her. Timberman and Sierra were on their honeymoon. Hawaii. But there was nothing she could do anyway.

"Talk to us, Dove," Martine hugged me and sat down at the kitchen table.

Schoe ushered Tim aside with, "No telling what time the police will make it out here."

"He's gone," overtly calm, I spilled the obvious. My shoulders rose and sank. "Gone."

Two kittens climbed on my lap, the other two bounded onto

the table to check for leftovers, but turned up their noses at the oats- the same kittens Cloud had roared over and had...healed?

Captain laid his head on my hand, commiserating.

Briefly, I explained to the persistent Martine how I'd returned from the reception around 10 pm and gone out to ride Cloud in the snow. I skipped the magical parts- too private to share, and I couldn't afford to be locked into a crazy ward. Death, I could deal with that, except I had too many critters depending on me. No option in the grave- not for me.

"I latched the gate afterward and went to bed. This morning...no Cloud," I heard the catch in my voice.

"Oh, honey," she rose and put her arms about my shoulders. "Don't worry, we'll find him. I can find anything- it's something I'm really good at."

With her affinity for networking, I knew she'd give it her all, turn up the ends of the earth; whereas the policeman, when he finally arrived, distractedly shook his head- defeated before he started.

Cloud. The magnificent, perversely-humored Cloud. Gone.

Alone, except for the critters. I'd sent Schoe off to fulfill his snow plow obligations. Resolutely, he complied, telling me he would check on me later, though I assured him it was unnecessary.

Martine had compiled lists of organizations to contact. She'd also put a notice on Creekside's web site about Cloud.

"You'll be flooded with supportive e-mails. Even more so than the ones that contacted you after seeing your fabulous ride with Cloud at the clinic," she did her best to bolster me.

I nodded to appease her; I needed to be alone. The haunts were looming, sucking me back...

Finishing the day's feedings, I returned Schoe's calls, falsified conviction to reassure him that I was ok, and pleadingly reminded him not to call Sierra.

IOU A HORSE

I wasn't fooling him, not at all. He ended the call with, "Wish I had a girl love me the way you love that Cloud."

Collapse into bed. Sadness magnetizes all other lonely, difficult times. Plunging me into the past until I am three years old again.

Cold penetrating everything I wear. No one can help. He'd left, Cloud had left. Why? I thought he was saying good night. Stupid girl! Stupid kid!

It hadn't made an ounce of difference that I'd said I loved him. Stupid kid, I hear my father berate me in the old rattletrap car. I cringe, waiting for the slap or worse.

My love was worthless. My worth...worthless... Too much pain... I held my shuddering sides together as I cried myself to pieces.

The man in the shadows restrained himself with dredged-up sheer determination, viewed the painful progression. The rest of the concerned- the kittens and dogs nuzzled her, mewling in empathetic distress which she could not hear. The horses in the stable had diligently nudged and nickered support, too, but their efforts fell on an isolated, numb soul.

She must survive this, he silently willed.

44

Martine was dead-on right. The Creekside web site burned up with a maelstrom of optimistic notes, prayers and stories to share. Though she constantly prodded me each day and reiterated a few of the anecdotes, I'd guardedly furnished myself with a suit of armor thick enough to get me through the day intact, and glossed over the notes without letting any of them penetrate my injured soul.

I couldn't speak of my feelings, despite all the kind people who endeavored to help by sharing. Only facts. I could do facts. Lists...

Tim, Ned and the other boarders and students continually asked for updates or stopped by if they had four-wheel drive vehicles as the snow continued on its merry spree.

Mr. Thorne offered a reward for any information leading to Cloud's discovery. I tried to tell him that wasn't necessary, but he'd used his speculative insights to figure me out and I had the distinct unease that more than anyone, except Teacher and Cloud, he did know me. Another person sharing a kindred past?

How much could anyone know about another unless they willingly shared highly personal information? Or had been personally 'there' before? Or, maybe an intuitive person might discern the wretched pains others hid in closet recesses of their minds.

I thanked him profusely and doubled his offer- I still possessed the insurance money he'd given me. But ultimately, deep in my heart, I knew it would come to nothing. Why? I couldn't explain, except Cloud...Cloud was not an ordinary horse. Not even close.

Auction houses were under surveillance. Thurman was contacted by the police, but his alibi was ironclad. And I never believed he'd done anything to make Cloud disappear, anyway- he didn't have the nerve.

IOU A HORSE

I knew Cloud, I thought I did. He'd managed to come and go. Maybe he was the Crocodile Dundee of the equine world and had merely 'gone walkabout'.

The snow spree was unabated, alternating with horrendous fits of ice. Lessons were cancelled. Ned had difficulty getting to Creekside at times, but Tim, Martine and Schoe were always there to help without being asked.

"Dove, answer your e-mails. At the very least compose something to tell all the folks who are genuinely interested and worried for you," Martine cornered me and berated my seeming indifference.

I simply nodded. Yes, there was time to do that. I put it on my list.

"Oh, no you don't, you can't brush this off. You're not exactly alone, even though you think of yourself that way. I'm not sure I can play Sierra, but here goes," she pushed me into a chair and pulled up the Creekside web site.

"Get your ass in gear! Read what some of these kind people have to say. Oh, and here, eat a f****** sandwich. How's that? God, I can't wait for her to get back here," exasperated, Martine loudly harrumphed.

I broke into a snort, somewhere in-between a laugh and a cry at her use of the f-word. So out of character for her. Tim would be appalled.

"Read!" And her expression stood guard, while she pulled up a chair and eventually a magazine and a sandwich of her own. My personal babysitter.

"Thank you, Martine, thanks for...being a friend," I croaked through a throat raspy with my nighttime crying.

Sierra's speech about species specific conversation came to mind as I scrolled through well wishes, personal anecdotes and well-meaning advice.

Some had lost horses to rustlers. The lucky ones had been reunited. Others never found answers and their stories of hurting hearts, stories of love...sharing, species specific...

Soon my eyes overflowed with the outpouring of expressed love. Of a certainty, I was not alone. Had I really believed I ever was? No, I simply had not thought at all. More importantly, why had I not let myself share my story with others?

I grasped at words to put together a synopsis of my initial meeting of Cloud and our ensuing relationship. For the first time in my life, words steamrolled out of me along with an unstaunched river of tears- for anyone to see.

I described our nighttime rides and the last one in the snow- the absolute, euphoric feeling of being one with another living soul. The magic of our telepathic communication I kept to myself, but part of me knew many of my supporters would have understood.

Once I finished my communiqué, Martine reading over my shoulder, I quickly hit the key to send my heart out to everyone- before I reneged, feeling like I'd transgressed some invisible line that only existed in my own psyche.

Others lived through hard times. No one was alone. No one. Unless they made it so. Teacher would be proud of me, and Cloud- I recalled one of his remarks which I'd glossed over at the time- 'Horses left to be are horses; shuck baggage and go on, freely!' Between Cloud and Teacher, could anyone have hoped for more in the way of mentorship? And a glimpse of heaven at the same time? Even if the magic had...gone, abandoned me, I'd received great gifts. I bowed my head to give thanks, wiped my sodden eyes and blew my nose.

Martine drew me into an empathetic embrace; she cried and I stood pat until she quietly left.

The stories of rustlers reminded me of something- the CatSkills and the small band of wild horses. Cloud missing. I dug out Bonnie's card after Martine's departure.

Murphy's Law- an answering machine picked up. I left a message telling her about Cloud's disappearance in case she hadn't seen the web site lately and I asked her to return my call.

In my heart, at least, I continually told myself, Cloud- that super special stallion, wherever he was, would be all right. I wouldn't think of the marks on his body...

IOU A HORSE

Into bed, I climbed. Two days had gone by and I made a resolution that I would not let the sadness defeat me. Right. I hugged Minie and saturated her kitten coat.

At some point, I fell asleep, but soon woke with a start, scattering critters.

One of the pictures Bonnie had reluctantly flashed of Cloud... In the corner... Something familiar... What?

I rubbed at my temples, think! Ah, a landmark Creekside boulder by a young cottonwood. The pictures had been taken...at least one had, at Creekside? What in the world did that mean?

Sheer futilely beckoned to accompany me.

"Sorry, Sheer, we'll wait until the ice is gone. Be ready, sweet girl. We'll be taking much longer walks- get you back in shape." I slipped her a peppermint and scratched her favorite spots.

Turn-outs, due to the ice-frosted snow, were relegated to hour bouts in the sand ring with amicable, equine buddies- this kept me pretty busy during the day. On one particular day, though, I reserved enough light to venture out.

The previous night's revelation irritated me no end. I headed out towards the boulder I thought I remembered from Bonnie's photo. Maybe I was making something out of nothing. I mean, they did have boulders and cottonwoods out west.

For some reason, like an itch I couldn't quite reach to scratch, I had to find the spot. It turned out to be a fruitless task as the snow shrouded everything. Nothing looked familiar. Even the denuded cottonwood with its snow-coat melded into the grayness of the day and the renewed snow swirls- would the winter never end?

I almost felt I'd been hornswoggled. Maybe the CatSkills were magic. Dare I ask?

"You're out there, aren't you?" Who was I talking to?

Teacher had not graced my dreams for days. He'd told me at times he'd be away. With his people. Sure, I'm not the only needy soul, but I wished with all my being to see him right then.

Teacher said he always kept an eye on his students. Did he know about Cloud? Could he help? Or was this a case of each has his own path? Are you out there, Teacher?

My sketch book slid off the chest at the foot of my bed as I grabbed another blanket.

How long since I'd opened its pages and allowed the magic to flow? Ireland? Sheer's accident?

A compelling sensation enjoined me to pick up my drawing pencil. I flipped the pages, sat up in bed with pillows braced at my back, and adjusted the light to shine on a blank section of paper. As had happened magically in the past, the pencil came alive with its own ideas and my pencil-held fingers danced on a ballroom floor of white drawing paper.

Two horses. As the shadings progressed, the biggest one undeniably became Cloud and the smaller, finer-boned one, joined him in a joyous full gallop. Stride for stride beside him. Who was the other horse? I almost cried; the magic hadn't deserted me! Though I had no idea what was portended, my heart skipped a beat in relieved gratitude.

I swept the snow off the chair under the pin oak. As late as a pin oak holds it leaves, the snowstorms had relieved this sturdy giant of any stragglers. The red-orange leaves were gone- all of them buried in the ice-shrouded snow.

I stared into Cloud's run-in, missing his catchy remarks, his well-defined, Cloud humor and our unscheduled rides. Not to hear him again... Not to...

BE STILL!! Roared inside my head. I swung about. No one. BE STILL AND YOU MAY HEAR!

IOU A HORSE

Casting aside my intrusive, scape-goat lists, I wavered at the questions sadness always plied me with. "Leave, please," I murmured to the tangled morass in my head.

Stillness. Quiet of mind. For a second. One cannot force a still mind. I took a deep breath and exhaled everything in my way.

'You are part of everything. Live. Do not retreat.' A clear message in Teacher's voice. Or was it Cloud's voice? A trick of my imagination?

"Please come tonight, Teacher," desperately I attempted to downplay the entreating note inveigling into my invitation.

For a response, I heard the snowflakes landing on my Carhart coveralls. Tears swelled my eyelids and my heart creaked to fall apart, but somehow I held it together. I'd always been a good student, if a quiet, reserved one- I just had to amend the 'quiet' in the direction Teacher demanded. I wanted Teacher's approval. Craved it.

The merest flicker of unfamiliar anger kindled and was immediately doused. I'd been given tremendous gifts. Critters to care for. An opportunity to ride the most magnificent stallion. Cloud. Cloud... Be in the here and now, I silently berated myself. Only the present mattered.

Sheer and all of our wonderful times together and all those ahead of us. She was still with me, telling me of her needs and wants. Needs. Wants.

What do you want? What did I want?

I shook that question off, I knew the answer now. Too late?

I had a coterie of species specific friends who, although I refrained from confiding in, they were there and not shy about letting me know of their support. I had a home. The sketch pad and... THE MAGIC STILL EXISTED!

Only time would reveal its tantalizing mystique.
"Thank you," I whispered to the late afternoon sky. "Thank you. I'll keep on trying to...be as I should be."

I thought I heard a 'You're welcome' in a deep, masculine voice. I thought I did.

45

"I f****** swear!"

No mistaking that irreverent voice. "Sierra?" Turning, I forced a smile.

What day was it? Was the honeymoon over already? Surely Schoe hadn't called her? I unfolded from my chair, to face the music.

"Why didn't you f****** call me? No don't answer. I'll probably only get really steamed! You didn't even hear me pull down the drive! Just sitting there in the snow, watching that f****** paddock! F***!"

I stood mute, let her have her say and finally, seeing I wasn't buckling, she resignedly sighed.

"You must be the strongest person I've ever met. Not a single tear, nor the slightest sign of anger. And I've talked to Martine, so I know more than you think I do- one cry'll do it? I think not. How do you do it? How do you keep from falling apart? How do you f****** stand it?

First your Aunt Vickie, then Sheer. Now that f****** stallion has disappeared, not to mention all the other happy horse shit you keep bottled up inside like some ass-backwards treasure. And not a hint of anger... You know what? I am desperately afraid of seeing the refurbished 'Do Not Disturb' sign popping up again. That f****** monster was good for putting that in f****** layaway, at least. F***!"

"Sierra," I interrupted her lambast and stood directly in front of her, craning my neck up. "Am I...a worthy...friend to you?"

She rolled her blue eyes under her winter Stetson complete with its crimson ear warmers.

"Are you f****** serious? You're my best friend. No one else, except Schoe and Timberman, accept me for the quirky, loud mouth I am. You listen to me. You're non-judgmental and I know,

IOU A HORSE

I know for f****** sure if I need something I only have to call you. Does that answer your stupid question?"

My lips trembled; I was about to...break.

"Sierra," my voice choked.

"Aw, Kid," Sierra's voice quavered, too.

"It hurts...hurts so bad," and I finally surrendered to the full heaving turmoil of emotion. Species specific, be damned!

She pulled me into her arms. "I know Kid. I...know."

I bawled like a baby, as I should have been able to do when I was a baby, into her chest- too short to reach her shoulders.

"F****** men!" she ranted. "And you can't even deck him! F***!" We cried, and I think we laughed, together.

Sierra left me much later in a chocolate-induced, comatose state. Too eager for the comfort of its insane richness, we denied the batch of brownies their full dose of cooking time.

Along with an entire bottle of chocolate syrup, we dropped spoon-fulls of the half-baked sweets on top of ice cream and added chocolate chips to boot. With every bite, the tears alternately retreated and flowed anew.

A few giggles set in when Sierra described Timberman's attempt at snorkeling. Instead of waiting to don mask and feet fins upon entering the water, he put on full snorkeling gear and stumbled and fell across the beach- numerous times. He wouldn't listen to Sierra's cackling advice and she simply chortled on at the spectacle of such a large man obliviously playing a comedy act.

Once in the water, he couldn't get the hang of not talking with the mouth piece in his mouth, causing him to nearly drown- numerous times. Sierra declined to participate as she had too much fun watching her inadvertently comedic, new husband choke up salt water, slip and trip on his fin-clad, big feet and disturb all other snorkelers and the shoals of canary-yellow fish.

"The Big Splash, the rest of our tour group called him. Earned us free beers, which I can tell you, after all the swallowed sea water, Timberman was more than ready for."

Sierra hugged me good-bye after the Big Splash called for the third time. "Kid, I want to be like you when I grow up. NOT! But I love ya. I'll call you tomorrow."

I fell into bed half-asleep. The half-awake part felt the tears trickle. Surely by now I should have been wrung dry.

"Cloud's all right. Cloud's all right. Please let Cloud be all right," I began my nightly mantra.

The deep breathing I practiced while riding coupled with the escalator descending from the chocolate high soon forced me to sleep.

Winter on the prairie. Why did my dreams keep returning to the windswept expanse lately carpeted in dried, golden wisps canopied by murderous-looking clouds?

"Teacher," I sighed in relief as his more-than-welcome height strode toward me.

Not a fraction of movement in his facial muscles, but his black eyes bore into me- seeking, gauging.

The closer he came, the higher my chin rose. A rush of emotion within my heart accompanied his fingers gently stroking from my temples to the curve of my cheek, and then they rested briefly under my chin.

"You've lost weight; you're not sleeping well," just like a teacher grading a composition and finding it lacking.

I knew he had to know, but nevertheless, "C...Cloud is...gone," my eyes gave up the water works.

Without expression, he imperceptibly acknowledged my nightmare.

Find another topic before you cry this entire dream away, I reprimanded myself.

"Why am I not cold? It looks cold here," I couldn't look away from him.

IOU A HORSE

"This is your dream." Was that supposed to be an explanation?

"Why aren't you cold?" His bare, scarred chest seemed impervious. My eyes fell on the space between his rudely- scarred, pectoral muscles and dropped to his...long, bare feet- how?

An idling at the corner of his mouth, "Shamans do not necessarily experience cold."

To ask why seemed inane. Maybe it was the lingering effects of too much chocolate. Too little sleep. Too much emotion.

He caught me as I crumpled.

"The stallion's leaving hurt you," he remarked, as my body fed off the contact with his skin- receiving a surety of balanced blood sugar and revivifying strength which emanated from him- warmer than what I assumed a mother's arms might feel like.

My lips trembled and like a kid, I sniveled as he supported me sitting upright on what should have been fiercely cold ground.

The wind battened the sails of his streaming, black hair, but he disregarded the interplay, continued to examine me with x-ray mirrors powered beyond technology's ability.

"Why did he go? Why did he have to leave?" I whimpered, tasting my tears through my words.

"You're learning. Not everyone's path is set to coincide with another's for unlimited time. Perhaps, he had another task."

I was only a task to him? A job?

"Do not denigrate the time you had; do not contrive silly questions," Teacher advised my thoughts.

I jammed a fingernail underneath another one for a suitable back-up to biting at the inside of my mouth- control...

"I still..."

"No. Tell me why you hurt?"

Why? I never thought of Teacher as dense. A first grader could answer that question and I didn't feel up to playing 'Are you smarter than...?'

"Are you upset because you enjoyed riding him? Wanted to show him?" he challenged me.

"Is that what you think? You don't know me at all," I shot back, struggling to rise. And run.

"Your love makes you vulnerable. Accept this. Will you stop loving him?"

"No, never," I defiantly vowed.

"Perhaps he had something important to do," Teacher suggested with great patience.

I suddenly, absolutely, deflated, miserable to the nth degree. "What do you want?"

That insidious question. I knew Teacher would rebuke me if I answered for Cloud to come back, but I could see in the solemnity of his eyes he knew what I was thinking.

"When you allow the numbness to overtake you, you give up your choice to feel, to access inner strength. In experiencing the full gamut of emotions we allow ourselves to live. Feeling joy, gratitude, sharing hard times and good times, all will help fill you with the means to get through the seemingly unbearable episodes," Teacher guided my spirit.

Yes, that made sense, but it didn't alleviate nor dispatch the excruciating, heart-wrenching pain.

"It's not meant to," he read me.

"I understand. I've received..." Did he know what e-mails were? "Many notes from people."

"Who share your hurting, who have known your joy, who consider you worthy to share with," he finished for me.

"I know," I admitted ruefully, playing with my fingernails and wanting so very badly to feel his arms holding me. "As humans, we're all in the same boat. What about shamans?"

Teacher seemed fractionally taken aback.

"Do you...feel, or just dispense wisdom and healing?" I asked.

IOU A HORSE

A definite grunt accompanied the upturn at the corner of his wide lips. "I am not inhuman," he finally remarked, his eyes sweeping the plains.

"What do you want, Teacher?"

"I'm here to help you," his voice tinged with impatience.

"Just to help me?"

Night after night Teacher appeared. Whatever we spoke of or if we simply ran together, a healing inexorably burgeoned inside me.

And it became evident to Tim, Martine, Ned- who I was mentoring to take on the beginner lessons- Sierra, Timberman and Schoe. All of them eyed me differently.

Schoe asked me out to dinner or a concert once in a while. I no longer rushed by to fulfill a list in my head; instead, I made an effort to connect with people, to shuck the tremendous isolating, self-restraint I'd saddled myself with, to grow strong in a new way, and 'be' mindful of every moment- not just those giving lessons or on horseback. I was joining my species specific humans, even as I loved on my critters.

"I will never completely abandon you, but my time here draws to...an end," Teacher hit me with. That last night.

"What are you saying?" An up-swell of panic stampeded through me.

"I believe you know," he impassively informed me.

"Is it because your people need you? Is there a barrier between us because of...our different heritages? If that is so, why? Is it you or something else that constructs it? Don't you believe we are all one?"

"What do you want?" he sidestepped my impertinence and drilled me.

I hesitated, near chickening out.

"Not to be alone. No!" I stepped right into his chest. "If it's true I drew you to me...I want to love and be loved, to need and be needed...by you."

There, I'd said it. Eye to eye. Soul to soul. Completely bared. The ultimate in vulnerability.

Sierra could deck the giver of the incorrect response, but I was not Sierra. My chin rose for the blow that would inevitably follow my truthful admission of what I wanted. The shadow of an unloved child stretched behind me.

"You have your work here," he lamely, finally replied.

"And your people need you," I cringed.

A definite grimace thinned his lips. He felt something!

"I want to love you and feel your love for me returned," I repeated, daring him to acknowledge what reigned between us.

Implacable, palpable blows fell as he stepped away, retreated.

"You'd give yourself to me," he stated with incredible, incomprehensible somberness.

I didn't tell him he'd already been ingrained in my heart for some time. Along with a certain dream stallion, since departed. I might be able to live without Cloud, but if Teacher...

Too choked up to reply or ask why the very idea struck him in such a way, I simply bobbed my head.

Black pools glittered at me. Reflections of my unshed tears. Perhaps it wasn't dejection, perhaps Teacher was...disgusted with me? Appalled? The typical sordid scenario- a concerned teacher unwittingly earns a besotted student's love- in the full male/female sense of the word.

I was about to flunk the final exam.

"Never that," Teacher murmured.

Like a startled raven, his black mane feathered about me as he swooped down, kissed my brow and fingered my cheek. And that was the last dream of him.

IOU A HORSE

46

"I thought I'd find you here."

"Shaman," the shadowed man inclined his head in respect.

"She looks good, considering her age," CatSkill admired the scenery.

"My thanks for your keeping her safe and healthy." Two pairs of eyes watched an older, roan mare and her pregnant companions as they nibbled the tremendous swathe of hay on the sage-brush tinted high plains.

"We've plenty, my Wife and I," the shaman shrugged, indicating the hay. As his protégé remained quiet, CatSkill chuckled. "I swear if you're not the broodiest man I've ever seen-any eggs hatching? I think I like you better in... Haven't the spirits presented you with the most precious of gifts? If you weren't feeling such genuine pain, I'd... Nevermind."

The shaman, CatSkill, shuffled his fingers through his dense, tangled mane and gracefully rose from his cross-legged position. He decided to give it one more try.

"You know the answer is not always bound up in flight or fight?"

The wild mares startled; heads flew up, preparatory to fleeing. CatSkill checked himself, camouflaged his scent and the mares eyed the agile individual with his disarrayed gold and auburn hair with its black highlights around his ears. Sensing they'd been mistaken and that they were indeed safe, they returned to avariciously devouring the hay.

"It is not that, Shaman. The spirits... Dove..." the shadowed man actually snickered in the vaguest sort of way.

"Did I hear what I think I heard?" CatSkill chuckled in surprise.

"Probably, it sounds too foreign to my ears. It didn't take long to divine the Lady Shaman's intent and the spirits' approval-one and the same with you."

"Then, what is the problem?" The normally, excessively patient CatSkill, relentlessly probed. "If you listen to spirit…"

"I can not…leave here."

"You do need a cuff to bring you to your senses- you are not bound by distance or time. Our people will expect your attendance as always; they've accepted my Wife," CatSkill reminded his student.

"She is a shaman."

"Are you so sure this woman is not? Check yourself," and CatSkill cast enigmatic, gold eyes on his intransigent, black-eyed disciple.

"I sense you have another question," CatSkill probed.

"Does nothing get past you?"

"Hey, I've been around…for quite some time," the mentor's dimple paraded full-force.

"When you are in…your other guise, are you wholly you or…?

CatSkill threw back his head and wholeheartedly laughed. "I always have a choice, as do you. A shaman's powers are ordained and guided by spirit so we remain true- but we are not slaves.

My first 'appearance' to Bonnie presented me with quite a conundrum, and nearly an impromptu snack. However, trusting in spirit, I'm very comfortable in my complete transformation to cougar- a oneness with my spirit guide. Spirit maintains a most interesting overall witty genius- that's my experience. Can't go wrong- even if you do not fully comprehend the supernatural intellect. No one is meant to know everything…right away.

It was a mare spirit sent to drag you away from your sense of powerlessness and isolation. You must continue your work on the isolation aspect, though. It's easier to help others if you're not hiding out in your cabin half the time. I'm impressed with the 'drawing' business, it harkens to Bonnie's…nevermind. I am proud to have you for a friend and my protégé. I repeat, check yourself." Catskill grinningly waved a see-you-later and vanished leaving a wake of equine snorts.

IOU A HORSE

Night after night I steal in to watch her sleep. Many are the trails of tears which cause my heart to pang. At times, she convulses in a trance-like pain. I hear her siren-call and more, I sense her physical desire. Mirrors...

I must choose. Funny, in reality, the choice has already been made. But I am the one who must openly accept what spirit suggests.

In this in-between, I'm of no use to others or myself. What do I want?

My student is indeed a shamanic teacher. My heart echoes her answer.

I take one day at a time. Force myself to continue in an outward friendly mode, otherwise, what did I learn? What was the point?

Surely, it would be the height of ingratitude to deny the magic's intent?

I'd made progress in the species-specific role. Why had it taken an amazing stallion and an enigmatic, Native American shaman to push me to do what Sierra had always urged me to do?

Magic.

I enjoyed the inroads of sharing when I spoke with my friends, although I balked in the thinking about it- a crazy apprehension which I forced myself to discount and continue on.

Teacher would be...proud...of my living as I should, of denying the past its chain-like hold over me, even if nights remained difficult. Friends were one thing, but I missed that long, strong barefooted stride into my dreams at night.

I page through the sketches. I have Cloud on video, but the only likeness of Teacher is the one I drew. Or the magic drew for me.

Teacher. Muscled chest. Scars. I know how he'd gained those scars. Hadn't I been gifted with visions into his past?

Scars? I flicked the page back. Cloud. Scars. Two on his chest. Two above his shoulder blades.

Teacher would have scars on his back, though I never actually saw them in my spirit-inspired vision. I knew the weight of those buffalo skulls hanging from piercings under his black hair...

Shamans. Hadn't I read somewhere about shamans and shape-shifting? The events drawn in caves leading to... Ceremonies of shamans incognito- in other animal forms. Was it possible? Teacher and...

With the magic, everything was possible.

I longed to search for more details of shamanism, (I could almost hear Teacher smirk) but the pencil, the drawing pad...those scars held me in place while my bewitched mind whirled. Fingers shaking I turned pages back and forth, seeking answers reality scoffed at. Magic!

Befuddled, I twirled the drawing pencil and shuffled to a blank page. Hesitated. Would it be right, presumptuous, to draw him...back to me, if his destiny called him elsewhere?

Was fate relegated to one across a divide from...another, unable to...be with the mirror of my soul?

Teacher spoke of the inter-connectedness of everything. Hmmm... I held the sketch pad, pencil poised, deep in thought.

Midnight. My whole being yearned for... Valentine's Day, nearly a month since... I wondered if I would ever see him in my dreams again.

5 am Captain barking non-stop! Too early to rise. But Captain never wakes me unless...

IOU A HORSE

I shoot up, heart pounding horrifically. All the critters are looking at me with...expectation? Captain barks and prances to the door and back to me, Bosun and Mate mimicking him and whining.

In my awkward rush, I fall out of bed, scramble to my feet, throw on coveralls, forget the buttons and slide into my winter boots.

"What's wrong?" I stop for a second to ask all the eager, upturned faces. The dogs brush against me, forcing me to the door. I don't hear anything. Wait...horses neighing! Dear God!

Grabbing a phone, I look out the window- no flames, but that doesn't mean...

Flying out the door, I race toward the sound of the entire barn clamoring.

Sheer thrusts her muzzle out the stall. 'C'mon, hurry' she imperiously calls. The rest of the barn echoes her command.

Slipping and sliding in my haste, dogs and cats providing a flanked runway, I flounder along as fast as I can go.

"Sheer?"

Thrusting aside the latch, I step into her stall.

'Surprise!'

At the moment, it doesn't register who shouts. My knees knock together and I grasp the stall wall to fend off collapse- in absolute astonishment! Surprise- the word is completely insufficient!

Sheer nuzzles my pockets. All pockets are receptacles for snacks and therefore a horse's domain. Absently, I pull out a handful and let her indulge.

'My sire said you'd love me.'

I choke. Cloud! Before me a tiny, whiskered black muzzle pushes into my chest- a foal!

Cloud- you sneak!

What had he said- the Amazon wasn't his type... Indeed!

Black feet and legs, except for the right front white fetlock with ermines, black mane, a twitching, black tail, black tipped ears turned in creating a heart shape...and Sheer's white body, except for a streak of that glorious, red-bronze running like a badge of honor down the length of the right shoulder- the mark of Allah!

A colt! Shades of Cloud! And I'm crying and shaking and praying and thanking the magic and completely out of my head all at the same time.

"I...I love all my...my critters," I manage to gasp, realizing- OH, MY, GOD!!! I hear, actually hear, the saucy little fellow as clearly as I'd heard Cloud!

Sheer exhales into my hair, 'She most certainly does.'

"Sheer!" Am I still dreaming?

Had the pencil's magic created...again? In a flash I consider the other horse I'd drawn running next to Cloud. This colt? Think about it later...

I throw my arms around Sheer's neck, sobbing, choking, thanking.

"Sheer, I can hear you! Are you OK? I should call Dr. K..." I cry- let the damn tears roll- there is still magic in my life!

No Cloud or Teacher, but...magic!

'You always heard me, Dove, just not in this way,' Sirocco nuzzles my cheek and the foal mouths at my Carharts.

"You and Cloud?"

'I was his type,' Sheer softly, proudly whiffles, arching her perfect neck.

'I'm hungry,' the foal's little black nose bumps against Sheer's abdomen.

In response, she begins nuzzling his haunch as he latches on for nourishment, his baby tail swinging happily. He's going to be taller than her...

"I'll have to think of a name for you," I muse, leaning against the stall wall for support, considering whether to call Dr. K- Sheer nixes the idea- and watching just as greedily as the colt suckling.

IOU A HORSE

The feeding abruptly breaks off, 'I'll let you know if you get it right.' His retort rings out- the spitting image of Cloud with his unbridled sense of humor.

The congratulatory nickers have mostly died down- the orders for breakfasts will be fast on their heels.

Sheer leaves off ministering to the colt's hide, her attention drawn elsewhere. She nickers a welcome.

Welcome? I about-face.

The magic has another surprise for me.

Teacher! In lieu of his bare chest and feet, an open, faded blue shirt, jeans and moccasins. An unfamiliar look of contentment softens his face as his eyes absorb the maternal scene and then, I fall into the limelight.

I actually pinch myself. Hard. Ouch! Real. No dream.

Those wide lips curl, his usual grunt bleeds into a vague sort of chuckle. Unfathomed black eyes enchant me.

"I know you," I whisper.

"Yes, you do," his deep, masculine voice- the one I yearn for-now here in my head, in my ears, in this stall.

His arms rise from his sides and I step within the magic come to life. A perfect fit.

Another attempted chuckle on his part and my arms sweep around him as they'd wanted to do for so long. Overwhelmed, I step into a magic-come-to-life euphoria.

For a crazy half-second, I picture how I'll introduce him, especially to Sierra. His chest vibrates with unrestrained laughter and I join in. Whatever! The magic will take care of it- the magic of us together. Mirrored souls.

He turns me so we both face Sheer and the foal, his arms round my waist and my hands atop his. Nuzzling my neck in expert fashion, "The way I figure, I owe you a horse."

Thankful Acknowledgements

My horses- my dreams and teachers!

Gillian Bath- your advice 'Create your own bible when working with horses' is the best!

OLDSTONE Riding Center for the innumerable happy hours!

Cathy and Mary for getting me started in dressage!

Dagmar Zimmerman- you gave me the finest appreciation of 'the basics' and their paramount importance!

All the grand horses and their persons I've been honored to work with- thank you for your trust, and for all you've taught me!

Dr. Kraushar- for the suggestion of infected tendon sheath and for your patient bedside manner with my horses!

Dr. Leick, veterinarian also practicing chiropractic work, acupuncture and herbal medicine- a shaman in his own right!

Gary Stern, farrier extraordinaire, and a wonderful horse lover- my girls love you!

Susan Fortney-Harlan- for brainstorming with me on Dove's character!

Brian Busse- friend and computer genius!

The muses that fascinate my life!

Thanks to all for sharing your time with me!

For those wishing to know more of Riordan and Bonnie CatSkill and Cloud please check out the CatSkill Trilogy as listed in the front of the book

Correspondents welcome at: lisaannettepowell@gmail.com

Please check out the CatSkill Trilogy Facebook page for more pics of Ahlam, my soulmate, and other goodies. Many thanks for sharing and liking!

IOU A HORSE

My Pride and Joy, and she knows it!
Photo courtesy of Nan Rawlins Equimage.com